PRAISE FOR

Everything Comes Back to You

"Heartbreaking. Healing. Hilarious. This book is everything I want in a coming-of-age novel. Lennon is one of my favorite main characters in recent memory, and reading her journey with her own identity, and each person in her life over four years, was so touching, so entertaining, so rewarding. Taking full ownership of your own future requires courage—a reality Khalilieh masterfully presents here. A thousand stars!"

—JESMEEN KAUR DEO, author of *Reasons We Break*

"A beautiful and achingly emotional story filled with raw yearning and perfect storytelling that deftly captures so many ways a heart can be broken and healed. I adored getting lost in Lennon's world. Jackie Khalilieh continues to write some of the most genuine, vulnerable, and incredibly loveable autistic characters I've ever read. A perfect read!"

—CG DREWS, *NYT* bestselling author of *Don't Let the Forest In*

"A sweet coming-of-age story of falling in love, but also falling in love with yourself. The world can feel too big and demanding when you're a teenager and Khalilieh's depiction of what it feels like as an autistic teenager navigating family, love, and dreams is raw and unapologetic."

—ZOULFA KATOUH, bestselling author of *As Long as the Lemon Trees Grow*

"An exceptionally honest unfolding of teenage girlhood over the course of four years. The particularly nuanced depictions of intimacy and romance that don't shy away from the realities of shame, pressure, and judgment facing young women are standout elements, only elevating the ways in which readers might relate to Lennon's highs and lows with love. Khalilieh has crafted a timeless narrative through this authentic exploration of all the ecstasy, embarrassment, introspection, and messiness that comes with growing up and into oneself."

—RACQUEL MARIE, award-winning author of *Ophelia After All*

"With deft prose and a sensitive touch, Khalilieh delves into the weight of parental and cultural expectations, autism, and identity. Lennon's emotional world is beautifully rendered, and it's profoundly rewarding when Lennon finds her truest self. A gorgeous bildungsroman."

—ALENA BRUZAS, award-winning author of *Ever Since* and *To the Bone*

Everything Comes Back to You

JACKIE KHALILIEH

tundra

Tundra Books, an imprint of Tundra Book Group, a division of Penguin Random House Canada Ltd., 320 Front Street West, Suite 1400, Toronto, Ontario, M5V 3B6, Canada
penguinrandomhouse.ca

Published simultaneously in the United States of America by Tundra Books of Northern New York, an imprint of Tundra Book Group, a division of Penguin Random House Canada Ltd., P.O. Box 2040, Plattsburgh, NY 12901, USA

Library and Archives Canada Cataloguing in Publication

Title: Everything comes back to you / Jackie Khalilieh.
Names: Khalilieh, Jackie, author.
Identifiers: Canadiana (print) 20250270978 | Canadiana (ebook) 20250270986 | ISBN 9781774884782 (hardcover) | ISBN 9781774884799 (EPUB)
Subjects: LCGFT: Novels.
Classification: LCC PS8621.H3375 E94 2026 | DDC jC813/.6—dc23

Library of Congress Control Number: 2025946192

Edited by Lynne Missen with assistance from Katie Heeps
Designed by Zeena Baybayan
Typeset by Daniella Zanchetta and Six Red Marbles
The text was set in Filosofia.

Printed in Canada
1 2 3 4 5 30 29 28 27 26

tundra | Penguin Random House
TUNDRA BOOKS

Dear Reader,

This story is for people who see themselves in Lennon. And for those who, regardless of age, want a safe space to read about the evergreen issues that can stay with us long after our teen years.

I should know.

This novel contains the following:

Teenage pregnancy.

Discussions of prenatal options.

Alcoholism in an adult.

Mature subject matter, including scenes depicting consensual sexual activity.

Recreational teenage drug and substance use.

Emotional abuse.

Disordered eating.

Depression.

Please take care if any of these topics are sensitive to you.

With love,

Jackie

to anyone who has ever been shamed for their dreams, desires, or being who they are.

you are good.

(also, shame on them)

"I can't stand it to think my life is going so fast
and I'm not really living it."

—ERNEST HEMINGWAY, *THE SUN ALSO RISES*

The moon and I have a complicated relationship.
Kind of like my father and me.
And the first boy I fell in love with.
The only boy I ever truly loved.
It's an undivine trinity.
The moon,
my father,
and him.

AUGUST 7

The red-and-white bucket seat rocks back and forth. I place my hands, palms down, on either side of my body to center myself. A cool breeze swirls between my father and me. I suck in the salty air, hopeful that when I blow it out it will release some of my nerves.

"Why are we stopped?" I ask my father, who has both arms stretched out on the back of the seat, his head turned to the ocean. California seems to bring out a different side to him. A more relaxed side. Something I rarely see back home.

"Because, habibti, they have to let people on and off the ride. It's a slow process, but it's part of the experience." Dad grins as his eyes continue to take in the sights. The L.A. coastline serves as our backdrop, with a multitude of sailboats in the distance. Below us, the Santa Monica Pier is tightly packed with tourists, my mom and older sister among them. The baby blue sky meeting the teal blue of the ocean makes the earth seem, for a moment, endless.

"Feeling like a caged animal is part of the experience?" I mock, my eyes the only part of my body that seem to move at the top of the Ferris wheel.

Dad's smirk softens into a smile. "We spend most of our lives working toward a goal, for that one moment of glory, and then, just like that"—he snaps his fingers—"the moment is over."

Our bucket seat rocks again and we jerk down a level.

"Did you hear that? I think maybe we lost a bolt."

Dad laughs and slides over to my side, nodding at me to remove my hand from the seat. I pry it off and wipe my sweaty palm on my shorts. "This is what you wanted, isn't it?" he asks, draping an arm around my shoulders.

It's true. I pushed to go on the Ferris wheel. Mom didn't want to mess up her hair, and Georgie's fear of heights stopped her.

We started our day at the beach and spent the afternoon exploring the pier. My dad, Georgie, and I even reenacted the show opener for *Three's Company*, Dad's favorite show from when he was young. A show he watched in the basement, away from his strict and conservative parents. We ate delicious seafood for lunch and took so many pictures that our phones' batteries collectively drained. I begged Dad to ride the Ferris wheel even though he was clearly exhausted, and he agreed. For me.

"You're right. I'm sorry," I say. "I know you were looking forward to a nice, long shower and room service." My toes wiggle in my flip-flops and granules of sand come loose from the soles of my feet.

"I didn't bring my family to California just to lie on a hotel room bed. I'm glad you insisted on this." Dad leans in, and his eyes dart around as if to make sure no one can hear us. "I'm going to let you in on a little secret. But you can't tell anyone."

I nod, my big brown eyes opened wide to his.

His lips stretch into a wide grin and the skin around his eyes forms multiple crinkles. "You're my favorite daughter . . . by a hair," he says, pulling on a lock of my frizzy black hair.

Dad's words—though perhaps appeasing or, one might argue, unfair—still manage to light me up from the inside.

We rock again and move down another level as the sun begins its descent.

"What if we can't find Mom and Georgie once we finally get off this ride?"

"You worry too much," Dad says, waving me off while clearly taking in the experience much more than I am able to.

"Me?" I point a finger to my chest. "You worry more than anyone I know."

"You're right," he says, with a far-off look in his eyes. "I passed that on to you."

My father is a big man who puts up a strong front. He immigrated to Canada with his parents and older brother from Palestine as a child. In his early twenties, he met and fell in love with my mother on a visit back home. They married the following year, and she moved to Toronto, where they eventually had two Canadian-born daughters. By the time he was thirty-five, he'd lost his older brother and both parents—all to cancer. He turned to music when his brother died, and loves the Beatles, John Lennon especially. My father is a man of many talents but he pays the bills by working as a chartered accountant.

Our household thrives on rules and structure. And I thrive on making my father happy and proud. I already knew I was his favorite daughter. He didn't need to tell me. I'm the easy one. I don't question the rules. I do as I'm told. I seek out his validation. Always have.

Dad shifts in the seat and faces me. I swallow as the unbalanced bucket continues to rock back and forth. "Promise me something."

"Okay?" I say, looking into his eyes to ground myself, to forget for a moment that I am suspended in air.

"Never forget who you are and where you come from."

"Dad!" A blush rises to my cheeks. It isn't often he gets sentimental, but whenever he does, it makes me uneasy.

"I'm serious, Lennon. Next month you'll be in high school. There will be many temptations. People who want you to break the rules. Boys," Dad says, heaving a sigh.

"Dad!" I say again, because I don't know how else to respond. I'm a few months away from turning fourteen. Boys are definitely on my radar whereas in the past they've only been on the periphery. But Dad has nothing to worry about. All day today I noticed boys noticing Georgie and other girls. Girls with long, flowing hair and an unequal skin to clothes ratio. Not me in my knee-length board shorts and baggy T-shirt. It's fine though. It allowed me to do what I do best: observe. And what I observed was disappointment in my father's eyes as boys glanced at Georgie's full chest and bronze skin in her short shorts.

Dad would be so displeased if he knew how much I yearn for at least one boy to look at me the way they look at my older sister. I want to feel wanted. Special. It's almost like this need that is engrained deep inside me—to be perceived in a way that would bring shame to both my parents. And it feels like if I don't get that need fulfilled soon, I might die.

My father, however, wants something completely different for me.

"You must stay true to who you are and always remember our values. And it wouldn't hurt if you promised never to love another man more than you love your father." With those words he laughs, but I don't.

Instead I nod, while avoiding his stare. Waves crash against the pier, and people scream in mock horror as the roller coaster below us takes a sharp turn. In the distance, Nirvana's "The Man Who Sold the World" plays. It's a song I recognize only because of my father's extensive vinyl collection—which I hope one day to inherit.

My eyes fall, once again, to the part of the ocean that meets the sky. The sun is setting and now the divide between ocean and sky is much starker, not as endless as it once felt.

"Still scared?" Dad asks, pulling me out of my trance.

I shake my head as he settles next to me, throwing his big arm over my shoulders again and pulling me in. "Can you knock on my door . . . ?" he sings, his fading Arabic accent making the theme song for *Three's Company* sound even more ridiculous.

"I've been waiting for you . . ." I sing back, both of us mixing up the lyrics so the song can be a duet instead of a threesome. After all, it's just me and my father up here. And in this moment, no one else in the world matters.

Part I

NINTH GRADE

find the mask that fits best
never perfectly
The acceptable version.
it will make it easier on them
and eventually it will become your second
foreign *skin.*

Chapter One

SEPTEMBER 5

When I need grounding, I look up at the night sky. Amidst the twinkling stars I search for the moon. She's my refuge from the storm inside the walls of my home. In my backyard, with headphones on, music blasting, I lie on the grass, the cool blades tickling my skin, and look up. Just like that, I'm transported, thousands of miles away.

There are times it takes me a minute or two to find her. Buried behind dark skies and gray clouds. Even on the nights when I can't spot the moon, I know she's up there, going through one of her phases.

Relatable.

The sliding door at the back of the house slams shut, pulling me back to earth. Georgie paces around the patio, her breathing heavy, her sobs loud. I sit up, bringing my headphones to my neck, waiting for her to notice me. She mumbles and curses, wiping her tears with the backs of her hands, then screams this loud, visceral scream that sends a shiver through my entire body.

I spring to my feet. "Georgie," I say, slightly above a whisper.

She freezes. Then her eyes meet mine and a breath leaves her body.

“What’re you doing out here?” She asks it so casually I almost forget a moment ago she was unraveling next to my mother’s beloved hydrangeas.

“It’s where I go,” I say with a shrug. “When you and Dad fight.”

“You missed a good one.” A sad laugh escapes her as she wraps her arms around herself.

I walk to her, looking past her shoulders to see my father at the family room window, eyes searching. As he spots us, he offers me a small nod before turning away.

“Want to go for a walk?” I ask.

Georgie’s eyes flick down at her bare feet.

“Okay. Then come with me,” I say, reaching out my hand. Together we walk to the darkest spot in our backyard, a place the indoor lights don’t reach. I release her hand and lie down. She rolls her eyes as she lies next to me.

“Look up,” I say. “Do you see her?”

“Her?” Georgie asks.

“The moon.”

“You’re one of those girls who romanticize the moon, aren’t you?”

I turn to meet her discerning eyes. “What’s wrong with that?”

“Nothing.” She smiles. “It’s sweet that you’re still optimistic about love and life and all that shit.”

“*Love, Life, and All That Shit*, the title of my first memoir.”

“*An Autistic Girl’s Guide to Existing*,” Georgie adds. We laugh as my sister shimmies closer. “So why’s the moon a she?”

“Because,” I say, “men let you down. But the moon, she’s always there. Dependable. Even when you can’t see her, you can feel her.”

Georgie turns quiet and I glance at her. More tears escape from the corners of her eyes.

"It'll be okay," I say, holding her hand in mine. "He just needs a minute to work off the anger."

"No." She shakes her head, the movement so slight. "It's different this time. I really screwed up."

"So you'll stay in a few nights. Keep your room clean. Drive me to school," I say, bumping shoulders with her. "Are you super excited to have your annoying baby sister attending high school with you, finally?"

She smiles, then cries again. I shift on my side, propping my head up with my hand. "Okay," I say. "I'll take the bus."

"No." She matches my pose, and I study her beautiful face. Hazel eyes. Golden skin. Plump lips. And thick, dark brown hair that somehow shines even brighter under the night sky.

Then there's me. Tall. Lanky. Black hair that hasn't decided if it's straight or wavy. Muddy brown eyes. Pale skin. Stubborn round cheeks that somehow didn't get the memo that I'm almost fourteen.

"I can drive you," she says, sweeping hair from my face. "For a while. But then you'll have to start taking the bus."

"Are we going to keep talking in circles or are you going to tell me what's wrong?" I ask, sitting cross-legged on the grass now. Georgie matches my pose again and wipes her tears, looking even more gorgeous despite her nose and cheeks being puffy and red.

The sliding door opens and the click-clack of Mom's slippers sounds on the patio stones. She stands with her hands on her hips, scanning the backyard. I glance at Georgie, asking her what we should do using only my eyes and a bit of sister telepathy. She rises and offers her hand to help me up. I follow her to the patio.

Relief washes over Mom's face as we come into view. She's been crying too.

"Come inside," she says to Georgie, completely ignoring my presence.

"I don't want to fight anymore," my sister says, her voice soft. Little.

"How long have you known?" Mom asks, looking down at Georgie's stomach.

She shrugs. "Not long."

"Who?" she asks, her expression gone slack.

I watch, examining my mother and sister for clues. The fighting is as normal as can be between strict Arab parents and a daughter who continually pushes the envelope. Every week it's a new battle. Extending her curfew. A third piercing in her ear. Dropping math. Freedom to wear what she wants. Georgie has never colored inside the lines. My dad has aged twenty years since she turned thirteen. And now that she's about to be a senior in high school, she seems to think the rules no longer apply. But this fight is different. The current silence is unsettling. I'd almost prefer the shouting.

"Don't tell me you don't know who the father of your baby is," Mom says, her icy tone so jarring it's unrecognizable.

"Baby?" I ask. My eyes move to Georgie's taut stomach.

"Go inside," Mom says to me, her gaze fixed on Georgie.

I look at my sister and she nods slightly, suggesting I follow our mother's orders. I open the sliding door and close it quietly behind me.

The light in Dad's office is on. I rest my phone and headphones on the kitchen table and walk to his office, knocking gently on the open door. He's seated at his desk, head resting in his hands.

"Hi," I say.

He looks up and clears his throat before waving me in. I sit on the chair across from him.

I take in the neat stacks of files on my father's large oak desk. Behind him, matching oak shelves are lined with accounting texts, books by Arab philosopher Edward Said, Paul McCartney's memoir, all the classics, and of course framed photos of our family. Below that, his impressive vinyl collection rests.

"Is Georgie . . . is she really . . . ?" I twist my hands into each other. "What's going on?" I finally ask, knowing my father will be the one to give me answers.

"Your sister decided to ruin her life and bring shame to our entire family because she couldn't keep her legs closed."

My wringing hands freeze, and my eyes widen. I swallow down the tightness in my throat at my dad's choice of words. I've never heard him speak this way before. I wouldn't call him a feminist, but he's always treated us—the women in his life—with the highest regard.

"So she really is pregnant?" I ask, the last word coming out like a whisper. Like it's a bad word.

"It's my fault," Dad says, rising from his office chair and walking to the window that looks out over the front yard. "I gave her too much freedom. She acts like one of *them*, forgetting her moral compass. *Our morals.* And now she has embarrassed not only herself, but all of us."

"People make mistakes, Baba," I say. "No one is perfect."

He turns from the window, a slight smile tugging at his lips.

"No. No one is perfect. But you," he says, walking to me and tucking a rogue hair behind my ear, "are still my sweet angel."

I look down, my stomach in knots. I'm not sure why I feel guilty. I haven't done anything.

But I've *thought* about doing things. In fact, it's all I think about lately. Boys. Kissing. More than kissing. I can't *stop* thinking about it.

I'm a walking hormone, and somehow the pining feels worse than the actual doing. Because when you're doing, at least someone else is involved. Someone else wants it too. Your desires are matched. Validated. When it's just you obsessing over a kiss, a touch, a feeling, it's kind of pathetic.

"Now what?" I ask Dad.

He raises his shoulders. "We pray to God for answers, and we hope He will guide us on this journey."

"What about . . . what if she doesn't want the baby?" I ask.

I shrink into myself, expecting to receive a tongue-lashing. Instead, there's hesitation.

"She wants the baby," Dad says, his normally perfect posture hunched.

When it comes to me, I'm pro-choice, but my parents, I never thought they'd . . . I guess, I never thought.

This changes everything.

This also gives today's holiday, Labor Day, an entirely new meaning.

"Pick an album to mark this occasion," Dad says dryly, and I almost have to bury a laugh. Dad says retaining a sense of humor helped him get through his hardest times. The loss of his older brother when he was ten. The racism he faced as the only Palestinian boy at his Canadian high school. The back-to-back losses of his parents. And now this: a pregnant teenage daughter.

I rise and walk to his collection, running a finger over the narrow spines before making my selection. I slide the record out of its sleeve with care, just the way Dad taught me when I was seven. Placing the vinyl on the player, I gently lift the needle to the right track. "Let It Be" by the Beatles plays.

"Come," Dad says softly.

I nod as I walk to him, my steps mimicking the keys of the piano. I wrap my arms around him like I did when I was little. We hug with my cheek pressed against his broad chest. Dad cries in my arms after the chorus as we sway back and forth.

Back and forth, while I carry the weight of his worries, his fears, and his heartbreak.

Chapter Two

SEPTEMBER 13

Andie saunters up to my locker, her large green eyes expectant. *Hopeful.* She's the first, and only, friend I've made since starting high school last week. She's so different from me, and so fun. Like, she makes faces at our English teacher when he's turned to the whiteboard writing down a meaningless quote from some old book written by a dead white guy. And she flirts so outrageously with older boys that no one takes her seriously, but she gets away with it because she's so, so pretty. Her light brown hair is down to her waist. She styles it with sporadic skinny braids that frame her heart-shaped face and light brown skin. Her mom was a prominent Black model in her youth, and her dad was the Swedish Canadian photographer who shot some of her mom's biggest campaigns. They were pretty much Canadian royalty in the '90s and now they run one of the top modeling agencies together. Andie just oozes cool. Makes me wonder why she chose me.

And she didn't just choose me. She plucked me from obscurity and wrapped me in a shield of her braided wings.

Andie has the kind of freckles you only see with filters, and somehow her long and lithe limbs are like one continuous line that flows as peacefully as a warm breeze on a perfect April afternoon.

"Did you ask them yet?" she asks.

"No," I reply. "This is definitely not the best time to ask for their blessing to go on an overnight trip with a bunch of teenage boys."

Andie has been my savior through all of this. I didn't mean to tell her everything about me and my family. At least, not every last detail. I have this tendency to overshare and scare people away. But with Andie it's different. I feel safe around her. No masks. No fake personas. Just me.

"That's not how you pitch it, Lennon." Andie clears her throat before nodding, her expression switching from playful to serious. "This retreat is an opportunity for ninth-graders to become familiar with the faculty and meet their peers through a series of get-to-know-you games and fun outdoor challenges that promote health and socializing in a safe—emphasis on chaperoned—setting."

"Maybe you should ask them," I say, slamming my locker shut.

"Do you really think they'd say no? It's a school-sanctioned event!"

I shrug as my eyes look past Andie, focusing on the older students who roam the halls with a seemingly endless amount of calm and confidence. Georgie hasn't started senior year yet. She's not even showing but she feels awful all day long. When she's not throwing up, she wants to throw up. Her peers keep coming to me, asking where she is. *When will she be back?* I don't even know if they know.

Zach's been at school, though. It's like his life has barely changed.

"Lennon?"

"What?"

"Are you going to ask your parents about the retreat tonight or not?" Andie asks as she runs a lip gloss wand over her lips. "Tomorrow's the last day to submit the form."

"No. Yes. I don't know," I say, shaking my head as I let out an exasperated breath. "I just don't want to make them any more upset than they already are. It's like walking around a land mine. The other day I didn't close the cereal box properly and my dad lost it on my mom. Saying how they raised ungrateful, spoiled girls." His scathing words had felt like a dagger. I'd done nothing wrong, and yet I was being lumped in with Georgie's mistake anyway. It's not fair. None of it is.

"I wouldn't take what your dad says in a fit of frustration too seriously, you know? My parents are always losing their shit."

"Yeah. You're probably right," I say.

Andie offers me her lip gloss, but I shake my head. Zach walks past us and nods at me ever so slightly. Andie and I look at one another, both scrunching our faces in disgust.

"Do you think your sister will marry him?" she asks.

"Ugh. I never even thought of that."

"Come on." Andie locks her arm with mine as we walk down the hall. "You *need* this break. Ask them tonight. Or sign the form and ask for forgiveness later."

"I'll try."

"Good. Let's take the scenic route to class. The football team has practice in the gym this morning." She giggles as she tugs on my arm to walk faster.

☾

I'm in the kitchen, washing the dishes left over from dinner. Zach and his parents are out back with Georgie and our parents. Hot water from the tap turns warm as it runs over my hands. I've been scrubbing the last pot for well over five minutes while watching events unfold through the window over the sink. The parents alternate between resting their hands on their hips and crossing their arms over their chests. Zach and Georgie sit on separate outdoor sofas, avoiding eye contact with everyone.

Dinner started off pleasantly enough. There were hugs. Tears. Compliments about the food and the house decor. Mom even smiled. Tonight was the first time my parents had met Zach's parents. We knew about Zach. He was the reason Georgie and my father had fought most of her junior year. But they'd given in, eventually, and allowed her to see him. They'd set ground rules. Georgie ignored them all. And then some.

When Georgie ran off to the bathroom to throw up during dinner, the table fell silent. That's when the facade of acceptance dropped. More like shattered.

I went to check on Georgie, mostly to escape Dad's angry tirade against Zach. His parents stepped in to defend him, as parents do. Once Georgie came back, Dad's anger turned on her. Zach spoke up for her, or spoke for her, not really sure. His parents told him to stay out of it. The most civil of fights broke out after that and ended with more tears. Mom suggested coffee out back. Some fresh air. And now they're at it again.

I'm not sure what they're saying to one another. All I know is that there's no one solution that will make everyone happy.

Once the last dish is washed and put away, Georgie comes through the sliding door and runs upstairs to her room, leaving the door open in her haste. As I walk to close it, I notice only my parents remain out back. Zach and his parents must have just left through the backyard gate.

Mom and Dad are talking now and doing a poor job of keeping their voices down. Mom worries how to tell her family back home about this. That's when she's not lamenting about how the women at church will react to the news. Dad keeps saying "What does she want from us?" over and over. Like he's offered Georgie his best deal and is angry she won't accept it.

A text from Georgie lights up my phone screen. Come to my room.

I stall, phone in hand, watching my parents, my heart aching for them. The atmosphere around here since Georgie revealed her pregnancy has been so stiff. Guarded. But if I'm being honest with myself, it's been building to this for a while. It used to be that no matter what I was dealing with at school, I knew that when I stepped inside my home I could leave it all behind me. I was safe. Loved. And now Georgie had to ruin all of that by having unprotected sex with some average white guy. I can't even blame my parents. It's not just the disappointment. They're completely heartbroken.

All the years of hard work raising us, instilling their morals and values, have dissolved with one moment of impulse. Or passion. Maybe boredom? I wonder if it was her first time. Imagine getting pregnant the first time you have sex? That's for sure a sign that God's punishing you for having relations before marriage.

Sex and God. It's like they're one in the same sometimes. Can't think about sex without thinking about God. Religion. Culture. Disappointing my parents. *The guilt. The shame. How does Georgie live with herself?*

My parents are now seated on an outdoor sofa, side by side. Quiet. My phone is still in my hand, lit up with Georgie's text. Releasing a deep breath, I walk out of the kitchen and up the stairs toward Georgie's bedroom and knock on the door.

"Come in," she says. She's seated on her bed, legs crossed,

texting on her phone. Likely to Zach. They're both probably venting about how terribly everything went. Or maybe they're coming up with a plan to either run away together or break up. I wonder what would be easier. On everyone.

"Sit," Georgie instructs as she puts her phone down next to her.

I sit on the edge of her bed, wedging my hands in between my knees, eyes on the frilly white rug covering the oak floor.

"Well, that was a shit show," Georgie says, with the smallest release of laughter. "Can you believe both sets of parents want us to get married?"

I clear my throat, carefully raising my eyes to meet hers. "You don't want to?"

Georgie exhales as her gaze moves around the room. "I've barely accepted the fact that I'm pregnant. I can't even think about getting married. Oh god," she says, her face contorting.

"What is it?"

"Oh god," she repeats as she jolts out of bed and into the bathroom attached to her room. The toilet seat squeaks as she raises it. I get up to hold her hair and rub her back. It's not even a thought, no matter how disgusting it all is. Watching my sister's tough, foul-mouthed, tell-it-like-it-is demeanor crumble as she's become restricted to either her bedroom, due to exhaustion, or the toilet, due to nausea, makes me want to be there for her. But then there's the other part . . .

I'd never say this out loud, but on the night we found out, I prayed to God that Georgie would lose her baby. In a natural way so she wouldn't feel guilty for making the wrong choice and so everything could go back to normal. I'm such a terrible person for wishing death upon a fetus but this fetus has destroyed everything.

And I hate it. I hate this baby. I hate Georgie for getting pregnant. I hate my parents for making Georgie feel like she did something wrong. Almost everyone has sex (eventually). Why is it such a sin for us to even think about it?

But then, Georgie did more than just think.

"Can you get me a towel?" Georgie asks after flushing the toilet. Her arms remain draped over the seat, strands of her sweat-filled hair framing her face. I get up and grab a face towel from the stack on the marble counter, turning the faucet on, waiting for the temperature to reach hot before wetting the towel and bringing it to Georgie. She releases a heavy breath as she wipes her face and pats down her neck and chest.

I help Georgie up, holding onto her arm as we walk back to bed.

"What're Mom and Dad doing?" she asks as she climbs in. I cover her with a blanket before sitting by her feet.

"They're in the backyard. Talking."

"Talking," Georgie repeats, before clearing her throat. "So, how's grade nine been?" she asks, the subject change so jarring I find myself sitting up straighter.

"Mostly uneventful."

"Make any friends?"

"One. Her name is Andie. I really like her."

A smile lights up Georgie's face. "That's amazing, Len. I'm so happy you found someone. I told you high school would be better for making friends."

"Friend. Just the one."

"That's all you need," Georgie says.

"Are you coming back to school?" I ask.

“Eventually.” She nods. “Just need to talk to the principal. Make sure there’s some flexibility, given appointments and, you know, my need to run to the toilet on a moment’s notice.”

“That will pass. I mean, from what I’ve read.” I turn in my spot to face Georgie, who is less pale than she was a moment ago. “Andie really wants to go on the ninth-grade retreat, but I haven’t asked Mom or Dad because . . .”

“I fucked everything up. It’s okay, you can say it. It’s true,” Georgie says.

“Do you think it will make them mad if I ask? There’s no point, right?”

“There’s always a point. Your life shouldn’t stop just because of my actions. It wouldn’t be fair to you.”

“Okay, but there’s fair and there’s reality. What do you think my chances are?”

“It’s all about timing,” Georgie says. “Wait until the mood is right.”

“The form is due tomorrow.”

“Lennon.”

“I know. I have a tendency to put things off.”

“Do you want me to ask for you?”

“No.” I shake my head. “I can do it. I *should* do it. I really like Andie, and I don’t want to lose her as a friend.”

“You won’t.”

“That’s not true. Every friend I’ve ever made, I’ve lost.”

“No. They’ve lost,” Georgie says with a smile.

“I’m trying not to come on too strong with her, you know? But if she goes on this retreat without me, she’ll probably make new friends and I’ll be left behind. Again.”

Georgie whips the blanket off and gets up. She reaches for my hand. "Come with me."

I nod and follow her down the stairs.

Our parents are in the kitchen now. Mom's wiping counters as Dad sips on a cup of tea.

"Lennon is too afraid to ask you because of everything going on, but I think it's important that she goes."

"Goes where?" Mom asks, dishcloth in hand.

"The ninth-grade retreat," I answer. "It's up in Muskoka. Just one night. At the end of the month."

"Is it mandatory?" Dad asks.

My eyes find Georgie's.

"It's not," Georgie says. "But it would be good for her. She's made a new friend, who wants her to go. You know as well as I do that Lennon needs to learn how to foster relationships."

What Georgie is on the verge of not so eloquently saying is that my parents, who have been desperate for me to make friends and live a normal life, should jump at the chance for me to go on this retreat so I can hold on to this one friend for dear life, or else I'll return to my "concerning" loner ways.

"Why didn't you tell us about a new friend?" Mom asks.

"I don't know," I reply.

"We'll think about it," Dad says as he returns his cup to its saucer.

"The form is due tomorrow," Georgie says, before I have a chance to. "It's a school trip. Teachers will be there. I went on this retreat when I was in ninth grade."

"And look where that got you," Dad says quietly.

"This isn't about me," Georgie replies, her tone even. "It's important Lennon be pushed out of her comfort zone. This would be a good push for her."

"Where's the form?" Dad asks, shoulders dropping.

I reach into my pocket and pull out my phone, opening the email with the form attached. "They sent it to you, too," I say as I hand it to him. I don't know why I said that. My parents are not the type to open school emails.

Georgie stands behind me as we both wait for our father to make his decision.

"What do you think?" he asks our mother.

Mom offers a small smile. "It would be good for Lennon to make more friends."

Dad breathes out a sigh before nodding. "Print this out and I'll sign it."

"Okay. I'll be right back," I say to my parents before looking at Georgie, who has regained some of her sparkle.

"And Lennon," Dad says as Georgie and I are walking out of the kitchen. We both stop and turn to look at him. "Promise me you'll be a good girl on this trip."

Georgie shakes her head slightly and walks on. Her footsteps pad up the staircase. A moment later, a door slams shut.

"I promise," I say.

Dad smiles, and pride swells within me.

Still good. Still pure. Still untainted.

Chapter Three

SEPTEMBER 30

I wanted so badly to go on this overnight trip with the rest of my grade. And part of me is glad I did. Andie and I got to spend uninterrupted time together. Well, mostly. There were of course the mandatory get-to-know-you activities, which only served as a reminder of how terribly I fit into large group settings. Even though Andie stayed by my side (when we weren't forced apart), it was obvious that people, mostly boys, were intrigued by her. One boy in particular, Dean, seemed to be cutting through the noise of the others.

"Bad news," Andie says, sidling up next to me outside the school bus waiting to take us home. "Hopper is set on adhering to the seating plan like it's the Bible or some shit, so I have to ride back in Bus A."

"Why is he such a prick?" I ask, peering over her shoulder at the vice-principal.

"He said if the bus crashes, they'll need to refer to the seating plan to identify the bodies." She chews her pink wad of gum and blows a big bubble. I pop it with my finger. "At least you have your headphones. I have nothing. Not even my phone," she says, sighing so dramatically that her brown hair rises with it before falling off her shoulders.

I tug on one of her braids. "I told you to charge it last night."

"The charger was on the other side of the cabin, and I was tired," she whines while pouting. Only Andie could be both annoying and endearing at the same time.

"Are you still coming home with me?" I ask. We called our parents last night to see if Andie could sleep over when we got back since it's Friday. Having her sleep over was also strategic on my part. My hope is that Andie's presence will act as a buffer before the tension swallows me whole again.

"Of course! I can't wait to meet this family you've spoken so fondly of." She laughs and her head falls back, drawing the attention of three boys standing nearby. I'd be jealous but it's not as if I met any guys on the retreat that even vaguely interested me. They were all so juvenile. Especially together.

Every moment I spend with a neurotypical peer makes me more steadfast in my belief that autistic people are superior in many ways. I just can't admit that. It would make me seem too autistic, and people don't like it when you're too much of anything.

"Remember not to judge me based on the impression my family leaves on you. We're going through . . . things," I say, reminding her and myself. The tension is already rising up my legs. It won't be long now.

"Chill, Lennon. Your parents will love me."

A horn sounds and Mr. Hopper claps, reminding everyone to get in the right bus line. Andie takes off to her bus and Dean waves her over to his spot. I guess she won't need her phone to entertain her after all. I wait as the line ahead of me inches forward. Just as I'm about to step inside, a tall guy with shaggy brown hair cuts in front of me.

"Do you mind?" he asks, without giving me a second look.

"Go ahead," I reply dryly, but he doesn't hear me. He's already halfway up the aisle. I take my assigned seat in the middle of the bus and, thankfully, no one is seated next to me.

Two hours until we're back in civilization. Or Varley Village, a medium-sized suburb an hour north of Toronto. I can picture my parents now, chomping at the bit to get me back under their roof, where I'm safe and more easily monitored.

But I kept my promise to my father and was good—an easy promise to keep. I'm not like Georgie, or the kids who snuck out of their cabins in the middle of the night to do god knows what. *If only*.

There is literally a couple kissing in the seats across the aisle from me and no adult has said a thing about it. So much for adhering to the seating plan. I study the teachers at the front of the bus, chatting away like they're just grateful not to be stuck inside a classroom or on the same bus as Mr. Hopper. Are they really this clueless or do they just choose to look the other way? I figure it's because they probably don't give two shits about morals and purity.

Just as I'm about to put my headphones on, a fellow ninth grade boy makes an obscene gesture at the kissing couple. The bus erupts into laughter, causing one of the teachers to clap his hands loudly as he makes his way up the aisle. His behind blocks my view as he reprimands both the kissing couple and the obnoxious boy.

As things settle down, I put my headphones on and sink back into my seat. It's so easy to be invisible as a girl. You just close your eyes and stay silent, waiting for the boys to take up space. Which they will. If you don't challenge the status quo, if you slither off into quiet corners, you can almost, possibly, make it through four years of high school completely undetected. As much as I'd like to believe

I want that, a part of me so badly wants to be seen. But then I'd also have to be perceived, and the idea of that kind of makes me sick to my stomach.

A few songs into my "never show anyone this playlist" playlist, my eyes blink open to find the guy who cut me off in line staring down at me with a crooked smirk. His only saving grace is that he's wearing a Smashing Pumpkins T-shirt. I place my headphones around my neck and pause the song on my phone.

"What is it?"

He slides in next to me. "Do you realize you were singing loud enough for the entire bus to hear?" His body is angled toward mine. His left arm hangs over the green vinyl bus seat in front of us, and I feel caged in. But it doesn't bother me as much as it should.

"I was not."

"Hey." He pokes the head of the girl sitting in front of us. She turns around. "Did you hear her singing a minute ago?"

The girl looks at me, her face pinched. When her eyes connect with his, she noticeably softens. A smile grows on her face as she nods. Just as quickly, it disappears when her gaze flits to mine before turning back in her seat. Guess I'm not as invisible as I thought.

"See?" he says.

I fold my arms over my chest. I couldn't have been singing that loudly. Between the mix of conversations and most of the windows being open, letting in the crisp fall air, it would be hard to hear much of anything.

"Can I help you?"

"Yes, actually." He leans against the seat, looking defeated. "I got into a little fight with a friend and I need somewhere to sit."

"So, you come to me in desperation." I glance to the back of the bus, not bothering to be discreet, and find a group of girls comforting a beautiful blonde. "What did you do?"

He faces me, eyebrows furrowed. "I didn't do anything. I just said her stories about her horse were kind of boring. Then she told me to sit somewhere else."

"Lucky me. So did you . . . ? Never mind," I say, shaking my head before staring out the window.

"Did I what?" he asks, and he's sitting so close I can feel his warm breath on my neck.

I turn slowly so as not to bump noses with him before pressing my back against the window, trying to put space between us. "Did you and horse girl meet on this retreat?"

He buries his laugh. People are always doing that around me. "Her name is Avery. We actually met over the summer. At a party."

Ah. Parties. Heard about those. I've never been.

He leans back again, pulling at the stuffing coming out of a hole in the vinyl seat.

"Why are you even here?" I ask.

"I just told you."

"No. Not why are you sitting next to me. The retreat was for ninth-graders," I try to explain. "And you're clearly not in ninth grade."

A corner of his lips turns up and he raises his brows. "So, you know who I am?"

I roll my eyes before looking straight ahead. "Yeah. You're the person annoying me on the bus."

He laughs, and what's even more annoying is that I don't hate the sound of it. "My homeroom is ninth-grade Geography. Kind of goofed off last year. Anyway, I was given a trip form and filled it out.

No one stopped me from coming, so here I am. Got out of school for two days."

"And you had no problem being at a get-to-know-you niner retreat?"

"Well, I *was* kind of seeing Avery. Was? Am? I don't actually know right this second."

An exasperated sigh escapes as I fight the very strong urge to roll my eyes, again. "If you don't mind, I'd like to put my headphones back on." I try to raise my headphones, but he stops me.

"I do mind, actually." He smiles, and instinctively I slap his hand away.

"Don't touch my headphones." My words come out louder than I was expecting. Within seconds, Ms. Weaver is barreling down the narrow aisle, her hips grazing the sides of the seats.

"Lennon, is everything okay?" Her eyes dart between me and my seatmate.

"Yes." I swallow, trying to ignore the fact that almost everyone on the bus is watching. "Just a misunderstanding."

"Those always seem to happen around you, Mr. Brody, don't they?" Ms. Weaver narrows her eyes at the guy, and he shrugs slightly. A smile stretches tightly over her teeth in response. I can't believe she's falling for it. "Try to keep it down. We'll be back at school soon." She returns to her seat at the front of the bus, seemingly more bothered that we interrupted her conversation with the other teachers.

"Your name is Lennon?" my uninvited guest asks, head tilted.

"Yeah. So?"

"As in John Lennon?"

"Yes." I shift in my seat to face him, preparing myself for the typical questions.

He smirks, again, and this time I can't help but notice his blue eyes. His brown hair that can't seem to stay tucked behind his kind of big ears. And his broad shoulders that he hasn't quite grown into yet.

"I've never heard of a girl named Lennon. I've never heard of *anyone* named Lennon."

"Didn't you know it was big with the hipster sect of millennials?" I say. "That and Bowie."

He laughs again, studying me like he's trying to figure out if my attempt at humor is on purpose or if I'm just awkward. In this situation, it's likely my autism.

"Your parents are hipsters, then?"

"No. There's nothing hip about my parents. And technically they're Gen Xers."

"Then why Lennon?" He clenches his jaw in this masculine way that sends a pulse of something unfamiliar through me.

"My dad is a big Beatles fan." My answer comes out dry, like I expected him to have pieced it together by now. I'm always doing that. Expecting too much from people. "And I was born on John Lennon's death day, December eighth."

A laugh escapes him. "That's morbid as fuck."

"I think so too," I say, trying my best not to laugh or smile. It's this personality I've built for myself. Distant. Tough. Very different from the role I play at home. And it has never made me the most-liked girl in my grade. Elementary school was hell. Once I finally learned why it was so much harder for me than others, I stopped trying to be like everyone else. My autism diagnosis by the end of sixth grade was a relief. But it also made me guarded.

"Want to know something funny?" He shimmies himself closer as if he's about to tell me a secret. His knee comes into contact with mine and it's exciting in a way I hate myself for admitting. "My name is John. So, like, together we're . . ."

"John Lennon," I say, completing his sentence, as deadpan as possible. It's either that or let my mind decide we were destined to be together. There's a romantic in me. I try to tame her but she's annoyingly persistent. "Awesome." I hold in another smile while ignoring the warmth quickly rising up my body.

"Do you have any siblings?" he asks. "And are they also named after members of the Beatles?"

I can't tell if his question is him being a smart-ass or if he's genuinely interested. I decide to answer because something about him intrigues me. "I have an older sister. Her name is Georgie, but she's not named after George Harrison. At least that's what my dad tells my mom."

"Then who's she named after?"

"My dad. George." I say it without much inflection because talking about my dad to this very attractive boy is weird. Like I'm doing something I shouldn't do.

"And what's your mom's name? Yoko?"

I give him an unamused look. "Mary."

"No way. *My* mom's name is Mary."

"No way," I repeat with less emotion than John.

He smiles, and I smile back because my body sometimes acts of its own accord and betrays me by responding to stimuli without checking in with my brain first.

"My dad is James. My sister's Valerie and my little brother is Mikey."

"Any pet fish you want to tell me about?" I instantly regret the sarcastic tone of my question. Sometimes the words slip out before

I have a chance to think about how they might sound out loud. I wish I weren't like this, but also, I don't know how else to be.

"I did have a fish named Harvey when I was younger. But he's dead," he answers.

"RIP Harvey."

John leans in slightly, a smile decorating his face like the smallest but most beautiful ornament on a Christmas tree. "What was that song you were singing?"

"I wasn't singing any song."

"So, you're not going to tell me?"

"No." I grin. "I don't share secrets with people who cut in front of me in line."

He sizes me up, his mouth forming an O as if he's just realized his blunder. "What can I say? I was looking for an in."

"False flattery doesn't work on people with more than two brain cells, *Mr. Brody*," I say, mocking Ms. Weaver's tone.

"I'll wear you down one way or another. Besides, you can't deny all the coincidences. We're connected." He leans in slightly as his eyes sear into mine. It makes me forget how annoying he is. Because he's not annoying. He's challenging me in a way I'm not used to. And maybe, in some small, dark corner of my mind (or body), I don't want this ride to be over so soon. I want to stay in this moment. The moment before I have to get off this bus and enter my parents' car, breathing in the stale air left behind on my ride to school yesterday. I kind of want John Brody to keep asking me questions. To keep "accidentally" pressing his thigh against mine. To keep me from remembering who I really am.

"John."

His eyes peel off mine and he jerks his body toward the aisle. The blonde, Avery Morgan, from the back of the bus, stands there with red-rimmed eyes. We're in two classes together. She's the kind of pretty that an instruction manual on how to be a perfect girl would use as a model. Hair this way. Makeup like this. Dress in these clothes. *Warning: results may vary.*

"Will you come sit with me again?" She pouts and stretches her hand out.

John exhales as he rises, taking her hand. He looks back at me. "I'll leave you to your music. Or whatever it is you're *not* listening to."

"I guess you'll never know," I say, biting back a smile as he begins to walk away.

John stops and releases Avery's hand before turning to me. He lowers his head and says, quietly, "Someday I will."

Before I can muster up another clever reply, he's already at the back of the bus. He shoots me a grin as he places his arm around Avery's shoulders. I turn around and sink into my seat.

Someday.

Doubtful.

I bet that's the last time the two of us ever exchange words.

People like John don't make friends with people like me.

"Connected" or not.

We're as far apart as the moon and the ocean. The sky and the sea. He's up there and I'm . . . I'm down here. Behind iron gates.

Chapter Four

OCTOBER 2

"Thanks for coming on this walk with me," Georgie says, tucking her hands into the sleeves of her hoodie. The autumn leaves crunch beneath our feet; the sun has already set. There's something about a Sunday night. The anticipation—or is it the dread?—that makes it feel like a ticking time bomb.

"I didn't have any homework so no excuse to say no," I reply, a bit too honestly. But it's Georgie. She doesn't require my forced politeness.

"Fresh air is good for you." She nudges me with her elbow as we turn the corner. "So, Andie seems really nice."

I bend down to pick up a bright red maple leaf, struck by its deep color and smooth texture. "Yeah. She is. I'm not sure if Mom and Dad like her, though." I pass the leaf to Georgie, who looks at it briefly before smiling at me.

"They probably weren't expecting the first friend you brought home from high school to be so beautiful. And loud. She can also really shovel back the food."

We both let out a small laugh.

"They're the ones who want me to have friends, and then when I finally find someone I'm excited about, she doesn't meet their impossible standards." I quiet for a moment, my angry and accusatory words twisting around in my stomach. "It's not like they said that to me, but . . ."

"Their faces say it all." Georgie's glance flicks to mine before she releases what is either an exasperated breath or a defeated one. "Besides, they'll never think anyone is good enough for you. Friend or lover."

"Lover?" I shudder at the word. "Gross."

Georgie smirks as she passes the leaf back to me. "Aside from some quality time with Andie at the retreat, did you make any other connections?"

"Is this your way of asking if I have any crushes yet?"

"Maybe." Her smile widens. "Nobody crushes like you, Lennon. It's been a while, though."

"That's because I went to school with the same kids for ten years. The novelty wore off by sixth grade."

"And now? New school. New options," she says.

"Maybe."

"No one on the trip caught your eye?"

"No one in ninth grade."

"An older boy?" She stops walking to look at me, eyes brimming with excitement.

"He's in tenth grade. We only spoke for a few minutes. And he has a girlfriend. A really beautiful girlfriend."

"What'd you talk about?" she asks as we circle back to our street.

"Nothing really, but the thing is, it didn't feel like work, you know? Which was nice."

"Maybe he can be a friend."

"Yeah. Maybe."

A friend.

"So, listen," Georgie says as our street comes into view again. A cool breeze whizzes by and more leaves fall off the trees as we walk beneath them. "I'm not coming back to school tomorrow."

My feet halt and Georgie traces her steps back to where I've stalled.

"Why?"

She lets out a deep breath. "I'm not ready. I'm finally starting to feel better physically, but mentally I can't handle the looks and the questions. They all know. Everyone knows."

I shake my head. "How do they know? I don't tell them when they ask me."

"It got out. Somehow."

"Zach?" I say, a coolness to my tone.

"Maybe."

"Are you two still together? Because I saw him talking to that redhead last week. The one he dated before you."

Georgie rolls her eyes. "Tell me exactly what you saw."

Georgie always does this. She asks me to go into detail when I'm recounting an event. She doesn't realize that I know the real reason she does this is because she doesn't think I can read situations correctly. But I can. From a distance, anyway.

"They were standing face-to-face. And then he said something that she must have found funny because she kept throwing her head back and laughing like this," I say, and I demonstrate.

"She's such a pick-me."

And he's such an asshole. But I keep this to myself.

"To answer your question," Georgie says, cutting through my thoughts. "Yes. We're still together."

I nod, and she points her chin ahead of us. We begin walking the final steps until we're back home.

"Would you choose him again?" I ask once we're at the foot of our driveway. All the exterior lights are on, and our house looks like a model home: you can look but don't touch. Deep-red bricks. Black-framed windows. Three-car garage. Meticulous lawn. Not a stray leaf in sight.

"I don't know. Doesn't matter anyway." Then a tiny grin appears. "How about this?" she says. "When people ask you where I am, tell them I'm being homeschooled. In Switzerland. With our rich aunt. And that I send you selfies with the French Alps in the background. Daily."

"Okay. But if you're in Switzerland, it would be the Swiss Alps."

"My mistake." Georgie chuckles before wrapping her hand around my wrist and pulling me up the driveway with her. I release the red leaf in my hand and allow it to fall to the ground. An imperfect speck on an otherwise pristine canvas.

A couple of days later, I'm crouched, searching through a pile of novels at the bottom of my locker. I need something to keep me and my falafel sandwich entertained for the next forty minutes. Andie's off with Dean, the guy she's been "talking to" since the retreat, but I don't really mind. It means I can spend my lunch in the library, reading. And, more importantly, decompressing.

"Lennon."

I look up at the sound of the familiar voice. Zach.

"Yeah," I reply as I make my selection and stuff the book into my backpack.

"We need to talk."

I sigh before bolting up and slamming my locker door shut. "What is it?"

Zach glances around before clasping my arm and moving us to a quieter spot in the hall. I twist out of his grasp, narrowing my eyes at his. To think I will now be tied to this person for the rest of my life. No one asked me. No one ever asks me.

"Are you telling your sister that I'm flirting with other girls?" he asks, his blond hair hanging in front of his face. Every time he comes over, my dad stares at the diamond studs in his ears. Neither of us understand what Georgie finds appealing about him. When Georgie first showed me his picture, I thought he was cute enough, but then I met him. He's not funny. He's not smart. He's just some mediocre guy who got my sister pregnant.

"No. I said that I saw you flirting with a girl. Not girls, plural."

"Lennon." Zach exhales a heavy breath as he pinches the bridge of his nose. "You can't go around making up lies. Are you trying to break us up?"

"I wasn't lying. I told her what I saw. You and that redhead were talking over there," I say, nodding my chin to the bank of lockers down the hall.

"Right. We were talking. Not flirting. Just because a guy and a girl talk doesn't mean they're into each other. Grow up."

"You grow up, asshole," I shout. Then I push him away.

"What the fuck, Lennon?" He doesn't respect the boundary I tried to enforce and returns to where he was, looking down at me.

"You've ruined my sister's life," I say, through gritted teeth. "And you've ruined my life. Just go away."

Zach straightens, surveying the hall. He steps even closer then and says, in a quiet but stern tone, "You're causing a scene. Your sister doesn't want everyone to know. Keep it down."

"You're right. She didn't want everyone to know, but somehow, they do. Tell me, Zach. Why is that?"

His eyes lower to mine as a frown appears on his face. "I'm not the one telling people."

I huff out a laugh. "Well, it's out there, and people know, and now she doesn't want to come back. And you're to blame. For all of it."

"That's not fair," he says.

"Fair?" I say, feeling my eyes bulge out of their sockets. "You want to talk about fair? Georgie is at home, alone, missing her senior year, while you get to pretend, at least for seven more months, that everything is normal."

"You don't think this affects me too?" he asks, pointing a finger to his chest.

"I don't care how it affects you," I retort, my voice rising with my words. People are slowing down around us, and it freezes me in place, but not enough to stop the words from coming out of my mouth. "You're nothing to me."

Zach shakes his head and gets in my face. "You may want that to be true, but it's not. And telling your sister lies isn't going to make me or the baby go away. You're not a kid anymore. Stop acting like one."

"Go away." My hands form into fists. I want to scream. I want to cry. I want to shut my eyes so tight that when I open them I'm back in my room, away from Zach, away from school, and away from all these bystanders witnessing my very public meltdown.

"You heard her." A voice cuts through the silence and I open my eyes. John. He's standing in front of me, blocking Zach from getting any closer. "Leave."

Did I just dissociate long enough that I conceived this moment? Because how could this be happening?

"Whether you like it or not, I'm in your life," Zach says to me.

"Leave," John repeats. He continues to stand in front of me like a shield, even after Zach has walked away. When the small crowd that has gathered begins to disperse, he turns around, and I immediately look away.

"Thanks," I say, my voice just above a whisper.

"Who is that guy?" John asks. When I don't answer, he cups his hand around my arm, lowering his gaze and forcing me to meet his eyes.

"My sister's boyfriend."

"He shouldn't speak to you that way."

I nod.

John looks down, sees he's still holding my arm, and lets go. "You okay?" he asks.

"Yeah."

Except I'm not. It's hard enough to deal with rehearsed interactions, but being confronted by Zach took me completely by surprise. Even before the baby news, I never let myself get close to him because I figured he was temporary. Add that to the list of things I was wrong about.

"I'm glad I ran into you," John says, somehow knowing the exact perfect thing to say.

Unsure how to reply, I don't, and I adjust my backpack instead, almost losing my balance.

"Do you need help with that?" he asks, seemingly fighting a smile. "What have you got in there? Bricks?"

"Books."

"Are you taking extra courses?" he asks.

"Not textbooks. Just books. To read. For fun?"

He leans in and raises his brows. "Like smut?"

"Yeah. Smut," I say. "Anyway, thanks for your help, but I'm fine now."

"Are you? Because you still look a bit not fine to me."

"That's just my status quo," I say. "I have RSF: resting sad face."

John laughs so loud it echoes down the mostly empty hall.

It's like, I want John to keep talking to me, but I also want the conversation to end so I can dissect it in my brain, line by line, look by look, touch by touch.

"Sing any good songs lately?" he asks with a smile so wide it shows off his perfectly white teeth. There's a tiny gap between his two front teeth that I didn't notice on the bus. It's incredibly endearing. Why are the most annoying guys the best-looking ones? Not that he's annoying. He's just annoyingly out of reach.

"No. I reserve my public concerts for school buses," I say, a response so witty that even I'm impressed.

He grins as he runs his fingers through his hair. This time the motion brings my eyes to his arm.

"So, the reason I'm glad to run into you is because I want to apologize," he says, seemingly out of nowhere.

"For what?"

"For cutting in front of you in the bus line. And then for bothering you on the bus."

"It's fine," I say. "You didn't bother me that much."

Don't get obsessed. Don't get obsessed. He's just being polite.

"Good. I'm glad."

We remain in the hallway, alone, my backpack strap on its way to leaving a permanent indentation on my shoulder. Every time I think John's going to end the conversation and walk away, he keeps going. He must really feel bad.

"So, you probably—" I begin, taking a step back, but John cuts in.

"What's your favorite Beatles song?"

Despite the weight of my backpack, a lightness comes over me at his question. After getting off the bus the day we met, I did a little investigative work. More specifically, I cyberstalked him. He's an Aries. He's in a band. He likes old-school rock and indie music.

"You get three guesses," I say, sucking in my cheeks to prevent John from witnessing any more unbridled vulnerability.

"Okay." He nods and rubs his hands together. I hear my father's voice warning me that boys never approach a girl without an ulterior motive. But John said he wanted to apologize. Which he did.

"'Let It Be.'"

"Nope. Down to two."

He runs a hand down his face before blowing out a dramatic puff of air. "Based on the little I know about you, I'm fairly certain it's not one of their more popular songs. And it's got to be something romantic, because you're a girl and you like to read."

"You're saying a lot of words. Some of them gender stereotypes. None of which are song titles."

"Okay, okay," he says. He looks up and our eyes lock with sudden intensity. "'I Want to Hold Your Hand.'"

"Sorry?" I ask, swallowing, my eyes frozen to his gaze.

"It's my second guess. 'I Want to Hold Your Hand.'"

"Oh." I shake my head with a bit too much vigor. "No."

"Shit. I'm down to one," he says before biting on his lower lip.

Ulterior motive. But what could it be?

"Kurt Cobain," I say.

"Kurt Cobain?" he repeats.

"It's a clue," I say around a swallow while focusing my gaze on the floor tiles.

This is the part where I'm supposed to tell him to come find me if he ever figures it out and walk away like the cool girl I'm not. But if I did that, I could be walking away from the last conversation we ever have.

Why do I care? He has a girlfriend. Not to mention he's completely out of my league.

"'And I Love Her,' right?"

I lift my head to meet his gaze. There's a proud smile on his face, but I'm not quite buying that he figured it out that quickly.

"You're right," I confirm. "So do you know the song, or did you just find the answer via Google?"

"I don't. And I did Google." He blushes and holds his phone up to show me his screen. "I'm in a band," he says, extending the conversation even further. Every time I try to come up with a valid and not-rude reason to walk away, the slack on his rope extends. Softening the newness of our relationship. Friendship? Acquaintanceship? "Maybe I could learn this song," he goes on.

"If you'd like," I say.

He grins, unfazed by my apparent lack of enthusiasm. But inside, I'm enthused. Deeply.

"Let's shake on it," he says, stretching his hand out.

I place my hand in his and the wall I build to keep people out transforms into a fence. An old, rickety one that looks like it could collapse with a strong—or not even all that strong—gust of wind.

"What are we shaking on?" I ask, hearing the tremble in my voice.

He laughs. "That I'm going to learn the song and then I'll perform it for you. I know, if I'd like. And yes, I would like."

"Okay," I say, removing my hand from his.

John clears his throat. "So, you heading downstairs?"

"Yeah. To the library."

"Right. Books. Non-smutty ones." The curve of his smile brings my eyes to his mouth. He's got a tiny scar above his lip that's shaped like a tidal wave. *I wonder if you can feel it when you kiss him.*

"I like reading love stories," I blurt out. "It's fun being on the outside, looking in, witnessing two people fall in love. And the thing about romances is that you're always promised a happy ending. With the world on the verge of collapse every day it's kind of nice having a sure thing you can escape into."

John's mouth is slightly open, his eyes studying me. I said too much. I was creepy. He probably thinks I'm the sort of girl that stalks guys on the internet after one small interaction.

"I get that, but I'd argue that there's one thing better than witnessing a love story," he says, his eyes on mine again. "Experiencing your own."

A buzzing comes from the phone in John's hand, and it saves me from trying to come up with a smart response, because how do you respond to something like that?

John looks at his phone and sighs. "I've got to run. You sure you're feeling okay?"

"Yeah. I am."

"Good." He nods. "I'll see you around."

I watch as John walks away. He turns back to smile at me before rounding the corner. A breath goes in easily, despite my accelerated heart rate. I pull my earbuds out of the front pocket of my backpack and quickly put them on. I search through my phone before hitting play on "And I Love Her" and allow myself to smile as I enjoy the remaining bits of dopamine.

Chapter Five

OCTOBER 21

Before high school, Friday nights meant the start of a hibernation cycle. I'd come home from school, change into comfortable clothes, tackle homework right away, and then settle in for a couple of nights of gaming, movies, writing, and/or whatever special interest was occupying my mind at the time. Of course there were also the familial obligations. Meals together. Sometimes church on Sundays. Occasionally being dragged to some Arab person's home or party. But now that I'm in ninth grade and have a best friend, my Friday nights belong to Andie. And tonight, she's asked me to tag along to the movies with her and Dean.

There's just the small formality of asking my parents for their permission. Ever since Georgie's pregnancy, I try not to ask for too much, but it always feels like there's something I need or want from them.

"So what time is Dean the teenage dream meeting you?" I ask from my desk, where I've gotten a head start on my homework. Andie is lying on my bed, scrolling on her phone. I put my pencil down and let a breath out. "Sorry," I say, turning to look at her. "That came out rude."

She sits up and smiles. "Don't apologize. It was funny. Dean is meeting both of us," she says, emphasizing the last three words, "around seven."

"I guess I should ask my parents," I say.

"Yeah," she says, like *Duh* but kinder, and with a twinkle in her eye.

"How are things going with you and Dean?" I close my textbook and then squeeze in next to Andie, who makes room for me on the bed.

She stretches her arm out and takes a selfie of us. Her face, full and bright, contrasts sharply with my sad eyes and still expression. "We're just having fun," she says.

"Do your parents know about him?" I grab her phone, grimacing at the sight of myself before deleting the photo.

"I told my mom that I'm talking to a guy from the retreat. And she knows we're meeting up with him tonight."

"So they're okay with you having a boyfriend?"

"Technically I'm supposed to wait until I'm fifteen, but my parents are realists. They know that I'm going to do what I'm going to do, so they'd rather I just be smart about things and not lie."

"Can't relate," I say, almost to myself.

I give Andie her phone back and she takes a new series of photos, with only my shoulder making it into the frame of these ones.

It sometimes feels like everyone else is on a conveyor belt that is progressing steadily, hitting the easy-to-reach markers, while I'm off to the side maneuvering past boulders and other unexpected obstacles, trying and just barely managing to keep up with the pack.

I wish I could return to being the kid who didn't care about being on par with my peers or falling in love, but lately it's all I can think about. To the point where I wonder if I'm even normal. I share so much with Andie, but part of me is afraid to admit to her how often John crosses my mind. Because I know what she'll say: "You've had two conversations with the guy. You're reading too much into it." "He has a girlfriend." "He was just being nice." "Pitch closer to home." Okay, maybe that last one was my own inner critic.

The door to the garage closes with a thud and I sit up. "My dad's home."

"Do you want me to wait here while you ask?"

"Yes. Who knows what kind of mood he's in." I swallow before clenching my jaw. "If you want to go alone with Dean, I really don't mind staying home."

Andie props herself on her elbows and playfully scowls at me. "You're not getting rid of me, Lennon. So stop trying."

Andie knows I'm autistic. And not only that, after I told her, she read books and watched videos about autistic people. She's not afraid to call out my self-sabotaging ways. Outside of my parents and sister, no one else has ever been so determined to break down my walls. And yet I still can't shake the fear that I'm going to lose her one day.

I know that's part of why I push her away, so that I don't let myself get too close. I've seen what happens when I put too much trust in others. I go all in, and then one day, when they tire of me or get upset at something I did or said, they walk away. No conversations. No fights. No goodbyes. Just silence that feels like a slow death.

"Okay, I'll be right back," I say.

I close my bedroom door behind me as I leave and race down the steps. Mom's in the kitchen cooking and Dad's sitting at the island, cupping the open beer bottle next to him. I greet my father with a kiss on his cheek, and he wraps one arm around my waist, squeezing me closer.

"Yalla, dinner will be ready soon. Set the table," Mom says in Arabic without even looking up from the stove.

"Can I go out tonight?" I blurt.

"Out where?" Dad asks, releasing me from his embrace.

Mom shoots me a *you shouldn't have asked that* look, but I don't care. I've been in high school for almost two months, and I've had next to no social life outside of Andie coming over.

"To the movies. With Andie."

"I don't like this girl," Mom says in Arabic. "She's silly and loud. Don't her parents ever wonder where she is? Always here and there."

"You wanted me to make friends, and now that I have one, you don't like her?" I reply in Arabic, for fear that Andie might hear us.

Mom clicks her tongue like I said the wrong thing. With Mom, I always seem to say the wrong thing.

"Let her go," Dad says, taking a sip of his beer.

"But what about dinner? I made kibbeh," Mom says.

"We'll eat first and then go," I respond. "Andie knows how to use the bus, so you don't have to worry about driving us there."

"Bus? You think we'd let you use the bus?" Mom's eyes are wide like saucers at the very idea of taking public transportation.

"I'll take her and pick her up," Georgie says as she enters the kitchen, wearing her lavender sweats. She's somehow even more beautiful since becoming pregnant. She's still not showing. My stomach is bigger than hers. "I have some errands to run anyway."

"Errands." Dad scoffs. "You mean seeing Zach?"

"No. I mean errands." I can tell Georgie is biting her tongue. We're all learning that not every battle is worth fighting.

"Can I go?" I look to Mom for her approval. I already have Dad's. And a ride.

"Will there be boys there?" Mom asks.

"Lennon doesn't even like boys yet," Dad says, before taking another sip of his beer.

I choose not to reply. That way I won't have to lie.

After Mom finally agrees, I run upstairs to tell Andie the good news. We wolf down dinner with the rest of the family and then return to my room to get ready. Which for me means running a brush through my hair and packing my portable phone charger, small notebook, pen, and wallet. Andie changes into a different outfit and puts on mascara and a fresh coat of lip gloss.

"Want to borrow some makeup?" Andie asks.

"If I look like I'm trying too hard, my parents will think I have an ulterior motive."

"Your parents think everyone has an ulterior motive," Andie says, her lips curving up.

"You do catch on quickly."

As Andie and I come down the stairs, the muffled voices of my parents and Georgie grow louder. I hold in a breath, avoiding eye contact with Andie. It won't be long before another fight erupts.

Georgie storms out of the kitchen, her gaze widening when she spots me and Andie. "Let's go," she says, grabbing her bag from the coatrack and slipping into her Uggs.

I pop into the kitchen to kiss my parents goodbye. It's hard leaving them when I can clearly see how upset they are. I try not to take sides, especially since I can sympathize with both. But all that does is put me in the middle of an impossible situation.

In the car, it's silent for the first few minutes. I don't dare touch the stereo since Georgie is super serious about the terrible music she listens to.

"So, am I really taking you two meatheads to the movies?" Georgie asks.

I shake my head. "Where else would we go?"

"It's a miracle I got Lennon to agree to even leave the house tonight," Andie says, tugging gently on my ponytail from the back seat.

When we arrive, Georgie pulls into a parking spot. "Andie, can you give us a few minutes?" she asks, turning in her seat.

"Sure. I'll meet you inside," Andie says to me. "Thanks for the ride."

"No problem," Georgie says.

We sit in silence as we watch Andie cross the parking lot into the movie theater.

"You know why Mom doesn't like Andie, right?" Georgie asks.

I don't respond because I know Georgie is going to tell me regardless. She's good at reading people. Brilliant, really. She's just very, very impulsive. She was the kind of kid who touched the stove right after being told not to because she had to see for herself how hot it was. She learns things the hard way, but I also feel like that's the *only* way for her.

"It's because Andie is like me," Georgie states.

"They barely even know her. Judging people is their hobby."

It's quiet again. I want to use this opportunity to ask Georgie questions. How is she feeling? What's the plan? But how do you ask someone questions about their life when their life is falling apart?

I never told her about Zach confronting me at school. I figured I'd poked my nose in their business enough after blabbing and maybe embellishing about the redhead.

"Do you want to come to the movies with us?" I ask. "My treat."

Georgie doesn't answer. Instead, she shifts in her seat to face me. "I want to tell you something."

I unbuckle my seat belt and turn to her. "Are you okay?" I ask, even though I know there's never a simple answer to that question. Especially with everything going on. And that's the thing. No matter how devastating something is, life continues to go on. You still have to eat. You still need to shower and answer simple questions like "How are you?" You still have to *be* when being seems like the hardest task of all.

"Yeah." She wipes at the corners of her eyes and laughs. "Don't worry. I'm not going to off myself or anything like that. I'm just . . ." Her voice trails off and she runs her hands down her face before they land on her stomach. "I want this baby. I really do. I know that messes up Mom and Dad's plans for me, and your life, too, but I want her. And I'm going to have her."

I nod, because my throat is constricting too much for anything coherent to come out. It isn't often Georgie shows her vulnerable side, and when she does, admittedly, it makes me a little uncomfortable.

"Are you going to marry Zach?"

"I don't know. I don't think so."

"Are you *ever* coming back to school?" I ask.

"Not sure. Online learning feels a bit safer, you know?"

"Yeah." I stop firing off questions because she looks exhausted. And not the kind of exhausted that goes away with sleep.

"I'm sorry I did this to you," she says quietly. I can almost hear her fighting to hold back tears. She's so strong. Even now.

I'm the one who should be apologizing. I wished this baby away. A baby my sister clearly wants and loves. A baby she's already started calling "her," like she knows it will be a girl.

"I just want everyone to be happy," I say, not realizing how naive my words sound until they're out of my mouth.

"If you never hear anything else I ever say to you, hear this," she says, looking deep into my eyes. The blue glow of the building's lights shines into her car, reflecting off the light layer of dust on the dashboard. "Stop worrying about making other people happy. It's impossible. The only thing you can control is your own happiness, and even that is questionable. Okay?"

"Okay," I respond, but only because you can't really turn away advice like that. You can't say, "No. I won't run myself into the ground making sure others are happy" even though it's basically how I've lived my life so far. I just have a really hard time feeling joy when my parents are upset. Especially when that anger is directed toward me. I don't understand people who can go on living life like they exist in an alternate timeline. One where the earth isn't dying and children aren't losing their lives at the hands of taxpayer-funded military forces while so-called democracies resort to fascist extremes to control their citizens. Couldn't be me. I feel too much. I wish I didn't, but I'm soft. I'm sensitive. And to the outside world, it makes me look like a big, weak baby. It's probably why so many people infantilize me.

My phone buzzes. "It's Andie," I say, holding it up.

"Go. Have fun. I'll be here at ten, okay?"

"But the movie will probably end before then," I say.

"Then find another way to kill some time." She grins, and I smile back at her before leaving the car and walking to the theater.

"Lennon!" Andie squeals from the foyer, like she didn't see me just a few minutes ago. She runs to me, her enviable waist showcased under her crop top. She locks arms with me, and Dean trails behind us as we step onto the escalator.

"What movie are we seeing?" I ask. The scent of popcorn and fake butter is so strong, I can almost taste the salt on my lips.

"The one with what's-his-face? The guy who played Spiderman."

"That narrows it down," I scoff.

"Here." She slides a card into my hand as we get off the escalator. "Can you get us some popcorn and Cokes and some fruity candy for me? My treat. Pin is 2235."

"Sure," I say as she joins Dean who is talking to a group of guys. My eyes latch with one of them.

It takes me a second—my brain sometimes struggles to recognize people out of context—but it's him.

John breaks from the group and walks toward me. "Hey, how's it going?" he says with a nod as he keeps walking.

He keeps walking.

Frozen in place, I cover my open mouth with my hand. *Hey, how's it going?* That's it? Here I was searching my brain for the right conversation starter only for John to stroll right by me. Glad I didn't open up to Andie and tell her my true feelings about John. Saved myself some humiliation. I guess there really is nothing between us. Maybe I should just be happy he acknowledged my existence at all.

I really should have just stayed home. It's safer there.

A few minutes later, John comes out of the restroom and smiles as Avery and a group of her friends approach him. My eyes zero in on their hands and I watch as their fingers interlock. She's so lucky, and she doesn't even know it.

I force myself to leave this place where my feet seem glued to the carpet and walk to the concession stand. My heart is racing and I barely remember the order when the guy behind the counter asks me what I want.

"Miss?" he says as I struggle with the pin.

"There. Sorry," I say, looking up at him.

He doesn't accept my apology or even fake a smile. He only hands me the receipt, the snacks, and the drinks.

"Can I have a tray, please?"

He sighs heavily as he passes one to me.

I move to the side to gather everything. When the girl behind me places her order, the worker's face transforms. I turn back to see that it's Avery. Of course he's nicer to her. It's no secret that good-looking people are treated better. Just another hit for my confidence.

At this point, I'm ready to walk all the way home just so I can cry in peace. I hate it here. In the real world. Around people who instinctively know how to act and be. Just because I'm not a pretty blonde who knows how to place an order doesn't mean I deserve to be treated rudely. Maybe he wasn't rude, though. It can't be easy working at a movie theater on a Friday night. I shouldn't have let Andie talk me into this. God, I can't even go to a movie like a normal person without spiraling. But then, I was fine until I saw John. *Hey, how's it going?* It's NOT GOING WELL!

After dropping off the snacks and drinks to Andie inside the theater, I tell her I'm going to sit at a table and write. She offers to sit with me until I feel better. I'd rather be alone, though, and she knows that. I'm not trying to push her away, but I can't be around her and Dean right now.

There's a handful of small, round tables by the escalators. I sit at the cleanest-looking one and pull out my notebook. Maybe if I can get the words out and onto the page, I'll start to feel better. Exhaling a deep breath, I put my earbuds in and start writing.

"Lennon."

My hand shakes as I peel my eyes away from my notebook. Slamming it shut, I pull out an earbud.

"Sorry. Did I scare you? I was saying your name over and over, but you weren't responding," John says.

"I was listening to music," I say, removing the second earbud.

"Why aren't you in the theater with Andie?" John asks, still standing, hovering.

"I changed my mind about watching the movie."

"Is it a sensory thing?" he asks, rather astutely. *Too* astutely.

"How do you know I'm autistic?" I blurt.

He shakes his head. "I didn't. I just noticed you're often wearing earbuds or headphones. So I thought, maybe you don't like loud noises, or maybe it's so random guys don't bother you," he says, almost laughing to himself.

"I don't really get triggered by loud noises. And I don't wear headphones to keep people away. It's just . . . I like music."

"Me too. Speaking of . . ." He nods to the chair, and I nod back. John sits across from me as I grip my journal tightly in my left hand, the fingers of my right hand pressing into my knee.

"I've been practicing that Beatles song," he says.

"Alone or with your band?" I ask. It's a filler question. I wasn't ready for this interaction. I haven't rehearsed enough. Not that it would help. John never seems to ask me logical questions; our conversations are never linear.

"My band. Did I tell you about them?" he asks. "Theo Petropolis and Eddie Singh. Eddie's on drums. Theo on bass guitar."

"I know Theo." I grimace. "We go to the same church. He bullied me when we were younger."

"Want me to beat him up for you?" John asks, leaning in slightly, and even though I know he's joking, a part of me thinks he might.

"We haven't spoken in years," I say. "And with everything that happened to his father . . ."

"Right. He's a good guy now. I can attest to that. But your experiences are still valid, and I stand by my offer to kick his ass. How old are you?" John asks, his eyes flitting to my journal before meeting mine again.

"I'll be fourteen in December."

"Right. John Lennon's death day." He smiles, and I can't help but smile back. It's like a damn reflex—but only for him. Everyone else has to earn my smiles, both fake and real. "Can I ask you another question?"

"Okay," I reply.

"Are you masking?"

"How do you know about masking?" My hands fall still and I tilt my head at John. His more than base level knowledge of autism has me intrigued.

"My cousin, Nora, is autistic. She's only ten but she's way smarter than I'll ever be. Funny, too."

"I'm almost always masking," I say, replying directly to his question. "To a degree. Unless I'm alone. Depends on my comfort level. Sometimes it slips completely." Our eyes lock with sudden intensity, and instead of looking away, I hold it for a few seconds before picking up my pen. Just as something to do.

"What're you working on there?" he asks glancing at my journal again.

I tuck it toward me and shake my head. "Nothing. Just . . . why aren't *you* watching the movie?" I ask, deflecting attention.

"Avery wanted M&M's."

"The concession stand is over there," I say nodding to it.

"I tried to look you up on socials," he replies, ignoring my helpful direction. "Couldn't find you."

I swallow before straightening in my seat, willing my knee to stop thumping. "I don't have any accounts. What would I even post? Pictures of myself not smiling?" I say, putting the pen down and sticking my hands under my thighs. *Stop shaking.*

John laughs. "Can I have your number?"

"Why?"

"I'll need it to invite you to watch our band practice. You know, once we stop sounding like shit. You and I can't keep relying on timing and chance."

Timing and chance and the universe pulling two people together—it's the kind of thing I eat up. The kind of romance you only find in books. But this is real life, and if I want to stay tethered to John, giving him my number seems like the best way to do it. There's real life and then there's the lives we lead on our phones. I want to be part of both those worlds.

"Fine," I say. "Pass me your phone."

John unlocks his phone before handing it to me. His background is a photo of a small kid on a bike.

"Is this you?" I ask, holding it up.

He laughs. "Do you think I'm that in love with myself?"

"I don't know you well enough to answer that question."

"It's my little brother, Mikey," he says.

"How old is he?"

"Six."

"That's a pretty big age gap. Did everything change when he was born?" I ask, afraid to hear the answer.

He nods. "It did. In every way I expected. Mikey meant chaos. Milk and other stains on the couch. Toys everywhere. Nonstop crying the first year. But then it changed in ways I didn't expect. Like fighting over who got to give him his nighttime bottle. Racing up the stairs after his nap to bring him down. Teaching him to ride a bike." John rakes his fingers through his hair, his far-off glance meeting mine for a fleeting moment.

"That's sweet," I say. "But that's a baby brother."

"Is this . . ." He pauses before clearing his throat. "Is this about your sister?"

"Yeah." I look down at the table, the shame of the subject matter making it hard to once again look John in the eyes. But everyone knows by now. It is what it is. "The whole out of wedlock, teen mom thing makes the whole idea of her baby feel, I don't know . . . tainted."

"Once you all lay eyes on the baby things will change. For the better. Babies are the least of our problems now," he says, with a tight-lipped smile.

"There." I pass John's phone back to him.

"Perfect." He clears his throat again, and it makes the silence between us even more pronounced. "I'd better get that chocolate for Avery."

"Okay."

John nods a goodbye as he walks to the concession stand.

In his absence, his words from earlier echo in my head: "*We're connected.*"

I flip open my journal to a new page.

What if he breaks my heart?

And what if I let him?

Chapter Six

OCTOBER 30

I'm at church with Mom and Dad. Georgie stayed home. We don't attend every Sunday, but we go often enough that everyone knows who we are and vice versa. My father is on the board, which means he spends most of the service in the office at the back of the building talking with the other men. It's a boys' club. One of the last ones standing. I think that's why people hold on so tightly to religion, because it doesn't change. And I can understand how that could be comforting in a world that's changing so fast it's almost impossible to keep up.

I also think some people use religion as a crutch. Culture and religion are always being intertwined but they're not the same. It's not God that shames us.

Sitting next to my mother in the pew I can't help but feel a small level of satisfaction, knowing I'm doing something that makes her happy. I'm wearing the dress she picked out. My hair is styled the way she likes it. I really want to be the version of myself that my parents respect and are proud of, but I also want to be free to explore the things and people I want to. And the thing is, I don't think I can be both.

When the service ends, the priest invites the congregation to the basement for baklawa and coffee to celebrate another name day.

It's especially weird being here today without Georgie. Our once tight family unit now has a giant wedge in it.

I think my parents are still in denial.

At some point they will have to accept that a baby is coming.

At some point, so will I.

"Hey, Lennon."

I look up from the dessert table to find Theo Petropolis staring back at me. I've spent the last five years successfully avoiding Theo. It's easy enough to do since the only time we cross paths is at church, and I'm good at making myself invisible.

"Hello," I say, without the slightest hint of emotion. I continue to pile desserts onto my plate, hoping if I don't engage him any further he'll just slither away. But he doesn't.

"How's it going?" he asks as people push past me to get to the coffee station. It's super crowded down here, and loud.

"It's going." I look up to see a flash of disappointment in his eyes. But what does he expect? He bullied me at Sunday school. Who does that? It was a long time ago, though, and his dad did just die. Besides, he's friends with John. How bad could he be? "How are you?" I ask in return, allowing my edges to soften slightly. My words sound so phony, but that's pretty typical whenever I'm engaged in any form of small talk.

He leans in slightly, pointing to his ear to indicate that he didn't hear me. "Want to get out of here?" he says, almost shouting above all the voices.

I shake my head, struggling to process the fact that Theo thinks I'd go anywhere with him. But then an Arabic song blasts over the basement speakers and between the music, the body heat from the crowd, and the multiple scents of strong perfume and cologne, I find myself nodding.

With our tiny paper plates weighed down by Arab desserts, we exit the hall and walk up the stairs. We walk up another flight to the choir loft that looks out over the chapel. We sit next to one another on an old, dusty pew.

Theo loosens his tie before leaning back and shoveling an entire piece of baklawa into his mouth.

I hold my plate in my hand but can't bring myself to eat in front of this person. People can change, but it's hard to reconcile that with memories of how someone made you feel.

"So, I hear we have a mutual friend," Theo says, his words slicing into the air like an icicle snapping off a branch.

"Who's that?" I ask. Better to play dumb than give too much away.

"John Brody. He mentioned you and, well, there aren't many girls named Lennon, so I put the pieces together."

"Right." I nod. "He did say something about you being in a band together."

Theo's mouth stretches into a wide smile. "He's got us practicing that song you told him about. It's cool. I like it."

"Did you tell him how you knew me?" I ask.

"No. Because you already did," Theo says, his trademark cocky grin making its grand reappearance.

I look away, the plate of desserts shaking slightly in my hand. I place it next to me and turn slightly to face him. "It wasn't a lie."

"No." He shakes his head, his smile fading. "It wasn't."

"I should go," I say, thinking about how my dad's head would explode if he knew I was up here with a boy. I get up, taking my plate with me.

"Lennon," Theo says as I begin to walk away. I turn back slowly, trying to find a safe place to focus my eyes. "You should come watch our practice today." He says it so casually. Like we're old friends and not two people whose lives have orbited around one another's, barely ever intersecting.

"I'm not sure if I can," I reply, backing away slowly.

Theo rises and walks right up to me. "Are you saying that because of me? I'm not the asshole I used to be. I swear. I've grown up a lot. I've changed." Theo tips his head down, forcing eye contact. "I'm sorry if I said jerky things to you when we were younger. It was a long time ago, and I was a dumb kid who didn't know how to deal with the fact that my father was sick."

I nod, then shake my head. "I understand. And I accept your apology."

"Then it doesn't have to be weird between us anymore? You won't avoid me every time we're in church or at school?"

"I don't avoid you at school," I say. "I haven't even seen you there."

"Really? Okay." He lets out a small huff. "That's interesting."

"What's interesting?" I ask, even though I really need to put an end to this conversation.

"I see you all the time, and I thought the only reason you weren't making eye contact is because you were purposely avoiding me. But you seriously never saw me?"

"You know I'm autistic, right? Eye contact is a challenge on the best of days. But if it makes you feel better, I have spent the last five years dodging you at church," I admit, and Theo's laugh fills the space between us.

"Fair," he says. "I actually didn't know you were autistic. So thanks for telling me. Maybe now that we've hashed things out, you might say hi if we do cross paths?" Theo lowers his head again to meet my flittering gaze.

Hashed things out? He apologized and I accepted.

His eyes remain on mine as I think over his question. I just told him eye contact was hard, and yet his eyes are burning into mine like lasers.

"You're flustered." Theo smiles.

"No. I'm thinking," I retort.

"You're cute when you think."

Is he flirting?

"Then I guess I'm always cute," I reply.

Am I flirting?

"So come today," Theo says, his grin growing. "We're practicing at John's place. I'll text you the address."

"I really don't think I'll be able to," I say.

"Give me your phone anyway," he says.

I pass him my phone, unlocking it first, and Theo adds his number to it before sending a text to himself. He hands my phone back to me before holding his up. "Now I have your number."

I glance at my phone to see a missed call from my mom. *Shit.*

"Where were you?" Mom asks as we pull out of the parking lot. Dad's in the driver's seat, quiet.

"I was talking to Father Petropolis's son."

"Where?" Dad asks.

"At church?" I reply, hoping the vagueness of my response will be sufficient.

"In the basement?" Mom turns from her seat to ask me this. "Because I didn't see you there."

"No. It was too loud." I bite at my lip, tasting some of the honey from the desserts I crammed into my mouth as I scurried down the stairs to meet my parents in the parking lot.

"So where did you go?" Dad lowers the volume on the car stereo while glancing at my mom. Like she's to blame for letting me out of her sight.

"The choir loft."

"You went there alone? With a boy?" Dad's tone has shifted . . . slightly. So slightly that only someone who truly knew him would notice. I can feel his eyes peering at me in the rearview mirror while I focus mine on people in the cars we pass. People who can just drive away on this beautiful fall Sunday and listen to music and not have to worry about every single choice they make being judged and dissected.

"Theo is the son of a priest. He's like a brother," I say, even though I don't mean it. We're not even friends.

"You can't be going off with boys in the choir loft," Dad says.

"I didn't *go off with boys* in the choir loft. Theo and I ate our baklawa and talked for, like, five minutes." I sometimes wish I could force myself to shut up. Nothing I say will change the fact that they think I did something wrong. Something bad.

"What did you talk about?" Mom asks, her question like a test. Her eyes shift to Dad's as we reach a stoplight.

"I don't know . . . stuff. Theo goes to the same school as me."

"I didn't know that. He's a nice boy," Dad says as the light turns green.

"It doesn't look good," Mom cuts in. "Don't do it again."

"Do what?" I know I asked that with too much bite *and* spite, but what the hell? I didn't do anything wrong.

"Be alone with boys," Dad answers.

"Baba, we were at church. It's not like we were going to *do* anything."

"Khalas," he says, and Mom gives me a *cut it out* look from the front seat.

My phone buzzes and I exhale loudly before checking to see who it is. They may get the last word but I'm still allowed to breathe, aren't I?

Theo: Did you ask them yet?

Me: Now's not a good time.

Theo: everything ok?

Me: My dad found out I was in the choir loft talking to you

Theo: So?

Me: You haven't heard about my sister?

Theo: Oh.

Theo: I guess they're being extra protective.

Me: A high security prison is extra protective. George Hadid is Fort Knox. Thanks anyway for the invite.

Theo: You're funny.

Theo: 272 Langston Rd. John's address. In case you manage to get away.

Me: Not likely.

Theo: Can't blame a guy for trying.

Me: It's not you.

Theo: I know, it's your dad.

Theo: John will be bummed.

I look up from my phone as if I've just been caught doing something I wasn't supposed to. Thankfully my parents aren't paying attention to me anymore. But Theo's words feel a bit too . . . has John said something to him about me? Or maybe he's noticed me noticing John at school. Am I that obvious?

Me: John's just a friend.

Except that's kind of a lie. John has become all I can think about.

Every time we talk, I grow more attached to this idea of something that could never be. And yet, my mind keeps going back to all the what-ifs. Everything does. Every thought. Every idea. Every dream.

Everything comes back to him.

So, I stop myself from asking him questions.

I stop myself from thinking about him.

And I stop myself from dreaming as much as I want to.

Sometimes it feels like I stop myself from living.

And it's all because of him.

Not John.

The *other* him.

My eyes meet Dad's in the rearview mirror again and I look away. I can't stand the way he looks at me when he's disappointed. My stomach gets twisted up and all I want to do is fix it. But I never know how. And I'm tired. I'm tired of letting his anger seep through my skin and allowing it to affect me so much. Why do I give him so much power over me?

"Georgie?"

I knock gently on her door after changing out of my church clothes. I crack open the door to find her sitting at her desk. She's about twelve weeks pregnant now, and the morning sickness seems to have gone away.

"What're you doing?" I ask.

"Making a list. I'm going to the drugstore. Want to come?"

She seems to be in a good mood. I don't want to tempt fate by asking about it, so I blurt out my request instead.

"Can you drop me off somewhere?" I sit on the edge of her bed and swallow. "A friend invited me to watch their band rehearse. You could drop me off then go shopping and pick me up right after."

"A friend?" She turns in her chair and cracks a smile. "Which friend?"

I try to keep myself from smiling and blushing, but the body reacts how it wants.

"Do you remember Theo, Father Petropolis's son? He's the one who invited me, but the practice happens to be at the house of the guy I kind of have a crush on. And before you get too excited, it's nothing. He has a girlfriend." I am doing way too much.

"Theo?"

"No. John. The guy whose house you'd be taking me to."

"Is this the same guy you met on the retreat?" she asks with a smile.

"Yes."

"Where does he live?"

"Langston Road. There's a drugstore just outside his neighborhood," I say, hearing the hope in my voice. Or is that desperation? The idea of being on John's home turf thrills me in a way I don't want to admit.

"Fine. Go and tell your lover boys that you'll be there. I know you're just dying to," she says as she taps her fingers together in a mischievous kind of way.

Lover boys?

Clearly, she misunderstood. But I'll let her believe what she wants because I really want to go to this practice. No. I *need* to go.

Chapter Seven

Georgie drops me off, and from the driveway I get a view of John in his garage with his classic six-string acoustic guitar hanging off his body. The black strap digs into his shoulder in this almost intimate way.

There's an old couch in his two-car garage along with a drum set, mic stand, and a boxy TV, the kind I've only seen in my parents' old photos. There's also more stuff than a family of five could possibly need. It's piled in stacks against all three walls, seemingly seconds away from toppling over. This would make my parents, with their type-A tendencies, bug out. Their anxieties would have anxieties looking at this mess.

Our home is picture perfect. Shiny. Polished. A place for everything and everything in its place. Dad says he equates a clean home with a safe home, and I guess when you spend the first seven years of your life in Palestine, feeling safe isn't something you take for granted. As for Mom, she grew up with four messy sisters.

You would think two type-As together would be a perfect match, except they have different levels of insanity. Different reasons behind their need for control. Sometimes I find it so exhausting, all I want to do is scream "WHO CARES IF THE TOASTER ISN'T PERFECTLY PARALLEL TO THE WALL?"

"Lennon?" John's head jerks back at the sight of me, like I'm a flaw in an otherwise perfect portrait. Did Theo not tell him I was going to stop by?

"Hey." I turn back to watch Georgie drive away. "Theo invited me. Is it not okay that I'm here? You're probably not ready for an audience yet. I'm sorry."

John shakes his head. "It's fine. It's a nice surprise."

In my head, this was supposed to go differently. I would remember it one day as that time a cute boy asked me to watch his band perform my favorite Beatles song, the kind of moment that belongs in a Netflix teen movie. But standing here right now, my palms are sweaty and my mouth is dry. And there's no script telling me what to say or how to act.

I'm not wearing the perfect outfit to go with perfect hair and a perfect face of makeup.

John could butcher Paul McCartney's sweet lyrical voice, making me cringe on the inside while my face betrays me by communicating my unfiltered thoughts, like it always does.

My arms hang limply at my sides; I'm unsure how to stand or what to do with them. Regret floods me. Why did I agree to come here? Why did I push so hard for this moment to happen?

"Actually, I'm glad you came. It might force us to stop sucking," John says, with the sweetest smile I think I've ever seen. He could be everything wrong for me, but looking into his eyes, it feels right. So very, very right.

"Yo!" John shouts to get the attention of the guy sitting behind the drum set smoking a joint. "This is Lennon. Lennon, that's Eddie. He's high 90 percent of the time."

"Fuck off," Eddie says before taking another hit.

A moment later, Theo comes out of the house eating a sandwich. His black hair is slicked back. Or maybe it's just wet. He's wearing a white T-shirt and Dockers. He's this mix of '50s greaser and modern-day prep.

His face lights up as he swallows his bite. "You came."

I rock back on my heels and release a breath. "Yeah. Just for a little while."

"I'm glad," Theo says.

"We should start, yeah?" John interrupts.

"Did you eat my sandwich?" Eddie yells from behind the drums.

"Huh," Theo says before taking the last, gigantic bite. "I guess I did."

"I've told you not to touch my shit!"

"Next time, label it." Theo's challenging smirk is familiar, taking me back to those days when he'd single me out in our Sunday school classroom.

"Fuck this shit," Eddie says, rising from his seat. He picks up his drumsticks and walks out of the garage.

"I thought weed was supposed to mellow people out," I say in the quiet aftermath of his departure.

John and Theo both look at me, then laugh.

"I'll go. And you," John says, eyes narrowed at Theo, "don't mess with a high man's food." John places a hand on my arm and gives it a gentle squeeze. "I'll be right back. Don't leave."

He chases after Eddie, and it's just me and Theo alone in the garage.

I sit stiffly on the couch, praying the skunky stench of pot doesn't seep into my clothes. Theo sits at the other end, running his hands through his hair. It's just wet.

"That took a sharp turn. I probably shouldn't have come today. I'm sorry," I say.

He squints at me. "I asked you to come." Theo shifts so he's slightly closer and shakes his head. "I'm not sorry. And you shouldn't be either, okay?"

I nod slowly while looking into his glistening brown eyes, and it's like seeing him for the first time. "My dad was completely heartbroken when your dad passed away. Said he was one of the best."

Theo's face softens, and it makes him look younger than his fifteen years. In this moment, he looks like a boy who just lost his father. "Thanks. He was."

He opens his mouth like he wants to say more but clears his throat instead. Theo looks away from me as Eddie and John head up the driveway. Just seeing John again has my stupid heart pitter-pattering. Eddie approaches Theo with his hands in both pockets.

"Sorry, man," Theo says. "I'll buy you a burger after practice."

"It's all good," Eddie replies, shrugging slightly.

"Give me a sec," John says to his bandmates before taking my hand and pulling me up from the couch. He releases me and runs his fingers through his hair. "Avery just texted. She's coming over."

"Oh." I feel my face drop at his words. "Does that mean I should leave?" He doesn't respond, his silence telling me everything I need to know. What I should have known all along. I'm so stupid. "Got it." I swallow the burn in my throat, spreading fast like a forest fire. My eyes meet Theo's briefly before I head down the driveway.

I can't believe John just asked me to leave. After everything I went through to even come here. What a colossal waste of time. I text Georgie, telling her to meet me at the corner of Langston and Putnam when she's done. I'm so unbelievably embarrassed and angry that it's hard for me to get my message out without constantly typing the words incorrectly.

"Lennon." Someone calls my name as I reach the end of the street. But it's not him. It's not the voice I want to hear. John didn't chase after me like I half expected or pathetically hoped he would. I stop and shut my eyes tight, swallowing again as I wait for Theo to catch up.

"Can I walk with you?" he asks.

"I'm just . . . my sister is picking me up. I don't need—"

"But do you *want*?" His eyes are wide with the question, like he needs me to say yes almost as much I needed him to ask it.

I nod, and we walk together in silence, me with my arms crossed over my chest, Theo with his hands in his pockets.

"Guys our age . . ." He pauses, offering me a small smile before I look away. "We don't really know how to be. And we don't know how to be what you want us to be."

I glance at him sideways and let out a small puff of air.

"Do you like John?" he asks. It's such a simple question but also bold. And coming from his friend, it feels like a test.

I raise my shoulders slightly, not offering a definitive response.

"I think John sees you as a friend. You're just not really his type."

Theo's words are like a dagger to my heart. No one wants to hear that the guy they like would never, *could never* like them. I want to disappear. Or be woken up to discover this was all just one very bad, very vivid, very humiliating dream.

"I don't mean that in a bad way," he goes on as we continue walking. "He's the kind of guy that always has a girlfriend, and they're always the same kind of girls. You probably stimulate his mind in a way the others don't, but . . ." He stalls. "I don't see romantic feelings between the two of you."

"I didn't ask what you thought," I say, stopping mid-stride. "And if you're trying to make me feel better, you can stop."

Georgie's car pulls up to the corner. I walk to the passenger side and force myself to look at Theo one last time. He's standing on the sidewalk, his jaw slack. "If you ever see me in church, or school, and I'm not making eye contact, just know it's because I'm purposely ignoring you."

I get inside and slam the door without giving Theo another look.

"Is that him?" Georgie asks, nodding to Theo.

"Just drive. Please," I say, turning away, wishing this entire day could be wiped clean from my memory.

Chapter Eight

DECEMBER 17

"I'm thinking of giving John a letter I wrote," I say to Andie, seated at the kitchen island. My parents are at a Christmas party at the church hall. It's nice to be able to roam around the house without them poking their noses into our business.

"No, Lennon. Don't do that," Andie says as she closes the fridge. She passes me a can of pop and opens hers.

"Why not?"

"Because he won't get it. Trust me."

"What if I said it wasn't for him, but for me, to gain closure?"

"You're in your feelings because you just had a birthday and next week is Christmas, then New Year's. You're reflecting on the last year, and I get it, but John is better left in the past."

"I wish it were that easy," I say, opening my can of pop but not taking a sip. I get up to get a glass and fill it with ice. Andie sits in my spot.

"Is the letter in here?" she asks, glancing at my notebook.

"The page with the bookmark."

"Let me see what you've written."

I freeze by the cupboard and watch as Andie's eyes move through the three-page letter I've drafted. "Well?" I'm grasping the glass so tightly I'm afraid it might shatter.

"It's beautiful," she says, looking up at me, a slight frown painting her otherwise perfect face.

"But?"

"It's too much, Lennon. You spend an entire page comparing your relationship with him to an overused Rubik's Cube. He's not going to get that, sweetie," she says. "You're giving him far too much credit. He doesn't deserve it."

"Who doesn't deserve what?" Georgie asks, carrying multiple empty cups and plates from her bedroom. She has the most adorable bump now, small and perfectly round. She's decided not to return to in-person school for her final year, and I hate that for her.

Georgie unloads her dishes into the sink, and Andie looks to me for permission to answer her question.

I nod.

"Lennon wants to send a letter to a boy she had a situationship with."

"Not even that," I admit.

"What kind of letter?" Georgie asks, leaning against the counter, arms crossed over her chest.

"It just lays out my feelings and how I possibly read more into his actions than I should have. And how I think there is a connection between us, and how maybe we could try being friends again. I apologize for ignoring him after the band practice and for allowing myself to get upset, given that he'd been really clear with me about his girlfriend. I note how I did not respect those boundaries, and if we were to try being friends again, I would."

"And you also write 'I couldn't seem to help myself from forming a deep attachment to the idea of you. You, who suddenly became the boy in my story.'"

"That's really beautiful," Georgie says. "But you most definitely cannot give him this letter."

"Why not?" I ask again, putting my glass down on the island, looking from Andie to Georgie and back again.

"I'll take this," Georgie says to Andie. She peels herself off the counter and stands across from me. She's four inches shorter than I am but her presence has always felt much larger. "I'm glad you wrote the letter. It's a healthy way for you to process your emotions. That being said, it's too vulnerable to share with someone who you can't trust with your heart. If he has a girlfriend, it's also not appropriate for you to give this to him. Do you understand that?"

"Yeah." I nod. "But I don't say I like him *now*."

"Just because you don't come out and say you still like him in the letter, it's clear, babe," Andie says. "And as dense as most boys are, even they'd be able to see that."

"So, what?" I ask with a shrug. "I just do nothing? Wait for time to erase all memories of him?"

"No. You move forward. You talk to new people. You go out, have fun. Be fourteen. It doesn't have to be so serious," Georgie says.

"What if I don't want to meet new people? What if I want it to be him?"

"Does he want it to be you?" Georgie asks, her eyes searching mine.

"I don't know. Maybe if he reads this letter he'll change his mind."

"He won't, Lennon," Georgie says. "Words are not going to sway him. He's got a girlfriend. You have to respect that. Even if you truly believe he's your meant-to-be, then it will happen when it's supposed to. Until then, you need to give him space and live your life."

"Come on," Andie says, taking my hand. "Let's watch a sappy romance and cry our eyes out. It will make you feel better."

"Yes!" Georgie says. "It's been a while since I've had a good cry. Well, over someone else's poor life decisions."

I agree, because what else am I supposed to do? They think it's so easy. That I can just flip a switch and forget about John. But they weren't there. They don't know. They couldn't possibly understand how I feel when I'm around him. You can't just give up on something like that.

"Lennon?"

"Yeah?" I say, shaking away my thoughts.

"Where does Mom keep the microwave popcorn?" Georgie asks.

"In the pantry, next to the chips."

I walk to the kitchen island and flip open my journal to a new page.

It wasn't in my head. It was in my heart,
but it wasn't in my head.

Chapter Nine

APRIL 8

The thing about babies and pregnancies is that they serve as a real live measure of time. I watched all second and third trimester as Georgie's bump grew larger. Rounder. Harder.

On Christmas morning, Georgie bemoaned her swollen ankles as we unwrapped presents by the tree.

By Valentine's Day, Georgie's cheeks had completely puffed out.

And while bathing suit shopping together over spring break, I couldn't help but notice how her breasts had doubled in size.

It's like her growing baby belly is a clock counting down our remaining few moments of normalcy.

"No, no, Lennon, the parsley goes here," Mom says, taking the tiny garnish from my hand and placing it delicately over the homemade platter of baba ghanoush.

We're hosting a small baby shower for Georgie. This wasn't Mom's idea. She doesn't like flaunting Georgie's pregnancy in people's faces. She'd never want any of her snobby friends to think she condones my sister's actions. But when Mom learned Georgie's friends were going to throw her a baby shower at one of their homes, she quickly stepped in, taking hold of the reins. I think it's been good for her. To have this distraction.

The baby is due to arrive at the end of the month, and watching Mom frantically cooking, baking, and bossing around vendors kind of makes things feel almost normal. But also, very real.

Mom finally broke the news to her family over Christmas. Her parents didn't quite understand. Especially when Mom said Georgie and Zach weren't getting married. My grandparents blamed Mom, and then themselves for allowing her to move to Canada to marry my father in the first place. I know they're old *and* old school and say mean things in a fit of rage, but if they truly believe Mom would have been better off in Palestine then that means they'd be okay with the idea of neither Georgie nor myself existing.

While my mom and dad would never say something like that to me or Georgie, even in the heat of the moment, they do care far too deeply about what other people think.

Mom proceeds to straighten all the dishes on the folded-out plastic table that we rented for the "small" shower. This went from a gathering of about ten to somehow needing rented tables, matching tablecloths, and, of course, floral centerpieces.

Mom can never do anything small.

The guest list includes Mom, Georgie, me, Andie, ten of Georgie's friends, along with some of their moms, Zach's mom, his grandmothers, and a few of his cousins. Mom also invited her closest, least judgmental friends, most of whom do not attend our church.

"Are we all done here?" I ask, looking at our transformed backyard. The decor is subtle, but beautiful. Florals on every table. Some fun, but muted, balloons surrounding the dessert table. And even though it's early spring, Dad has had the backyard professionally tended to.

"Yes, yes," Mom says, examining the alignment of the multiple cake stands and rushing over to adjust them. "Go get ready."

I look down at my black T-shirt and jeans. "What's wrong with what I'm wearing?"

Mom's gaze snaps from the decor to me. "You can't wear jeans to a baby shower."

"But it's at home. I bet Georgie's friends will be in jeans."

"You are not Georgie's friends. You're the baby's aunt. Wear your paisley dress. The one I bought you last Easter."

I throw my head back. "I hate that dress. It's so corny."

"Corny?" Mom asks, giving me two seconds of eye contact before she rushes over to a table to recenter the florals.

"It's itchy and short. And I didn't shave my legs."

Mom breathes out a heavy sigh. "Fine. Wear dress pants, then. And a nice blouse. Go. Yalla."

What even is a blouse? This is not how I want to spend a Saturday in April. Especially when it's so nice out. But I'll suck it up. For Georgie. Seeing as I don't have a choice in the matter anyway.

I enter the house from the backyard to find Dad at the kitchen sink, washing dishes. "Made lunch for myself," he says proudly.

"You're not eating the catered food with the rest of us?" I ask.

Dad pats his slightly inflated belly. "Have to watch my sodium intake."

"What're you going to do during the shower?"

Dad's dressed in khakis and a polo. His hair is freshly washed, and the smell of his cologne lingers in the air.

"I was invited to Zach's home for drinks and cards."

"You're going?" I ask, my eyes wide at this revelation. Dad at Zach's home with Zach's dad? Weird.

"I said I'd stop by. Can't be rude," he replies, an obvious strain in his voice. Dad's not the most social guy, and this situation is sure to be awkward. I'd go with him to alleviate his obvious anxiety, but I'm expected here since I'm a girl and god forbid we upset gender norms.

"How're you doing at school?" Dad asks, almost out of nowhere, but it's not out of nowhere. He probably feels bad because all the attention has been on Georgie lately and my ninth-grade year is almost over.

"Good," I nod, walking over to help him dry dishes. "I'm really enjoying Music class."

Dad cracks a grin. I know he'd much rather I focused all my time on maths and sciences, but that's just not where my heart is.

"Don't worry," I say. "I don't have any grandiose plans of running off to be a singer. It's just kind of fun."

"Are you playing any instruments?" Dad passes me the last dish before drying his hands.

"The piano, a little. Mrs. Morales, my teacher, knows that I like to write and she's helping me turn some of my poetry into a song."

Even though it's faint, there's a small but proud smile on his face. We both speak the language of music. "Play it for me when it's done?"

"You'll be my first official audience," I say, putting the last plate away. "Outside of Mrs. Morales, of course."

"Of course."

"So, Georgie's due date is in ten days."

Dad's smile falters as he looks down. His nod is slight but it's there. "The baby could come any day now."

"Hard to imagine," I say. "A whole other human living here. Crying. Pooping. Crying."

My words manage to make him laugh a little.

"It will be an adjustment, but we have God with us, and we will figure it out. Together."

My dad leans on faith extra hard when life goes askew. But sometimes I feel like he uses talk of God and faith as a reason to cut a conversation short. To stop us from delving deeper. I want to know how he's really feeling about Georgie's impending birth because I'm scared, and it feels like I can't tell anyone that because no one else is admitting they're scared too, but I know they are. How can they not be? Life as we know it will never be the same. It hasn't been the same since the end of last summer.

"I have to go change," I say, tugging at my T-shirt. "Mom's orders."

As I begin to walk away, Dad calls out, "Lennon?"

"Yeah," I say, turning back.

"Want to grab ice cream tonight after all of this is over? Just you and me?"

"Okay," I say.

"Your treat?"

"Sure." I shrug. "The down payment for the castle in Ireland will have to wait."

"Ireland? Are you trying to kill me? You know I can't live without you right next to me." He laughs.

"Yeah," I say, not laughing back. "I know."

Chapter Ten

APRIL 13

Quarter to four. I've been waiting almost fifteen minutes for Mrs. Morales. She's buzzed into the music room over the intercom three times since I arrived, asking me to hold tight.

For the last three weeks, every Thursday, I've stayed after school to work one-on-one with Mrs. Morales. There's only so much time in a class period, and she's been giving me extra help. Learning how to transform my poetry into a song that tells a full story has been a fun challenge. Can I break someone's heart and put it back together in 360 seconds?

Mrs. Morales buzzes into the empty room again. "Lennon?"

I get up and press the speaker button. "Yes?"

"There's an issue at my son's daycare. Why don't you work on that verse some more and we'll reconvene at lunch tomorrow, okay?"

"Sure."

I release the button and sigh. I could leave right now, and Mrs. Morales would never know, but I am nothing if not diligent. And a people pleaser. I pull out the piano bench and sit. The sheet music is already propped up. Mrs. Morales helped me figure out which notes I needed when I hummed her the tune last week.

I hit middle C before clearing my throat. I hum at first to warm up my voice and because, even in this empty room, I'm afraid to hear myself. When you're raised to be quiet and obedient, you're sometimes afraid to be seen or heard.

But if there was ever a place to practice, it's the music room at school. The acoustics are a dream.

In here, I can forget about almost everything. Behind me is an audience, holding their breath as I captivate them with my song lyrics. *A girl can dream.*

Sometimes it feels like that's all I do.

On my thirteenth birthday, I decided to make a concerted effort to stop masking. I knew it would be risky. I knew it would mean opening myself up to an often unkind and harsh world. And people. I haven't been perfect. My default when I meet someone new is still to mask. I never want to let anyone in until they've earned my trust. But sometimes . . . sometimes the walls come down faster than I can put them back up.

Without all these conflicting emotions, without those intense yet confusing and sometimes embarrassing interactions with John, I wouldn't be sitting here, singing my heart out. Scribbling down lyrics to a song that didn't exist—wouldn't exist if I hadn't let John in. Even just a little bit.

I've spent the last six months trying to get over him. Instead, I find myself analyzing every single one of our conversations, which is just so unfair. While I'm sitting with my feelings, processing, John is out there, living his life. I don't even know if I exist in his memory. Maybe it was all one-sided. I do have an active imagination. I'm good at pretending. To be somewhere else. Someone else. Based on how skillfully we've managed to avoid one another since that deeply humiliating day in October, one might think we were strangers. It feels like that's what we're becoming. Of course, a big reason for that is me. I blocked his number as soon as I got in Georgie's car that day, and at school there may have been a few times where it looked like he wanted to say something, but I've always been quick to turn the other way or duck into the bathroom.

I play the final note and exhale, imagining a standing ovation behind me. What I didn't expect was to hear someone clapping by the open classroom door, the sound ricocheting against the walls. Jolting out of my seat, I almost trip backward in surprise.

"John."

"That was amazing," he says, leaning against the doorframe.

"It's not done yet. It was . . . I was just messing around," I say, folding my notebook closed. "What're you doing here?"

"Avery's got volleyball practice."

Feeling my guard go up even further, I grab the sheet music and stuff it into my folder. "Then why aren't you in the gym?"

John shrugs before standing straighter. "Sports aren't really my thing." He closes the door and walks toward me, his steps slow but purposeful. *What is he doing?*

"How have you been?" he asks, like my dentist who I see twice a year.

"I've been existing," I say with a nod. And then another nod. Why can't I stop myself from nodding?

Six minutes until my parents arrive to pick me up.

"Okay. Guess you really don't like small talk." There's a slight edge to his voice, enough that it makes me want to scream. What right does he have to have *his* guard up? "I thought we were friends."

"I don't have time to get into this right now," I say, swallowing down a lump of nerves.

He takes another step so he's standing across from me. Close enough that I can see the faint scar above his lip. "I'm sorry if my asking you to leave the band practice that day hurt your feelings. I just didn't think it would look good if you were there when Avery arrived."

Could he seriously be this clueless? I didn't imagine it *all*. He wedged his way into my life. And as soon as I let him, he pulled away.

"It was obvious that my presence wasn't welcome the second I arrived. Clearly, I'm only good enough to speak to when you feel like it."

John swallows so hard, his Adam's apple travels slowly down his neck. He takes a seat on the piano bench, and it pisses me off. He wasn't invited. No one asked him to stay. This is my territory. Just because he's a musician in a band doesn't mean he has any right to just barge in here and—

"I have a girlfriend, Lennon. You can understand that, can't you?" He says it so condescendingly, I could cry.

Four minutes.

"What're you doing here?" he asks as I shoulder my backpack.

"I'm planting a garden," I respond, my hands gripping the straps of my bag.

John watches me carefully, his eyebrows pinched. "Why're you being so hostile?"

"That fact that you're even asking me that makes me wonder . . ." I trail off. He doesn't deserve my truth. He never asked for it.

He stands, offering me a tight-lipped smile. "Then I guess I'll leave."

I get right in front of him before he can walk away, ignoring the small voice in my head telling me to shut up. The tips of my toes press against his. "I didn't ask you to leave," I say, shaking my head to stop the tears from falling. "I don't want you to leave." My voice cracks as I push the words out. Words I've been dying to say for months. "I want you to stay."

His face softens, giving me a sliver of hope that I haven't scared him away. And that he'll show me, with a kiss. The kind of kiss where he'll take me by surprise, grabbing my face and pulling me closer to him. The kind of kiss I've been fantasizing about since I got off the bus the day we met.

Two minutes.

"I miss you." The words, quiet and raw, tumble from my lips.

John shuts his eyes so tightly they turn into little slits. When he opens them, I'm filled with regret. No. I'm drowning in it. This isn't going to go the way I wanted it to.

"I'm not the one who walked away from our friendship," he says. "I tried to say hi to you in the halls. I even texted. You never responded."

"You kicked me out of your house."

His eyes shut slowly, and I can hear the smallest groan leave him. "You're misreading the situation. You're making it into something it never was."

"You telling a girl you want to sing a love song to her is telling her something, whether you want to admit it or not," I say, fighting back the tears that are begging to come out. "I take some responsibility here. I do. I let myself believe that there was something . . . I let myself fall, and that's on me. But you played a part in this too, and I think you need to admit it."

"You knew I had a girlfriend. I was always upfront about that. I'm not sure what you expected from me."

I am so tired of him and everyone else bringing up Avery. This isn't about Avery. If it were, he wouldn't be here right now. He wouldn't keep coming back.

"You can lie to yourself, John, if it makes you feel better about what happened . . . or didn't happen. But I was there. I was there too." I walk past him, willing myself not to cry. I open the door, but before walking through it, I stop and turn to face him. "I don't let my guard down for people easily. I just . . . don't. But I did, for you. I trusted you. I let myself let you in, and just like that, you made me feel like an idiot."

His eyes remain steady on me, even as I unravel in front of him. "That wasn't my intention," he says. "Maybe it would be different if you were a guy or had a boyfriend or if we really were just friends," he says, finally letting the facade crack.

"What do you think we were?"

"I don't know," he responds, shoving his hands deep into his pockets.

I nod, taking in his words, or at least trying to. "No one has ever made me feel the way you made me feel."

John rubs at his forehead. "I don't . . . what do you mean? Like, in a good way or . . . ?

A buzz cuts in from the speaker above. *"Lennon Hadid, your father is waiting for you in the office."*

"Shit." I turn to leave, but John gets ahead of me and blocks my path.

"What do you mean?" he repeats.

"My dad is here," I say, meeting his intense stare.

"He can wait."

"If I'm not there in sixty seconds, he'll come looking for me and if he finds me alone in a room with a boy, that's it. My freedom—the little freedom I do have, will be a distant memory."

"So this is how we're going to end it?"

"I guess so," I say, my heart racing too fast for me to speak more articulately. Not that John deserves more words. Or an explanation. He doesn't get to decide when that information is worth his time or attention. He doesn't get closure the second he decides he wants it.

He nods, almost reluctantly as he moves out of my way. Instead of bolting, I remain where I am, grasping for something, anything.

"Lennon." He says my name, but I can tell he doesn't know how to follow it up, and I'm not masochistic enough to wait and see if the right words do ever come to him. Because right now, I don't need words. I need him to show me how he feels and it's obvious that he doesn't know.

The way I feel, it can't be one-sided. It just can't. "Deal in or walk away. You don't get to watch the game from your golden perch, deciding when the best time to play is."

"I can't," he responds with a slight lift of his shoulders. Like anything more would be too much effort.

"Neither can I." Forcing myself not to look back, I walk out of the room. After turning a corner, I pick up my pace. I race past my father who's waiting in the foyer and get into his running car, slamming the door shut.

Chapter Eleven

SEPTEMBER 1

There was a full moon on April nineteenth, the night Paulina Hadid Spencer entered this world. All seven pounds, eleven ounces, with jet-black hair, glossy eyes, and an annoyingly cute, dimpled chin.

This tiny human being, who had once seemed like a parasite poisoning my family from within, was so breathtakingly beautiful that I fell in love in an instant. All the jealousy. The spite. The anger. It dissolved the moment my mom placed my niece in my arms.

Instant love.

They say it isn't real.

And maybe it wasn't instant.

I had spent nearly nine months trying to get used to the idea of her. Nothing anyone said helped prepare me for her existence. Mom's promise that my room would stay mine. Dad's insistence that the house wouldn't be overrun with toys. Georgie swearing she wouldn't ask me to babysit every spare second. No one's words were reassuring. No one's except John's.

Because he wasn't reassuring me by promising me things wouldn't change.

He told me they would, and he showed me that it would still be fine.

Maybe I'm romanticizing Paulie just like I do everything else. I'm not the one who has to get up every couple of hours at night to feed or change her. In some ways, my life isn't that different. I have the option to hide in my room and close the door. Georgie doesn't. And although my parents and I are dealing with Paulie's birth better than I expected, I'm not sure if I can say the same for my sister. Her emotions are all over the place. She cries *a lot.* But she also smiles a lot. And the tension that existed for nearly nine months has eased, like a slow leak in a king-sized air mattress.

Even Zach and I are getting along. Sort of. Better than we were. These things, I'm learning, take time. I'm also learning you can fight with someone and that doesn't mean it's the end of your relationship with them. Maybe it would have meant the end of Zach and Georgie if not for Paulina. But Zach is showing up. Surprising everyone.

He comes over every day, and sometimes the three of them look just like any other young, happy little family. Especially when they go on long walks with Paulie in the stroller. Georgie's attachment to Zach appears to be deepening. They're clearly in this together, and maybe they'll make it work. I guess it wouldn't be the worst thing. As long as it makes my sister and Paulie happy, because I want that for them. They deserve it.

My favorite thing to do with Paulie is take her for long walks. Long, but not far from the house in case there's a diaper situation. Just me, Paulie, my headphones, and my thoughts. Mom is completely obsessed with Paulie and won't stop talking about her upcoming baptism—I guess she got over worrying what the women at church would say. And Dad, I can tell he loves Paulie, but he hasn't fully let himself fall in love with her the way the rest of us have. Something is stopping him. Maybe he just needs a bit more time.

There's a knock at my door. I put down the book I'm holding but haven't yet opened. It feels kind of like a prop. Like I feel at school. Only there to fill a quota. Take up enough space to exist, but not enough to get noticed.

"Come in," I say.

Georgie enters, freshly showered, looking luminous. It didn't take long for her to return to her previous self . . . physically, anyway.

"Where's Paulie?" I ask.

Georgie smiles. "Having her third nap of the day, like the angel she is. What are you up to this last Friday before school starts?" she asks, sitting on the edge of my bed.

I sit up and pull my knees to my chest. My phone buzzes on my nightstand, and I sigh.

"Andie wants me to go to a party with her."

"Then go."

I bite down on my lip, studying my dry knees. I try to follow my sister's after-shower body butter routine, but I'm kind of lazy. Maybe that's my problem. I give up too easily.

"I don't know how to act at these things," I admit. "Everyone knows who Andie is, and when I'm with her, it's like I'm invisible."

"It's because you make yourself invisible. You started off high school strong. You met Andie. You let her drag you to things. But then you retreated. Somewhere around Christmas. I haven't seen you go anywhere in months. It's always Andie coming here. What happened?"

I swallow, wishing I could bury my face in my knees and make Georgie disappear. My entire existence is just so embarrassing, and

I don't want to talk about it. "What happened is what always happens. I misread situations. I come on too strong and I scare people away."

"I don't understand. Andie is still around."

"Not Andie," I say, as realization appears to dawn on Georgie's face.

"Oh. That boy. John. The one with the girlfriend." There's a beat of silence before Georgie goes on. "Did you tell him how you felt?"

"Feel," I say quietly, correcting her.

"That was brave," she says, nodding repeatedly, like she's searching for a way to make this humiliation I inflicted upon myself a positive thing.

"Yeah, well, brave or not, now all I want to do is avoid him. Which was easy enough to do with the school year ending and then summer, but it's September, and there's a good chance I'll see him if I go to this party with Andie."

Georgie nods for me to slide over and I do. She takes her spot next to me and places my hand in hers, leaning her head on my shoulder.

"I'm really, really terrible with boys," I say, tilting my head to hers.

"It takes practice. But also, when it's the right boy, it won't be this hard." She nudges her knee with mine.

"It's always going to be hard for me," I say, before gritting my teeth. "And Mom and Dad don't make things any easier."

"I'll take you. We'll tell Mom and Dad that I'm bringing you with me to Zach's."

"I think I'd rather stay home."

"You're going to lose Andie if you keep this up. She's been really patient with you so far, but there's going to come a point where she stops inviting you to things. And when she does, it will hurt your feelings. Relationships take work. Compromise."

"And what if I see him?"

"Do you want to see him?"

I shrug.

"I'll take that as a yes." She grins in that satisfied *I know you so well* kind of way only sisters can get away with.

I nod ever so slightly at Georgie's assumption, but really, what more is there to say? Haven't I already put my heart on the line? Wouldn't more words just be digging a deeper hole of despair and humiliation?

"I know life sort of feels endless now that you're fourteen—"

"Almost fifteen," I interrupt.

Georgie gives me a look. "You're always *almost*. Stop thinking about what you aren't or nearly are. Focus on the now. It all goes so fast. Having a baby has shown me that. My childhood is gone, and now every choice I make for my future will have to put Paulie's needs first. I don't know when or if I'll go to college or what I'll end up doing once Paulie starts school or even if I'll stay with Zach. The opportunities are not endless for me anymore. They are for you."

"Hello. Do you know who our parents are?"

"Stop living your life for them."

"So you think I should talk to him, or wait for him to come to me, or . . . ?"

"Stop overthinking." She smacks my knee and gets up. "Wear something cute. Brush your hair. Put on some mascara and get out there. Life is passing you by. *Your* life," she reminds me. "Also, I can't believe you like a guy named John. It's a little too on the nose, even for you."

Georgie smiles before closing the door behind her. I sink down into bed, my head resting on my pillow. I stare up at my white ceiling, the crown molding like a cage, trapping me in the four walls. There's a hairline crack in one. I study it, wondering what caused it.

After an exasperated sigh, I reach for my phone and tell Andie I'll meet her at the party. She texts me the address with about a million exclamation marks. When I reply asking her whose house it's at, she simply writes back: Theo Petropolis.

My stomach sinks.

"Just a few more steps," I say, with my arm wrapped tightly around Andie's waist. Andie decided to award my being there by spending most of the evening by the makeshift bar. She went from "I can handle my liquor" to "I'm more fun when I drink" to "I think I need to sit down."

We finally make it to an outdoor sofa. Andie flops onto it and struggles to hold her head up. I prop her legs on the table in front of her and position her body so she can rest without falling over or choking on her vomit. Ninth-grade Health class serving a purpose after all.

I glance at my phone. It's just after nine. Georgie isn't coming to get me until ten-thirty. She and Zach plan to drive Paulie around in her car seat in hopes it will put her to sleep.

With Andie seconds away from passing out, the anxiety inside me has gone from simmering to boiling over. Almost every time I push myself out of my comfort zone, I end up regretting it. I'm at a party with people I don't know at the home of a boy I have a complicated relationship with while my best friend is completely wasted. The old teen movies made parties look like a lot more fun than they actually are. But then those movies never followed around the autistic girl trying to keep her drunk friend from hurting herself.

Before I'm able to claim my seat next to Andie, two girls swoop in.

"We've been drinking," one says, barely able to hold back a string of obnoxious giggles. "We need this spot more than you."

The other girl locks eyes with me. *Avery.* I look away, praying she's too drunk to recognize me as the girl who pined after her boyfriend all last year . . . and lost.

"Bug Girl," she says.

My eyebrows pinch together. "Sorry?"

"You're the girl named after the bug group. What're they called again?" She slurs her words as she struggles to snap her fingers.

She knows their name and mine; we've had two classes together. She's just getting off on making me squirm. Isn't it enough that she has John?

Andie straightens from her sinking position, narrowing her eyes at Avery. "And what're you named after? Envelopes?" Andie laughs at her own joke before winking at me and slinking back down.

Avery and I exchange strained glances. She leans back in her seat, then whispers something to her friend.

As if the night couldn't get any worse, Theo walks by. It's my first time seeing him tonight and his gaze widens at my presence. Almost immediately, his eyes move off mine and land on Andie. He heaves a loud, dramatic sigh.

"Is she going to be okay?" he asks, as if I'm her keeper. I guess, in this situation, I am.

"Is there somewhere she can rest inside?" I ask, hopeful the two of us can stow away in a room until Georgie shows up. I'm going to have to bring Andie home with us. Her parents can't see her like this. My parents might not notice. They'll probably be in bed. As for why I'm with her, well, I'll just have to work on an excuse later.

A lie is not an excuse.

"Yeah, come with." His smile is sympathetic and his tone comforting. Or maybe it's the other way around.

"Can you help me?" I ask, nodding to Andie's limp body.

Together we lift Andie off the sofa. Avery's tense face eases into a Cheshire cat–like smile and she says to Theo, "Tell John I'm looking for him." I make fleeting eye contact with her, my heart dropping at her words, before heading inside Theo's bungalow.

"Where's your mom?" I ask as we walk through the quiet, dark halls of his home. It's cozy and modest from what I can see.

"Greece. She's there with her sisters." Theo opens a door. "You can chill in my room." Once inside, he very quickly grabs a plastic wastebasket and places it next to his bed.

"Thanks," I say, as I lay Andie down gently and take off her shoes.

Theo's bedroom is almost immaculate. It's weird being in a guy's room. Knowing this is where he gets dressed and undressed every day and every night. I think about him stepping out of his shower and entering his room in only a towel. His body dripping wet. His black hair hanging in front of his face. His kind brown eyes glistening. Like they were when we talked about his dad. My thoughts switch to him sitting on the floor of his bedroom, curled up, heaving sobs. I don't even know how to fantasize properly.

"So, you're on your own, then?" I ask Theo. "My parents would never."

"It's two weeks. I have family around in case of emergency or whatever." The ease of conversation we experienced in John's garage all those months ago no longer exists. I don't take full blame for that. He was a dick, although he's being less of one now.

I turn Andie on her side, tucking a loose strand of hair behind her ear. Without saying another word, Theo leaves.

I sit on the edge of the bed, running my hands over my face. Tonight was supposed to be fun. At least that's what Andie promised. A chance to put our tenth-grade selves on people's radar.

But I don't want to be on anyone's radar. After falling hard for John and getting rejected, my heart can't take being put through the wringer again. If I can't handle a crush, there's no way I'd survive a real relationship.

Why does everything always have to be so meaningful for me? Here I am, almost fifteen, and I still haven't been kissed. I've been waiting for that perfect moment, the perfect person, but I'm starting to think it was all an excuse to avoid experiencing something real.

Or maybe I'm just too afraid to learn that perfect moments don't exist.

A gentle knock at the door pulls me out of my thoughts.

"Lennon?" a familiar voice whispers, my name sounding like a tortured song as it travels to me.

I clear my throat and quickly stand, running a hand through my hair and down my body. "Yeah?"

The door cracks open and John hesitantly steps through it. "Is it okay?" he asks before walking farther into the room. Despite how much he's hurt me, he's still always so considerate and polite.

"Andie's asleep," I say quietly as my heart drums against my rib cage.

He nods and we remain standing across from one another, the distance at once intimate and infinite.

"Theo told me you were in here," he says.

"Oh."

"Oh?"

"I'm just surprised you . . . never mind."

"Finish that thought." He says it sweetly, and I feel myself reverting to that little girl with a crush. A crush that almost crushed me.

"I just figured if you knew I was somewhere, you'd go running the opposite direction."

John shakes his head. "Why would you think that?" His question sounds sincere, but the fact that he's asking it causes a spike to my blood pressure.

"Do you remember the last time we spoke?" I ask, my feet firmly planted as John takes another, slightly less hesitant step toward me.

"That was a while ago. You still thinking about it?"

I can't tell if he means for his words to come out like that. Like, if I'm *still* thinking about that day, that moment, *him*, then that would be pathetic. Clearly, he hasn't had that last interaction of ours etched on his mind. Or maybe enough time has passed, and he figures it doesn't matter anymore. That *I* don't matter anymore. But if that's true, then why is he here right now? And why is he looking at me like that?

"Why are you looking at me like that?" I ask.

"Like what?" His eyes narrow.

"Like that?" I say, throwing an accusatory hand in his direction.

"You look nice," he says simply.

Andie groans in her sleep, and before I can tell John to leave, he walks right up to me and speaks softly in my ear. His warm breath makes the hairs on the backs of my arms rise like little soldiers. He clearly still has a hold on me. I *am* pathetic.

"Let's go for a walk," he says.

"A walk?"

"Yeah, it's that thing you do where you put one of your legs in front of the other."

"I shouldn't leave Andie," I say, acting like the martyr I know I'm not.

"Andie's asleep. She's on her side. She'll be fine." He moves to the bed and props a couple of pillows against her back so she can't roll over. "Just a lap around the block," he says.

"What am I? A German shepherd?"

John bursts into a loud laugh and I cover his mouth with my hand.

"Andie," I whisper sternly.

His blue eyes look down at my hand pressed against his lips, my body closer to his than it has been in months. I remove my hand, wiping it on the back of my jeans.

"Fine." I cave. "A short lap. Woof."

He grins, grabbing my hand. He continues to hold it as he guides me through Theo's house. He moves through his home with such ease; it makes me wonder how long they've been friends and how close they really are.

We make our way back to the party and he doesn't let go. Not even when we walk past Avery and her friends. Her big eyes zoom in on John's hand holding mine and a tingle of satisfaction surges from my toes to the grin I can't hold back. This singular, quick-passing moment is a gesture so public it almost makes the last few months of torture worth it.

Once we're out front, I let go of John's hand and step away slightly, afraid to get roped back in. I've been doing just fine lately. Not okay, but fine.

We begin our walk. It's late, but there are streetlights posted every few homes, so it feels safe. Or maybe it's because I'm with him.

"I guess this means you and Avery broke up," I say, bringing up the obvious. I'm good at that. At not tiptoeing around things. One of my few strengths.

"Yeah. Last month. My decision. But I'm pretty sure Avery would have pulled the trigger eventually. All we ever did was fight. Then make up. Which was kind of fun for a while, but it got old."

"Fighting was kind of fun?" I ask.

"No." He blushes. "The making up part was."

I run my tongue along my teeth. "I see."

"I don't know." He shrugs. "She's nice enough."

"And beautiful," I say.

"Sure," John agrees. "But I need more than that. She and I could barely manage a real conversation. She doesn't get me, and I clearly don't get her. Besides, I'm not all that interested in being tied down anyway."

"Right. Why would you be?" I say, looking down at my feet while we walk.

"Did Theo invite you?" John asks.

"No. I came with Andie. Why would you think Theo invited me?"

John lifts his shoulders slightly. "Because he likes you."

I pause, mid-stride. "Who likes me?"

John retraces his steps back to where I stalled. "Theo."

"He told you that?"

"Not outright. But he asks about you. *A lot*." The way John says this, it sounds as though he's kind of annoyed that someone might actually like me.

"Did he tell you that we got into a disagreement at your band practice? Which also happens to be the last time we spoke."

"What's with you getting into so many disagreements with people?" John chuckles.

"Not people. *Boys*," I say, the word leaving a sour taste in my mouth. Because it's true. Boys. Guys. Men. They're all disappointing. They never say the right things. Never do what you wish they would. Can never read between the lines. They need everything spelled out for them. And it's exhausting.

"He said you were spicy."

I roll my eyes and continue walking. "Seriously?"

"Seriously."

I wonder if he meant it as "neuro-spicy," an annoying term that tries to make being neurodivergent sound quirky and fun. It's not.

"What else did he tell you?" Part of me wants to ask John if it's true that I'm not "his type" and he'll only ever see me as a friend. I still want to believe Theo was wrong, but once again, actions speak louder than words. And the lack of action from John says plenty.

He shakes his head, glancing at me quickly before looking ahead. "Nothing, really. He just kept asking if you were coming back to watch us perform that song."

"And what did you say?" I press.

"I didn't take notes or anything," he responds, appearing slightly agitated. "Just said I wasn't sure."

"Then what makes you think he likes me?"

"Because guys know when their friend is into someone."

And I guess that clears up any confusion I had about John liking me. Because if he had, Theo would have known.

"Why didn't you tell him to go for it?" I ask, biting back a smile. I'm being a petty little brat, and I know it.

He laughs. "I don't see you and Theo together. He's pretty experienced."

"The inflatable tube man at the car dealership is more experienced than I am," I scoff. "Does that really matter, though? When you got together with Avery, you were likely more experienced than she was. Right?"

His shoulders tense. "It's different."

I stop again and grab his arm, forcing him to face me. "How is it different?"

"You're just really innocent. And that's not a bad thing," he quickly adds.

"If you haven't noticed," I say, looking him in the eyes, "I've had to grow up a lot this year. I'm not the baby in my house anymore. And just because I don't throw myself at every guy I see, that doesn't mean I'm incapable of feeling things or experiencing love."

"See . . ." He pauses, raking his fingers through his hair as if he's choosing his next words very thoughtfully. "Even just saying that . . ."

"Saying what?"

"Love. For you, it *has* to be love, otherwise you don't want it."

"What's so wrong with that?"

"Nothing. Except most people our age aren't looking for someone to love. If it happens, great. If not, that's fine too."

Whenever I'm with John, there are moments when I want to tell him everything I'm thinking, and moments when I force myself to hold back, afraid to let him in. The logical part of my brain is the one telling me to hold back. Remain mysterious. My heart, however, wants to jump into the deep end, headfirst, so far down that the surface is barely a flicker in the sunlight.

We continue walking for a bit but eventually circle back and stop underneath a streetlight across the road from Theo's house. I stand on the curb and gather my hair into a ponytail, tying it up.

"How's life with the baby?" John asks.

"Paulina." I smile. "But we call her Paulie."

John returns my smile, and it feels real. Genuine. Like it was before things got messy.

"It's different," I answer. "Like you said it would be. But *good* different. It's weird, because before she was here, all I ever thought about was how her existence would interfere with my life. As if my life was this perfect thing. It wasn't. And now that she's here, it's like, I can't remember life before her. I mean, I can, but it feels like that was another version of me. A me from a long, long time ago."

"A long, long time ago." John stares back at me with an open-mouthed grin. "Has anyone ever told you that you should be a writer?"

"Why? Because I'm so corny?" I shake my head, fighting the blush I feel warming my neck.

"No. Because you're good with words. In this really relatable, accessible way. It helps me see and think about things differently."

"You're so full of it." I laugh.

"Don't do that, Lennon."

"Do what?" I ask, my eyes meeting his. There's a crease between his eyebrows. He looks disappointed. Not angry, just disappointed.

"Don't pull away just because I said something real. You're not the only one who can be honest."

Everything goes silent as I try to take in John's words. I beg myself not to ask the next question, but I need to know his answer like I need air to breathe.

"Why her?" I inhale then exhale, willing myself to go on, even though I'm pretty sure his answer will hurt my feelings. "Why Avery and not me?"

His jaw clenches. He twists a heel into the ground and his gaze falls. "It was easier, I guess," he says. "Being with someone like her. She just made sense."

"Because you were attracted to her?"

"Yes, I was attracted to her. But I was also attracted to you." He takes a step closer, and because I'm standing on the curb, we're eye-to-eye.

"Was?" I meet his gaze, my heart thumping against my chest so hard it reverberates in my ears.

"I tried not to think about you," he says. "I tried to make it work with Avery. I tried to push you out of my head. I tried so hard that I was able to convince myself that whatever it was we shared wasn't anything at all."

"That's harsh."

"It is harsh, but it wasn't that hard to do. You put up walls. Not to mention, you blocked my number."

His words sting. "I let you in," I blurt. "I lied to my parents just so I could go to your house and hear you play that song. I almost never lie to them. And then you asked me to leave. Do you know how humiliated I felt? And after all of that, having to listen to Theo tell me to my face that there's no way you'd ever be interested in me. I wanted to crawl into a hole and die."

John's eyes expand. "Theo said *what*?"

"When he followed me out of your garage, he made it clear that you'd only ever see me as a friend. I assumed you sent him to be the messenger."

"No." John shakes his head so fast it's dizzying. "I didn't. I didn't know he said that. Lennon, Theo was wrong. I never said that to him." He places his hands on my arms, gently squeezing them. "You're the most interesting person I've ever met. I love hearing you talk. And . . ." He stops abruptly, taking a step back, and I could die at the silence that lingers from his unfinished sentence. John uncrosses my arms and holds my hands, interlacing his fingers with mine.

"Do you like me?" he asks, his trademark smirk making an appearance.

I nod.

"Can I ask you another question?" he asks.

I nod again.

"Have you ever kissed anyone before?"

My eyes flicker away from his, focusing instead on the pavement below us, imagining a version of myself getting swallowed by one of the cracks. "Technically speaking . . . no."

Music flows to the street from Theo's house muting the noise of the people inside. A car passes every few minutes, hitting the same damn pothole. And crickets do their thing. In this moment, it's the most beautiful sound I've ever heard.

"Can I ask you a question?" I say, bravely meeting John's eyes again. My cheeks burn as my heart continues to race like the finish line is in sight.

"Yes," he answers, his gaze never leaving mine. His pupils are like the moon on a clear night. Full. Glowing.

"Will you teach me how to kiss?"

"Teach you? How would I . . ." He trails off before clearing his throat. "How would I do that?"

"By kissing me. Obviously."

He lets out something between a laugh and a breath. "Are you sure?" John licks his lips, probably subconsciously, but it does things to my body. Things I've never felt before.

"No." I smile as I lift my shoulders. "But yes."

He swallows before running a hand through his hair and looking away. "You're such an enigma," he says. "I never know where I stand with you."

"It's not me. It's the idea of us," I say.

"What about it?"

"The idea of us together . . . well, admit it, we'd combust," I say, clenching my jaw at the brutal truth.

He leans in, his lips brushing against my ear. "But those would be some wicked flames."

I exhale a slow breath and am otherwise entirely still. "So, will you be my first kiss?" The question comes out fast. I'm afraid if I wait too long the momentum, or rather the magic of this moment, will be gone.

"Yeah." John pulls back, looking at me now. He straightens his back like he's ready to go on a mission to Mars or something. "Step off the curb."

"Okay." I stand across from him, waiting for his next instruction. It's like the heavy fog between us has lifted and we can see the road ahead.

"We're going to have to stand closer. I'll take a step forward, then you take a step forward," he says.

I nod, following his cues. We stop once my forehead presses against the tip of his nose.

"What do you do with your hands?" I ask, holding them up to my chest.

"Sometimes you hold the other person's hands. Or the guy will cup the girl's face. Girls usually put their arms around me." A nervous laugh escapes his lips. The lips I am quite literally dying to feel on mine. "I don't know. I don't usually think about what my hands are doing, especially during a first kiss. People are still feeling each other out, you know?"

"Okay, well, maybe you can do the holding my face bit. That sounds kind of romantic."

"Sure." His cheeks turn crimson as I watch him fight another smile. "I'll just put this hand on the side of your face and my other one around your waist. Bridge the gap a bit more."

At his request, I take another step, standing as close as I possibly can without pressing myself up against him. His pinky grazes the exposed skin at my waist. "You smell really good," he says. "Is it vanilla?"

"No. Body butter. Georgie's always telling me to use it on my dry knees." *Shut up, shut up, shut up!*

"I like it." He leans in closer, tilting his head down, then stops himself. Talk about being on the brink of combustion. "If you're uncomfortable, we can stop."

"John," I say, almost sternly. "Please stop talking and kiss me."

He laughs nervously as he slowly strokes my jawline with his thumb.

"That feels nice," I say. *Nice* is an understatement. I might actually burst.

He moves his lips down to mine and places a gentle kiss on them. The taste of his minty toothpaste lingers. He pulls away slightly and kisses my bottom lip, then the top. My hands grip him tighter, and he leans in even closer, surprising me by pressing his lower half against mine. I part my lips, wanting the kiss to be faster, harder. John is probably trying to be respectful, knowing this is my first, so I slip my tongue into his mouth unabashedly. In response, John rests the tips of his fingers on my bare lower back. I bring my hand up and run my fingers through his beautiful hair. The hair I've seen him nervously run his fingers through what feels like a million times, killing me slowly with each pass.

We could be anywhere. My locker. John's garage. The street outside Theo's house. It doesn't matter. It never matters as long as I'm with him. And he's with me. John feels like coming home, and inside that home there's a secret room to which only we hold the key.

He stops kissing me first, and I can't help but look up at him in complete awe. He's so beautiful. That kiss was everything I wanted, wished for, dreamed of, and more.

It's in the surprises where life really happens, I think. Not the things we plan for. Or rehearse.

Perfect moments do exist.

But then John pulls away and sits on the curb. He's crouched, eyes to the asphalt. Distant.

"Was it that bad?" I ask, sitting next to him like a deflated balloon.

He looks at me in bewilderment. "No. It was amazing."

"Then what's wrong?"

"Nothing."

"*Some*thing."

His eyes won't meet mine, and before I can let myself get upset at the idea of him already being bored with me, I see it.

I bite the inside of my cheeks to fight back a grin and remain seated next to him, not saying a word. But my entire body is on high alert. Sensory overload. I want to touch him again. Hold his hand. Kiss his face. Here he is, sitting right next to me, after months of silence, and there's still a wall. Even after the truth of our words and the truth of that kiss, it's still there.

"Don't worry," I say, trying my best to play it cool. "I don't expect you to be my boyfriend or anything just because we kissed."

He turns to me, studying my face. *Enigma.*

My voice catches as I force the rest of the words out. Half truths. "I would like to be your friend again though. Or at least try. Look," I say, pulling my phone out. "I'll start by unblocking your number."

He laughs before pressing his shoulder to mine. "I don't kiss my friends like that, Lennon."

I look at him, at his lips that were on mine only a couple of minutes earlier. I've always wanted to know what it would feel like to kiss John. And now I do. I read once that a crush is just a lack of information. Unfortunately, for me, that isn't true. The more I know about John, the more I want to know.

"We've always been a little atypical," I say. "And I'm okay with that."

He smiles. "I guess I can learn to be okay with that too."

So almost perfect, it hurts.

Part II

TENTH GRADE

I'd trace a line
down your neck,
following the curve of your shoulder to your hand,
and I'd close my eyes,
imagining your fingers wrapped around mine,
pulling me away from the staleness of where I exist.
I'd trace a line from you to me.
Connecting us.
A string.
And I'd never let go.

Chapter Twelve

SEPTEMBER 3: LABOR DAY WEEKEND

John kissed me.

I kissed John.

And not just a kiss. But a *kiss.*

A defining moment.

One that will stay with me for the rest of my life. It's like the kiss opened a portal. Before, I didn't know what I was missing out on. Now that I do? I've become a girl obsessed. Woman? There's got to be a better word for the in-between stage.

"Lennon, you ready?" Dad calls from downstairs.

"One sec," I shout, slamming my journal shut.

"Yalla," he grumbles. This isn't the first time he's asked if I was ready to go. But Arabs run on different time. He should know that.

I've been writing a lot—random thoughts, poetry, song lyrics—and everything I write, even when I don't mean it to, comes back to John.

My poetry tries to encapsulate the bridges between infatuation, lust, longing, and love.

My journal entries express all the truths I'm too afraid to say out loud.

And my song lyrics try to capture the best moments. The ones that are always so fleeting.

I miss John. I want to kiss him again. I think I might even . . .

"Lennon!"

Like I said. Obsessed!

I switch out my ratty T-shirt for a clean one and my leggings for jeans. Dad doesn't like it when I wear tight pants outside the house. He doesn't even have to say it. I just know. That's the thing about my dad. His face speaks so his mouth doesn't have to.

"Where are you going?" Georgie asks. She comes out of the kitchen as I reach the bottom step, where Dad is not so patiently waiting. She's carrying Paulie, who's dressed in a jumpsuit with little smiling suns.

"Back-to-school shopping. Do you need anything?" The question leaves my lips before I realize the weight of my words. Georgie spent the entirety of her senior year online and growing a baby. She did get to attend her graduation—we even brought Paulie—but we had to leave early because Georgie was breastfeeding. Breastfeeding was a whole ordeal. My sister tried hard, and I think it put her into a low-key depression. Her breasts were making the milk, but Paulie wouldn't latch. Eventually, our family doctor convinced Georgie that "fed is best" and she transitioned Paulie to formula.

I kind of like it because it means I get to help with Paulie's feedings. We all fight over who gets to give her the bottle. Mom insists on being part of almost every bath time. And Dad gets on the floor and plays with Paulie. Well, as much as a five-month-old baby can play. Even though we didn't go on a family vacation this summer, we still spent a lot of time together.

And with Zach.

While Zach is starting university, locally, Georgie's life remains on hold. Which doesn't seem fair, but I guess this is part of the sacrifice she made when she decided . . . when she decided.

"What are you wearing?" Dad asks, examining my shirt.

I look down at the white tee I'm in. The same white tee I wore when I kissed John. The one that lands right around my navel. I didn't even notice.

"I'll go change," I say. I turn to go back to my room, but Dad takes my wrist, stopping me from going up the stairs.

"Where did you get this from?" he asks, eyes narrowed.

"It's just a pajama shirt I forgot to change out of," I lie.

"I've never seen this shirt before. Georgie," he says, turning to her. "Is this a pajama shirt?"

We exchange knowing glances. "Yeah. It probably just shrank in the wash. Cheap material."

"Bring it down with you after you change," Dad says.

"Why?" I ask.

"It doesn't fit you anymore. Mommy will donate it."

"I can still wear it around the house," I say, indignant.

"No." His tone is sharp now. "Not with Zach coming and going at all hours."

"Zach? He's like a brother," I say, scrunching up my face in disgust.

"Do you think of every boy as a brother?" Dad asks.

"Do you think of every boy as a threat?" My words are biting, angry.

"Go change, and bring this cheap shirt back with you."

I spent sixty dollars on this "cheap" shirt. Andie convinced me to buy it. It's the shirt that made John see me differently than he had before. It's a keepsake at this point, and my dad wants to take it away from me. It's the one shirt that helps me blend in with my peers. The one shirt—

"Go," he says, his thick black brows bunched together.

"Fine."

I stomp up the steps and slam my door. This is such utter and complete bullshit.

I throw on an oversized shirt, with long sleeves to make him extra happy, even though it's a million degrees outside.

When I come back down the stairs, he has his hand out, palm open, waiting for me to place the shirt in it.

"Good girl." He says it like I'm a dog that followed its master's orders. Except I don't get a treat for behaving. I don't get anything.

"The shirt wasn't tight. It wasn't see-through. It just didn't drag all the way to my knees," I say to Mom in the kitchen that evening. I'm cutting up veggies for the salad. Dad is out back grilling kebabs. "Dad went to high school in Canada. Why is he like this?"

Mom gives me a look, like the answer is right in front of me.

"Did he try to control what you wore?" I ask as she slides a cucumber to me.

"I was an adult, habibti."

"Just barely," I mutter. Mom was nineteen when she met Dad. He was twenty-four. I don't tell people this because they'd think he groomed her or something.

"He never gave his opinion on what you wore?" I ask.

"It's different. You're his baby."

"I'm not a baby. We *have* a baby in this house and it's not me," I say, sounding like a baby.

Dad comes in with the empty meat dish, raw juices and leftover marinade sloshing around. He washes his hands at the sink and quickly places a kiss on Mom's cheek. He bends down and tries to kiss me where I'm seated at the kitchen island, but I lean away. I'm still mad at him, and he needs to know.

He goes back out, closing the sliding door behind him.

"We were raised with certain morals and values. And with you and Georgie being born here, we must try harder to make sure you . . ." She sighs, and I know exactly what the sigh means. No matter how hard they tried with Georgie, she still messed up. She had sex. She got pregnant. She committed the ultimate sin.

"I'm not Georgie. I can make my own decisions. You raised me to make good decisions." I say the last line extra clearly, so she'll understand that all of their lessons weren't for nothing. Even if I don't fully agree with them all, or even truly believe what I'm saying. But in this moment, I believe it enough to say it because I'm desperate. Desperate to break out and be my own person and experience life like the rest of the kids I go to school with.

"And just because you're fourteen, you think we're done raising you?" she asks. She nods at the cucumber, and I peel off the plastic wrap and pass it back to her to wash.

"Almost fifteen," I remind her.

"This is when you need us the most," she says. "Every day we send you to that public school, you're surrounded by kids who have no religion, sometimes no good role models at home, who drink and do drugs. It's more important than ever that we keep a watchful eye on you."

"Look how well that worked for Georgie," I say, dryly.

"Georgie was always only ever going to do what Georgie wanted.

And now she's paying for it." Mom passes the cucumber back to me and motions for me to cut it in half-moon slices. "You and your sister are lucky. You have a mom and dad that love you very much and give you everything you need. You know how it was for Baba. His parents weren't there for him, mentally, after Yousef passed. And my parents are back home. I wish they were here to lecture me. One day you'll miss it."

It takes all my willpower not to respond with an eye roll.

My phone lights up in front of me. A text from Andie.

Andie: wyd

I finish slicing the cucumber and slide the cutting board back to Mom. "I'm done. Can I go watch TV for a bit?"

She shoos me away.

I pick up my phone and flop down on the couch in the family room. The TV was left on, but no one is watching it. On the other side of the window, where he's outside barbecuing, Dad raises his chin in a greeting to me. I force a smile and message Andie back.

Me: Counting down the minutes until I can move out of this PRISON!

Andie: lol. you're dramatic.

Me: Says the girl who has the freedom to wear what she wants and go out with boys.

Andie: yes and parents who work 24/7. Besides, all those things are overrated. I think I'll try being single this year.

Andie: Or not.

Me: lol. speaking of guys . . .

Andie: what about HIM?

Andie knows all about my first kiss with John. She slept over the night of Theo's party. In the morning, once she was sober, I shared every last detail with her. Every. Last. Detail. When we sat at the kitchen table for breakfast, we couldn't stop giggling. At one point she kept talking about how blue the blueberries were. I'm pretty sure my parents thought she was high.

Me: I've been thinking about asking him if he wants to hang out.

Andie: be more specific.

Me: OK. I'm not allowed to have a boyfriend. He doesn't want to be tied down. But that doesn't mean we shouldn't still explore the potential between us. KWIM?

Andie: Yeah. You're thirsty for him.

Me: OMG. Do you think that's how he'll read it?

Andie: Yes!

Andie: But that's not a bad thing.
It is risky though.

Me: Risky in what way?

Andie: Don't hate me for saying this but I'm your best friend and I have to look out for you.

Me: . . .

Andie: I'm just not sure you're emotionally mature enough to handle what this kind of arrangement might lead to. Or not lead to.

Me: How so?

I pull my knees to my chest and rest my chin on them, waiting for Andie's response.

"Emotionally mature" is a term I hear a lot as an autistic girl. It's what separates me from my peers, according to the psychologist who diagnosed me, the multiple books on girls and autism I read, and, of course, my parents. What I want to yell to all those people and all those books is that maybe it isn't about "girls" and autism. Maybe it's because we've been socialized to believe there's a difference between autistic boys and autistic girls, and, as a result, we're not only erasing the experiences of people who don't fit into those groups, but the girls are also treated differently by teachers, doctors, our own family members, and peers. These made-up marker points exist so that other people can try to make sense of our lived experiences and identities and plot us on some graph. But I don't buy it. I have felt more mature and in tune with my feelings than my peers since I can remember. Just because I may not be able to articulate my thoughts as well as allistics do, verbally, that doesn't mean I'm not fully aware of every single emotion that passes through me. It just sometimes takes me longer to process them.

Andie: I don't see a way where this situation ends without you getting emotionally invested in him. Especially considering you already are.

Me: You're always able to move on after a breakup.

Andie: That's because I've never loved any of the guys I've dated. We usually break up before things go too far and maybe that's part of why I haven't gotten too emotionally attached, but I know you, Lennon. John isn't just some guy. And whether you want to admit this to yourself or not, I think you want him to be your boyfriend and this is your way to lure him into a relationship.

I don't respond immediately. Andie's words are harsh. But they're true. Everything she has said is true. I don't just want to hook up with John because I'm attracted to him. I like him. A lot. I want him to be the person I run to with all my good news. And bad news. I want to have long, deep conversations that last until two in the morning. I want to wake up to texts from him and feel his strong arms around me in a hug when we see each other at school. I want to be the girl on the receiving end of his gaze. The fact is, Andie wasn't there. She didn't experience that kiss. She doesn't know what I do. No one does. Not even John.

Andie: the further twisted up you get in John, the harder it's going to be for you to walk away from him. Kissing him (etc.) is only going to make you more attached to this guy who I'm not sure is worth it.

Me: You don't like John?

Andie: I don't even know John.

Andie: but I do know and love you and you deserve the best. tbh I'm not sure if John is it.

My parents being against the idea of John and me is one thing. That I've prepared myself for. But my best friend not being down?

As much as I value Andie's opinion, at the end of the day this is my life. I don't need anyone's permission to make decisions regarding my body and heart. This is between me and John. What anyone else thinks doesn't matter.

Chapter Thirteen

SEPTEMBER 8

There's a buzz in the halls. Friday morning, the end of the first week back. Everyone else always seems so excited for the weekend, but not me. At school, I'm free. I'm not looking over my shoulder every few seconds, afraid my father might overhear my words. Read my face. Or worse, see what I'm doing and who I'm doing it with.

If only.

Starting tenth grade has felt like a fresh start. I never had a chance last year to be anyone but "that pregnant girl's younger sister." It's not like I was ostracized (at least, not in any obvious way) but the heaviness of Georgie's decision loomed over me and created this identity I never asked for.

And now I'm free to explore the things I want without an audience. Well, freer.

John and I haven't texted since the kiss.

No calls.

Nothing.

When we have seen each other at school this week, it's only been from afar. A fleeting moment when our eyes meet. A head nod that says, "Hi. I see you." And also, "Stay where you are."

Maybe Andie was right and the story I've built up in my mind is just a fantasy. At least in my head, I can control the ending.

"How's your schedule?" John appears, as if out of nowhere, leaning against the locker next to mine. His hair is freshly washed and his clothes, well, they're wrinkled as usual.

"It's not bad," I say, coolly. *Keep it together.* "English. Math. Lunch. Phys Ed. Music. Yours?"

"It fucking sucks." He smiles, and my eyes move to his lips. Those lips I kissed only eight days ago. "Math. Science. Lunch. Phys Ed. English."

"Phys Ed third period? I haven't seen you in the gym," I say, trying to figure out what to do with my hands now that I'm done fiddling with my lock.

"That's because Mr. Healy is making us run the outdoor track every day. He wants to take advantage of the nice weather. He also said sharing the gym with the girls might be too 'overstimulating' for some of us." John's eyes linger on mine as a tiny smile slips out. "He may have a point."

That was definitely something.

"And what does he say about those who don't identify as a boy or a girl?" Why do I do this? Why do I start conversations neither of us has the time to get into? My entire body pulses and I swallow as a prolonged and very awkward silence stretches between us. *I wonder if he still thinks about the kiss.*

"I don't think we have any non-binary people in our class?" John finally responds, a little unsure.

"But in all the school?" *Why do I keep pressing?*

"I guess it's up to them where they feel more comfortable

participating. You bring up a good point, though. Why do we still have gendered Phys Ed classes?"

"Because people like my father exist," I say bluntly.

A sudden and kind of loud laugh escapes from John.

"Since we have Phys Ed at the same time, we should go together." The words come out so fast, I don't even remember thinking them first. "I mean, whatever. If you're around." I let out a flirtatious smile, or at least what I think is a flirtatious smile. It's possible I look constipated.

"Whatever." A playful smile dances on his lips as he presses his finger to my shoulder. *That's* what I get after eight days of no communication? A finger to my shoulder?

The first bell rings and students rush past us, their bodies grazing ours, bumping and separating me and John.

"I'm heading downstairs," I say.

"I'm just down the hall." He nods past me.

I nod back and we part ways. With slow, heavy footsteps I become lost in thought. He never responded directly to my proposal. Was I too forward in asking him to walk me to class? Too desperate?

My phone buzzes in my back pocket. I pull it out to see a text from John. My first official text from him. I'll meet you at your locker after lunch.

Before I can react or reply, Andie appears and pulls on my arm. "What're you doing just standing here? Come on."

☾

I didn't tell Andie about my plans to meet John at my locker. Just said I had to grab my gym bag before class. I don't even have a gym bag.

Not wanting to wait around at my locker and come off as too desperate, I spend more time than I need to in the restroom before meeting him. The amount of planning and scheming and over-thinking I've had to do just to get the boy I like to walk beside me to the worst class imaginable should be studied.

My heart bursts when I come down the hall to see him leaning against my locker. He showed up. And he is just so effortlessly chill. Not to mention so, so good-looking. Those words don't even do him justice. I love how tall he is, his long hair and that easy smile.

"Ready?" he asks, straightening.

"For Phys Ed? As ready as one can be, I suppose." We make our way down the hall.

"What're you doing this weekend?"

"Paulie's baptism. You?"

"We've got band practice tomorrow. Might head to Theo's tonight. His mom is back from Greece and she brought me treats. I gave him shit, by the way."

"For what?" I ask as we head down the stairs together.

"For what he said to you about me. Us."

Us?

"Oh." I nod. "And what did he say?"

We stop in front of the girls' changeroom, and John falls silent as his eyes connect with mine. "He was unapologetic. He went on about how you're not my typical type and that he felt sorry for you."

"Wow. He *is* an asshole." We both laugh.

"I still think it's because he likes you and he's trying to keep us away from one another."

As we stand, mere inches apart, I can't help but let a smile slip out. "He's clearly doing a good job of that."

"A very good job."

"Speaking of—"

"I know," John cuts in. "Why didn't I call or text you after Theo's party."

"I didn't either," I say, choosing this moment to assert my feminism. "Actually," I go on, before he can say something that will make me lose my nerve, "can you drive me home?"

"Don't you take the bus?"

"I do. But I want to ask you something."

"Ask me now," he says, taking a step so he's standing even closer. Close enough that I can feel heat radiating off his body.

"I want to ask you in private," I say, meeting his intense and curious gaze.

He grins, looking off to the side before locking eyes again.

"I'll meet you in the parking lot. Okay?" I say, gripping the straps of my backpack like they're stress balls.

He doesn't respond instantly. Instead, he studies me for a moment that feels like forever but also, somehow, fleeting. He leans in and murmurs in a low, gravelly voice, "Yes, ma'am." His words and hot breath trickle in my ear, all the way to my toes, and because I'm the least cool person ever, I take a clumsy step backward.

To hide how flustered I am, I bring my finger up and give his shoulder a tap, but he cups his hand around my wrist and pulls me in. My eyes focus on the fading but mesmerizing scar on his lip.

"Enigma," he says quietly before releasing me.

To John I'm an enigma, but to me, he is the sun, the moon, and all the stars.

My entire body is jelly. I open the door of the girls' changeroom with my back, with John's eyes glued to mine until I'm inside.

Okay.

Breathe.

Okay? OKAY.

!!!!!!!!!!!!!!!!!!!!!!!

I hide inside the bathroom stall so I can have my stimming freak-out in private. Flailing hands. Racing heart. Rocking back and forth. My water bottle falling into the toilet.

"Shit!"

"Are you okay in there?" a girl calls out.

I stop myself from flapping my hands and cover my mouth. "I'm good."

"Okay," the girl says. I wait until her footsteps fall silent and the door to the gym closes.

I stare down at the toilet. There's not enough soap or hot water in the world to make this okay. "Sorry, buddy," I say as I pull the bottle out by its untainted lid. "This is where we part ways."

After school, John texted to say he'd be a couple of minutes late. His English teacher wanted to speak to him. The anticipation of his arrival might possibly kill me. The green metal back door of the school finally opens, and my heart skips a beat (or a hundred) as he steps outside. The parking lot is completely deserted and I'm unsure where to look as he makes his way to his car, and me, so I pretend to be enthralled by something on my phone.

"Sorry about that," he says, slightly out of breath when he reaches me. "Mr. Pine is a dick."

I laugh. "Can confirm. I had him last year. But he's easy to please."

"In what ways?" he asks. I can't tell if he's being suggestive or wants me to actually answer.

"By completing your homework," I state, in a matter-of-fact tone.

John squints at me as he unlocks his car doors, then he tosses his bag into the back seat. I keep mine with me, tucked between my legs on the floor of his car. His car is old. Dirty. Incredibly dusty. But it smells like him.

He sits, slams his door, tilts his head back, and releases a loud, suffering sigh. "I just got a one-day extension on some stupid *Hamlet* essay. He expects me to email it to him tomorrow morning. Saturday! First week of school and I'm already behind."

"At least he gave you an extension."

"What difference does a day make when you didn't read the play? I couldn't keep up in class. The guy moves at warp speed."

I spring into fix-it mode. "Do you have *Hamlet* with you?"

He nods and twists to his back seat, pulling it from his bag.

"What's the essay topic?" I ask, taking it from him and quickly flipping through the pages.

"We have to write about his famous 'to be or not to be' speech and the significance behind it."

I roll my eyes at how basic this assignment is. "That's easy enough."

"It is?"

"Sure. I can help."

"You've read it?" he asks.

"Yeah. I took Advanced English last year. The thing about these Shakespeare texts is that the pages on the left side decode what

Shakespeare is saying. It's basically a cheat sheet and road map to your essay."

"I didn't realize you took advanced courses."

"Not all of them. Just English and a couple of others. Definitely not Math. Anyway," I say, "we could probably hammer this out in an hour. We can even do it right here if you'll drive me to Andie's after."

"Why Andie's?"

"Because that's where I'm going to tell my parents I am," I say, smiling as I text my mom.

Mom: Okay. I'll have daddy
come get you at six.

Me: It's Friday night!

Mom: Six!

Me: Fine!!!

I shove my phone into his cup holder before sucking in a breath, hoping it will tame my thumping pulse as I search for the nerve to ask what I've been wanting to ask John since we kissed. "Do you ever think about that night? Theo's party." After a beat of silence, I press on. "The kiss?"

I pick at my sleeves, waiting for his response, knowing that his words will set the foundation for what I say next.

"We were supposed to pretend that didn't happen, right?" His voice softens as the lines of his face deepen.

"I don't remember agreeing to that."

It's quiet again until John clears his throat. His eyes land on the copy of *Hamlet* resting on my lap. "Did your mom agree to pick you up from Andie's?" he asks.

"Yeah," I say, remembering the offer I made. I toss him *Hamlet* before taking out my laptop and cracking it open. "I'll type, but you have to tell me what to say."

"But I didn't read it," he reminds me.

"What about Mr. Pine's lessons or discussions in class?"

"I didn't pay much attention."

"Well," I say, turning my face to his. "Pay attention now."

He runs a nervous hand through his hair and nods. "Alright. I'm listening."

☾

It takes just over an hour, but by quarter after five we have a pretty good essay for John to turn in. It took asking him a few leading questions to get John in the right headspace, but once he was warmed up, he came up with some thoughts and perspectives that I'd never thought of before. It's interesting how people's lived experiences can shape how they take in literature. Or anything, for that matter.

"I'll email this to you when I get home. Don't send it to Mr. Pine until at least nine. He might get suspicious if you turn it in too soon."

"Smart," John says as he sends me a text with his email address.

I put my laptop away and shift in the seat so my back is against the passenger-side window. "You never answered my last question."

John tilts his head. "What do you mean? The essay is done, isn't it?"

"Not about *Hamlet*. The one about our kiss," I manage, my heart in my throat. "Actually," I cut in before he can answer, "can you turn around?"

"What?" The question buries his laugh.

"Just humor me."

"Okay," he says, following my instructions. "I'm facing the window. Do you want to tell me why?"

"Putting aside what we said about forgetting we kissed, you liked it, right?"

He turns to look at me and I bring my hand to his face, forcing it back toward the driver's-side window. "Yeah. I liked it. But—"

"I liked it, too," I say, cutting him off again. "The way I see it, we have a couple of options here. One, we go back to being just friends. But to be honest, we were never really good at that."

John's shoulders rise in a laugh.

"Option two, we hang out and see what happens."

In the not so far-off distance, the custodian throws trash bag after trash bag into the rusty brown bin. I try not to take this as a sign.

"I'm not looking for a relationship," I say. "Just casual." I need him to know this isn't a ploy to get him to be my boyfriend. I also needed to say the words out loud to remind myself of that. "You can turn around now."

When John turns in his seat to face me again, his cheeks are blazing red.

"I'm down." He says it so simply, and yet his two-word response is more powerful than my own long-winded, over-practiced pitch.

"Cool." My shoulders fall as I try to copy his approach. John's arm brushes against mine on the center console and suddenly the temperature in this car is hotter than Mercury next to the sun.

"Just kissing, for now," I stammer out before my nerves take complete hold of me.

"That's fine with me." He leans in, but I bring my hand up to his chest to stop him.

"One more thing. If you meet someone—or I meet someone—the deal is off."

"Lennon," he says, intensity and longing in his blue eyes, "I don't see anyone else here I want to kiss."

"Okay. You can kiss me now. If you want to."

"Okay, because I have been wanting to," he says, tucking a piece of hair behind my ear.

My body melts at his touch, his scent, and then his mouth. I pull away, ever so slightly. "Me too," I say, my breathing already intensifying. "Obviously."

The back of his hand skims across my cheek. His mouth is a whisper away from mine. "I'll be whatever you need me to be."

Our lips meet again and it's all I can do not to climb over the console. I can't think straight. I've thought about kissing him again constantly since the moment our first kiss ended, and being here now, doing it so freely, I'm a complete goner. Useless to the world. As he wraps one arm around my waist, thrusting me closer to him, I feel like a matchstick that's just been lit. This is dangerous. This could get messy. But it's also exactly where I want to be.

"You're so good at this," he says, his lips touching mine as he speaks.

He kisses me again, and I can't believe this is happening. Me and John. John and me. I wouldn't trade this feeling for anything.

Theo and Andie have no idea what they're talking about. Everything about me and John makes complete sense.

I press my lips into his and John pulls me in even closer—the matchstick completely ablaze now.

Chapter Fourteen

SEPTEMBER 10

"Mom," I yell over the banister. "There's a hole in my tights."

"Try clear nail polish," she shouts from the kitchen.

"Nail polish?" I shout back. "I said tights, not stockings. *I'm not eighty*," I mumble.

Georgie comes out of her room, her eyes little slits as they adjust to the light. "Would you keep it down? Paulie's napping."

"Do you have any extra black tights?"

"Even if I did, they wouldn't fit your Amazonian legs. Go without. You're not twelve."

"My dress is short. Dad would have a cow."

"Dad always has a cow. Just ignore him. It's what I do."

It's the morning of Paulie's baptism, and Mom's in the kitchen preparing a fruit platter to bring to the restaurant where we're having lunch afterwards. Dad's already at church making sure everything is good to go. The baptism will follow the regular weekly service. Everyone is extra on edge because this will be the first time Georgie is setting foot inside the church since Paulie was born. I hope she doesn't burst into flames.

"When do we have to leave?" I ask my sister, twisting the holey tights in my hands.

"Once the guest of honor wakes up." She smiles sweetly. "Want me to do your makeup?" Georgie is already dressed in a modest white dress, her hair and makeup done.

"Could you?"

"I'll meet you in your room in a few."

Back in my room, I slip on my black dress, which is simple with its long sleeves and high neckline, but regardless, I know my father will think it's too short. I sit on my bed and read over John's texts as I wait for Georgie.

Friday night.

John: I submitted the essay
at 9:01 like you said to.

John: Thanks again for helping me.

John: I guess you're busy and Theo
is getting annoyed with me being on
my phone so I'll talk to you later.

Saturday.

John: do you have regrets?

John: I don't

John: just wanted to make that clear

This morning.

John: everything ok?

Me: Sorry. It's a bit hectic here. Paulie's baptism today. Been helping my mom since Friday night.

John: Do you want to hang out tomorrow?

Me: Sure. When?

Oh my god!

John: Meet you at your locker at lunch?

Me: Sounds good.

Sounds perfect.

Me: Got to go!

And then I add a ☺ so he doesn't misinterpret my tone. I wish I could carry around emoji flashcards in real life to hold up in conversations. It might help cut down on the number of misunderstandings due to my often deadpan delivery, lack of eye contact, and fidgetiness.

"Close the door," I say as Georgie enters carrying Paulie's baby monitor and her own makeup bag. I don't think my sister's hands have been empty since the nurse placed Paulie in her arms.

She pulls my desk chair over to the bed.

"I have to tell you something," I say, my words coming out quickly.

She grins. "Tell me."

"I kissed John. Twice."

Her smile widens and she leans in. "How was it?"

"So perfect. Like, seriously, perfect. Everyone always tells you it won't be, but it was. It is."

"*Is*? So, this is a current event?" she asks, with one perfectly arched brow.

"It might be."

"My advice," Georgie says as she empties out the contents of her makeup bag on my bed, "is keep it on the DL. The second Mom and Dad get a whiff that there's a boy lurking, they'll lock you up."

"I already feel locked up," I say with a groan, tugging on my dress.

"Do you have any questions?" Georgie asks as she blots concealer on my face.

"Kind of, but I can't ask you. That's weird."

She laughs. "Believe me, anything you've thought about doing, I've not only thought it, but I've probably also done it. Multiple times."

I guess there is something comforting about divulging your innermost secrets (and demons) to someone whose secrets and demons are no longer innermost but on display for the whole world to see. Except now disguised as an impossibly adorable baby.

I exhale, looking at the bedroom door, half expecting someone to burst through.

"What comes after a kiss?" I finally ask. "Like, say you've kissed a guy a few times. Then what?"

"Depends on what you're comfortable with," she says, blending the makeup on my face with a sponge.

"Say I'm comfortable with whatever comes next but not what comes after that." It's so cringe saying these things out loud, but I don't want to come off as completely inexperienced with John once things eventually get past just kissing.

"Touching," she says simply.

"Do I have to ask permission?"

Georgie laughs. "Maybe that's something you can discuss before. It's important he knows that he has your consent and how far you're comfortable going. Do you trust him?" She's applying blush to my cheeks now and my face feels heavy, like I'm wearing a mask, but I don't want to tell her that.

"With my body, yes. With my heart? That's to be determined."

"Isn't it always?" she says, the corners of her lips curving up. "Just be careful, okay? You don't want to end up where I did."

"No. Yeah. That's not even on my radar," I say, pulling my dress down again.

Georgie pauses, gazing at me thoughtfully. "It wasn't on mine either, but things can sometimes move quickly once they get going."

"Right. You're right."

"Part your lips," she says as she brings lip gloss to my mouth. She leans back once she's done, taking in her artistry, and grins. "You're really beautiful. I hope one day you come to see it."

I shake my head. My looks have always been a source of angst and insecurity and confusion. Every time I look in the mirror lately, it's like someone else is staring back at me. Someone I don't always recognize. My body is changing so fast, and whenever I mess around with my hair and makeup, I'm careful not to go too far one way, because I don't want people treating me differently. Especially Dad. But sometimes I want to express myself through my outward vessel. I just wish I could do it without my parents noticing.

Paulie's cries come through the monitor.

"Little Miss is awake." Georgie rises, gathering her things. "Don't forget to put on mascara."

"Thanks," I say. "For everything."

"You can thank me by babysitting the next time I ask." She winks before leaving my room.

I quickly put on some mascara and then stand in front of the mirror. I look way too good for a baptism. Thankfully my dad won't be able to punish me at church.

Mom, Georgie, Paulie, and I arrive just as the church service is ending. We sit in the last row, waiting for everyone to leave. Mom invited only a few people—close family and friends and, of course, Zach's family. The backs of my bare thighs stick to the cool wooden pew, and I yank my dress down, trying to cover my legs.

Dad makes eye contact and nods for us to join him and the priest in front of the altar as the congregation clears out.

As I walk up the aisle, I try to take a deep breath but it's like the air gets lodged halfway down. This dress felt like a better idea when I was in the safety of my room. My stomach twists as Dad's eyes move to my bare legs.

In typical Dad behavior, he shows his disappointment by not greeting me. Instead, he introduces Mom and Georgie to the new priest. I take the diaper bag from Georgie and place it on a pew near the baptismal font, waiting for things to get underway.

"Hadid," a voice calls out, startling me. I look up to find Theo Petropolis, dressed in full altar boy garb.

"What are you doing here?" I foolishly ask.

Theo extends his arms out to his sides. "I just really love wearing this long robe on Sunday afternoons."

I laugh, because sometimes he's funny.

"I'm helping with the baptism. Is that your niece?" he asks, nodding to Paulie and my family.

I take a step back from him so my dad doesn't find another reason to get mad. I hate it when he's upset with me.

I hate it when he's upset.

"Yeah. I'm her godmother," I say, standing straighter.

"Big responsibility."

I shrug. "It's just symbolic."

Dad comes over with the priest and looks me up and down before clearing his throat. He wants me to know he's unhappy. As if it's not already obvious.

"Lennon, this is Father Abraham."

I nod and force out a smile.

"Always nice to meet the youth of our church." Father Abraham smiles back. "Do you know Theodore?"

Theo responds "Yes" while I say "Not really," our voices overlapping.

I clear my throat. "We go to the same school." I side-eye him, praying he can read my face well enough not to bring up the one disastrous band practice I attended. Or his party.

"Nice to see you again, Theodore," Dad says, giving me a sideways glance.

"Theo is fine," he chimes in.

"Yalla, let's commence," the priest says, holding out his hands.

Theo and Father Abraham move behind the altar. I try and sneak away to where Mom is seated, but Dad takes my arm.

"I don't like this dress," he says curtly as more guests arrive.

"My tights had a hole in them. Georgie said to wear it like this."

"Did Georgie also paint your face like a clown?"

"She said I looked pretty." My voice comes out quiet as I feel myself shrink in his presence.

"It's too much. Go wait in the car."

"But the baptism," I say.

Dad cocks his head to my mother, who walks over. He whispers sternly in her ear. She speaks back to him, in an equally stern tone. I hear her tell him he's being crazy in Arabic. Reminding him that I'm the godmother and must be here. He grumbles about this being a church, not a nightclub. Thanks, Captain Obvious. Was confused there for a second. I swear to god, sometimes he regresses into this old-school, stereotypical Arab man, and I hate it. I hate him when he's like this.

Mom tells Dad the only person here who has a problem with what I'm wearing is him. He takes off his suit jacket and hands it to me, telling me to tie it around my waist.

I accept my father's jacket, trying not to huff and puff like a baby dragon as I tie the sleeves around me. My eyes meet Theo's at the altar as I'm aggressively tightening the knot. I wonder how long he's been watching. Theo, in a seemingly uncharacteristic move, offers me a nod of understanding, like he gets it. Like he can see that this isn't my fault. I'm not the villain my dad is making me out to be. I'm just a girl who doesn't know how to be the person my father wants me to be. Not anymore, at least.

But even Theo's kind face isn't enough to squash the complete humiliation and shame I'm drowning in as I walk to the baptismal font, my dad's coat working overtime as a tent.

Once everyone has arrived, the baptism begins, and Dad, the godfather, holds Paulie as the priest recites the service from his book. Theo stands by Father Abraham, somehow knowing what to do to assist him without being told. I remain still, next to Dad, kissing the cross when I'm told and nodding my head to reject Satan when I'm asked.

The priest breathes upon Paulie's mouth, brow, and chest as he says, "Expel from her every evil and impure spirit which hideth and maketh its lair in her heart."

How does a person expel all evil and impure spirits to achieve goodness? By turning the cheek? By closing themselves off to temptation? What extraordinary alchemy would be needed to turn evil to good?

Following the baptism, Dad and I ride home together so I can change before lunch at the restaurant. We don't speak. Fine by me. What more can he say? I already know he's disappointed.

They never stop to think about the mixed messages they send us. Mom encourages me and Georgie to dress up. To "look nice." How am I supposed to know when "looking nice" crosses the line into being dressed in a way that they don't deem appropriate? Especially when these aren't my rules or guidelines.

At home, I take off my dress and throw it into a corner of my closet. I'm so over this. I can't believe he treated me that way, and what makes it worse is that Theo was there to witness it. What if it gets back to John? He doesn't need another reason to pull away. Not when I have him where I want him. *Need him.*

I grab a pair of jeans and throw on a huge hoodie. In the bathroom, I wash all the makeup off my face and throw my hair into a messy topknot. Mom bought me that dress. She saw me walk out of the house in it. Make it make sense!

As I come down the stairs, Dad is waiting in the foyer. I expect him to give me a hard time for dressing so sloppily, but instead he looks relieved.

Despite myself, I'm happy to see that the ice has melted a little between us. Why do I care so much about pleasing him, anyway? It's always so fleeting. And if he knew the truth of what happened between me and John—what's *happening* between me and John—he'd never forgive me. I'm not Georgie. He expects more. He expects the impossible.

When Dad and I arrive at the restaurant, appetizers have already been set out. Mom rises from the table before I can sit and she grabs my arm. She nods for my father to join us at a quiet spot by the entryway.

"What is this?" Mom asks, looking me up and down.

"Dad didn't like my dress, so I changed." I say it so casually. Without emotion. Like I'm some robot that does whatever they want. An AI version of myself who can never get it quite right. Much like version 1.0.

"You're the godmother," Mom reminds me. "You can't show up here dressed like you just rolled out of bed."

"She's comfortable," Dad says, offering me a smile.

"I'd love to be comfortable too, but we've invited the priest to eat with us."

"So?" I ask. "Are you worried he's going to gossip with the women at church about how your daughter's fashion choices are confused?"

Mom sighs deeply. She shoots narrow-eyed glances at both me and my father. "We are trying to make a good impression here." She doesn't have to expand. I know what she means. She saw this lunch as an opportunity to prove to the priest that we are not Arab trash just because Georgie had premarital sex and got pregnant.

"Mom, he's a priest. A man of God. He forgives people for a living. Stop worrying so much."

"Listen to her, Mary. Is he here yet?" Dad glances back into the dining area while loosening his tie.

"He's downstairs washing his hands."

"Did he bring his wife?" Dad asks, as I try to slink away from the conversation.

"No. She wasn't feeling well. He brought the altar boy with him. Theo. And his mother, Petra, Father Petropolis's widow."

Dad nods in understanding while I try not to freak out at having to break bread with John's best friend in front of my entire family.

Of course, the only available seat at the table is across from Theo. I pull out a chair and sit. He's changed too. No longer in his altar boy threads, Theo is wearing a crisp white dress shirt, black tie, and dress pants. This teenage rebellion of mine is flopping as I move from one clothing-imposed insecurity to the next.

We both open our mouths to speak at the same time, then stop.

"Go ahead," he insists.

"So, like, are you and Father Abraham besties?"

Theo laughs. Good. He doesn't take himself too seriously.

"He's sort of taken me under his wing. I go along with it because it makes him feel good about himself, and it's easier. It's also good for my mom to get out. She and your mom seem to be getting along," Theo adds, cocking his head to the other end of the table.

"Easier than what?" I ask, as I try to ignore our mothers laughing and smiling together. My mother is good at peopling.

"Easier than letting them know the truth."

"Which is?" I ask.

"I'm fine. I don't need the constant supervision and check-ins."

I want to say *relatable*, because all I want to be most of the time is left alone. Trusted to make my own decisions. But then again, I'm not grieving like he is. I can't quite relate to what he's going through, and as much as my parents annoy me, I'd never want to be in Theo's shoes.

He spoons some hummus onto his plate and dips his pita into it. "I see you changed," he says, raising his eyebrows. His mouth widens as he stuffs in an enormous bite.

"You don't have to pretend you didn't notice that whole thing at the church."

He lifts his shoulders, unbothered, as if it wasn't as big a deal as I'm making it out to be.

I grab a warm pita from the basket and rip it in half.

"Not that I agree with your father's reaction, but all that stuff—the makeup, fancy clothes—it's all a distraction. And you don't need it."

"Because it's easier to say mean things to me when I'm ugly?"

"That's not what I meant. At all." He shakes his head, looking almost upset. "You're *not* ugly."

Georgie nudges my knee with hers under the table. I glance sideways to see a grin on her face.

My phone buzzes in my hoodie pocket. I pull it out.

Georgie: He's flirting with you.
Flirt back.

Me: He's John's best friend!

Georgie: He's cuter. And Dad might actually let you date him.

Me: You think he's cute?

"Are you texting each other about me?" Theo asks, his voice light. Playful.

"God, egotistical much?" I say, dipping my bread directly into the shared hummus bowl.

"God, table manners much?"

"Khalas with using God's name in vain," Dad groans from the other end of the table.

Everyone bursts into the kind of laughter that cuts away the remaining tension. Well, most of it. I look across the table to find Theo blushing. The contrast of the rose-colored hue of his cheeks against his porcelain skin makes him look like one of those expensive handmade dolls. Objectively speaking he is very good-looking, but in a non-exciting way.

"So, are you Greek or . . . ?" I ask, trying to figure him out. We attend a Greek Orthodox church but most of the congregation are Arabs.

"My mom's Greek. My dad is . . . was, half Greek and half Lebanese."

"Oh." I nod, taking it all in. "I didn't know that."

"Yeah, well, you and I never really got a chance to talk much." He smiles. "I know I didn't leave the best first impression on you."

"Or thirtieth," I say, referring to the garage band practice. *Time to get our stories straight.* I write out a text and clear my throat, nodding to his phone on the table.

Me: My parents can't know about that practice.

Theo: Hello.

Me: Hi.

Me: I lied to them about where I was that day.

Theo: tsk tsk

I glance up to find him smiling down at his phone.

Me: Just don't say anything.

Theo: I guess they don't know about the party either.

Me: No. Or that Andie got drunk.

He looks up from his phone and laughs as his eyes meet mine. I squint at him before looking down at my phone again.

Theo: You and Andie seem mismatched.

Me: She's my favorite person outside of my family.

Theo: Not John?

I suck in my cheeks to stop my smile from growing.

Theo: I guess I was wrong about you not being his type.

Oh god. What does he know?

Theo: Do you want him to be
your boyfriend?

Me: I'm not allowed to date.

Theo: Even boys from church?

I'm biting the insides of my cheeks so hard, I'm about to take out a chunk as I vigorously type my response.

Me: Especially boys from church!

Theo puts his phone on the table and picks up his glass. He looks right at me as he brings the cup to his lips and says, "We'll see," before taking a sip.

Chapter Fifteen

OCTOBER 7

"Lennon?" Mom's voice calls from my bedroom doorway. I turn from my desk, where I'm writing in my journal, to find her with wet, dull eyes.

"What's wrong?"

She sits down on my bed, and I join her there. Mom takes my hand and holds it in hers.

"Did I interrupt your homework?" she asks.

"No. I was just writing. For fun. What's wrong?" I ask again.

"I can't seem to ever get it right with your sister," she says, her voice low.

"Did you fight again?"

Before Paulie was born, the tension between Georgie and my father was so thick around here that it was hard to breathe some days. But since Paulie's birth it's been mostly Mom and Georgie who have been butting heads. Mom tries to help, but I think Georgie just sees it as her not trusting my sister's motherly instincts. She lectures her about dressing Paulie warmly, especially around her tummy. And not letting her sleep too long because she needs to eat. She guilts Georgie whenever she asks Mom and Dad to babysit so she can see her friends. I think they expected Georgie would turn into a full-grown adult the moment she became a mom, but that transition hasn't fully happened. She's still a teenager. She wants to do the things her friends do. Hang out. Be free. Stay up late.

Mom nods. "I just keep thinking, if I'd done something differently, Georgie would have made better choices."

My eyes flick to the open door.

"Don't worry. She's out with Paulie and Daddy."

"You can't think that way. Besides, it's not like anyone hands out an instruction manual on how to be a good parent. And even if they did, you were so busy keeping us clean and fed that you wouldn't have had time to read it."

"There's a difference between small mistakes and big ones."

"Are you calling Paulie a mistake?" I ask, my eyebrows raised at the thought. This household is obsessed with that baby.

"It's not so simple. Of course we love Paulina. But I'm worried about your sister. I never got to go to school or work. And when I had you girls, I gave everything of myself to make sure you would have all that you needed to build a life even better than mine."

"Did you marry Dad because your parents wanted you to, or because you loved him?" I ask.

"Because I loved him."

"And how many suitors did Teta and Sedo bring to your home before and after you met Dad?"

"Too many," Mom says with a laugh.

"Did you ever feel pressured to choose someone else? Someone who lived in Palestine? Do you ever regret leaving?"

"No." She shakes her head, seemingly answering all of my questions at once. "I don't regret. But I do grieve the loss of my old life.

Maybe I should have gone to school when I first got here or found a job. If I had set a better example, for both of you . . ."

"You have four sisters. And are you and your sisters the same or different?"

"Very, very different."

"And I'm very different from Georgie. It's not because of anything you did or didn't do. You made our home beautiful. And the consistency you provided, being there to manage my meltdowns and tantrums, hugging me tight after another terrible day of elementary school, helping me get diagnosed when Dad resisted, it saved my life."

Mom's eyes fall to her lap, and she grabs both my hands and squeezes them.

"I don't think you're giving Georgie enough credit," I say, straightening. "She's going to do big things. Just give her time. God wanted Paulie to come into the world when she did, we have to believe that, and so we also have to trust in Him to guide us to our destinies."

"My girl. So smart. So wise. So beautiful."

"Meh. Two out of three isn't bad," I say around a smile.

The silence that follows is thick. Heavy. Broken only by my phone vibrating on my lap.

"Andie?" Mom asks.

"Yeah." Unfortunate that I have to follow up such a nice mother-daughter moment with a lie.

"I still think she's a bit loud and silly, but she's been good for you. I'm happy you have her."

"Me too."

"Okay," Mom says, wiping under her eyes and sniffling. "I'm going to prepare dinner. They'll be back soon. Do you have any plans tonight?"

I glance at my phone, where a message from John is waiting.

"Andie's house. After dinner, if that's okay?" I ask.

"Sure." Mom nods. "I'll take you."

Mom leans over to kiss me on the cheek. I watch as she rises and walks out of my room, closing the door behind her.

After releasing a breath, I flip my phone over.

John: Are we still good to meet
at Andie's at 7?

I bite on my lip, trying to do the math in my brain.

Me: Make it closer to 7:20. Please.

John: Okay. See you then.☺

Me: can't wait!

"I think this is the first time you've ever been in my car at night," John says a few minutes into our drive. It's funny how he's just coming to that conclusion when it was the first thought I had climbing into his car at Andie's. I invited Andie to join me and John, but she's recently started seeing a new guy and he's coming over once her parents go out.

At the light, he reaches over and takes my hand, entwining his fingers with mine. His smile never fails to make my heart race.

A horn sounds behind us breaking the silence.

"Oops," John says, releasing my hand and driving. "I thought we could go for a walk on Main Street."

"Sounds good."

We turn in to a gravel-filled parking lot and John parks. He shifts in his seat. "Wait," he says, before I pull on the door lever.

We've been keeping things casual for about a month. Which means a lot of kissing but, also, a lot of talking. He still keeps parts of himself guarded, and I'm trying to be patient, but it's hard. Especially when you want to know everything about a person.

"What is it?" I ask.

He brings his hand up and cups it around my face. Our eyes meet, and before I can say anything his lips are on mine. It never gets old. I've kissed John so many times now that I've lost count, and yet the thrill of the moment before his mouth reaches mine cannot be beat.

"Sorry. Just wanted to do that before we go out there," he says.

John understands that if we're out in public I can't hold his hand or kiss him. I have to always be aware of my surroundings. Even though there's nothing I'd love more than to hold his hand in front of the entire world.

"It's okay," I say, not bothering to hide my grin.

He gets out first, then opens my door. We walk out of the lot and to the sidewalk. It's a Saturday night and there are lots of people out. The patios are still open and bustling. John offers to buy me ice cream, but I settle on a Diet Coke instead, extra ice. Our arms brush as we walk, and I want to toss out all of our rules, but I know the second I do I'll get busted.

"Theo told me your moms are becoming good friends," John says, stealing a glance.

"Yeah." I nod. "It's good for my mom. She needs someone who will get her out of the house once in a while. Most of her friendships kind of fell by the wayside after Paulie was born."

"It's good for Theo's mom, too. He says people were there for them a lot in the beginning, but after a while they stopped calling and visiting."

"People are weird when it comes to death. Or maybe that's just my community. What are your parents like?" I ask. The question tumbles out. I regret it almost immediately, but John seems unfazed.

"My dad's in construction. Eaves and gutters. Mom stays home, because of Mikey. But before that she was a daycare teacher."

"And Valerie?" I ask. I've only ever seen John's sister in passing. She graduated last year. I don't think she and Georgie were friends, or even acquaintances.

"Typical firstborn daughter. Straight-A student. Got a scholarship to the University of British Columbia."

"Do you miss her?"

John nods. "She was a big help around the house, and with Mikey."

"Is he a lot of work?" I smile at the thought of a little John running around his house, annoying him, interrupting our texts. Asking John to play.

"Oh yeah. But he's in school now so he's starting to mellow out?" He says it like a question and we both laugh.

"You don't like to talk about your family, do you?" I ask, trying to meet John's eyes. Hard not to take note of all his short, almost rehearsed responses.

He shrugs at my question. "We're just not all that interesting."

"Right. *Your* sister didn't have a baby last year," I say, deadpan.

"We're your typical working-class family. Doing the best we can. Val's scholarship was one of the biggest wins we've had in a while."

There's a heaviness surrounding his words. But why?

"Every family has their load. No one goes through life unscathed. Even before Georgie got pregnant, we had our challenges."

"Like what?" John asks.

"My dad is really strict, and he butts heads with Georgie constantly, has for as long as I can remember, really. He also has a hard time talking about certain things. He lost both parents and his only brother when he was still young, but he never speaks of them. My mom, I think she regrets not doing more with her life. And on top of everything with Georgie, having an autistic daughter has also been hard for them," I say, looking at the ground as we continue walking.

"I have a hard time believing your parents are anything but proud of you."

"I try," I say. Sometimes I feel like that's all I ever do. "And thank you."

I raise my eyes to John's but stumble to a stop.

"Hadid. Brody," a familiar voice cuts in.

Theo. And some girl I don't recognize.

"Hey, what's up?" John asks, bringing his hand to Theo's for an aggressive handshake/side hug.

"This is Cassie," Theo says, pointing to the pretty brunette next to him. "Cassie, this is my friend John and his friend Lennon."

"John and Lennon. That's so cute," she says with a wide and toothy smile.

"It's sickening," Theo says. "You guys want to hang out?"

John hesitates.

"I actually have to get back to Andie's," I say, reading the situation correctly . . . I think.

"Right." Theo smiles, then nods. "Because your parents don't know you're out with John."

"Theo," John says.

"It's all good. Cassie and I were going to a movie anyway. I'll talk to you both later," Theo says.

"Bye! Nice meeting you," Cassie says, trailing behind Theo, who is already steps ahead of her.

"He still likes you," John says after Theo has walked away.

"I don't think he ever liked me," I retort. "Seriously. He made my life hell when we were in Sunday school."

"What did he do?"

"Just said stupid stuff about how I looked or acted. The autism mask wasn't so strong back then. I was awkward and weird, which made me an easy target."

John shakes his head as people walk around us on the sidewalk. "I wish you didn't have to mask."

"We all do, to some degree," I answer. "It's easier now because I have an outlet. People I can be myself around. Andie. You," I say, stepping closer to him.

"I really like you," John blurts, and my heart almost stops.

"Yeah." I look down, smiling. "Me too."

John lowers his head and takes a sip of my drink, eyes on me. "This tastes disgusting."

"And apparently it's terrible for me."

"Just because someone says something isn't good for you, that doesn't make it the truth."

I reach for John's hand and, without hesitation, his fingers twine with mine. He nods and we continue walking, holding hands and talking.

Sometimes the fear of the risk can't compete with the high.

Before getting into his car, John kisses me goodnight under a full moon. I wish I could freeze time. It's too good. My life is never this good. I'm scared of losing him. This moment. This version of myself. Us. Everything.

Chapter Sixteen

DECEMBER 7

A mischievous smile dances on John's lips as he walks to his car, where I'm waiting. Like I've done every Friday for the last three months. John slows his gait as he approaches, and he opens the door for me. He takes my backpack and tosses it into the back seat. He doesn't even have to say anything, nor do I. It's like we know how to be around one another. In a constant state of real-life reverie. He's chivalrous in this low-effort kind of way that feels natural.

We've slipped into a comfortable routine together, one I try to savor, because some days I still can't believe it's real. We're pretty reserved within the school. No hand-holding or kissing. We don't even eat lunch together. I reserve that time for Andie. But John will stop by my locker between classes, sometimes walking me to mine. Then we part with a quick hug before we go our separate ways, living our separate lives. At night we text, sometimes FaceTime if my parents are out. But Fridays are ours. We drive around. Get something to eat. Kiss. Talk. Kiss.

Lately, though, I've been wanting more.

John climbs into his seat and starts the car. It doesn't always catch on the first try because it's so cold out.

"Let's go somewhere," I say, once the car engine has successfully turned. "My mom isn't getting me from Andie's until nine."

"Okay." He nods. "You want to go to the mall? It must be fun Christmas shopping with a baby in the house. Won't be long before Mikey will be trading in toys for video games." John takes my hand, intertwining his cold fingers with mine.

"Too many people there. How about your garage?"

He tilts his head.

"I just think, with it being December, we should move to an indoor location."

"My garage isn't any warmer than my car," he says. "Besides, my mom and Mikey are home."

"Right." I nod.

"Do you want to get pizza or burgers?" he asks.

"Not really hungry," I say, my tone doing a poor job of hiding my disappointment.

John runs his free hand through his hair. "Something's on your mind."

"Yeah."

He shifts so he's closer, leaning in, still holding my hand. "Tell me."

I pull at my earlobe, looking out to the parking lot. I'm jarred by the sight of students and staff getting into their cars. Sometimes when I'm with John I have such tunnel vision that I forget there's a world that exists outside of us.

"I hate that on Friday nights I walk out of your car and don't get to see you for two days."

He smiles this sweet smile, his cheeks pink, and I'm relieved that my truth-bomb didn't scare him away. For now, anyway.

"And I guess," I say, continuing, "a part of me is worried that on weekends you go and do whatever it is you do, and maybe you forget about me. Or you wish you weren't tied up with me in the way you are tied up with me." I've practiced this conversation with him in my head and in front of the mirror so many times, and already I'm veering off script.

"What makes you think that?" His thumb strokes my hand, and it helps calm my racing heart.

"You've been with other girls. And you've *been* with Avery. And I guess I thought because of that you might expect more from me, and I'm okay with that," I say quickly. "But every time I slide my hand up your thigh, you pull away. Not like you're disgusted—at least, I don't think so. But enough to tell me you don't want to go any further. Maybe you're just not that into me, because if you were, you'd want to do more. And I was thinking that maybe on weekends, when we're not together, you get your . . . fulfillment elsewhere?"

John lets go of my hand and leans back in his seat, facing forward. He exhales a long breath. His fingers run up and down his thighs. His face is stoic. *Too far, I guess.*

He shifts suddenly, facing me. "First of all, I don't get my 'fulfillment' elsewhere. Unless my hand counts." He says it so factually, without a hint of embarrassment. "Second of all, we agreed that we wouldn't hook up with anyone else while we were . . ." he pauses, looking me in the eyes, "doing this."

"I know, but . . ."

"But what? You thought I'd do that to you? Lennon, I would never betray you like that."

I freeze at his words. Those are not the kind of words someone in a casual relationship says to the other person. I try to read John's face to see if he regrets what he just said, but it's hard when his face is on its factory default setting. So I stay silent, waiting for him to clarify, or take it back. But he doesn't.

"Is there a *third of all*?" I ask, knowing my question is laced with both hope and desperation.

"Yes." He sighs. "You're fourteen, Lennon. And I'll be seventeen soon. I just don't feel right about us doing anything more than kissing right now."

"Are you serious?" My voice comes out louder than I expected. "Your birthday isn't until April. Which means you don't turn seventeen until I'm fifteen. Besides, Avery is in the same grade as me."

"Avery's birthday is earlier in the year than yours is. Besides, she's different. She'd . . . I wasn't the first guy she was serious with."

"It's my lack of experience, then?"

John releases another heavy sigh.

"John, experienced or not, you have my consent. This isn't illegal or anything. I'm really trying hard to wrap my brain around this so-called logic of yours."

My heart is racing so fast and my chest is burning, but I need to chill out. I can't let this conversation get away from me, from us.

John swallows, hesitation flickering in his eyes. "I just don't know if you can give me consent in a way where you fully understand what it is you're consenting to."

"Because I'm autistic?"

"No." He shakes his head. "I'm happy just kissing you."

"Well, I'm not," I say, like a frustrated, sulky child. "I want more than that."

John brings his hands to his face, pulling them down in frustration. "I don't think we're ready."

"No. You don't think *I'm* ready."

I can already tell I'm going to hate whatever it is he says. He's looking at me the way adults look at children when they want to explain something to them and they're trying to figure out the path of least resistance.

"Once you start doing those things, you can't go back," he says. "And feelings start to get really twisted up."

"Then this is your way of, what, keeping me at arm's length? To stop me from expecting something from you? From this?"

"I like being your friend," he says simply.

"And you think if we do other things we won't be friends anymore?"

He nods.

"Okay," I say, before letting out a long, dramatic exhale. "What if I told you that it's already too late?" I immediately regret my words, but only kind of, because I needed to say them. I needed to release them from where they lived, inside of me. "What if I told you my feelings are already twisted up in you? I don't see us, this, as just a fun thing I do between classes. I kiss you because I want to. Because I like you. Because it's all I can think about. Because you're *all* I ever think about."

"See?" he says, releasing an impatient breath. "This is what I didn't want to happen."

"I don't understand."

"You're the one who set the guidelines," he reminds me.

"So, you're going to pretend that when we kiss, when we text back and forth all day and all night, when you smile at me the way you smile at me, it means nothing to you? That this is in fact a casual . . . thing?"

"It's what we agreed to, isn't it?" He says it like I'm his lawyer and he's repeating the contract back to me. But I don't buy it.

"I don't buy it," I say.

"What don't you buy?"

"That *you* are impervious to everything I'm experiencing. That *you* are not feeling what I am. That *you* are not falling in love with me in the exact same way and with the exact same force with which I am falling in love with you."

"I don't know what you want me to say."

"The truth. Obviously."

He lifts his eyes to meet mine. They are full, beaming. He loves me. I know he does.

"I don't feel the same way."

The car goes silent aside from the faint ringing deep inside my ears.

"Bullshit," I snap, returning to the scene of the crime. This isn't just a situation I misread. This isn't my autism failing to read the signs. I saw the signs. All of them. He's lying.

He goes on, his voice breaking. "I think, in order to preserve our friendship, that we should, um . . . this should stop."

"I'm going to make this really easy for you," I say as tears prick my eyes. "I'm no longer your friend. I'm nothing to you."

"That's not true."

I reach into the back seat to grab my bag before opening the car door and stepping out. I slam the door shut and head back to the school building. I need to get as far away from him as possible. I can only handle so much humiliation in a lifetime.

Another car door slams and John calls after me. While this is what I'd want to happen in one of the romance novels I consume,

I don't want it to happen here. I don't want him to see me like this. What he's turned me into. I don't want him to know he has this power over me. I'm so sick of men having power over me and my emotions.

"Lennon," he calls again, and I can tell he's getting close. "Let me drive you home. Please."

I keep walking, and he catches up, grabbing my arm.

"Let go," I demand, turning to him, the movement like whiplash.

He does as I ask and stands across from me, his own eyes rimmed with red.

"I just don't know how you want me to be," he says, a deep frown in his forehead, his voice raw.

"I literally told you."

He shakes his head, like he's telling himself *no*. "I'm not the person you think I am. I'm not the guy you want."

"Says who?"

"Says the universe," he replies, arms outstretched like he's mad at the world.

"Where is this coming from? Did Theo get in your head again?"

"No. It's not Theo. It's me. It's you. It's everything." He rakes a hand through his hair so forcefully, it looks almost painful.

"What aren't you telling me?" I ask, wrapping my arms around my body.

The battering December winds howl in the aftermath of my question. John's gaze is focused on the ground below us, and just as I'm about to ask him again, he finally looks up.

"I saw where you live, okay?" John says. His Adam's apple moves around a tight swallow. "Theo told me you were rich, and I didn't believe him. I said you didn't act like you were. That you don't wear expensive-looking clothes or things like that. But we were driving around, and he pulled up to your house and I saw it."

"We're not rich. And my house isn't all that special," I say, hiking my arms up farther.

"Do you not realize how much nicer your house is than mine? Than, like, 99 percent of the houses of people who go to our school? Do you not see your privilege?"

"We're comfortable, yeah," I say, shrugging off his awkward observations.

"Your house looks like a palace compared to mine. Tell me you didn't notice a difference when you came over that day."

"I've never even been inside your house."

"Come on, Lennon. You don't need to see the inside of my house to know that our families are not on the same level financially."

"Sure," I finally admit. "But it doesn't bother me."

"What happens next?" His jaw clenches as he exhales through his nose. "We fall in love, then what?"

"Then we figure it out."

His eyes search mine, like he's trying to make me see what he does. "We don't belong together."

"Because I live in a nice house?" I ask, incredulous.

"It's not about the house, it's what the house represents. What it so clearly highlights."

"What does it so clearly highlight?"

John clears his throat and straightens his posture. He glances around the parking lot as if he's searching for something. Answers, maybe. The right words. "Do you really want your first relationship to be with a guy that your father would never accept? That doesn't fit into your lifestyle? Face it, Lennon. You and I exist in different worlds. Eventually, the outside forces are going to creep into our relationship, and they're going to pull us apart. And I'd rather not have to . . . I don't want to put you through that. We were fooling ourselves thinking this," he says, pointing a finger between us, "would be okay as long as we kept things casual. I can't do it anymore."

"You're just scared."

He shakes his head again, and I step up to him.

"You are. You're scared of letting yourself feel something real, so you're pulling away. Making up excuses to feel better about ending things. But it won't work. It's too late," I say, my sharp tone punctuating each word. "I'm not only in your head, I'm in your heart. And you can try to bury me, and the idea of me, away. You can probably even convince yourself that we're nothing. But you can't lie about the fact that you love me back. Because I can feel it. And you're just too afraid to admit it."

"If you stepped outside of this, us, you'd see realistically . . ." His voice trails off as his eyes trace over me softly.

It's silent again. The days are short. Daylight is creeping away. A motion-sensor light outside the school building turns on, spotlighting John and me, like we're actors on a stage.

"Maybe we are different," I say, cutting through the quiet. "Because, to me, you're worth it. All of it."

"I can't make you happy, Lennon," he says, his eyes glued to the ground. "It's not me you want or need."

I swallow down the anger that his words are responsible for. "You don't get to tell me what I want or need. No one does." I take in a breath through my nose and let it out in a quiet exhale. "By the way, I turn fifteen tomorrow. But you already knew that, didn't you?"

"I'm sorry," he says, his shaky voice causing a tear in my heart.

"You don't have to be sorry," I say passively, all hope drained out of me. "Truth is, you were never mine."

Chapter Seventeen

DECEMBER 27

It's surprisingly easy shutting someone out of your life in the winter. Even when you go to the same school. You learn people's patterns, and I know which routes John takes to get to his classes. I used to use this knowledge to my advantage, to orchestrate "chance" encounters with him. We'd brush shoulders, exchange secretive glances and smiles. John would sometimes grab my hand in his and squeeze it before gently letting it go as we passed one another.

Now, I take the routes less traveled. The ones that get me to class on time and come with fewer risks.

I've spent most of December trying to be the best sister, aunt, and daughter I can. I help Georgie with Paulie, do my homework, and spend time with Dad in the evenings, mending the fractures our relationship has suffered since I started high school, most of them invisible but still painfully felt. To other fathers and teenage daughters, these would just be growing pains, but for us, it feels like we're growing apart.

"Where's Georgie?" I ask Dad. I've just woken up from a couch nap—a perk of being on holidays for two weeks. But even in sleep I can't seem to escape thoughts of John.

"She's shopping with Mommy. And Paulie. I think Zach and his mom were meeting them there too. They want to see if there are any good after-Christmas sales. I think Georgie is looking for a bed for Paulie."

"So soon?" I sit up and turn my head to look at Dad, who is seated on the other sofa watching TV.

"It's good to be prepared. Paulie won't be a baby forever."

"But she's literally still a baby." Paulie is months away from turning one and already they're out looking for a bed? "Why didn't they invite me?" I ask, suddenly annoyed at being left out. Again.

"You were sleeping. They only left about twenty minutes ago."

"Whatever," I say, reaching for my book on the coffee table and flopping back onto the cushions.

"You're better off at home. It's warm, and you get to spend uninterrupted time with me," he says. I can almost hear the smile on his face. "I spoke to your friend, Theodore, at church after Christmas service."

The change in subject is so jarring that I sit up and turn to look at him.

"I forgot to ask," he goes on. "How did you do on that Algebra test? The one you took before break."

"Midterm," I correct him. "I got a 79."

He sighs impatiently. "Did you study?"

"Yes. I always do. I'm just not good at math. I keep telling you this."

Dad changes the channel and I stare at the pages of my open book, not reading, just anticipating his next words.

"This is a myth," he says. "Being good or not good at math. Math is practical. With proper training, anyone can be good at math. All those books you read are making your brain soft."

"How are my books any different from you watching TV every night after dinner? At least with books, I'm forced to think critically."

He glances at the young adult romance novel in my hands and chuckles. "*Our Last Summer*. This is garbage. All of it is."

I slam the open book down on my lap, bending its spine.

"Reading romance books doesn't put food on the table," Dad says, tossing me a dismissive sideways glance.

"But writing them does."

"My cousin Rania is an author. She says if it weren't for her husband's job in tech, they wouldn't survive. It's a hobby for her."

"I have a hard time believing she works that hard for something she sees as a hobby."

"How is it hard work to write? You sit at a desk, click-clacking on a keyboard, writing down the images you see in your head."

"You sit at a desk all day," I remind him.

He laughs at my argument as if it has no bearing. What he does, in his mind, is so much more elevated than what artists do. "Habibti, if you want to be a writer, go ahead. Just make sure you marry a very rich man."

"I would never depend on a man," I say, squinting at my father.

"I know." He nods. "I raised you right."

I roll my eyes as I bring my book back up to my disgruntled face.

"You know who's good at math? Your friend, Theodore."

I see we're circling back to Theo again since I didn't take the bait the first time.

"He's not my friend," I say.

"Maybe he can tutor you. It's just him and his mom, so he could use the money. He can come here and help you a couple of times a week. Stay for dinner. It will be good for both of you."

I lower the book. "Dad, you don't need to pay some guy twenty dollars an hour to teach me formulas."

"Twenty-five."

"Twenty-five dollars an hour?" I say, incredulous. "Wait. Did you already . . . please tell me you didn't."

"He's starting after winter break. You're welcome."

"I guess I forgot to thank you," I say.

"We need to bring your average up to at least an 85 to get into the Civil Engineering program at University of Toronto."

"I already told you, I want to be a writer. Besides, I'm only in tenth grade."

Dad clicks his tongue. "You'll need a strong foundation in all maths, especially algebra, before studying calculus. I'm not saying no to writing. You can minor in English if you want. I understand what it's like to enjoy creative endeavors. It's healthy even. Universities appreciate a well-rounded student. But it's important in this climate to graduate with a degree that will result in building a career. Not a job."

I sink into my seat. I suppose a minor in English isn't the worst compromise. It's something to fall back on when I eventually flunk out of Civil Engineering. Whatever the hell that even is.

"Do you have any plans for New Year's Eve?" Dad's question feels like a test. Before I can answer, he goes on. "Theodore is having a New Year's Eve gathering at his house. He asked me if it would be okay for you to attend. With your silly friend, Andie." His tone is so casual, it's completely throwing me. I can't read him. At all. And then, a horrendous thought pops in.

"Oh my god, Dad. Did you make him invite me?"

"Why would you think that?" he asks, wide-eyed.

"Because it's something you would do."

"It was his idea," Dad says, raising his shoulders ever so slightly, his eyes still on the TV screen. "I like him. He's a good boy. You should go."

I put the book down and grab my phone without responding to Dad. I text Andie.

Me: What are we doing for new year's?

Andie: We? Are you allowed out of your cage?

Me: Theo Petropolis is having a "gathering" and he's invited both of us. My father says I can go. Can you believe it? Theo asked my father to invite me. And I have my dad's blessing. Weird, right?

Andie: Theo invited me too?

Me: Apparently. You in?

Andie: Definitely

"I'll go to Theo's party if I can stay out until one," I say to Dad after putting my phone down.

"Twelve-thirty," he replies. "And you need to arrange your own ride home. I'm taking your mom out. But it has to be someone I approve of. Not just anyone gets to drive my baby around."

"What's Georgie doing?" I ask. Maybe she can come get me during one of her midnight rides with Paulie.

"Zach is coming over. They're going to spend New Year's Eve together."

Unchaperoned, I want to point out, but, well, seems a bit silly to worry about that now. I'm fairly certain Georgie wouldn't have minded if I hung out with her and Zach, but the fact that she didn't invite me makes Theo's party an even more alluring option. I never want to be anywhere someone doesn't want me. Whether they admit it or not. I know how to read silence. *Most of the time.*

"I'm sure Andie's mom will drive us."

"Don't be sure. Be positive," he says, nodding to my phone.

I pick it up to check with Andie but end up texting someone else instead.

Me: I hear you and my dad are bros now.

Theo: I didn't hear a thank you.

Me: For what?

Theo: It's an intimate affair.
I'm not just inviting anyone.

He's so full of himself.

Me: what's the dress code

Theo: Why? Worried you'll show up under or over dressed again?

Me: Yes. So what is it?

Theo: Casual.

I effing hate that word.

Me: Ok.

Theo: does that mean you're coming?

Me: Yeah. Andie too.

Me: Will John be there?

Theo: probably

Me: Does he know I'll be there?

Theo: don't know.

Me: Do you think I should tell him?

Theo: if you want to.

Me: this has been a super helpful conversation. thx.

Theo: 👍

Chapter Eighteen

DECEMBER 31

Strings. When your father uncharacteristically gives you permission to attend a New Year's Eve party with people who don't share your DNA, there are always strings attached.

First, I must check in hourly via text. My parents also warned me they may call periodically. And without warning. Of course, if they do, I'll be expected to respond within two rings.

Second, I had to arrange a ride with Andie's mom, who promised to bring me home by twelve-thirty, which, if I were Andie, I'd be pissed about since her curfew is much later. But she's going to spend the night at my house, which she loves doing for some reason.

Third, and this may be the most embarrassing one yet, I have to bring over a dish of ghraybeh, which are basically just shortbread cookies with nuts.

Dad didn't ask if Theo's mom would be there tonight, which seems odd. Unless maybe Theo already told my father she would be.

The number of things my mind has to consider to "enjoy" one night out makes all of this feel not worth it. But then I think, *What if John's there?*

Mom and Dad drop me off at Andie's before their night out. My parents need this time alone to rebuild and get back to a good place. There was a lot of fighting when Georgie announced her pregnancy. My father blamed my mother. My mother blamed my father. They took turns taking the blame.

At some point I think it clicked for them that if they didn't get on board, they could lose both Georgie and the baby. A few months into her pregnancy, things shifted, and my parents focused most of their attention on my sister. Maybe that's what gave me room to even allow myself to think I had a chance with John. I let my daydreams manifest into a quasi-reality. When things were good, they were so good. But now, sometimes I wish I could go back to before. Before I met John. Before Georgie was pregnant. When it was just the four of us in our safe little bubble and I didn't want for more than that.

In Andie's room getting ready, she tries to convince me to go without the cardigan I'm wearing, but I don't care enough about impressing anyone tonight, and I don't need to feel self-conscious about my skin showing. I do experiment with a bit with makeup, though. It doesn't always have to be all or nothing. A happy medium can exist.

Once I've found my makeup happy medium (and Andie has approved it), we tell her mom that we're ready to go. Andie sits in the back seat with me, and her mom makes a joke about being an Uber driver. Andie's seated so close that our legs are pressed together, and she's giggling as she shows me pictures of a guy she's been talking to. I hold in an audible gasp as she shares a picture of him in his underwear, which makes Andie laugh even louder.

"What's so funny back there?" Andie's mom asks.

"Lennon farted," Andie says as she turns her screen off.

"I did not!" I say, completely aghast.

"Stop being such a brat," her mom playfully chides. "We don't want to lose Lennon. She's the only good influence in your life. Me included."

They both laugh, and I sit quietly, trying to make sense of their comment. I wonder sometimes how Andie's mom, once an in-demand international model, feels about chauffeuring her just as stunning teenage daughter around. Andie says her mom is adamant about her having a normal teenage experience, since she never got one. Part of me can relate to that. I'm afraid of looking back twenty years from now and feeling the same sense of loss. In exchange, Andie's mom got a modeling career. And what do I get? I'd say my father's approval. But lately, that's been a moving target, and just as I think I've reached it, another one appears in the far-off distance.

Once we're dropped off, Andie grabs my arm to stop me from ringing Theo's bell. "I have to ask you something."

"Can you ask me inside?" I say. My bare hands are freezing carrying the tray of foil-wrapped cookies.

Andie fixes one of my stray hairs and focuses her gaze on me. "I'm kind of into Theo. But I want to make sure it's okay with you if I, you know, go there."

"So it's not ever after with the underwear guy?" I ask. Then I pause to take in her question and scrunch up my face. "Why wouldn't it be okay with me if you liked Theo?"

"Lennon." Andie's face softens. "Can't you see what's happening here?"

"What's happening here?"

She fails to fight back her smile. "Your dad is basically paving the road for you to fall into Theo's arms."

"You think?" I ask.

"One hundred percent."

"But I'm not even allowed to date."

"No. But your dad is all about 'laying the foundation,'" she says, laughing. And I laugh too, because it's one of his go-to lines in almost every conversation that has to do with my future. "He's slowly integrating Theo into your life in the hopes that one day, when you're 'ready,' aka when *he's* ready, you and Theo will just"—she snaps her fingers—"fall in love."

If anyone else spoke to me the way Andie does, I'd tell them to stop treating me like a child, or what I am, an autistic teenager who sometimes needs things explained to them. Especially people things.

Sometimes, being autistic is like sitting too close to the movie screen and focusing on one detail. Other times, it's like I'm in the back row, with too many distractions between me and the screen, and I'm unable to properly process what's happening. Having Andie as a best friend is like always having the best seat in the house.

"In that case, he's all yours," I say, reaching my finger to the doorbell. It lights up and a bell chimes. "Seriously. My heart unfortunately is stuck on someone else."

Andie grins as she presses her shoulder against mine.

The door opens and my mouth drops at the sight of him. "Speaking of," she says quietly before entering the house. She squeezes past John and turns back to look at me, covering her open mouth with her hand in excitement.

"Lennon." My name coming out of his mouth is like hearing a song I love but haven't played in a while.

"Why are you answering the door?" I ask, instead of saying "Hi" like a normal person.

John's lips curve up as he takes me in. It's quick, but I've clocked it. "Theo is otherwise occupied." He cocks his head to the family room behind him, where Theo is talking to a group of people, making big, showy movements with his arms, commanding all their attention.

I return my gaze to John, who these days I spend more time fantasizing about than actually being in the same room with.

"Come in," he says, stepping away from the door.

Once inside, I ditch my shoes and drop my coat onto the pile on the front bench. Awful music is playing, loudly, and the lights are dim. Voices stream into the foyer from the kitchen and sitting area. Theo's house is cozy. Lived in. A perfect party house. I wonder what it's like when it's just Theo and his mom.

I glance at the fancy dining room to my left, which doesn't match the modest decor of the rest of the home. I imagine big dinners with Theo's large extended family, where Theo and his dad led prayers and Theo's mom smiled proudly off to the side at her men. You can tell this home has had a lot of good memories, and some not so good ones.

"How are you?" John asks, hands deep in his pockets. He's wearing a long-sleeved tee and jeans, and he smells the way he always does. Musky, with a hint of lavender. His sister's shampoo.

"I'm okay," I reply, careful not to let the tray of cookies shake and reveal how not okay I am in this moment.

"Happy belated birthday, by the way," he says, nodding as each word leaves his lips.

"Where can I put this?" I ask. It's not that I'm ignoring his belated birthday wish, I just don't know how to respond to it. "My mom made me bring these cookies for Theo and his mom."

"I'll take them." He grabs the tray and places it on the dining room table before returning to where I am, unmoored by the front door. "Can I get you something?" he asks. "You want pop or water?"

"Is that what everyone else is drinking?" I say, pulling off my cardigan to reveal a sleeveless top. My cardigan slips out of my fingers and falls to the floor. I will myself not to flinch. I want John to believe that I am unbothered—by him, by the draft running across my bare arms, by the loud music—everything.

John picks my cardigan up off the floor and hands it back to me. "I don't really pay attention to what others are drinking. I don't drink."

"I've never noticed," I say, my shoulders dropping. "I guess I just assumed you were like everyone else."

"Not when it comes to that."

Not when it comes to anything.

"Are you two going to stand by the door all night or actually join the rest of us?" Theo shouts from the family room, drink in hand.

John lifts his chin to the party, and I nod, twisting my cardigan in my hands.

In the kitchen, John presents me with a beer, a bottle of water, and a can of pop. It feels like a test. I swipe the Diet Coke and take a long sip, then cover my mouth to conceal a small burp.

Theo wasn't completely lying to my father. This *is* more like a "gathering" than a party. Just about twenty or so people, including Eddie from their band, and a few other eleventh-graders I recognize but don't remember the names of. Well, "remember" would suggest I knew their names to begin with.

I take a seat on one of the couches. John sits on the arm of another couch across the room. I try not to look at him, but it's almost impossible. When John's in the room, my entire body knows it. Magnetic forces from deep within pull me to him. Our eyes meet, and it feels like he wants to say something to me, but every time he seems as if he's about to get up and sit in the empty spot to my right, someone starts up a conversation with him.

"Having fun?" Theo flops down next to me, throwing an arm around my shoulders. I squirm and push him away. He reeks of pot and beer.

"It's fine."

"*It's fine*," he says, in a tone that could be interpreted as mocking, but I don't take it personally.

"I never know what to do at these things."

"Just be yourself." He looks down at me. "You have goosebumps all over your arms. Are those from me?"

"No. I'm just cold," I reply, clasping my cardigan with one hand while taking a sip of my drink with the other.

"Then put your sweater on, genius." When I don't respond, he nods. "Ahh, I see. You want to look good for him. I'm going to let you in on a secret," he says, leaning in, his breath warm and yeasty. "You could be dressed in trash bags, and he'd still be staring at you the way he's been staring at you since the second you walked in."

"Has he?" I ask, almost whispering. Theo smirks, and I study his face. His conventionally yet annoyingly handsome face. "How much do you know about us?"

Theo fist-bumps some guy who squeezes by on his way to the kitchen.

"A gentleman never tells," he replies.

"We're not talking about gentlemen. We're talking about you and John," I say, placing my drink on the table in front of us.

Theo licks his lips before his eyes land on mine. "To be honest, he won't tell me anything."

"That's because there's not much to tell," I say, throwing my cardigan back on and slumping against the couch with my arms crossed.

"Did he try something?"

"No. That's the problem," I say, shifting to him.

"Really?"

I nod, wide-eyed, like I still can't believe it either.

"Do you want me to see if Eddie will screw you?"

I sit up and shove him.

"So is your mom here?" I ask, glancing around.

Theo lets out a small huff before taking another sip of his beer. "What do you think?"

"Did you tell my dad she would be here?"

Theo's eyebrows furrow at my question before he shakes his head. "No. Because that would have been a lie." I nod at his reply, trying hard not to overthink it. "She's working the overnight shift at the hospital."

"Hey guys," Andie says, sitting on the coffee table across from us. She and I exchange knowing glances.

"Where's your bathroom?" I ask Theo.

"You don't want to use the one out here. Fendelman was in there for like an hour. There's a bathroom in my room you can use. I can show you where it is."

"No thanks." I shoot up and smile at Andie. "I remember."

Andie squeezes into the spot on the couch where I was, and Theo throws his arm around her. He does it in a different way than he did with me. He's more careful with her. Less playful.

Theo watches me walk away as Andie flashes him one of her signature smiles that he hasn't yet noticed.

I admire that Andie so simply goes after what she wants. She doesn't waste time overthinking things. And when things don't work out, she moves on. She doesn't linger.

Maybe I've been trying to force something that isn't there. Maybe John Brody just isn't that into me.

Because it shouldn't be this hard, should it?

Chapter Nineteen

Theo's room is clean yet lived in. He's made his bed, imperfectly, which is kind of cute. The best part of his room is the floor-to-ceiling sliding doors, which look out to his backyard. I love the accessibility of bungalows. Everything on the same level. No one is ever too far away. But for some reason, in here tonight, I feel separate from everything happening out there.

Snow covers his backyard pool and pavers. A few lawn chairs are also covered in snow, cushions and all. I wonder if putting those chairs away had been his father's job and Theo didn't do it in time for the first snow. It must be hard having little reminders of someone's absence pop up in the most unexpected ways. Especially in the first few years.

It's a great backyard. I remember thinking so the first time I was here. I can picture myself out there on a warm summer day, sprawled on a lawn chair reading, in-between laps in the pool. Theo and John at the barbecue. Andie strolling past in her bikini. Me covered up with a large towel.

I have to stop including John in my daydreams. I foolishly let myself believe the connection we had was written in the stars just because of our names. I must stop feeding myself these false beliefs. The second I do, I'll be able to at least start the process of moving on.

I check my phone for messages from Andie. Theo isn't even Andie's type.

Me: Do you want me to come back
or should I stay away longer?

Andie: Stay away longer 😉

I tuck my phone in my back pocket as my eyes land on an impressive bookshelf next to Theo's closet. I examine the titles, running my fingers along the spines: Edward Said, nonfiction books on Palestine by Ilan Pappé, and, of course, a Bible. In a wooden frame on the top shelf sits a picture of Theo with his dad. I bring it down and wipe the light layer of dust away with my sleeve.

In my house, death is a subject that's almost as taboo as sex.

"Did you know him?" a deep voice asks.

I look up to find John standing across from me. "Father Petropolis?" I ask, gripping the frame.

He nods.

"We never officially met. My dad knew him, though. He's on the church board of directors or whatever. My dad, I mean."

"He was a great guy. Theo was really broken up about it," John says, glancing at the photo in my hand. "Wouldn't talk to anyone aside from me and his mom for months."

"Fourteen is too young to lose a parent," I say as I place the frame back on the shelf, studying Theo's wide, genuine smile. "He'd been sick for a while. Maybe Theo feels some relief now, as terrible as that is to say."

"No, I agree. Watching someone you love suffering long term—to me, that feels worse than a quick death. Everyone's life in limbo. In a state of anticipatory grief and being paralyzed by both the known and unknown." John's eyes find mine again before he looks away. "What're you doing in here?"

"Theo told me his bathroom would be less contaminated," I say.

Anticipatory grief?

John laughs and sits on the foot of Theo's bed before running both hands through his hair. "I fucking hate New Year's."

"Me too," I say, moving to lean against the chest of drawers across from Theo's bed.

"Yeah? How come?"

"Because . . ." I breathe out, and John's eyes latch onto mine. "It's like this actual tangible marker of time passing, but in a sad way. Once a year is over, that's it. It becomes an instant memory. And with everyone's lives seeming to move at warp speed, all New Year's does is make me feel kind of inferior about where I am." *And where I'm not.*

"What's so wrong about where you are?"

A beat of silence passes over us. "Right now?" I ask, allowing a smile to sneak out. "Nothing. But it's fleeting."

John smiles back, his hands gripping both knees. "I'm surprised your dad let you come here tonight."

My father is not exactly who I want to be talking about while I'm in a room alone with John. But somehow he always manages to make it into my most intimate conversations.

"He doesn't see Theo as a threat," I say, point-blank.

John chuckles. "Theo is a good guy, but he's not exactly the altar boy image he portrays."

"Aren't we all pretending to be someone we're not?"

"Are you pretending now?" he asks, tracing the lines of my face with his eyes.

"To my detriment, I struggle to hold back around you. The words come out, never the way I rehearsed them, and I say too much, and I feel too much, and I'm always just too much."

"You're perfect," he says simply.

"If that were true then we wouldn't be here right now, dancing around all the heavy subtext. We'd be together," I say, taking slow, cautious steps toward Theo's bed. I sit next to John, my hands clasped together on my lap.

He turns to look at me. "I lied. When you said . . ." He clenches his jaw, then swallows. "When I said I didn't feel the same way you did. Because I did. *I do*."

"But . . . ?" I ask, because I know there's more. There always is.

"But," he continues, "everything else I said still stands. It's why I couldn't say the words then. I wanted to, more than anything. I wanted to tell you I felt the same." He pauses, releasing a deep exhale before locking eyes with me again. "While you were fighting for me to admit the truth of how I felt, I was already grieving the us that could never be. That's why I didn't say it back. It's why I walked away." His voice trails off, and he looks down at my hand holding his.

Could never be.

I look at his face. Those stunning blue eyes. The scar that runs slightly jagged above his lip. His soft brown hair. The way his neck curves into his broad shoulders.

If only I could read his mind.

If only.

In the silence, I search his eyes for the truth. To cut through all the rules we seem to think we have to follow. Rules invented by other people.

"John," I begin to say, but his voice is louder.

"I love you."

His words, a literal dream, ignite me. Blood rising. Skin flushing.

I take in breaths, covertly, trying to steady my racing heart.

"Since the moment we met, I've been trying to get over you," I confess. "But I couldn't. I always felt tethered to you."

"We're connected," he says, repeating his words from the day we met.

John leans in, his warm breath tickling my lips. "We shouldn't," he murmurs, as if to himself. He moves back, creating a draft between us, but I lean in closer.

"I love you too." My words come out softly, but without fear. "I love you," I say again, this time against his mouth. A euphoric aura surrounds us.

We're so close that I can feel his resistance fading. Silence lingers as I run a hand through John's hair, still wet at the roots from his shower. He almost groans at my touch as his mouth grazes mine again. He lets out a strangled sound before kissing me with an intensity he never has before. It's hungry and breathy and I lose myself in it, in him. But then, just as suddenly as the kiss happened, he pulls away. From blatant need to obvious restraint in less than five seconds.

He bolts up and walks to the sliding door, looking out over Theo's backyard. A light from outside shines on his face, illuminating both his imperfections and his perfections.

"If you want me to leave, I'll go," I say. When he doesn't respond, I nod slightly before getting up.

"Lennon," he calls out as I reach for the doorknob.

I take in a deep breath, knowing whatever John says next will change everything.

"Stay. Please."

His words steal the air out of my lungs. Before I realize it, my fingers twist the lock on the door. John is turned away from the glass doors now. The moon lights up the sky and reflects off the snow, creating this ethereal royal blue haze around him. He looks like a mirage.

He pulls the drapes over the door, shielding us from the world outside. We walk in slow paces, inching our way closer to one another. It's not too late. I could still leave. I could do the right thing. Be a good girl and do what my parents have taught me to do: stay away from boys. But I don't want to. I want to be in this room, alone with John. Every inch of my body knows this. My heart knows this. It's only my inner voice—speaking the rules that have been instilled in me since I was taught there's a difference between boys and girls—that hasn't quite accepted what I'm going to do. What I so desperately want to do.

We're face-to-face, our chests inches apart. I stare at John's lips, breathing him in. The lavender scent of his shampoo wafts from his body to mine.

"I don't drink because my dad's an alcoholic," John says. "And I don't want to end up like him."

My lips part at his reveal, but I don't respond right away. All our past interactions play like a highlight reel in my mind. The hesitation, his insecurities—the clues were there all along. He just wasn't ready to tell me until now. Not until he felt safe enough.

"You're not your father."

John's open palm moves to my cheek, and I lean into it. His lips find mine, kissing me as if it's the first time. He moves with care, delicately, his warm mouth gentle against my top lip, then the bottom. With every kiss, his love radiates, of this I am certain.

My arms wrap around his body, this body I know so well but which also feels like a stranger. It's electricity and sparks and butterflies all in one. If I could make myself invisible to exist inside of him, I would.

Our kiss deepens, but he pulls away again, looking down at me, at my body, like he's seeking permission. I nod, then watch as he brings his hands up to delicately unbutton my cardigan. He slides it off and a chill passes over me as it falls to my feet. John places tiny kisses on my bare, goosebump-covered shoulders. His fingers travel up and down my arms, making the hairs stand at attention.

I swallow as warm, soft kisses on my neck turn my knees to jelly, making me forget who and where I am. My heart beats in sync with John's and I've never wanted anything more than I want this. Him.

But then, like clockwork, the intrusive thoughts slip in. I try to push them away, squeezing my eyes shut.

This is wrong.

They would be so ashamed.

No one will want you if you do this.

He's just using you.

You're a slut.

Bad things will happen if you let this continue.

"Hey," John says, his eyes level with mine. "Are you okay?"

"Yeah." I remove my top then take his hand and lead him to the bed. I lie down and John lowers himself onto me, carefully. I pull at his shirt, helping him remove it, as if I'm unwrapping the biggest present under the Christmas tree. My fingers caress the skin of his bare chest and I'm weak taking him in.

His cheeks flush watching me. It's all so vulnerable and intense, but I don't want to hold back anymore. John places one arm around me and grabs my thigh with his other hand. He kisses my neck, then my shoulders, then just below my collarbone. I bite on my lip, shutting my eyes and absorbing every single touch.

You're not the only teenage girl who does this.

Andie does this.

Georgie does this.

Paulina is the result of this.

John has done this with other girls.

There are probably people doing this right now, under this roof, in different rooms.

This is okay.

You can do this.

You don't need to feel bad about it.

He loves you.

You love him.

I press my fingers into his back, pulling him in closer. Feeling brave or confident, or maybe just ready, I bring my hands to his waistband and unbutton his jeans. He stops kissing me, his eyes searching mine, like he's making sure. I nod, and then he nods in agreement before kissing me harder. I need to remove the layers between us. I want to feel all of him against all of me. John slides his jeans off and I thrust my hips up slightly, removing mine at the same time.

We're both down to our underwear, and his body covers mine like a warm blanket. A tingle pulses between my legs as I watch his eyes flick across my body. Our kisses are needy, almost desperate, and my pulse reacts by thumping like a horde of happy elephants.

I don't feel pressured: to say the right thing, to do more than I'm comfortable with, or to act a certain way. All of that is gone, and I just want to exist in this moment with him.

"Is it okay . . .?" He pauses, then looks down.

I nod again, then say, "Yes," to absolve us of any misunderstandings. His hand finds its way to my inner thigh, and I can no longer think. His fingers feel like visitors to a foreign country. Each touch is new and more intense than the last. As he moves around me, I can barely catch my breath. It's all so fast and uncontrolled. I turn my head, burying my face into the pillow to muffle my heavy breathing. One hand grasps the side of the bed, while the other hangs limply, trying to take in every single touch, reminding myself to just be.

Just be.

When the roller coaster subsides, John's eyes freeze on mine before placing a gentle kiss on my lips. Still, butterflies.

"I . . ." John begins before brushing his lips over mine. I run my hand down his bare back, wishing I could freeze this moment. John opens his mouth to speak but a heavy knock at the bedroom door breaks the spell.

"Shit," John says, leaping off the bed.

"Who's in there?" Theo shouts from behind the door, the knob rattling.

John grabs my clothes off the floor and passes them to me. As I'm getting dressed, he ducks into Theo's bathroom. I can hear him splashing water on his face.

"What should we do?" I whisper, straightening Theo's sheets and myself out.

John uses his shirt to dry his face before pulling it back on.

"Why is this door locked?" Theo shouts again, frustration seeping through the walls.

The tone of his voice makes me freeze in this moment. I hear my dad. Feel his presence. *How does he know? How does he always know?*

"Lennon? Lennon?"

"Huh?" I manage, returning to the present.

"It's okay. Open the door," John says, blinking repeatedly.

I swallow, then walk past John both shakily and quickly. When I open the door, Theo and Andie are standing on the other side.

Theo storms right past me to find John by the foot of his bed. "Did you have sex on my bed?"

"No," I say, my eyes meeting Andie's. *The truth.* "We were just talking." *A lie.*

"Bullshit," Theo says, ripping his curtains open.

"Relax," Andie responds.

"Why are you even here?" Theo snaps at her. "I invited Lennon. Not you." Theo's tone is scorching, but I know his anger is directed at John and me.

"Fine. I'll leave," Andie says. "Lennon?" she asks, expecting me to follow. But the fading adrenaline has made me jittery. And weak.

"Apologize," John says, stepping to Theo. "You can't speak to people that way. Drunk or not."

"You'd be the expert, right?"

John shakes his head. "Andie has the right idea. Lennon?"

"I'll be right there," I say to John while looking at Theo. I wait for Theo's eyes to find mine. He's better than this and he knows it.

John's jaw clenches before he exhales loudly. He hesitates, his eyes moving between mine and Theo's. I give him a reassuring nod, and he responds with a tight-lipped smile as he follows Andie out of the room.

"I gave your father my word that you'd be safe here. Looked after," Theo says once they're gone. His eyes shift to his slightly mussed up bed.

"I didn't realize you were on babysitting duty." I cross my arms in front of me.

"This is my bedroom. How do you think it makes me feel knowing you were in here with him?"

"It's not like . . ." I inhale then exhale. "We didn't have sex."

"I'm not an idiot, Lennon."

"I wouldn't do that in here, on your bed." I say the words because I mean them, but I'm not sure if I believe them.

"You shouldn't do it here or anywhere else with him. He's not for you."

"He's not *for me*?" I repeat. "Do you realize how much you sound like my father? You're a snob, just like he is. But worse, because isn't John supposed to be your best friend?"

"And yet I thought *we* were friends. Or at least trying to be."

"We are. But I don't need your protection. I have enough people in my life protecting me. It's suffocating. I thought you got that."

Theo's body unstiffens, slightly. "You really didn't have sex with him?"

"No. Not that I owe you details about my personal life," I say, wrapping my cardigan around my body.

He breathes out slowly as his eyes meet mine again. Softer. Kinder. "Sorry for blowing up at you. I've had a lot to drink."

"Yeah, I can see that," I say. "Do you want me to bring Andie back?"

He shakes his head. "I don't care about her."

"Theo."

He takes an intentional step so he's standing directly across from me. "I don't care about Andie or any other girl. I only care about you."

"What?" My stomach sinks as the cold rush of adrenaline returns. Where did this come from? "You don't mean that. You're just drunk."

Theo brings up a hand and tucks a piece of hair behind my ear before following it down to where it ends. My heart feels like it's going to burst out of my chest as he sweeps his fingers across my waistline. I don't understand what's happening. I was confident John was wrong. Did I lead Theo to believe I could feel the same? *Could I?* Theo's vulnerability, his eyes, his touch, all of it is making it harder than it should be for me to walk away. To tell him to stop. To tell him I don't feel the same. Because I don't.

"I have to go," I say, taking a step back. "Just sleep it off."

"Lennon," Theo says, his lips quivering. He drops to the floor and begins to cry, his hands cradling his head. "I don't want to be alone. My dad . . ." His voice trails off.

I kneel next to him, taking his hand in mine as he rocks back and forth. "It's okay. I'll stay with you."

He lets out a loud, heaving sob, and I grab his hand tighter while running my other hand up and down his back. I can't leave him here like this, so I stay.

My phone lights up on the floor next to me. A text from Andie telling me she's waiting outside and called her mom to come get us early, and one from John asking me to meet him.

I tell Andie I'll meet her in a few minutes. I tell John that Theo needs me.

Andie responds.

John doesn't.

Chapter Twenty

JANUARY 8

I've changed.

And I haven't changed.

I feel bad.

But I also feel good.

I promise myself never again.

And then I practice all the ways I can bring up the subject of *us* to John. Not the *us* that tries to figure out what we are to each other. That's a conversation that feels endless and exhausting and not really that much fun. But the *us* we were on New Year's.

With winter break over, I figure enough time has passed that we can talk again. Face-to-face. Any more time that stretches between us will only make an already awkward situation even more awkward. All our texts since that night have been muted. Whenever I message him, he's about to "head out" or he'll "get back to you asap" but then . . . crickets.

Sometimes I wonder why I bother.

And then I close my eyes and picture his mouth on mine, and it all becomes clear.

A spark. Magic. Fireworks.

"We need to talk," I say as John heads out of the boys' change-room. I rushed to catch him as soon as class was over, not even bothering to switch out of my gym clothes first.

A few guys come out behind him, and he takes my hand, moving us out of the way.

"You're pissed, right? Because I stayed with Theo? It was only for a few minutes. I left with Andie right after. I couldn't find you."

"We talked about this," John says, his eyes struggling to meet mine.

"No," I say, assertively. "Not really. We texted and you responded with short sentences, which isn't talking. But it did send a message."

I can almost see him grit his teeth. "What message?"

"That you're pissed at me."

"Well, I'm not, so you can check that worry off your list," John says, straightening while simultaneously laying the foundation to build a brick wall between us.

But I knock it down, taking another step closer. "He needed someone, and I was there. We're barely even friends."

"Lennon, don't do this."

"Do what?"

He runs a hand through his wet hair, releasing a labored breath. "Insult my intelligence. You and Theo are more than just barely friends."

"My parents got friendly with his mom after the baptism. So now he's, like, tied to me via my family, which makes it harder to ignore him."

"Are you trying to ignore him?" he asks, slightly lowering his head, bringing his eyes level with mine.

"Okay," I say, looking to the ceiling for a moment. "*Ignore* isn't the right word. It's just . . . he's your friend and I'm your friend and

Andie wanted to be 'friends' with Theo, so it's kind of difficult to navigate all of you without bumping into each other, so to speak," I say, shrugging at my poor attempt to explain things.

"Want to know what I think?" he asks, crossing his arms.

"Yes!" I say, mirroring him.

"I don't think Theo needed someone that night. I think he needed you."

My arms drop at his words. "How was I supposed to walk away from someone who was on the floor, crying about his dead father?"

"I didn't know it was that bad," John says, his brows furrowed in concern.

"It was."

His jaw visibly clenches as he takes a moment to choose his next words. "He's into you."

I wave off his accusation. I really wish he would stop saying that. It sometimes feels like he's trying to force us together. And I already have one man in my life doing that.

"The thing is," I begin, cranking my neck, "my father hired Theo to tutor me in algebra. Just until my exam at the end of the month." I rock back and forth on my heels, trying to read John's face. "I don't regret what you and I did on New Year's Eve." The words spill out of me as the last-period bell rings. Neither of us budge as the remaining students rush off to class, leaving us alone in the hall.

John's eyes flick up before landing on mine, a small smile tugging at his lips. "Me neither."

I breathe in before taking another step closer. "I think about it. *All* the time."

"You think about 'it' all the time?"

"It. You. Us," I clarify.

He bites down on his lip, shaking his head slightly. "We can't be having this conversation here." His gaze sweeps across my face as his open-mouthed grin taunts me. "I think about it all the time too. And I also think about what might have happened if Theo hadn't interrupted us."

"Do you think we would have . . ." I pause, swallowing down a nervous flutter, "kept going?"

"I don't know." He shakes his head. "You and me, it's like making a pie with all the wrong ingredients, but somehow when it comes together, it's the best pie I've ever had."

"What're you saying?" I ask, as a wave of anxiety flows deep through me.

"I'm saying what we both already know."

"But that was before we . . . we both said 'I love you,'" I say, as if he needs to be reminded. "And then . . . even after all of that, you're still stuck on the belief that we can't be together? You can't still think that way after everything that happened."

"I don't take back what we said or did that night"—he stalls, his eyes flitting across the empty hall before meeting mine—"but it can't happen again."

"What?" My heart drops. The emptiness following his words echoes inside and all around me. He's slipping away.

"I'm sorry," he says, sounding like he means it. "I really, really care about you, but I think this is what's best."

"Why is it you keep making these decisions for us?"

"Because somebody has to," he says, the words coming out quickly. "You belong with someone like Theo, and if that's where your heart lands, I won't hold it against either of you."

"Why are you doing this?" My eyes fill with tears, one blink away from releasing the geyser. "Why are you like this?"

"I'm sorry."

"You're sorry that you told me you loved me? Or are you sorry that you ever got involved with me? Sorry that you let yourself get lost in a moment? What is it, John? What exactly are you sorry for?"

"This isn't easy for me either," he says, releasing a deep breath.

"Then stop making it so hard."

"I'm trying to. We can't keep doing this back-and-forth thing. This is me cutting the string. I'm sorry. I'm really sorry." His jaw clenches as he stares into my eyes. Before I have a chance to respond, he turns and walks down the hall.

Shame grips me by the throat, making it hard to breathe. I let him in. I trusted him. I told him I loved him. And now he's walking away.

I am so fucking stupid.

Chapter Twenty-one

JANUARY 25

Theo is sitting across the kitchen table from me, and he's chewing on his pencil. It's this annoying habit I've noticed. It's kind of hard to ignore. He does it when he's trying not to get frustrated at me for being unable to "get it." Math is logical, he says. How hard is it to follow a formula and arrive at the right answer? He's such an ass.

Not according to Mom and Dad, though. They think Theo walks on water. He's the son they always wanted. He's been tutoring me for three weeks and he doesn't even knock anymore when he comes over, he just lets himself in.

He's always so polite. To them.

To me he's still a bit of a dick.

Which I kind of prefer. It makes pretending New Year's Eve didn't happen easier. Neither of us talk about it—about the crying or what he said about liking me. At this point, what happened that night is buried so deep in my mind that it's almost as if it were a dream. The guy sitting in front of me, chastising me about my piss-poor math skills, is not the same guy I held weeping on his bedroom floor.

"No. You're not getting it. Try again," he says, sliding back my practice sheets aggressively. He grabs baklawa from the dish my mom laid out for him on the kitchen table.

I accept the papers as my gaze flits over Theo's shoulder to the window. Giant snowflakes fall ever so slowly. Is there anything more romantic than a winter sky lit up by fresh snow and a full moon?

"I followed the formulas," I say, refocusing my attention. There is red pen all over my page. Really encouraging.

"Did you follow the rule?"

"Oh. I guess I missed that."

"This is your last practice before exams, Hadid. Let's go." He narrows his eyes at me like he's the coach and I'm the quarterback and this is the Super Bowl and it's the final inning. Or last down? I have no idea.

"You're obnoxious, you know that?" I say.

"You're just wound up because John cut you loose."

I freeze at his words. "What did you say?"

"Nothing." He shakes his head.

"What did John tell you?" I ask, quietly. My parents are in the other room, never too far away.

"Just that you're not talking anymore. 'Talking,'" he says, making air quotes with a smug-ass grin.

"It was more than that," I respond, almost in a whisper.

"You sure about that?" Theo asks with a contrarian smirk. "Look, the way I see it, if John really was—"

"Shh," I say, my eyes shifting to the next room.

"Sorry," he says, more quietly. "If John really was serious about you, he wouldn't have let you go. Fool's move. Someone else's gain."

Before I can try and decipher what the hell Theo is trying to say, Dad strolls in.

I pull away from my huddle with Theo and sit up.

"Working hard?" Dad asks, his tone level.

"She's getting there," Theo says.

"Thanks to you," he responds. "Her head is in the clouds more than usual these days."

"I think we're all just kind of tired of winter. January is a long month." Theo offers me a smile. The kind that speaks volumes. *You're welcome. I saved your ass. Watch how easily I have your father wrapped around my finger.*

"You're very patient. More than I could ever be," Dad says. "Is your mom picking you up? I didn't see your car out front."

"No," Theo says, at the same time pointing aggressively to a calculation on my page. I exhale loudly and erase it. "A friend is."

"Who?" I ask, looking up from my practice sheet.

"John."

"John's coming *here*?"

"We're going to Eddie's to figure out our set list for the Valentine's Day dance."

Dad's eyes shift to the kitchen window. "I don't think you're going anywhere. The snow is coming down pretty hard. The drive home from work was ugly. Maybe call your friend and tell him to stay home."

"Are you suggesting Theo spend the night?" I ask, flabbergasted.

"Lennon, look outside," Dad says, throwing an arm toward the window. "No one is going anywhere in this weather. At least not in one piece."

“Of course.” I sink into my seat, tossing my pencil to the table. It bounces, and Theo stops it before it rolls to the floor. “Why don’t we just offer him my bed while we’re at it, and I’ll sleep in the basement?”

“Don’t be rude. Theo comes here to help you. He’s the one who’s stuck.”

“He comes here because you pay him to,” I say, avoiding eye contact with my father as I erase another wrong response. I feel both his and Theo’s burning gaze on my bowed head.

“Actually, I come here for the Paulie cuddles,” Theo says, instantly defusing the situation.

That’s the thing about Theo. I don’t have to explain to him why the mood around here can change within seconds. He understands. He knows how to read my father, and he also knows how to take the heat off me. He does it by charming my family. The only person he hasn’t managed to charm is me.

Georgie comes into the kitchen holding Paulie, who’s just woken up from her third nap. Her shiny, black hair is matted against her rosy cheeks. “Did someone say something about Paulie cuddles?”

“Paulie,” Theo almost sings. He rises from the table and reaches out to my niece, who grins a gummy smile in his presence.

“Clear the table, Lennon,” Dad says as he joins Theo by the kitchen island, gently squeezing Paulie’s chubby fingers.

I quickly gather my homework into a pile. Mom enters the kitchen and nods for me to clean up after Theo as well.

“Excuse *me*,” I grumble as I squeeze past everyone and make my way into the foyer, where I deposit everything on the hallway table. I’m sure Mom will have something to say about this as well, but right now I don’t care.

The doorbell rings.

I try to shake off my frustration as I open the front door. John is standing on the other side in a blue toque covered in snowflakes. A gust of wind drifts snow into the foyer.

"Sorry," he says, taking responsibility for the mess on the front mat. His cheeks are red. His bare hands are so white they're turning blue. He tucks them into his not warm enough for January in Canada coat pockets.

"Come in," I say, waving him inside and closing the door behind him. "Theo is in the kitchen being fawned over by my family. Oh wait, no, they're fawning over Paulie." My words come out kind of forced as I try to process the fact that John Brody is inside my house. Considering our last conversation, I didn't picture this ever happening.

John doesn't laugh at my attempt at humor. Good. I hope he's as miserable as I am. I hope he's seething with jealousy. I hope he's been thinking about me every second like I've been thinking about him, and I hope he hates himself for what he did and what he said and who he is and how he is.

"Lennon, who's this?" Dad asks as he steps into the foyer. My body seizes. Dad is meeting John. John is meeting Dad.

"This." I clear my throat. "Theo's friend. This guy. He's John."

"Do you need some water?" Dad asks, studying my face. John cracks the slightest of grins and I have to suck in my lips to hold back my own nervous version.

John keeps his hands in his pockets and nods. "Hi. Hello. Mr. Sir."

Dad sighs, rolling his eyes not so discreetly. "How are the roads?"

"Pretty shitty."

My eyes widen at John's rough-around-the-edges response. It's not something I've ever noticed before, but standing in the foyer of my home there appears to be a very definite line that's been drawn dividing *him* and *us*. The *us* that includes Theo Petropolis.

"Well," Dad says, glancing at me like it's my fault that Theo's friend swore, "I don't think Theo will be joining you. He's decided to spend the night."

"Dad," I say.

"What?"

"If the roads aren't safe enough for Theo, then they're not safe enough for John."

"He got himself here, didn't he?" Dad says, looking at John while responding to me.

"No, it's fine, Lennon. I'll go home."

"John," Theo says, entering the foyer, and for once in my life I'm relieved to see him. "I meant to call. Looks like I'm spending the night." Theo turns to my dad. "George," he says, "this is John Brody. He plays guitar in our band. He's also really good with his hands," he adds, unironically.

Dad nods. My father is a smart man, and I can tell he senses something is up between the three of us. Or more like the two of us.

"I just like to build things, with wood, when I have some free time," John says. I can't help but notice how his eyes move around my home.

"Did you learn this from your father?" Dad asks, crossing his arms in front of him. I wish I could blink and open my eyes to find that this was all just a very bad, very weird dream. The vibes are way off.

"Yeah, but I'm also taking woodshop at school. My dad, he, um . . ." John visibly swallows as his eyes search for somewhere to land. "He had an accident. He fell off his ladder a few years ago, so now he's on disability."

My heart drops. Why did he never tell me this? I try to make eye contact with him but he's looking everywhere but at me. There's a sense of foreboding in the air. Something I can feel but can't explain.

"Yalla. Tell this boy to leave," Dad says to me in Arabic, his voice low and gravelly. The fact that he doesn't even bother to respond to John tells me more about my dad than I want to admit. Up until this point, I always gave my father the benefit of the doubt. Somehow John knew not to.

Dad turns and walks back to the kitchen, his footsteps loud and purposeful.

"I'm sorry," I say quietly and to no one in particular.

"John should leave through the garage," Theo blurts. "To avoid letting the snow in. I'll walk with him. And you can come show us how to open the garage door."

"It's literally just a button next to the door," I say, completely deflated.

Theo clears his throat in a theatrical way. "I think you should show us," he says, brows raised, eyes opened wide.

"Oh. Right."

The three of us enter the garage from inside the house. John immediately surveys the new surroundings. An Audi. A Range Rover. And Georgie's car, Mom's old Mercedes SUV.

Theo gets inside Mom's car and closes the door, giving John and me privacy. I'll have to thank him for this later. Maybe not such an asshole.

"I didn't know that about your dad," I say.

He shrugs in response.

"I'm sorry. It must be hard having a parent who isn't well."

John sits on Dad's workbench and nods. "His drinking got worse after he was put on disability. His entire identity was tied to his job. When he lost the ability to work, he lost himself." John runs his hands up and down his thighs, eyes downcast. "There's so much on my shoulders, and I can't complain because my mom really tries to keep the household running, but we obviously need money, so I do a lot of cash jobs on the weekends to help out. My dad's friends hook me up. And I take care of Mikey when Mom needs a break. We're all just barely hanging on by a thread."

His eyes lift to meet mine and I can't help but see him differently than I did the first time we met. Instead of the confident, cocky guy who took up space next to me on the bus, there's a vulnerable, sad boy who seems to want to be part of my world but doesn't know how. All those times he pushed me away—he was doing it to protect himself as much as he was doing it for me.

His eyes, little half-moons, return their gaze to the garage floor. "I come here, and your house is so perfect and your family is so perfect and *you* are so perfect. And I miss you so much, Lennon, and I hate myself for what I said to you after New Year's, but being here makes it clear that we made the right decision."

"We didn't make that decision. You did." I sit next to him. The silence between us grows as I try to process everything that's happening. Our timeline. The back and forth. The push and pull. This whole time John was dealing with so much at home and never wanted to tell me.

"We're trying to get my dad help," he says, cutting through the quiet. "But it's hard because he doesn't always want it. Mom has threatened to walk away but he knows she won't because she can't.

His disability checks keep us afloat. Just barely, but she doesn't really have any other options. And she loves him. We all do. We don't want to walk away from him. We want to help him." His eyes are glossy now. I want so badly to wrap my arms around John, to wipe his tears away, but just being in this garage with him is dangerous enough.

"I didn't realize you were going through all this. I've known you for a year and a half. How am I just learning this about you now?" I ask.

"I didn't want you to know this side of me. I kept it from you on purpose. It's not who I want to be. I want to be the me I am when I'm around you. That guy doesn't worry about all this shit. But unfortunately," he sighs, "being around you has gotten hard. It's hard in the same kind of way it is if you take a pill to forget your problems but once it wears off you're left feeling even worse. The relief is temporary. You don't deserve to be wrapped up in all my bullshit. I just need some time to figure things out."

Dread fills me at John's words. My heart is racing so fast it feels like someone set it on fire. I'm not a safe space for him, and that idea paralyzes me.

"Where do you see yourself in five years?" he asks.

I tuck my cold hands into the sleeves of my sweater. "New York City. Getting an undergraduate degree in Creative Writing from Columbia."

"Sounds amazing."

"It does, doesn't it? But I may as well dream about sprouting wings and buying a condo on the Equator."

We laugh quietly.

"What about you?" I ask.

He shrugs and it's so delicate. Gentle. "I want my dad to be healthy. I want my family to be comfortable. And I want the person I'm with to be happy and proud of me."

"I'm happy when I'm around you," I say, no longer worrying about saying the right or wrong things because the truth is always right.

"Same."

We don't say anything for a couple of minutes. The howling winds outside draw closer. We're on borrowed time. Time always feels borrowed when we're together.

Theo steps out of Mom's car and looks between us. "We should probably head back inside."

John nods, rising from the bench.

"Can you text me?" I say to John as I stand. "To let me know you got home safely?"

"Of course."

John walks to the front of the garage and I press the button of the garage opener. He looks back at me and Theo and offers us a slight nod before disappearing into the snowy skies.

Twenty minutes later he texts that he made it home. I catch Theo's eye across the table after checking my phone. He offers me a warm smile and I return it.

I "heart" John's message but don't respond.

He's the right person, I know this with everything inside me. But it's not the right time for us.

Both things can be true.

Chapter Twenty-two

AUGUST 8

Clarity. Peace. The ability to walk through life without the shame or guilt of my decisions weighing me down.

I've had all three the past seven months.

Time has absolved me of all my sins. Sort of. Depends on who you ask, I guess.

And all I had to do was give up John.

Wouldn't recommend.

Because the clarity isn't real.

The peace is forced.

And the lack of shame and guilt comes at the expense of a large, gaping hole in my heart.

But life still goes on.

Paulie turned one.

Tenth grade is over (and all I got to show for it was an 89 in Algebra).

Dad signed me up for Calculus next year without my consent.

And Zach and Georgie are getting married next week. He proposed on Valentine's Day. I knew things were going okay between them. Good, even. He was always around. To the point where my parents eventually accepted him as part of the family. But I didn't expect the proposal. As it turns out, I was the only person who was surprised. Zach had already asked both my parents for their blessing. Even Georgie suspected a proposal was on the way.

"He was acting weird," she said to me after it happened, studying her modest engagement ring with a wide grin. "He kept fidgeting over dinner and checking his pockets. He practically gave it away. His dress shirt was completely soaked through!"

I didn't want to think about what Georgie getting married would mean for me, since it wasn't about me, but that didn't stop the thoughts from creeping in. I knew I'd have to watch as she packed up her bedroom and moved the never-opened boxes containing Paulie's big-girl bed into her new home; I'd never get the chance to set it up with her. I knew it would mean spending even less time with my sister, who was already stretched thin between caring for Paulie and spending time with Zach.

It's August now, and Georgie, with the help of my mom, is going over all the last-minute wedding decisions. They're a bit behind because last week Georgie and Zach finally secured a condo in downtown Toronto to rent, and between lawyers, bank appointments, and filling out paperwork, that ate up a lot of time. They can't afford a home in our town. They can't afford anything, really, with Zach in college and Georgie on Mom duty, but both sets of parents have agreed to help them out with rent. Instead of putting money into a big fancy wedding, they've planned something small. Actually, in Theo's backyard.

It's just all so much, so soon. The thought of living in my home without my sister keeps me up at night. Even though we haven't spent as much time together as we used to, just knowing she was next door helped. It helped.

As the wedding day approaches, Mom and Georgie are once again talking through all the boring details with Theo's mom, Petra, while I lounge in the pool with Paulie. We both love the pool.

Theo worked at a golf course most of July, but his hours got cut and so he's been joining us pretty often. His company is a good distraction from the changes headed my way. Forced proximity has shown me there's more to Theo than his textbook good looks and abundance of self-confidence.

We didn't mean to become so friendly, and I wouldn't have let him in to the degree I did if he and Andie hadn't made up. At my urging, he apologized to her at the end of January for the way he spoke to her on New Year's Eve. Andie accepted his apology without much drama. I guess not everyone holds onto grudges. And now the three of us are friends. I was kind of worried he and Andie would hook up and ruin our non-polyamorous triangle, but she's been seeing this guy Kiefer since April. And anyway she's spending most of August at her cottage.

Then there's eleventh grade, less than four weeks away. My biggest goal this year is to go on the school trip to New York City in the spring. Which means I'll be on my best behavior as I lay the groundwork to make that trip happen. Even if it means continuing to keep my distance from John. I thought by now it would be easier, but it's not. I still search for signs of him. Ask Theo leading questions. Ruminate over every interaction we've ever had. I sometimes wish there were a pill I could take to forget him.

Paulie is floating in her inflatable sprinkled donut with built-in umbrella to protect her delicate skin. I'm playfully splashing water around her when Georgie opens the back door off the kitchen. She kicks off her sandals and sits at the side of pool, dangling her feet in the water. Georgie doesn't quite have the deep tan I've acquired this summer. I bring Paulie over and we play for a bit, making obnoxious baby sounds together.

"Are you all done in there?" I ask.

"No." She sighs. "Mom and Petra aren't happy with the floral centerpieces. Or the cake. We're going out to meet with the vendors in about half an hour." She smiles at Paulie, who's busy splashing water with her tiny, chubby hands. Paulie grins and shows off her eight teeth. The whole family has had to suffer through late nights and excessive crying because of those new teeth. "Paulie's going to need her nap soon. Petra said I could use Theo's room. I have my monitor, so if you don't mind hanging around here until we get back? Theo is setting up the playpen now."

I straighten while adjusting the straps of my bathing suit. "Theo is here?"

"Yeah. He just got back from work. He's, ah . . ." She smiles, raising her brows without an ounce of subtlety.

"What?"

"You haven't noticed?" Georgie asks, spinning Paulie's donut around with her foot.

"Noticed what?"

Georgie drops her shoulders, tilting her head. "How hot he's gotten. Like, I know I'm about to be a married woman and all, but damn, someone's been hitting the gym."

"He has a physical job, and he swims a lot," I say, sticking to the facts like he's an athlete I represent or something.

"You'd know, right? Spending all that time in the pool with him."

"I don't like him," I say preemptively.

"I know." She says it like she's disappointed. "If you did, you wouldn't wear those boring one-pieces all the time."

"Like Dad would even let me wear anything else."

"Dad doesn't come here. He also doesn't mind you hanging out with Theo."

"Yeah. It's kind of unsettling how lax he is around him. I guess you mellowed Mom and Dad out, or broke them." I laugh.

Georgie studies my face, like I said something wrong.

"I guess from your perspective things do seem pretty good between us."

"Am I missing something?"

Georgie nods for me to release Paulie from the flotation device while she grabs her a towel.

I lay Paulie on the lounger on top of her cupcake-patterned towel. She squirms, reaching for the pool, but I distract her with a toy.

Georgie gets to work like a pro, removing Paulie's bathing suit and drying her before putting her in a fresh diaper. I grab a summer onesie from the diaper bag and dress her while my sister tidies up, placing the wet swim diaper in a plastic grocery bag. Then she pours warm milk from a thermos into a clean bottle.

It's so seamless now. For both of us. There were times over the last year when at least two of the three of us would cry doing something this complicated.

"I'm going to miss this," I say, as I pass Paulie to my sister.

Georgie is cradling Paulie while feeding her the bottle. "They don't look at you the way they look at me." The words are unexpected. My sister's tone is stark, almost monotone. But she's got my attention.

"You're virginal," she continues. "Pure. Angelic. They speak to you like you're still worthy of their respect." She smiles sweetly at Paulie, whose eyelids are falling prey to the temptation of sleep. "There may not be epic screaming matches anymore, but Dad's strategy has never been as pedestrian as shouting. His weapon of choice is more sophisticated. Shame. Just one look and I knew exactly how much I had screwed up. I could see through his eyes the depths of his disappointment in me. That everything between us would be changed forever."

I know the look myself, though I've never been on the receiving end of one as intense as the one Georgie received.

"But don't you think Paulie being here has fixed some of that? You can't deny that Mom and Dad love Paulie. They're practically obsessed with her," I say, running a hand over the baby's wet hair.

She shakes her head. "The damage is done. No matter how many years pass or how much good I do, he will never forgive me for sleeping with Zach before marriage. It wasn't even about the pregnancy, Lennon," she says, her eyes searching mine. "It was the act behind it. He's angry that I ignored all their lessons and warnings about premarital sex, and that I discovered the one thing he hoped we wouldn't learn until we were married, if ever—that sex isn't just about pregnancy, or for married couples to keep the husband satisfied. The unforgivable sin is that I, his daughter, actually wanted it. Because we're not supposed to. We're not supposed to grow up. We're not supposed to want to experience pleasure, with or without a partner. *That's dirty. It's bad*," she says, in a voice like his. "So maybe you were surprised by how 'well' they took it, but you weren't on the receiving end of those looks. You didn't suffer through the cold, blank stares when I said good morning to him. You didn't feel the pang that came with being ignored when I tried to talk to him about myself, my pregnancy, anything at all. It's emotional abuse, Lennon. I'm calling it what it is."

I don't respond. Even though I believe her. Even though I understand. Even though I've lived a version of it myself. Because hearing her call it emotional abuse stings my heart. I never thought of it that way. I just thought my dad was the way he was because . . . just because. And that's probably what he wanted. He wanted us to accept his words, his beliefs, as truth. Our truths. Since that was the way it had always been, and that was the way it would always remain. Until someone broke the cycle.

Georgie puts the bottle down and tries to burp a half-awake Paulie. "Even if there are moments when he softens his exterior for me, they are fleeting, and they'll never fix the hurt he's caused. It is what it is." Her lips form a straight, tight line as Paulie releases a tiny burp. "And you know what? It's okay, because I'm getting married, and I'm going to start my new life with Zach. I'm going to raise Paulie to be whoever she wants to be. To love whoever she wants to love. To never have to feel an ounce of the shame that we both grew up with." As Georgie rises with Paulie I gather all her things, placing the diaper bag on her shoulder. "I will not make my trauma hers. It ends here."

She begins to walk toward Theo's sliding doors but stops and turns back to me, Paulie's head resting on her shoulder.

"You're never going to please them. No matter what you do. It's never going to be enough. So you may as well do whatever the hell you want anyway."

I nod and give her a forced smile. The three years between us feel more like lifetimes.

Theo slides open his bedroom door for Georgie. He places a gentle kiss on Paulie's forehead before walking out to the patio.

"Hey," he says, smiling.

It feels nice knowing that smile is just for me. His presence instantly eases the heaviness of my interaction with Georgie.

Theo is in his swim trunks, holding a towel and the baby monitor. "Is it too late?" He nods to the pool.

"No." I shake my head and allow my own smile to come through. "I was actually hoping you'd show up."

"Really?" He wiggles his brows obnoxiously. "Are you saying you enjoy my company, Hadid?"

I could be obnoxious right back and continue playing that game where we banter, masking deeper emotions, but in this moment, I'm happy that Theo is standing here and that we're going to spend the afternoon together.

"You know I do."

He puts the baby monitor and his towel down before taking a step toward me. He points a finger at me before booping my nose. "I knew I'd get under your skin eventually."

"This is why I don't give you compliments. It just feeds your already massive ego."

"To go with my massive muscles," he jokes, kissing his biceps.

Deciding I've had enough with niceties, I push him into the pool. He goes down with a resounding splash.

When he resurfaces, his body glistens under the strong August sun. He runs his hands through his thick, black hair, and a stirring from deep inside freezes me in place. Water droplets stream down his face and drip onto his tanned chest.

A sudden yearning takes over.

It's like someone has finally removed the blinders and I can see what's been in front of me all summer. Theo Petropolis. All six feet of lean muscle, big brown eyes, and a smile that could end wars.

I dive into the pool, skimming close to the bottom, hoping the coolness of the water will extinguish these intense new feelings. Resurfacing, I swipe strands of wet hair away from my face.

"You pushed me in before I had a chance to put on sunblock," Theo says, treading water in front of me.

I flutter my eyes at him playfully while pouting. "I'm sorry."

"You know I'm a sucker when you do that."

"Do what?" I ask, even though I know exactly what it is I'm doing.

"Act like a girl."

"Please. I'm nothing more to you than a sparring partner who sucks at math," I say, floating on my back and squeezing my eyes shut at the bright sun rays.

From the front of the house comes the sound of a car pulling away. I switch to treading water. "Did everybody just leave to go meet the vendors?"

He nods. "Yep."

"Wow. My parents must really trust you."

"Why?" he asks, swimming around me like a shark.

"Stop that," I say, splashing him. He pulls back, treading water across from me again. "Because they left me here. With you. *Alone*. I guess they don't see you as a threat."

"Should they?" he asks, moving in closer.

"I haven't decided yet."

His cheeks redden, and I dive under the water again, swimming the length of the pool and back.

He meets me at the back corner of the pool where I've got one hand on the coping, catching my breath.

Theo tilts his head. "What're you thinking, Hadid?"

I smile, looking him up and down. "I'm thinking about how I'm starting to hate it less and less when you call me Hadid." I bite my lower lip, glancing around us. "It's pretty secluded here. I mean, you wouldn't even know you had neighbors with all the tall trees and spaced-out homes."

"Yeah?"

"Have you ever . . . you know?"

He studies my face. "No. I don't know."

"Skinny-dipped?" I whisper.

"All the time." He answers like it's no big deal. "Have you?"

"No. Never. I never even thought about it until right this second."

His face lights up. "Because you want to see me naked?"

"Get over yourself," I say, pushing him with my free hand. Instead of moving away, he wraps his arms around my waist and pulls me beneath the surface. Our eyes meet under water, and he smirks before removing his trunks. He floats up and I catch a glimpse of him—all of him—before I rise.

"Theo!" I say, shaking the water off my face.

He throws his shorts out of the pool. "Did you get a good look?"

"No. I'm not a pervert."

He swims up to me, and my heart races so fast I'm afraid I may go into cardiac arrest. *Eyes above the surface.*

"Wanting to see me naked doesn't make you a pervert, Lennon."

I look away, feeling my throat catch. "That's not what my dad would say."

Theo swims closer, snaking one arm around my waist while the other hand traces the strap of my bathing suit. "I don't really want to talk about him right now."

"What are you doing?" I ask, studying his hand on my shoulder.

"Can I slide this down?"

"I . . . I don't know."

"Don't think. Just answer honestly." His eyes bury deep into mine. "Do you want me to slide this down?"

I shake my head, but the word "yes" comes out.

"I need a clear answer," he says. His tone is so level, as is his stare.

I swallow, thinking it over, but truly, there isn't much thinking happening in this moment.

"Yes," I say, nodding.

He keeps his eyes on me as he slides both straps of my bathing suit down. He stops just above my breasts.

Without thinking, I wrap my arms around his body and kiss him. With my mouth on his mouth and his bare body up against my almost bare body, I'm very aware of how much he wants this, and it feels so good knowing he does. But that's not the only thing that feels good. Being wanted after seven months of wondering, analyzing, obsessing over what it was I did to push John away really messed with my confidence.

We pull apart and he looks at me in complete awe. "You don't know how long I've wanted to do that."

I don't say anything back because I don't want to lie to him. The attraction I'm experiencing is new. It's intense. And it's different from the way I feel around John. It's like Theo can satisfy this part of me that John was never able to. With John, too many words and feelings got in the way of us coming together fully, and with Theo, we both just want each other on a physical level. And in this moment, I'm not afraid to act on it.

"Can we go inside?" I ask, almost breathless.

His jaw clenches as sun-glistened droplets of water trickle down his neck. Theo nods and we swim to the stairs. I get out first, adjusting my straps and passing him his trunks. I turn away as he puts them back on. We grab our towels and the monitor before heading inside.

"Paulie's in my room," he says, dripping wet, his body this impressive specimen I can't believe I've only recently come to appreciate. "The basement."

He takes my hand, leading me to the stairs. It's cold and damp down there but it's also dark, and private.

We kiss again in front of the couch. His kisses are different from John's. I didn't realize kisses could be so different. Theo's tongue is a lot more active, and he kisses harder, like he wants to consume me. I can't tell if I like it or not. I'm experiencing way too much at once. All my senses are currently battling for first place. We drop our towels and lower ourselves onto the couch. He begins moving my straps down again and I let him. He stops once my suit is at my waist and he swallows as he takes in the sight of me, half-naked, in front of him.

He kisses me again while simultaneously removing his soaked trunks. His body is wedged between my thighs and he presses himself up against my lower half, his hands caressing my goosebump-covered skin. He thrusts against me in a slow, rocking motion and it feels indescribably good.

"I need to . . . you know," he says after a few minutes, nodding at me as if I'm supposed to understand. He looks down, his breathing heavy. "Are you okay if I . . . ?"

"Oh," I reply, realization dawning, along with some disappointment. "Yeah."

He pulls himself off me and goes into the basement bathroom to finish. I sit and put my suit back on, then pick my towel up from the floor and wrap it around my body, shivering.

Did that just happen? Did I just hook up with Theo?

A noise comes from the baby monitor. I grab it while making my way up the stairs, which creak with every step. I sneak into Theo's room to check on Paulie, who is thankfully sound asleep. Her angelic face fills me with both love and another feeling I can't quite name. My gaze falls to Theo's bed, and I shut my eyes tight, trying to erase the memory of John from my mind. It doesn't work. It never works. Instead, I sit on the edge of the bed, burying my hands in my face, and cry as quietly as I can, rocking back and forth.

Regret.

The other feeling is regret.

Part III

ELEVENTH GRADE

I hang on to his words.
I hang on to his gaze.
I hang on to all our moments.
Collected like memories, in a glass,
invisible to everyone, but us.

Chapter Twenty-three

SEPTEMBER 2

Early September, and both time and daylight are slipping away. Theo and his mom spent Labor Day at our house. My parents invited them over for a barbecue. Georgie was also here visiting with her family. *Her family*. I'm still trying to get used to the fact that my sister has a family. She's married. And she no longer lives with us.

The lead-up to Georgie and Paulie moving out was worse than them actually being gone. Or maybe that's just a lie I tell myself to deal with the truth, a "truth" the logical part of my brain says is just my insecurity speaking, or my tendency to create situations that don't exist. But I can't help wondering if maybe there's a reason why people keep leaving me.

Having a baby around brought a lightness to our home. Now that they're both gone, it's sad. I think we all feel it. The loneliness. At least my parents have each other. And I guess the other truth is, I'm not completely alone either.

When I was helping Mom clean up after dinner, Theo asked my dad if it would be okay if we went to Main Street to watch the Labor Day fireworks. Theo said it was an immediate yes. It is unbelievably easy going out with him. So much so that I almost feel guilty about lying to them about our relationship status. Because maybe they *wouldn't* mind?

After that first time we hooked up, I hid out in Theo's room until Mom and Georgie returned from their vendor meetings, saying Paulie was fussy and needed me to be with her. Theo and I didn't speak again until Georgie's wedding, one week later.

He asked me to dance, and I accepted, because the truth is, I wanted to. There was something so romantic about the entire setting. Theo's backyard. The moon and the stars and the music and the general ambiance of love. It felt like, for the first time in a long time, we were all happy. And I realized part of my happiness was due to Theo.

"I'm sorry if I made things weird between us," he whispered as we danced to a slow song.

I shook my head slightly, taking in the scene. Twinkle-lights hung along the wooden fence. A wedding cake, half of it gone, sat on a small table, surrounded by gifts. My sister and her new husband appeared to be blissfully in love. My parents were chatting with family and friends, smiles on their faces. Petra held baby Paulie. On the surface, everything looked perfect, and I allowed myself, in that moment, to believe it was.

"It's not your fault. I started it," I said, taking responsibility for ruining our friendship.

"I'm glad you did," he said, his eyes locked on mine. They were so clear; a tiny version of me was reflected in them. If anyone had seen how Theo was staring at me right then, they'd have known there was something going on between us. We were one spark away from setting the entire backyard on fire.

"It was . . . I wasn't planning . . . I guess I just . . ." I scrunched up my face. "I don't know what I'm trying to say."

"You think too much, you know that, right?" he teased.

"Yeah. I do," I said, looking down.

"You also worry too much," he said, lowering his head to meet my eyes.

"I do," I said around a swallow.

"And my guess is that when you and I were together, you weren't thinking or worrying too much about anything. Correct?"

"Correct." *At least in the moment.*

"So why can't we just go with that?" he asked, as his lips grazed my ear.

"You mean, just hook up?"

"No." He shook his head as his eyes traced over me softly. "I don't want to just hook up with you. I like you, Lennon. A lot. And I want you to be my girlfriend."

My body tingled at his words. No one had ever asked me to be their girlfriend before.

My gaze met my father's. He was at the other end of the backyard, and he was smiling, watching me and Theo dance. My mind flashed forward to our own wedding. It would be all the same people and probably two hundred more. Theo makes sense. He just does. And I like the fact that even though my parents think he's perfect, he's different around me.

"I can't stop thinking about you, Lennon. I've never . . ." He cleared his throat. "You do something to me. Something no one else has."

I pressed my hand into his shoulder, watching as his chest rose with every breath. His fingers gripped me tighter, and I was back to that moment in the pool when all I wanted to do was kiss him.

"Say we do this," I replied. "I want to do it the right way. I need you to tell John, so he's not blindsided by the sight of us together."

"What about our parents?"

"When we're both ready and we know that this is something real, we can tell them together," I answered.

"I already know it's real," he said with a confident smile.

Something about being around a person who felt so sure about me made me want to take the plunge.

"Regardless, we should wait. Maybe October? That way they won't think anything happened between us this summer. We don't need them connecting the dots."

"Whatever you want."

"Okay." I nodded, meeting his eyes.

"Okay." He gently pressed his forehead to mine. "Does this mean you're my girlfriend?"

"I think so," I said, sucking in my cheeks.

"You don't know how happy you've made me." He placed a soft kiss on my temple as the song came to an end, and it made me feel as if I'd made the right decision. For once.

We spent the rest of the night apart so as not to draw attention to our new relationship status, but we couldn't stop gazing at one another across the backyard, like we were the only two people in on this secret.

And in that moment, we were.

"So, are we really going to Main Street to watch fireworks?" I ask Theo now.

"We can do whatever you want," he says, stealing a glance at me as he drives. "You want to go for a night swim instead?"

"I don't have a suit," I say. "And what about your mom?"

"Haven't we already established that you don't need a suit?" He says it in this arrogant, suggestive way, but it still causes a small fleet of endorphins to rush through me. "Your father invited my mom to stay for cards. You know how they get when they play. They lose track of time."

Theo and I haven't done more than steal a kiss here and there since that day in his basement. After the wedding, I felt ready to try with him again, but we haven't had the opportunity. Georgie and Zach went to Niagara Falls for their honeymoon, which meant I was on Paulie duty. I'd bring her to Theo's, or he'd come over with his mom, but people were always around us. Theo has sent me a couple racy texts, pictures too, but I'm too much of a wimp to return the favor. Besides, I really want this thing between us to be more than physical. I'm sacrificing a lot by choosing him, and it needs to be right. For both of us.

"What about my hair?" I ask. "I can't exactly come home with wet hair."

He holds a hand to his heart. "I promise not to dunk you."

I snort laugh, and he grabs my thigh, shaking it. "Come on. You can wear your bra and underwear. I'll throw them in the dryer after we're done. Or we can save that step and just . . ."

"Okay, fine. Let's go night swimming."

Theo smiles a victorious little smile.

Once we arrive at Theo's, I go straight to the backyard from his bedroom while he grabs us towels. I undress quickly, leaving my clothes in a splash-free zone, and step into the pool before Theo can view my half-naked body.

"Damn. You're fast, Hadid. I didn't even get to sneak a peek."

"That was the point," I say, moving methodically through the pool, making sure to keep my head above water.

Theo squints at me before putting down the towels. He turns on the pool lights and plays music over the Bluetooth speaker.

"Not too loud," I say. "We don't want to draw any attention."

"Yes, ma'am," he says, lowering the volume slightly. He steps into the pool carefully, and it warms my heart seeing him try so hard. He nods up at me and smirks. "Come here."

Theo watches with sharpened focus as I make my way toward him. He's got this look on his face like he can't believe I'm his, and as I study his strong jawline, long eyelashes, and the hard edges of his body, I can't believe he's mine either.

I practically glide over to him in the shallow end, making sure to keep my shoulders above the surface, my dark hair safe in a messy topknot. I've already timed out in my head that with my curfew we only have an hour to hang out here before heading back.

"Why were you so mean to me when we were kids?" I ask, never one for small talk.

"I was mean to everyone," Theo says, snaking an arm around my waist and pulling me to him.

"Not true. I'm very observant, and I observed that you were tougher on me than everyone else. Was I really that weird?"

Theo rolls his head before his eyes find mine. "I was going through a lot. My dad was sick. In and out of the hospital. Mom was a mess. I wasn't getting the attention I wanted at home, so I acted out in public. The thing is, everyone else fought back, but not you. You just sat there and took it."

I think about that younger, lost version of me. "You weren't the first person to be mean to me. By the time you came around, I'd learned how to dissociate. To the point where I was mostly able to block out your words. Your looks. All of it. At least as it was happening."

"God." Theo shakes his head. "I'm so sorry. It crushes me knowing that I was just another asshole who made your existence harder."

"You were young and dealing with something you probably didn't know how to process."

"But you didn't know that then. It also doesn't excuse my behavior."

"I forgive you," I say, locking eyes with Theo.

His lips curve in a smile as he pulls me in closer. "For the record, you *were* really weird but also really pretty. Even with the unibrow."

"Shut up," I say, pushing him away playfully, but he pulls me back in.

I wrap my legs around him as he continues to hold me close. He places a kiss on my shoulder, then my neck. His finger traces the skin below my collarbone. "*M-I-N-E*," he spells out, and my heart swells. Just as he's about to kiss me, I pull back slightly.

"How many girls have you been with?" I ask, my autistic timing on point.

He shrugs. "Like, girlfriends?"

"No. Like been with sexually."

He flushes, swallowing hard before clearing his throat. "What kind of sex are we talking about?"

"All forms?" I ask. My voice sounds like a twelve-year-old's. I don't know why I'm so nervous.

"I've had sex with four girls, and I've fooled around with a few others."

Four?

"What does 'fooling around' entail? Like what we did?"

Theo cranks his neck, his shoulders rising with the motion. "Lennon, come on. Can't we just enjoy this moment?"

I cross my arms in front of me and he sighs. A space growing between us.

"No," he finally answers. "More than what we did."

"You mean oral sex, right?"

He laughs. "I love how to the point you are. Yes. Oral sex. Hand jobs. Etcetera."

"Girls did that to you, or you did it to them?"

"Both." He answers the question so casually, like he's being interviewed by a nighttime talk show host.

I swim away to the pool stairs and sit. I'm so self-destructive. Every time things feel too good, I swipe away the surface and dig below, trying to find the buried truths, in an attempt to reveal that none of this is real.

"I don't know why you're so upset," he says, swimming to me. "All of that was before we were even friends. You don't see me grilling you about what you and John did, or didn't do."

Just hearing his name causes my entire body to react. I shrink into myself, and I have to force my eyelids open when all I want to do right now is squeeze them shut and disappear. Old habits die never.

"Come on," Theo says, reaching out to me.

"Where?"

"My room."

"Why?"

"Because you're my girlfriend and I want to be with you."

"This feels more like you placating me," I say, rolling my eyes as I press my folded arms closer to my chest.

"Come on," he says, still holding out his hand.

I think about it for a second. About his offer or suggestion or request . . . I'm not sure which it is. But I'm also kind of intrigued to see if Theo can make me feel the way John did. As quickly as John did.

"Fine," I say, placing my hand in his. I rise from the pool step, pulling my wet bra and underwear away from my body, as if that is going to help hide anything.

His eyes take me in. "Yes, you are."

I push him away, but he pulls me to him, and we kiss again like we did that first time in the pool. I move my lips off his and take his hand, grabbing a towel and walking into his room.

"Turn around," I say then, and Theo rolls his eyes playfully as he obeys. I undress and wrap the towel around me, then hand him my wet things. "I need you to put these in the dryer first," I say, thinking practically as he closes the door behind us. No matter how worked up I am, I must always think practically. I need to walk through the doors of my home looking like I did when I left.

Pretty.

Put together.

Clean.

He takes my things to the laundry room, and I wait on his bed. I check my phone. A few texts from Andie. She wants to know what I'm wearing tomorrow. Then a text from Mom.

Mom: Georgie and Zach are going to
Main Street too. Text her so you can
be together.

Me: Ok.

"Shit."

"What is it?" Theo asks as he enters his room, a towel wrapped around his hips.

"My mom just texted. She said Georgie's on Main with Zach and to text her."

"So, text Georgie and tell her the truth. She'll cover for you," he says, sitting next to me.

I nod and start typing furiously to Georgie, explaining that I lied to Mom and Dad about Main Street and that I'm out with Theo.

Georgie: Where are you and Theo?

Me: Hanging out with his band in John's garage.

Georgie: That's boring. Come here.

"She wants us to meet her there."

"Tell her you can't."

"I don't want to lie to her again," I say, frowning at Theo and my phone.

Me: I don't really want to go to Main. It's too loud and busy. You know how easily I can go into sensory overload.

Georgie: Are you lying to me?

Me: No.

Me: Yes. Theo and I are hanging out alone.

Georgie: I knew it!

Me: Can you cover for me?

Georgie: Yes. Just don't do anything stupid. Like get caught.

Me: So if mom asks you'll tell her we met up, right?

Georgie: Yes. Don't worry.

Me: thx

Georgie: ♥

I exhale a shaky breath and place my phone face down on his night table, making sure to turn on sound notifications first.

"All good?" he asks.

"Yeah. But now Georgie knows about us. Which means Zach will too."

Theo smiles and leans in to kiss me.

"Wait," I say, leaning back. "Can you turn off the lights? And close the curtains?"

"Sure." He gets up and does what I ask, his towel barely hanging on.

"And lock the door. Just in case," I demand, my nerves taking over. It's like speaking to my family broke the spell. We said we didn't want to sneak around, and yet here we are, sneaking around and lying and getting other people to lie for us.

Theo returns and sits next to me again. He runs a finger over my lips, studying my face. "I've thought about this a lot," he says, his voice low. "You, here, with me, in my room."

"Oh yeah?" I say, nodding casually like he just told me he enjoys pineapple on his pizza.

"You're so funny." He kisses me and it's hard. Passionate. Intense. I wish he would ease in. Maybe take it easy with the tongue.

But I can't tell him that. It's Theo Petropolis. He doesn't need kissing lessons from me.

I start to feel my body moving back. He's trying to get me to lie down but it's hard to move my legs with the towel wrapped so tightly around me.

Theo stops and licks his lips, his eyes flicking down. "Can I take this off?"

"Do you have a T-shirt I can wear?"

"You want to put clothes *on*?" he asks.

"Just a shirt."

"Okay," he says, like he gets it. I hope he does.

Theo walks confidently to his dresser to find me a T-shirt. He passes it to me, and I throw it on before finally removing the towel and tossing it to the floor.

"Can I . . . ?" I reach out, my hand resting on the part of the towel that meets his hip.

"Yeah, I mean, if you're sure?" he asks, standing across from me.

I nod and remove the towel from around his waist. My lips part at the sight of him. I'm not sure what I was expecting. I've never seen one outside of textbooks. That time in the pool didn't really count, and by the time I realized what I was looking at I was already above the surface. Even though I'd been tempted to look online, something always stopped me—probably the fear of getting caught. I swallow, forcing myself not to freeze up.

Taking in a deep breath, I gently wrap my fingers around him. He places his hand over mine, tightening my grip. "It's not as delicate as we make it out to be." He laughs, and it helps lighten the moment. A little.

Theo shows me what to do by keeping his hand wrapped around

mine. Eventually, he closes his eyes and his breathing intensifies. "It's starting to chafe," he says, pulling away slightly after what feels like an eternity. Could have been one minute or ten. Time is a construct, especially in these kinds of situations.

"I'm sorry," I say, removing my hand, cheeks flaming.

"Don't be sorry. We could try the other thing," he says. "If you want."

I nod and take in a deep breath. I open my mouth and go through the motions, trying not to gag. He guides me through it. I can tell by the soft moans he's releasing that I'm doing something right, but it's actually a lot of work. Just as he seems to be getting really into it, I pull away, wiping my mouth. I try not to think about what I just did. How quickly things can change. How I went from never having done those things to being someone who has done those things. Things I can't even articulate. Things I shouldn't be doing.

"That was good," he says.

I know it couldn't have been *that* good because he didn't finish—not that I wanted him to. Theo kisses me again, and this time we lie back on the bed. The T-shirt is bunched up at my waist and a gust of cold air from his AC passes over me. Theo's body slides between my thighs, and he moans as he presses himself against me.

"Can I touch you?" he asks. I nod and it isn't long before his fingers start fumbling around my lower half. I try to make myself relax. To give myself permission to enjoy the moment. But it doesn't feel like it did when John did it. Theo's touch isn't as soft, and he keeps missing the spot that feels good, but I don't know if I should tell him. I didn't have to tell John. Maybe it's like this the first couple of times. It's not like I know what I'm doing either.

"I can't hold it much longer," he says, and, finally, relief as he removes his hand. But not the kind of relief either of us was expecting. "Are you good?" he asks, his hair hanging in front of his face.

"Yeah."

He kisses my forehead before pulling himself off me and disappearing into the bathroom. I bring my legs together, squirming at the discomfort pulsing below. I'm not sure what he was doing down there but whatever it was did not feel good.

His dryer buzzes and I reach to check my phone. It's later than I thought. I run out of his room to grab my things from the machine, and that's when I hear the front door open. *Shit.*

"Theo, I'm home," Petra calls.

I slip into the laundry room, my back against the door, trying to get my stupid heart to stop beating so loud.

"Theo?" she calls again, her voice fading as she heads in the opposite direction. *Thank god.*

I open the dryer quickly and with the care of someone holding a Fabergé egg in a room full of lasers. Grabbing my things, I put them on as fast as I can, throwing Theo's T-shirt on top, pulling at the hem. I prepare a story just in case Petra catches me. *We decided to go swimming. A whole bunch of us. The others just left. I didn't have my swimsuit, so I swam in Theo's T-shirt and I was just drying it with my other things.* Where is he? I don't have my phone so I can't text Theo, and I also can't stay hiding in this laundry room all night because my curfew is looming.

This is what I get for allowing my desires and curiosity to take control of me.

This is what I deserve.

And it wasn't even worth it.

"I'm going out," Theo says to his mom.

"Out? It's almost ten and you have school tomorrow. Wait," she pauses. "Where's Lennon? I thought you were together."

"She met up with Georgie and Zach and I came home."

"Why?" his mom presses.

"John and Eddie were going to come here, but plans changed and we're grabbing burgers now." Theo lies with precision. He's slick. Calm. Believable.

Once his mom appears satisfied with his responses, Theo enters the laundry room with my balled-up clothes, phone, and flip-flops. My heart is still racing too much for me to experience any relief at the sight of both him and my things.

I get dressed, then mouth, "Now what?"

He whispers. "I'll go to the kitchen to distract her. I'll text you when it's safe to go out the front door. Meet me on the corner."

"Okay. But hurry. It's late."

"Better late than caught."

"Right."

Theo heads to his kitchen and texts me when all is clear. I tiptoe to the front door, opening it as little as possible before wedging my body through the gap. Closing it behind me, I slip on my flip-flops and run down the street. One of my flip-flops slides off and I trip on my own foot, falling face-first onto the pavement.

That fucking hurt. I run my tongue over my teeth and taste blood.

I manage to get up and assess the damage: scraped-up bloody knee and elbow and what is sure to be a fat lip.

I am never, *ever*, doing this again.

Headlights appear around the corner, and I hobble to Theo's car as he pulls over.

"Jesus Christ, Lennon, what happened to you?" he asks as I open the door, bloody and unbalanced.

Karma happened.

Chapter Twenty-four

SEPTEMBER 3

It's the first day of school and I'm kind of excited to start eleventh grade with a boyfriend, though it sounds so shallow that I'm almost embarrassed to admit it. I always believed I was above that vapidity. Clearly, I'm not. I'd only convinced myself that those things didn't matter when they felt out of reach.

Theo wanted to drive me to school today, but I told him it would be better if I went with Andie since we haven't seen each other that much lately. The entire ride, I listen as she whines about the end of summer and how sad she is that Kiefer goes to another school. I've missed listening to her complain about things that we both know are trivial but feel huge. And I've missed her.

Andie has always been careful not to leave me behind when she has a boyfriend, even including me in her dates. Now that I'm with Theo, it's important for me to continue to be there for her. It was easy in August to split my time between Andie and Theo because she was at her family's cottage for a good chunk of it or hanging out with Kiefer. And I was on babysitting duty for most of the month.

I'm still not sure how she really feels about me and Theo together. There was a moment where they almost . . . well, who knows what might have happened. But if she told me to break up with him, he'd be history. She comes first.

Is any guy worth all this anxiety?

If I'd been asked this question two years ago, I would have said no.

If I'd been asked this a year ago, I would have said yes, if the guy was John Brody.

Faced with the same question now, I'm not so sure.

"Hey, Andie," I say as she pulls into the school parking lot. My heart races as I spot John's parked car next to us. It's been over six months since we last spoke. The night of the winter storm.

"Yeah?" she says. She pulls down her visor to check her reflection in the vanity mirror, then scrunches up her face and grabs her makeup bag from her backpack. "I look like shit. Do you want something for that?" she asks, nodding to my fat lower lip.

"It's fine." I run a finger over my mouth and attempt to swallow the knot in my throat. "I have to tell you something."

"What is it?" she asks, applying her lip gloss. She inspects her sunburnt skin. "Ugh, I'm peeling again. You'd think the melanin from my mother's side would save me from this."

"Things went pretty far with Theo last night."

She whips her head at me and cracks a smile. "Did you sleep with him?"

My jaw clenches as I take in a breath. "No. But just about everything else. I got this fat lip from tripping over my feet as I ran out of his house after his mom got home. Do you think he thinks less of me now?" It's such a black-and-white question, but sometimes—often—my autistic brain needs to ask direct questions to get direct responses. Anything else is too confusing.

"Oh my god, Lennon. No. And if he did, well, fuck him." She closes her lip gloss and tosses it back into the makeup bag before shifting to face me. "Did he say anything to make you feel that way?"

I twist my fingers through the hook of my backpack. "No, but it wasn't . . ." I swallow. "I didn't really enjoy it."

Andie sits, quiet, her green eyes downcast. "It can sometimes take a bit to find your groove together."

"It didn't with John," I say softly.

"Oh, sweetie. Are you still hung up on him?" she asks, lowering her head to meet my eyes.

"We don't talk anymore. And I really do like Theo. But it's not the same."

"Give it time," Andie says. "And if it still doesn't get better, then maybe it's less that Theo doesn't know what he's doing, and more that your heart is not in it."

The cold, hard truth I've been trying to push down. Leave it to Andie to see through me.

We're silent as more cars pull into the parking lot, followed by doors slamming, horns honking, and music suddenly cutting out along with engines.

She glances over my shoulder, then back to me. "Does John know about you and Theo?"

"Theo said he'd tell him. Do you think he'll be cool about it?"

She seems lost in thought for a moment. "I think he'll play it off like he doesn't care, but deep down he'll be devastated."

"But John's the one who ended things."

"Only because he didn't see a future where the two of you could be together. Not because he didn't care about you."

I suck in my lips, then wince at the pain. I've already bitten off the scab three times due to nerves. It will never heal if I don't leave it alone. Mom seemed to buy my story about tripping on Main Street last night and landing face down on the ground. It was partially true, I guess. After getting home from Theo's I headed straight to the shower to scrub the night off my skin, and I lay in bed fighting off tears, unsuccessfully, until I fell asleep.

"Come on, let's go in," she says, offering me a reassuring smile.

I nod and sigh as I step out of Andie's car.

"He's just a boy, Lennon," she says as we walk hand in hand past John's car. "He's just a boy, and you are the sun, and the moon, and the stars."

I squeeze her hand. "I love you."

"I love you more," she says with a smile as we head into school together.

Homeroom goes slowly. I forgot how tedious the first couple of classes in the new school year can be. The teachers look bright-eyed and well rested as they excitedly share the syllabus. Turns out that not only do I have to take Calculus, I have to do it at eight-thirty in the morning. Thankfully I have Music second period to recover from this dad-inflicted trauma.

Mrs. Morales insisted I continue taking her music class even though I can't really play the piano all that well. She says my singing voice is raw (a nice way to say mediocre). But she says where I really shine is in my songwriting skills, and she wants me to work at learning music theory. It feels nice knowing someone thinks you deserve to be heard.

I choose a seat at the back since my focus isn't on learning how to play an instrument. Familiar faces trickle into the room, greeting one another with smiles and hugs. By now I know everyone in my grade, but only on a superficial level, and it's starting to show as they all seem to have this bond and closeness that I don't share.

Growing up, it was easy for me to identify my autism as the reason I so often felt like an outcast. But sometimes, I wonder if I'm just as much, if not more, to blame for the distance between me and my peers. It takes effort to get to know people. Maybe part of the problem is that those I do put forth the effort toward consume all my focus, time, and energy.

I open my backpack, searching for the new notebook I bought specifically for Music class. I didn't write as much this summer as I had hoped to, but last week I had some free time and started messing around with song lyrics. Theo and his mom were beginning the painful process of clearing out his father's belongings. I decided to give Theo space as he worked through that difficult milestone in his grief. He wanted me close by regardless, so I hung out in his backyard, writing. My attempts at writing lyrics were awful at first. I was rusty. Writing is a skill that improves with consistent effort, and I hadn't been consistent. Once I allowed myself to open up, *awful* transitioned into *cheesy*. But the last few verses I've written have been soul-baring. The muse was gone for awhile, but it feels like it's back, or possibly just around the corner.

"Mind if I sit here?" a deep voice asks.

I look up to find John standing next to my chair. I force my mouth shut and nod, probably a little too aggressively. He smiles before taking the seat to the right of mine. He leans back, smirking as he watches me get my notebook and supplies all lined up.

"What?" I ask, squinting back at him.

"You're such a type A."

"Old habits," I say, letting my gaze linger a second too long. His hair is a bit shorter now. Styled. It appears even he made an effort on this first day of school. His last first day of high school. A pit grows in my stomach at the thought.

"How was your summer?"

He shrugs. "Not bad. My sister was home for most of it and we took Mikey all over Toronto whenever I was off work. Wonderland. CN Tower. The aquarium. All the touristy places."

"Just you and Val took him?" I ask, digging delicately for answers.

"My mom too."

"What about your dad?" I can't help myself. I need to know.

"He wasn't around this summer," John says.

"Oh."

He straightens, then clears his throat. "For a good reason. He's in rehab. Two months down. One to go."

"Wow. Wow," I say again, shaking my head as I take in his huge news. "How's he doing?"

John's eyes glisten. "Really good. We visit every weekend, all of us, and he's like the dad I grew up with. But I don't let myself get too excited. Sometimes I think it's better this way. Him there, where it's safe, and we get our fill on weekends."

"That wouldn't be fair to him, long term," I say, lifting my gaze to meet John's. "You have to trust him eventually."

"Yeah." He nods.

"But it's still scary. I get that. There's a lot riding on this. Can I ask how you were able to afford three months of rehab?"

"Did anyone ever tell you that you should be a journalist?" He smiles sweetly. "It was subsidized by the government, and I've been working a lot."

"I guess that's why I never saw you this summer."

"Yeah."

We both know his work schedule was not the reason we didn't see or talk to one another.

Before I can ask John more questions, Mrs. Morales walks in and claps to get everyone's attention. John and I face the front of the class, and a sense of calm, one that has been missing for months, takes hold of me. The humming in my head settles and I let out a breath that I've been holding for what feels like . . . seven months.

He was everything.

Every breath.

Every thought.

Every other beat of my heart.

There's danger in allowing one person to be everything.

It leaves you with nothing when they're gone.

When class is over, Mrs. Morales calls on the first chair orchestra students to sign out their instruments. The rest of us will get our instruments tomorrow. I got assigned the clarinet. Mrs. Morales said that because I would be the newest clarinetist, I'd be the last one in the section. Seated at the back. Thank god.

I turn to speak to John again, hopeful to catch up some more, but I eye Theo in the doorway, waiting for me. Or John. Or maybe . . . us?

"Did Theo talk to you?" I ask John as he begins to pack up. I can feel Theo's gaze on us.

"About what?" John asks.

He doesn't know. And now Theo is standing outside the classroom.

"Lennon," Theo calls out, annoyance ringing through his voice.

I look at Theo and then at John. We can't do it like this. We can't tell him together. It isn't fair.

"What does Theo want?" John asks. Because of course he doesn't know how close we've gotten this summer. To him, Theo waiting outside the classroom for me doesn't make sense. My feet stay planted as John nods to the door, like he wants us to head out together. I can't walk out that door and let him see Theo take my hand or kiss me. I won't do that to him.

"I have to tell you something," I say, ignoring Theo's obvious growing irritation.

"What is it?" John asks, resting his bag on a chair.

"Lennon," Theo calls again.

"Give me a second," I say, my words cutting through my teeth. I narrow my eyes at Theo until they're little slits, until he's just a blur. *I can't believe him.*

"What does Theo want from you?" John asks again.

I swallow, trying to find the words, but they catch in my throat. "Theo was supposed to tell you."

"Tell me what?" When I don't answer, he tilts his head to me and repeats himself. "Tell me what, Lennon?"

I have to say the words. I have to say them before Theo's actions reveal the truth in a way that will hurt John. He needs to hear it from me first.

"Theo and I are together," I finally say.

John's face remains unchanged. He glances over his shoulder to Theo, then back at me, nodding slowly.

"Congrats," he says with a slight shrug. "Is that all?"

Is that all?

I shake my head slightly, seeking realignment or something. "Yeah. That's all."

"As long as you're happy, Lennon, I'm happy."

"Do you mean that?" I ask, absentmindedly grabbing his arm.

He nods in response but I'm not sure I believe him. "I've got to run," he says. I release my grip, moving back. "There's a problem with my schedule and I have an appointment with Mr. Monroe to fix it."

"Okay."

"I'll see you tomorrow." He offers me a smile that feels foreign. Like it's in a language I don't understand.

John grabs his bag and swings it over his shoulder as he heads down the carpeted steps. He and Theo exchange something between a hug and a handshake while I watch, unmoored.

"You coming or what?" Theo calls again from the doorway once John has walked away.

I pick up my bag and come down to meet him, my feet fast, furious. "How could you do that?"

"Do what?" he asks, oblivious.

"I thought you were going to tell John about us."

He raises his shoulders. "Guess I forgot."

"Bullshit."

"Lower your voice," Theo says, stepping inside the now empty room and closing the door behind him.

"You did that on purpose. You wanted him to see us together," I say, all but pointing my finger to his chest.

"I'm not that sinister, Hadid. Relax."

"No? Then why didn't you tell him?"

He looks away, a forced smirk on his face. "It slipped my mind."

"I don't believe you. He's your best friend. Didn't you think about his feelings?"

"What feelings?" he asks, his brows cinched together in an angry frown. "What exactly do you think the two of you had? You messed around a couple of times. It wasn't that deep."

A puff of air escapes me. "How would you know how deep or not deep it was between us?"

"Are you telling me you still having feelings for the guy?"

"Do you know how condescending you sound?"

"Hey. I'm not anything," he says, patting his chest. "I'm just trying to figure out why my girlfriend is so concerned about my friend's feelings."

"He's my friend too, Theo."

"Apparently so."

We stand in the music room, our voices trapped inside the four walls.

"Do you still have feelings for him?" Theo asks again. This time his voice is raw.

There's the truth and there's the right answer. I give him the right answer. "No. I just didn't want to hurt his feelings."

"It's not that serious with guys, Len. Like, he wouldn't have cared. For real."

I don't believe that. I don't think Theo believes it either. But I also don't want to fight about this anymore. Because if we do, I won't be able to hold back.

The feelings I keep trying to bury away.

The feelings that won't stop rising to the surface.

The truth.

The real, honest truth that revealed itself like a shock of cold water the second John took his seat next to me in class.

I still love John.

And at this point, I wonder if I always will.

Chapter Twenty-five

OCTOBER 8

"What's wrong with you?" Theo asks, pulling away from our kiss.

We're in his bedroom. My parents think I'm at the library. His mom is working the night shift at the hospital. Sneaking around doesn't even really feel like sneaking around anymore. It's gotten too easy. Stale. And it's only October.

"You kiss too hard," I say, the words slipping out.

His face contorts while simultaneously turning red. "Are you saying you don't like kissing me?"

"No. I'm just saying you need to ease up on the tongue."

Theo rolls off me, staring up at his bedroom ceiling. "Didn't realize I was kissing an expert." Just as quickly, he turns on his side, resting his head on one hand. "How many guys *have* you kissed?"

"What does it matter?" I ask, pulling my shirt down.

"It doesn't. Forget it," he says, releasing an obnoxiously loud breath.

I turn on my side, mirroring his pose. "Is John mad at you? Because he stopped sitting next to me in class and hasn't spoken a word to me since I told him about us."

"I don't *think* John's mad at me. And even if he is, he'll get over it."

Said just like a guy who doesn't overthink everything.

"Hey." Theo pulls me closer to him, a playful smile tugging at his lips. "When are we going to move beyond this?"

"What do you mean by 'this'?" I ask.

He sighs and lies back on his bed, his hands clasped together at his chest. "All we ever do is kiss."

"That's not true," I say quietly.

"Okay. Once in a while you let me touch you under your shirt. I'm not sure what happened between us. We started off hot and now it's like we're in a Disney movie or some shit." He flips to his side again, a look of vulnerability on his stunningly handsome face. "Are you not attracted to me? Did I do something wrong the last time we . . . ?" He nods to my lower half.

"No. I am attracted to you. It's just complicated." I sit up, tucking my legs to my chest and wrapping my arms around them.

"Tell me." He sits up too, crossing his legs.

"You'll think I'm fucked in the head."

"Try me," he says, sweeping his thumb over my cheeks.

I nod, taking in a breath and letting it out slowly. "Sometimes when we're together, like *together* together, I feel guilty."

"Because we're sneaking around?"

"It goes deeper than that." I pick at my fingernails, and he takes my hand, stopping me from hurting myself.

"Is it, like, faith-based guilt?" he asks, which is pretty intuitive, but I shouldn't be surprised since he *is* an altar boy.

"No." I shake my head. "At least, I don't think so." He strokes my hand and looks up at me, patiently waiting for me to continue. "It's kind of hard to explain. Like, it's not you I feel guilty about, it's the act."

"Okay."

"I'm sometimes overcome with these feelings of shame and guilt when I give in to temptation. It can be so overpowering that I can't let myself enjoy it." I can't believe I'm saying these words out loud. Andie doesn't even know about this. Probably because this is the first time I've ever tried articulating these feelings to another person.

"Where does this come from?"

"My dad."

He tilts his head, confused.

"It's not what you think. I don't tell him about us or talk about my sex life. God. Eww."

We both laugh.

"It's just the messaging I've grown up with," I say. "Good girls don't have premarital sex. Good girls don't even think about sex. Good girls definitely don't do what we did in your bedroom on Labor Day."

"Oh." He nods, taking my words in, almost like he understands. "So because you sometimes feel bad about doing those things, now you don't want to do them anymore?"

I'm not sure how to answer this question, because some days the answer is yes, I don't want to do those things anymore, or at least I convince myself I don't. Like, if I stop, I can wipe the slate clean. And other times, my curiosity and hormones win. Especially when he's being sweet and understanding, like right now. But when he comes at me, like my body is just a means to an end for him, it reinforces all those doubts. It also makes me feel icky.

"I think maybe in order for me to move past that mental roadblock, I have to first feel safe," I say.

"I don't make you feel safe?"

"No. I mean, yes, you do."

His expression falls. "I'm not sure I understand what you're saying."

I don't blame him. I'm not making any sense.

I wasn't like this with John. Sure, sometimes I felt a bit guilty after, but never enough to hold back. Never enough to stop myself from experiencing pleasure. Never enough to try and convince myself I'd quit sex altogether. What makes things so different with Theo?

"Tell me what you want," I ask. "I won't be mad. I just need to know what it is you want us to do together."

He raises his shoulders, his cheeks turning pink. "Everything."

"And if I can't give you everything?"

"I'm not going to lie. The physical aspect of relationships is important to me. In the past, that's all I've ever really had. I think we have a strong enough foundation that this stuff shouldn't matter so much, but if I'm being honest," he says, rubbing his hands up and down his thighs, "because of that, it makes me want to be with you even more. So it's hard not being able to express that with you in the way I want to."

"I think I understand," I say, biting on my lower lip. "What about a compromise?"

"I'm listening."

"Everything but sex."

"Everything?" There's a light back in his eyes.

"For now."

He leans in, running his hands through my hair before kissing me softly. "Is that better?" he asks, looking to me for approval.

"Yes."

"I want you to feel safe with me, Lennon."

The intensity of this moment makes it so I have to force myself to look into his eyes. But it's not easy. Right now, I want to be anywhere but here. I'm not sure if I'm capable of being in such a mature relationship. Sometimes I think I only want this so that I can prove to everyone, including myself, that I'm normal.

Theo takes my hand and squeezes it, breaking me out of my thoughts. "I love you."

My throat catches at his declaration. Love? How is that possible? I'm nowhere near perfect, but I pride myself on not lying about the big, important things. Since I can't say the words that he wants me to, and because I don't want to ruin this moment of closeness, I lie down and allow myself to connect with Theo on a deeper, more physical level. I do everything in my power to stay in the moment and be present. Reminding myself that this is okay. That he loves me. That my parents love him. That so many girls would kill to be in my place. That if I can just get past this wall, maybe there will be something waiting for me on the other side.

The peace and calm I am so desperate to find.

After a few minutes, I'm able to dissociate enough from the thoughts in my head to be there for Theo in the way he so desperately needs me to be. I just wish I wanted it as much as he did.

Chapter Twenty-six

OCTOBER 19

Mom calls me into her room. I walk across the threshold of the bedroom where I spent mornings cuddled in bed with my parents, playing games on my mom's phone, while Georgie slept in. The bed where Georgie and I watched as Mom got dressed for weddings, and where I tried to hold in my envy as Mom let my older sister experiment with makeup. The room where I heard my dad cry, alone, on every anniversary of his brother's death.

Mom tells me to close the door, then pats the space next to her on the bed where she's sitting.

Immediately my mind cycles through all the possible reasons I could be in trouble.

Theo.

Sneaking around with Theo.

Maybe Theo's mom found out we've been hanging out at his house when she's at work.

Maybe she caught me on camera.

Do they have a camera outside their house?

Shit. What if they have one inside their house?

What if I left behind a piece of clothing?

Or she found Theo's condoms.

Not that we've used them.

But she could have made the connection between him having condoms and me being the girl he spends the most time with.

What if they somehow know about the night swimming in my underwear?

Or all the things we did under Theo's roof that would not only devastate my mom but cause my dad to never speak to me again?

I walk slowly to Mom as all these thoughts race through my mind, making my stomach twist and turn.

"I want to talk to you about Theo," she says.

Greatest fear unlocked.

I sit, facing forward, too afraid to look her in the eyes.

"What about Theo?" I ask, trying my best to sound innocent. I know the role they want me to play, and I play it well. Soft, high-pitched voice. Clothes that aren't too tight but are still current enough, so I don't embarrass my superficial mother. A good girl but not a social outcast. They want someone who is perfect. Someone who smiles when smiled at. Someone who blends in so well that a person might be surprised to learn about my diagnosis. A perfectly normal and nice girl. Someone I can never be.

It's not like they don't acknowledge the autism; if anything, it makes them more protective. But they don't see my being autistic as an excuse not to be their perfect daughter.

"You've been friends with him for a few months, yes?" she asks.

I open my mouth to respond, not sure what I'm going to say after "Yes," but before I can say anything, she continues.

"Do you like him?"

I respond with something between a shrug and a nod. I figure that will cover all the bases, depending on what she wants or doesn't want to hear.

"I think the two of you would make a nice couple."

Instead of being relieved over the idea of no longer having to sneak around with Theo, my thoughts can't help but go to John.

"Mom, was there ever anyone before Dad? Not just a guy that came over 'for coffee' with his parents. But someone you actually liked?"

Her lips part slightly, and she pauses. "Yes. Kind of. But Teta and Sedo didn't approve of him."

"Why not?" I study my mother's expression to see if I can read her, but her face hardens faster than cement. There was a second there where her mind had drifted to the past, but she pushed it back. She's probably gotten good at pushing away certain memories.

"He wasn't a good boy."

"Why?"

"Lennon."

"I want to understand what makes a boy 'good' or 'bad.'"

Mom clenches her jaw. She wants me to drop it. But I'm so sick of this game my parents play, where they put people into categories and write them off. It's archaic and elitist and shitty.

"He didn't come from a good family. And he'd been engaged before. Sedo didn't like him."

"But you did," I say.

Mom rises from the bed and walks toward her mirror. She stands in front of it and fiddles with the hem of her shirt. "It didn't matter. I couldn't be with someone my parents didn't like. That's how it is."

"No." I shake my head. "Maybe for you. But not me."

She turns around. There's a strained smile on her face. "I don't know why you're getting upset. Theo is a good boy. We like him."

"There's someone else," I blurt. "I like another boy more. John. He's Theo's friend."

"No." Her tone is brash. "Daddy doesn't like this boy."

I rise from the bed. "How do you know?"

Mom's eyes dart to the bedroom door, then back to me. "Baba is smart. He told me about this boy after he came over. He sensed there was something between you and him. I told him he was being paranoid and that you liked Theo."

The brutal truth of her words both slaps and stings my cheeks. The room spins and I swallow, trying to steady myself by breathing in and out, slowly.

"Theo came by this morning when you were shopping with Andie," Mom says, seemingly putting an end to our conversation about John.

"He came here?"

"Yes."

"Why?" I ask, standing in front of my mother, almost towering over her in my curiosity.

"He wanted to know if me and Baba would be okay with you and him spending more time together." She smiles. "It was very sweet. He said he respected us both too much to sneak around."

I drag a hand over my face. "No, he didn't."

"He did," she says with a proud grin.

"And where was Dad during all of this?"

"Buying meat for tomorrow's barbecue."

Of course.

I can't believe Theo. We said we would do this together. We agreed to do this together when the time was right.

I take in a deep breath and release it. "Does Dad know?"

"Yes. He said Theo could take you to the Fall Fair tonight."

"We already had plans to go together. With Andie and her boyfriend. Dad knew that. What's the big difference?" I ask.

"The big difference is you don't have to hide how you feel about one another anymore. We're not dumb, habibti. You don't go from just friends to more than friends without something happening."

I examine my mom's face. This feels like a test. Like I'm supposed to either admit she's right or deny that Theo and I have been sneaking around.

"I thought I wasn't allowed to date," I say, folding my arms over my chest.

She holds her hands out before clasping them together. "We make an exception for Theo. We know him. We know his family. And we know his heart. He will honor and respect your father's wishes and take good care of you."

A puff of laughter escapes me.

"It's this or nothing," Mom says, straightening. Her tone has shifted slightly.

I grit my teeth. "I guess it's this." I turn away and give the biggest behind-the-scenes eyeroll I can before forcing myself to open and close Mom's bedroom door without slamming it or stomping away like the angry, petulant child I am.

Fuck. This. Shit.

And fuck Theo.

Theo texts me multiple times to confirm that he'll be by at seven to pick me up for the Fall Fair. He keeps hinting at a surprise. All I can muster up in response is a "k."

I am so annoyed with him.

He thinks he's so clever. He thinks he's fooled both me and my parents.

I'm not even sure who I'm madder at: him or myself. Clearly, he doesn't know me as well as he'd like to believe he does. If he did, he'd have known not to do this.

"Lennon," Dad calls, his voice strangely cheerful. "Theo is here."

I check my reflection in my bedroom mirror, forcing out a breath in hopes it will unclench my jaw. I thought about faking sick, but why should I be stuck at home because Theo pulled some Neanderthal move behind my back?

Dad and Theo are smiling in the foyer, looking at me as I come down the stairs. Theo has flowers. He brought me flowers. How am I supposed to stay angry at him when he brings me flowers and looks so sweet and earnest standing next to my father? *If Dad only knew.*

Constantly living in fear of being found out is going to end me before my father does.

Mom takes my flowers, and Theo promises Dad that he'll bring me home by ten-thirty. Dad throws up a hand and says with a wink, "Eleven is fine."

Once we're in Theo's car, I put on my seat belt and try to find my center of gravity. I don't want to start a fight, but I also don't know if I can pretend like everything is okay.

"You're quiet," Theo says, reversing out of my driveway.

"I'm just trying to process the fact that you went behind my back," I say, a razor-sharp edge to my voice.

"So they told you?" he says casually, no change in his tone.

"Yeah, Theo. My mother told me. But even if she hadn't, the flowers would have been a big enough clue."

"It's great, right?" he says, stealing a glance at me and smiling. When I don't respond, his smile falters. He continues driving, but I feel his eyes drifting in my direction every couple of minutes or so. When we arrive at the fair, he drives onto the grassy lot and parks before turning in his seat to face me. "You're mad I didn't run it by you first, right?"

I unbuckle my seat belt and meet his eyes. "Yes, I'm mad about that. We're supposed to be in this together. But you keep doing shit like this, completely disregarding that I have a voice in this relationship too."

"What do you mean, 'shit like this'?"

"Like when you said you'd tell John about us. But then you never did, and I ended up having to tell him before he saw us together."

"So what if he had? Do you think he would have cared that much? You really have blown up whatever it was that happened between the two of you."

"You don't know what you're talking about," I say.

Theo's eyes burn into mine as he shakes his head. "Are all autistic girls like this or is this just a Lennon thing? You attach yourself to the first boy who ever paid attention to you? Romanticize him like he's some brooding hero in a romance novel? Open your eyes, Lennon. John is not into you. *I* am. *I'm* your boyfriend. *I* love you. I'm the one who's been there since the beginning, looking out for you. John is just this idea you've built in your head. He doesn't feel one ounce of the love for you I feel. Have you ever thought to ask yourself, if John loved you as much as you seem to believe he does, why he isn't here? Why isn't he fighting for you?" He turns to face his steering wheel, striking it with both hands. "This is such bullshit. I know you're autistic. I know your brain operates differently than mine. But you're living in a fantasy world if you think you and John could ever be together."

I grab my things and open the door, slamming it so hard his car shakes. Theo gets out, calling after me, and I can't seem to make my feet move fast enough to get away from him. There are too many people. And muddy puddles to dart around. And sounds. Why is it so noisy?

"Lennon," Theo calls again. Fainter this time.

I push my way through a family, locked arm in arm, taking up the width of the path, then make a sharp left until the entrance is in view. My feet move faster now. At the gate, I pull out a ten-dollar bill, ready to pay my own way inside.

I don't need Theo.

I don't need my father.

I don't need anyone.

My phone keeps buzzing inside my jacket pocket, but I ignore it. He can't speak to me that way. He can't treat me like that. He just can't.

I zip my fleece jacket, wishing I'd chosen something warmer. It's chillier out here in the open. No buildings to shield me from the crisp October winds.

I text Andie to tell her I'm here. She says she's in a long line for the haunted mansion with Kiefer and will text me when it's over. I wish it were just me and her here tonight. Part of me wonders if this obsession with boys is just so I can prove something to myself. To my parents. That I can still be someone worthy of their love while being allowed to explore all the things I want to explore. It doesn't have to be one or the other. It shouldn't have to be.

Except, I seem to have developed a tunnel vision of sorts. John. Theo. Theo. John. Theo. Theo. John. John. John.

"Lennon?"

He calls my name and time stands still. John. I whip my head around to find him standing just a few feet in front of me. He's studying me just as intensely as I'm studying him.

He takes a step closer. "Are you here alone?"

"Yes. No."

"Which is it?" he asks with a hopeful smile.

"I'm here alone."

"What about Theo?"

"I don't—I don't want to talk about him right now," I say, and John nods, understanding. "Are you here alone?" I ask.

"I came with Eddie and his girlfriend, but they're in line for the haunted mansion and I couldn't be bothered to wait that long, so," he shrugs, "here I am."

A chuckle escapes me. "Eddie has a girlfriend?"

John laughs. "Yeah." He stuffs his hands in his pockets, rocking back and forth on his heels, an adorable crease in his forehead. "Do you want to hang out for a bit?"

"Sure. I've never been here before," I say as we start walking.

He turns to me and there's a look of bewilderment on his face. "Not even in elementary school on a trip?"

"My parents didn't see the educational value in coming here. I think they were worried about me getting lost in a big, open space.

Or maybe they thought I might run away once I got the smallest taste of freedom." I let out a strained laugh, but John doesn't join in.

"Then I will take this as an opportunity to show you around." He offers his elbow for me to slip my arm through, and I hesitate. His gentle gaze finds mine. "So you can't run off or get lost."

"Got it," I say, looping my arm through his.

John shows me the cows and the chickens. The pigpen and the horses. We watch little kids take pony rides and we stop for hot chocolate–my treat. After the demolition derby, which John seems to really enjoy, we eat corndogs—his treat.

I responded to Theo's texts by telling him I needed space. He hasn't texted since.

Being here with John tonight, I feel like I'm in some sort of weird multiverse. Getting to experience what it would be like to be on a date with him. The ease. The comfort. The peace.

Is this what true happiness feels like?

"Ferris wheel?" John asks, pulling me away from my thoughts.

"Sure."

We enter the rides section of the fairgrounds. We haven't said anything in minutes but it's okay. It's kind of nice being close to him and not having to fill in all the silences with small talk.

"We got lucky," he says as the carnival worker lifts the rope and lets us in. "No line."

"Yeah," I say, smiling to myself at the irony of it all. How lucky and unlucky I feel in this moment. Timing and chance once again dangling a piece of fruit in front of me, almost within reach.

John leads and I nervously sit on the seat belt buckle. He gently pulls the belt from underneath me and buckles us in.

He watches me and laughs. "You're scared."

"No."

"Lennon, you're stiff as a board."

"Okay, fine. I'm not the biggest fan of heights."

"You could have said no," he says, a small frown on his face.

"I know. But I wanted to."

"You've never ridden a Ferris wheel before?"

Our seat rises to accommodate the next riders, and I grip the silver lap bar with one hand, trying to pretend I have an ounce of cool. "I have. With my dad. The huge one at the Santa Monica Pier. The summer before ninth grade. But it was before dark. It'll be nice to experience it at night with all the lights. It'll be pretty, don't you think?"

"Yeah." He smiles, his eyes on mine. "Very pretty. So how was it then?"

We continue to be jolted up as the seats fill with passengers below us. The line is growing quickly.

"By the time we got on, the sun was almost setting, and it gave us the most beautiful view of the coastline. We were stopped for a while, right at the top, and I was a bit anxious." John looks down at my hand still gripping the bar and smirks. I release it, wiping the sweat on my thigh. "Okay. I was scared out of my mind. My dad sang the theme song to this old show he used to love to distract me."

"Oh yeah? What show?"

"I doubt you'd know it. It's really old."

"Try me," he says.

"*Three's Company*."

John laughs. "I know that one. It plays on the old comedy channel at midnight. Eddie and I watched it a few times. High."

Now we both laugh.

The ride begins and we go around. Admittedly, the view of the rural fairgrounds, even at night, doesn't quite compare with southern California, but it's still nice.

"Can I ask you something?"

"Sure," John replies, his hair blowing in the breeze.

"Why did you change seats in Music?"

He shifts around slightly, his thigh pressed against mine, as a noticeable silence lingers. "I thought it was the right thing to do," he says finally.

In the distance, some Celine Dion song plays, filling the quiet that follows his response.

"Why are you like that?" I ask.

"Like what?"

"You're always doing the 'right thing.' Doesn't it get exhausting being so damn virtuous?"

He shakes his head. "If you knew what I was thinking half the time, you wouldn't be describing me as virtuous."

"What're you thinking right now?" I ask as we come to a stop at the top of the Ferris wheel. "The cold, hard truth. Screw being virtuous."

"The mouth on you," he says, a smile tugging at his lips. "Does your father know?"

I squirm in my seat, pulling my leg away from the warmth of John's. "I don't want to talk about him. Okay?"

"Alright. No Theo. No father. Any other topics off-limits?"

"You tell me," I say, looking out over the fairgrounds. It's funny, because right this second, I don't want to be up here stuck with John, but I also want to be here more than words can express.

"The truth is I'm thinking about how much I'm enjoying being with you tonight," John says simply.

"I never said we had to stop being friends."

"Come on," he says, his head tilted. "You know we can't."

"Because of Theo?"

"No."

"Then why?" I ask, turning to him.

"Because of us."

Us. I didn't realize there was still an *us* to be discussed. At least from his perspective. John and everything we shared together will always exist in my heart and my memories. And probably, years from now, he'll be the giant cloud that hangs over me, asking *What if?* The thought of that alone cracks something deep inside me.

"What are you doing after you graduate?" I ask, because I want to change the subject and because I really want to know. I *need* to know. I keep thinking if I learn more about John, he'll be less of this perfect specimen my mind has built him up to be, and more of a real, flawed human I could possibly convince myself I don't love.

"I'm not sure. I'm applying to colleges." He shrugs, looking out into the distance. "My dad's friends tell me I can get a job with them. But I don't want to be one of those people who wake up every day dreading going into work. I want to love what I do."

"What do you love?"

"Love doesn't pay the bills."

"Is that what you think we were put on earth to do?" I ask. "Pay bills?"

He shakes his head, looking at me as if I'm a child who still dreams of a fairy-tale prince who will save her from herself.

"I want to do something that will pay enough that I don't have to worry about bills. I want to be able to travel. I want to be able to spoil the one I love with whatever they want or need." He looks at me as he speaks, his voice rising slightly to punctuate the end of every sentence. "I want to wake up every day excited for what's to come, instead of counting down the hours until I'm free. I want to look at the time and think, shit, I only have a few minutes left. That's what I want."

"Sounds perfect," I say, allowing my leg to fall against his again. We drop down another level, slowly, methodically. The carnival worker continues the long process of unloading and loading passengers. "You can do anything you put your mind to," I say. "Guitar. Carpentry. Making friends wherever you go. Taking care of your family."

"I get by. That's my special skill. That and being able to adapt."

That's funny to me, since I'm probably the least adaptable person that ever existed.

"You still want to go to Columbia and get that Creative Writing degree?" he asks with a small smile.

"More than ever. I've been working to build up the nerve to ask my parents about the school trip to New York City this spring. One week in New York without my parents hovering. Exploring the city. Visiting all the tourist attractions I've only ever seen in movies or online," I say, feeling myself grow excited.

"I hope you get to go."

"You should come too!"

"We can't afford extras like that," John replies, his jaw clenching. He doesn't believe that he deserves a life with frills. I think he deserves everything.

"I happen to know they have a scholarship seat available. All you have to do is apply. You meet all the qualifications. You're enrolled in an arts class. You're an upperclassman. You're—"

"Poor as dirt."

"I didn't mean that," I say, my eyes downcast.

"I know." He nudges his elbow with mine. "I'm just being an insecure asshole."

Our seat rocks and I grab the metal bar with both hands.

"It's okay," John says reassuringly. "You don't have to be afraid." He unspools my hand from the bar and holds it in his, squeezing it. Without thinking I rest my head on his shoulder as we sit in silence, looking out over the fair as our bucket seat continues to descend, level by level. It's like a clock with a timer. Running down.

Tick.

Tick.

"Hey, Lennon."

My eyes flick up to see a mischievous grin on his face. "Yeah?"

He breaks into song. "Would you knock on my door?"

I laugh, stopping short of a snort. "Those aren't the right lyrics."

"Then sing them to me," he says sweetly, his eyes locking with mine. So I do. Eventually he joins me, making up ridiculous ad libs, and we both laugh so hard there are tears in our eyes.

Maybe these fairgrounds *can* compete with the ocean waves and bright lights of the Santa Monica Pier. Or maybe just being anywhere with John makes everything infinitely better.

We run into Eddie and his girlfriend after the Ferris wheel, and I make up a lie about meeting Andie by the food trucks. Instead, I text Andie and tell her I'm leaving early and will call her later to explain. Then I head toward the parking lot. My home screen is filled with new texts from Theo. Apologizing.

I find him sitting in his car, waiting. He straightens when he sees me approaching. I walk to the passenger side and let myself in.

"Hey," I say, closing the door.

"Hey," he says, looking out the window.

It's just after nine. He's been sitting here for almost two hours. Alone.

"You didn't have to wait," I say. "I walked out on you."

He shakes his head solemnly. "I told your parents I'd take care of you."

I tuck my hands into my lap, and we both turn to look at one another at the same time.

"When you act like that, Theo, it reminds me of my father, and not in a good way."

"Like what?" he asks genuinely.

"Like how you went behind my back to ask for his blessing to date me. I felt completely blindsided. You took away my voice. My option to have a say. I can't be with someone who does that."

"I'm sorry." He nods. "I thought I was making it easier for both of us."

"You need to treat me like an equal. We're partners, okay? We make decisions together."

"Okay." It's quiet for a moment before he leans in closer. "I'm sorry for what I said about you and John. I was there. I know you guys shared something special. And I think I was trying to gaslight you into thinking it was nothing so you'd finally get over him."

"Theo, I'm—"

"It's fine, Lennon. I know you still have feelings for him, and I can accept that. As long as you keep an open mind, and heart, with me." His eyes widen. "Can you do that?"

I nod because I think I can. I know I want to. It would be so much easier if I could.

"Good. Cause you know what? Eventually your memories with John will fade away and what we have will fill up all those cracks in your heart that John left behind." He picks up my hand and kisses it. "But that's not going to happen unless you let him go."

"I know."

He leans in and kisses me softly on my lips, running a hand over my cheek. "I love you so much. And I promise to do better."

I tip my forehead into his, staring into his soulful eyes. If I look long enough, if I let myself, I can almost see a future with him.

Almost.

Tick.

Tick.

. . . Boom.

Chapter Twenty-seven

DECEMBER 25

Mom and Georgie are in the kitchen preparing brunch while I take care of the aftermath of present opening in the family room. Georgie spent the night back in her old bedroom with Zach and Paulie so we could all celebrate Christmas morning together. Zach's trying to put Paulie down for a nap before they go to his parents' house.

It's been nice having Georgie here overnight, even if it means Zach's here, too. I've come to accept that he's part of the deal now. It's not that I don't like him. He's Paulie's dad and my sister's husband (as weird as that still is to say). But I can't help sometimes looking at Zach and seeing him as the person who disrupted our flow. And that's putting it mildly.

"Lennon." Dad sits on the couch and watches me tidy, my arms filling up with all the paper and mess, mostly from Paulie's presents. "Come here," he says softly. "Put all that down. It can wait."

I do as he says and sit next to him. "What is it?"

"I have another present for you." He smiles, his eyes crinkling at the corners. Instead of being excited, I swallow down the pit rising up my consistently tight esophagus. "You've been working hard in school and I'm proud of you. An 86 on your Calculus midterm report is very impressive."

It is. I busted my ass to get that grade. It helps having a boyfriend very skilled in mathematics. But it's not lost on me that my father didn't point out my 96 in English, my 88 in Biology, or my 91 in Music.

Well-rounded. It's what I aim to be. For them. But it doesn't come naturally. My profile, like that of many autistic people, is spiky. I excel where I excel, and I struggle when I don't care about the subject matter. Unfortunately for me, I don't have the option of not caring.

I know I'd be so much happier if I could focus all my attention on my actual passions. Master them, instead of spending my energy trying to find solutions to complex equations in Calculus. But I also understand that my life is not just my own. So I play along, as best I can. Some days are easier than others.

"You really want to go on that school trip to New York, yes?" Dad asks before bringing a small espresso cup to his mouth.

I become lit from within at his question. I've been asking my parents for their permission to attend at least once a day since the end of October, only to hear "We'll see." I half expected they'd give me their blessing on my sixteenth birthday earlier this month. When they didn't, I almost gave up all hope.

"Yes. More than life itself," I say, sucking in my lips to stop myself from saying everything else I want to say. They don't know yet about my dream to study at Columbia University. I figure one devastating upset at a time.

"We're going to let you go," he says, and before he can even finish smiling, my arms are draped around his neck and I'm covering his cheeks in kisses.

"Thank you, thank you, thank you!"

He pats me on the back with his free hand and says, "You've earned it. You're a good girl."

The light from within dims at his words and I pull away. I don't want him to see how those words deflate me, so I nod, forcing another smile to come through before I return to cleaning the mess at our feet.

☾

Theo's mother went all out for Christmas dinner. Fireplace. Music. A roasted lamb with every imaginable side. I regret not wearing stretchy pants, but Mom made us dress up. Like, really dress up. I'm in a dark green dress with a pleated skirt and long sleeves and black stockings. My parents, who are also overdressed, are in the kitchen helping Petra clean. Theo made up a story about wanting to show me his new gaming system in the basement, and Dad's clearly had one too many alcohol-infused eggnogs because he doesn't flinch as Theo takes my hand. We disappear together, almost giddy.

"Did I tell you how adorable you look in your Christmas dress, Hadid?" Theo says once we reach the bottom of the basement steps. "I just want to unwrap you right here." There's a deep hunger in his eyes as his cute words transform into something more R-rated. He kisses me passionately, and almost immediately his hands are under my dress.

"Our parents are upstairs," I say as his lips trace my neck. I don't push him away even though I know I should.

We stumble to the couch and he flicks on the TV and gaming system. He sits first and I straddle him, our lips never leaving each other's. Being here, alone, after having to sit through dinner on our best behavior, is the exact release we both need.

He runs his fingers through my hair, his kisses like tiny bites up and down my neck and shoulders. He pulls me in even closer, his hands under my dress again, trying to remove the layers between us. When he attempts to pull my stockings down, I stop him.

"Clothes stay on. Parents upstairs," I say almost breathlessly as I return my lips to his.

But he pulls away, exhaling an annoyed breath. His jaw clenches, body stiff as his arms fall to his sides. I slink off him, sitting on the cold spot to his left.

"I'm getting really tired of having to finish the job myself," he says, his tone sharp. Harsh almost.

"Are you serious right now? It's Christmas. Can you take one day off from thinking about sex?"

"And what will tomorrow's excuse be? It's Boxing Day? Then it's New Year's Eve? It's Tuesday? I thought we were both ready to move beyond this," he says, waving his hand between us.

"I don't know what you want me to say." My arms are crossed over my chest now as Theo adjusts his crotch.

"I've been patiently waiting for you to be ready, and I thought when you turned sixteen you would be."

"Why? Did you think there'd be some chip inside me that would activate at 12:00 a.m. on December eighth to spread my legs open?"

He gets up and paces behind the couch. Footsteps from the floor above. Chairs being pulled out or tucked in. A toilet flushing. Instinctively, I straighten myself out. Just in case.

Theo comes back around, sits next to me, and takes my hand.

"I don't see what the big deal is," he says, his voice soft now. "We've been together almost five months. We've known each other forever. Our families are close. I'm not going to use you and walk away. I'm in this, Lennon. For the long haul." He leans in and says more quietly. "We've done everything else. Why can't we do this?"

My eyes squeeze shut as I release a breath through my nostrils. "The way I feel about you is not contingent on whether we have sex. I wish you could see that."

"I wish you could see how much I want to be with you."

"I understand," I say, turning to look at him. "I do. I'm just not sure that this next step makes sense for us."

"Why not?" he asks, brows furrowed. "Are you planning on going somewhere?"

"No. But you are. You're graduating in six months and you've applied to schools all at least two hours away. If we sleep together, I'm only going to grow more attached, and for what? All so you can leave?"

He shimmies closer, grabbing my other hand and holding it even tighter. "No. I won't leave you. We'll stay together."

"You can't promise that. You're moving away for school and I'm . . ." I pause, sighing. "I haven't told you this yet, but I'm hoping to study in New York."

He pulls back slightly. "New York? Do your parents know?"

"Not yet. But I'm working on them. The trip is step one."

He releases a deep laugh, obvious relief flooding his face. "Good luck with that."

Anger pulses through me as I rip my hands away from his. "So it's okay for you to consider schools as far away as B.C., but you expect me to stay put, waiting for you? You can't even handle me being here and not having sex with you. Am I supposed to believe you'll actually abstain once you move away? Let's be real."

"Why would you think anything else?" he asks, legitimately perplexed.

"Because everything comes back to sex. You're not going to be able to stay loyal to me for four years while you're wherever you are and I'm . . . wherever I end up. And I don't expect you to. Which is why I don't think it makes sense for us to do that."

"So what're we doing, then?" he asks.

"To be honest, right now, I don't know."

His face contorts, like I just said the worst thing possible. I probably did. But it was the truth.

Our relationship since October has been a series of passive-aggressive comments, followed by bigger disagreements, followed by making up. Over and over. It makes me understand a bit more why John and Avery stayed together as long as they did.

The basement door opens, and heavy footsteps come down the unfinished stairs. Theo and I move way from one another on instinct.

"Everything okay down here?" Dad asks, his eyes flicking to Theo, then me. "I thought I heard yelling."

Theo turns to my father and switches into his altar boy persona. "I was just showing off the sound system." He nods to the console, his eyes seeking mine for the briefest of moments; I can see that he's still hurt by my words.

"Let me see that," Dad says, sitting next to Theo.

I get up from the couch and sit on a chair and unlock my phone. There are messages from Georgie complaining about her mother-in-law's cooking. A pic from Andie posing with her new boyfriend, Reid. And a text from John.

John.

My heart pounds against my chest as I open it, my dad and Theo just feet away.

John: Merry Christmas, Lennon.
I hope it's a good one and you
get everything you want.

John: Also, happy belated birthday.
Sorry I didn't say it sooner.

I reply immediately.

Me: Merry Christmas. And thanks.
Was Santa good to you?

The three dots appear and my heart races.

John: Yeah. My entire family together.
Dad's sober. It's been pretty much
perfect.

John: Except for one thing.

My throat catches, and I glance up at my father and Theo, lost in some video game.

"Lennon," Dad's voice calls out after what could be seconds or minutes.

"What?" I shoot back, prying my eyes off my phone screen.

"We should get one of these, yeah?" Dad asks.

I watch my father and Theo playing a video game together and the pit in my stomach grows bigger. If Theo and I break up, how would it play out? Our lives are so intertwined. The fact is, my dad has been nicer to me since Theo and I started dating officially. For some odd reason, he trusts me more. Allows me more freedom.

Theo is probably the reason my father agreed to New York. There are advantages to Theo being my boyfriend.

And then there are disadvantages.

The number one being: he's not John.

It's not fair for me to keep stringing Theo along when my heart so clearly belongs to someone else. The reason I don't want to have sex with Theo isn't because he's going to be moving away. It's because I don't want it to be him.

I close my message with John and open my text window with Theo and type:

Me: We need to talk.

Chapter Twenty-eight

DECEMBER 31

I broke up with Theo.

I didn't even have to say anything. He knew it was coming. I saw it in his eyes as he read the "we need to talk" text with my dad still seated next to him. And once it was done? There were no tears. No screaming matches. No begging or promises to change. He basically shrugged and said, "Okay." Had me almost believing it was.

But the last few days he's gone out of his way to post pictures of himself living his best life, his arms around a new girl in every photo. I know exactly what he's doing. Unfortunately, it's working. I feel like shit, and it's coming from all angles. Because my father? He's taking it worse than Theo and I combined.

"You've made a mistake," he says to me over breakfast. "You won't find someone better than him."

"What if it's not about finding someone better?" I challenge, looking up from my plate. "Besides, Theo is graduating soon and moving away. It was going to happen eventually."

"You could have stayed together while he was at school." Of course Dad would say that. How perfect would it be if his daughter's perfect boyfriend lived hours away?

In his mind, my relationship with Theo was nothing more than a lengthy dinner reservation, so that one day, when we were both of marrying age, we'd default to one another. It's laughable that he thinks Theo, of all people, could abstain from sex for all those years. I don't understand how such a smart man, a man who lives in constant fear of my purity being tarnished, could be so oblivious to Theo's true colors. Not that Theo is a bad guy. He's not. He's just not the person Dad thinks he is.

Then again, neither am I.

Shakespeare was right. "All the world's a stage, and all the men and women merely players . . ."

"I hope you don't expect your mother and Petra to stop being friends," Dad says as he brings his plate to the sink.

"Why would I expect that?" I ask, shoving a forkful of scrambled eggs into my mouth.

"If you keep an open mind, you could find your way back to one another." He stands at the sink, rinsing his dishes.

What I want to say to Dad is that I've already wasted too much time with the wrong person and I'm not going to do it again.

"We're going to Petra's tonight for New Year's. You should come instead of staying home alone. Maybe Theo will be there."

"Theo will definitely not be there," I say. "And I'm not spending New Year's Eve alone. I'll be here babysitting Paulie."

"Right, right," he says. "Can't blame your old man for trying." He comes over to the table, where I'm squishing the small pieces of leftover eggs under my fork. Dad ruffles my hair and places a kiss on the top of my head before walking out of the kitchen.

I hate how much I crave his affection. And how good it feels to receive it.

I have to hand it to Georgie. Looking after a one-and-a-half-year-old is exhausting. I feel like I've aged five years in one night.

Me: Your adorable monster is finally asleep.

Georgie: It's almost eleven! Her bedtime is seven!

Me: I know!!! She wouldn't go down. You're welcome!!!

Georgie: You know this means she'll be up earlier than usual tomorrow morning.

Me: How does that even make sense?

Georgie: Trust me.

Me: Better get your butt here early then. With iced coffees and donuts.

Georgie: You got it ♥ happy new year xoxo

Me: yeah yeah happy new year

Me: ♥

I flop my tired and wretched-looking self on the couch, taking in the mess before me. How does one toddler create so much disaster? I *could* leave this for my mom to clean up in the morning, but I really don't want to start off the new year with a lecture about how I need to pull my weight around the house.

I let out a loud sigh and start picking up Paulie's messes. I'm always going to be the girl who doesn't want to upset my parents. I'm always going to seek their approval. And all I ever want to be is accepted and loved and valued and appreciated for who I am—but for who I *really* am. Not this sanitized version of myself where I remain the same girl I was before my diagnosis.

That girl was lost. Confused. A people pleaser.

I guess not that much has changed.

After tidying up, I move to the kitchen to heat up the Greek takeout I didn't get to enjoy with Paulie hanging off my arm. My phone buzzes as I'm wiping up the rice I spilled.

Andie: You've got to see this.

I press play on the video she sent to see Theo drunk out of his mind at a party.

Me: Who's he there with?

Andie: Eddie.

Me: No John?

Andie: Not that I've seen.
He's completely fucked.

Me: Can you tell Eddie to
bring him home?

Andie: Eddie is also completely
fucked.

Andie: And before you ask me to do it,
I am bordering on completely fucked.

Andie: He's sloppy as hell too.
Telling everyone you dumped him.

Me: I don't know what you want
me to do with this information.
I'm babysitting Paulie.

Andie: idk but someone's got
to get him out of here before
he gets his ass kicked.

Me: I'll try John. Keep an eye on him.

Andie: lol yeah k I'll try

The microwave dings. I ignore it and return to the family room instead. I think about texting John, but my fingers are too shaky. I call instead, hoping he'll pick up. I never responded to his Christmas text. Well, that's not totally true. I responded by breaking up with Theo. I just didn't know what to say to John about it.

"Hello?"

"John. Hi. It's me. Are you busy?"

"No. Everything okay?"

"Andie texted. She's at Abby Windsor's party and Theo is there. She said he's really messed up and pissing people off. Do you think you might be able to bring him home?"

"What about Eddie?"

"Eddie is apparently not in any shape to drive either."

"God, they're such idiots." I can almost hear him raking his fingers through his hair. A pang of something fierce flows through me, even now, in the middle of this Theo-inflicted drama. "I'll try."

"Thanks. Let me know how it goes."

I pace around the house, carrying the baby monitor with me and checking my phone every fifteen seconds. No longer hungry, I toss my leftovers into the compost and give the kitchen a good scrubbing. Wiping down cupboards. The floor. Cleaning the fridge. Stove top.

Headlights flash through the front door window. I peek out to see John's car pulling into my driveway. Theo gets out of the car and stumbles up my front path. I open the door before he has a chance to ring the bell and wake Paulie.

"What are you doing here?" I ask as he struggles to stand upright. John comes out of the driver's seat, bags under his eyes, no jacket, hair cropped short. "Why would you bring him *here*?"

"He wouldn't let me take him home," John says, closing his door before circling to the passenger-side door and slamming it shut. "He said your parents are there?"

"Okay, then bring him to Eddie's," I say, like they're both lacking any common sense.

"I don't want to go to Eddie's," Theo says, pushing his way past me and into my house.

John and I exchange glances as he steps through the doorway. There's a hesitation in the way John moves, like he doesn't feel welcome here. I try to tell him with a look that I want him here, more than anything, but I'm not sure my message is coming across. Not with Theo being a complete disaster a few feet away.

"At least take your shoes off," I say to Theo. He turns around and, with a toothy smile, kicks off his shoes before falling face-first onto the sofa.

"I'm sorry," John says, "but telling Theo I'd bring him here was the only way I got him out of the party. I thought when we got to

Eddie's I could trick him into going home with him, but he wasn't having it. He's even more of a stubborn asshole when he's drunk."

I run my hands down my face, hoping an idea will come to me if I think hard enough. Anything to get Theo up and out of my house before my parents return.

Although . . .

Maybe it would do them some good to see Theo like this. To see for themselves that he's not the perfect altar boy they think he is.

"Leave him," I say, coolly.

John's brows pinch. He's glancing between Theo, whose long limbs are hanging off the couch as a trail of drool drips from his open mouth, and me, arms crossed.

"Want a drink?" I ask, nodding to the kitchen.

John looks around, eyebrows still furrowed. "I don't think I should stay?"

"How else am I going to explain how Theo got here. Unless . . ."

"Unless what?" John asks, still standing in between the family room and foyer, undecided.

"Unless I'm keeping you from something or *someone*?"

"I was hanging out at home. Alone."

Relief floods through me at his response. *Alone.* "Why didn't you go to the party with Theo and Eddie?"

He swallows, burying his hands in his jean pockets. "Lennon, Theo and I aren't really close anymore."

I stall, thinking over the last five months. I just thought Theo was spending all his free time with me because that's what couples do. God, I can be so self-involved.

"Is this because of me?" I ask, already knowing the answer. "Wait, did Theo ask you to stop speaking to me?"

He shakes his head slightly. "I didn't just do it for him. I did it for you, too."

"Oh." I laugh. "How commendable. I just love it when men make decisions on my behalf."

"Did you really think you and Theo could be a couple and I would just . . . what? Hang around as a spare tire on all your dates? Watching the two of you fall deeper in love?" John takes a step closer, his voice quieter. "When he asked me to respectfully keep my distance, I agreed, because I knew it was the right thing for all of us."

"You're no better than the rest of them," I say, waving an arm in anger. "Deciding what's best for me as if I don't have a mind of my own."

"But you chose Theo."

"No." I say it with everything inside me, as if that one simple word had been buried under the weight of a lifetime of bad decisions, begging to come out. "No," I repeat. "I broke up with him after you texted me on Christmas."

"I didn't ask you to do that," he says.

"I know you didn't. But I wanted to. What's the point of—?"

The front door opens, and John turns quickly. Every single pulse point in my body throbs. My mouth snaps shut, jaw clenching. I try to move away from John, but I appear to be in a frozen state of shock.

"What's this boy doing here?" Dad asks, Mom behind him. He probably saw John's car in the driveway and drew his own conclusions even before turning the knob.

Mom closes the front door as Dad removes his boots. He comes up to where I'm standing. Even in crisis mode, Dad is careful not to dirty his precious floors.

"Answer me right now," he demands in Arabic.

A loud moan from the family room disrupts the impending volcano eruption here in the foyer. Mom walks past all of us and gasps when she finds Theo on the couch, passed out drunk.

"Why is Theo sick on the couch?" she asks in Arabic, looking back at me like all of this is somehow my fault.

"He's drunk," I say.

Dad turns to John. "Did you let him get this way?"

"What?" I snap at my father. "You can't be serious."

"No, sir," John replies. "I was trying to get Theo home safely. He was at a party."

"If you were a good friend you wouldn't have let him get this drunk in the first place. You should have been looking after him," Dad says.

I watch as John's face goes white at the accusation.

"He wasn't even at the party with Theo. Theo did this all on his own," I say, my words coming out fast and furious.

"You know New Year's Eve is a hard day for him." Dad's tone is sharp, his glare sharper. "And his mother tells us he's still heartbroken over what you did." Dad eyes burn into mine. "Did you leave Theo for this boy?" he asks in Arabic, like he's connecting the pieces.

"George," Mom calls from the family room. "He's in bad shape. I'll call Petra and let her know he's spending the night."

"Why is this boy in our house?" Dad asks me again, this time in English.

"Oh my god! Do you even listen? John brought Theo here from the party. Theo clearly couldn't drive himself home."

"Why *here*?" Dad's eyes flick from John to me. "So he could have an excuse to see you? Make a fool of Theo, to turn you against him?

This is what a friend does?" he asks, now staring at John as if he's some sort of criminal.

"I should go," John says quietly.

"No. Don't go. You didn't do anything wrong." I take a step toward him before turning back to Dad. "I asked John to pick Theo up from the party. Andie told me Theo was drunk and needed to leave. John only came here because Theo practically forced him to."

"I don't understand your story."

"No." I shake my head. "You're just choosing not to listen. Because you don't want to believe Theo is anything but the perfect future son-in-law."

"Khalas. Tell him to go home," he says in Arabic, his words quieter but fierce. "We'll take care of Theo."

"I get the message." John nods. He turns and walks back to the foyer, puts his shoes on, and opens the door. He looks back at us. "Sorry for any trouble I've caused."

The door closes, and the rage that has been simmering inside me for months rises and spews out of my mouth. "You can't talk to people like that!" I tremble. "John didn't do anything wrong. He saved Theo from getting hurt or from hurting someone else. If you would just step outside your own prejudices, you'd see that John is the good guy here. John is the one deserving of your respect. John," I pause, swallowing before locking eyes with my father, "John is the one I love." The words pour out of me before I can stop them.

Dad's eyes narrow as his face stiffens. "You do not speak to me this way. That boy doesn't belong here. He is not for you. Love," he spits. "Give me a break. You sound like a stupid child."

"I hate you."

"Lennon," Mom cries from the couch, where she's propping up Theo's head.

I grab my coat and jam my feet into my runners before storming out the door, without a plan. My heart steadies at the sight of John's car idling in our driveway. I pound on the passenger window, simultaneously relieved and afraid. He reaches over and unlocks the door.

"Sorry," he says as I get inside. "I need the car to heat up before driving. Otherwise—"

"Take me with you. Please. I can't spend another second inside that house."

John shakes his head, his eyes red. "I can't. I can't," he says, his words breaking both our hearts.

"I don't want to go back there. I don't want to spend another New Year's Eve without you. I don't want to start another *day* without you. What's the point of all this? Knowing you're here, *you're right here*, and I can't be with you."

"I know."

"Why did you let me go?" I ask, my voice quiet. "Why didn't you fight harder for me?"

"If I fight, no one wins," John says, looking down at his lap.

I lean back in the seat, squeezing my eyes shut. "I feel like I'm in a cage. And it's a beautiful cage with vines and roses. Every day I wake up to the sun streaming in, and for a moment, just before I open my eyes, I forget that I'm locked inside this cage made of petals. Locked away from experiencing the world outside. Locked away from you."

Horns sound in the distance. I glance at the dashboard. Midnight. I turn to John, running my hand along his jaw and feeling the scruff against my fingertips. I close my eyes, breathing him in as he leans in closer, his warm breath on my lips. My eyes open to find his shut tight, a few tears running down, stopping at his mouth, right above his scar.

"You never told me how you got this," I say, wiping his tears away, my thumb lingering on his lip.

His eyes lift to mine. "It's not important."

"It left a permanent scar. Something significant must have happened," I say, almost regretting the words even as they come out. I push too hard. Sometimes my need to know things, to have an answer, outweighs the part of my brain that considers other people and their feelings.

"My dad," John says, his voice low, chin tipped to his chest. "A few months after he was injured at work, he got really drunk. He dropped his beer bottle on the kitchen floor and didn't even flinch. I saw he was barefoot and about to step on a piece of glass so I dove for the shard, but I guess his reflexes kicked into gear because he swiped it before I could and waved his hand at me, not realizing how close I was." He sucks in his lips as he takes in a deep breath. "Sliced my lip right open. He was too drunk to drive me to the hospital and my mom wasn't home, so he told me to go to the neighbor's and ask them for a ride. He made me lie. Said to tell them I fell off my skateboard. He said if they knew the truth, the police might come after him. Or separate us."

I watch as his breath stills to a slow, steady beat, and I take his hand in mine.

"When your dad said that thing about me not trying hard enough to keep Theo from drinking . . ." His voice cracks. "It was like a shard of glass slicing through me again, because the truth is, all I ever do is try."

I run a finger over his scar, staring into his eyes. My need to be close to him is stronger than any fear I have of being caught. "He's wrong. I would choose you over them. Every single one of them," I say, each word punctuated, in slow, steady beats.

"I know." He nods, pressing his forehead to mine. "But I can't let you. They love you, Lennon, and they're just trying to protect you."

"From what? Happiness? Love?"

"It scares them."

"No. *You* scare them. They know that you are the one person I would leave them all behind for."

His eyes shut tight again as he exhales a deep sigh. "You need them more right now than you need me," he says, looking at me. "There is so much out there waiting for you. So much life to live. They're your foundation. You need them to set you up for the life you deserve. I can't do that, Lennon." I shake my head, but he holds it steady in his hands, grounding me. "It kills me. I wish I could. I wish I could be like Theo. I wish your father looked at me the way he looks at him. I wish he could see that I love you as much as he loves you."

"Screw him," I say, the tears spilling out. "I don't care about him."

"Yes you do. He's your father. He's trying his best. They're all trying their best not to mess us up."

"Why? What do we owe them?"

"Eighteen years?" He says it with a forced laugh as he tucks hair behind my ears, gently. "Then you'll be free."

I laugh. "I'll never be free of him. Not until—"

"Don't say something you'll regret."

The exterior lights turn on, spilling into John's car. He pulls away from me like it's a learned behavior. I guess it is. I look up to see my father standing in the front door, arms crossed.

I place my hand on the door handle and turn back to John. "You cut your hair."

"Yeah." He runs a hand through his short locks as if he's just remembered.

"I fucking hate it."

He laughs. "I fucking hate it too."

I open the door and get out, closing it gently behind me. Taking in a deep breath, I walk toward my father. Our shoulders brush as I step inside. He takes my wrist, stopping me.

"You made the right decision." He says it so smugly. Like he's just so sure of himself. Like he knew I'd come back. I always come back.

"When are you going to open your eyes?" I ask, pulling away from his grasp. I can hear the lack of emotion in my voice, so flat it's bordering on pathological. Dad's expression shifts from self-assured to shocked. I half expected a slap across the face for my tone, but he just stares at me, eyes wide. "Theo is not who you think he is. He's got both you and Mom fooled. Is that really who you want me to end up with?" I ask, throwing an arm to the family room, where Theo remains passed out.

"People make mistakes when they're hurting," Dad replies.

"This isn't about him being drunk. It's about how he treated me when we were together. Like I was his to own." I exhale sharply as I search for my filter. I have to be careful not to say too much, but I also have to say something. I'm so tired of them thinking that Theo is some sort of hero. The ideal. He's not. He's human like the rest of us, flaws and all.

"He loved you very much."

"He did." I nod, breathing in and out, slowly. "But loving someone doesn't give a person the right to . . ." My heart races again as

I struggle to find the right words. This isn't a conversation I had planned out in my head. My points aren't rehearsed. My emotions are too jumbled up with my thoughts, with the message I want to get across. "You judge people on a really superficial level, Dad. Theo. John. Me. We're more than what you see. There's so much you don't know about us, about the situation."

"If you are finished with Theo, fine, be finished with him. But I will never accept this John character. He's not right for you."

"No." I shake my head. "He's not right for *you*." Dad and I stare at one another, the quiet floating between us like thick fog. "Theo can't be here when I wake up tomorrow morning."

I take off my shoes before running up the stairs, back to my beautiful cage, where I cry myself to sleep on a bed of withering petals.

Chapter Twenty-nine

JUNE 7

John and I haven't spoken since I walked out of his car on New Year's. That wasn't intentional. I did draft messages, but I couldn't send them. They were too angry. Self-centered. Downright depressing. There was nothing I could write or say that would change things.

John is right. He has always been right about us. It's just taken me longer to get here. But the thing is, I don't want to be here. I don't want to reach acceptance. Because if I do, it's like admitting that it's over, and I refuse to believe it is. No matter how much time stretches between us.

But time is going to pass regardless of how set in my ways I remain. So instead of stewing or forcing myself through the stages of grief, I just keep going. I go to school. Get good grades. Hang out with Andie every Friday night. Spend weekends in my room reading or writing, usually both. I've kept a low profile these last five months, mostly because I didn't want my trip to New York City to be ripped away from me. And now the trip is only two days away.

Dad made it abundantly clear that he would not accept John, and I couldn't let New York become another loss. Although I never officially apologized for yelling that I hated him on New Year's, Dad also never apologized for how he treated John. It's kind of like we broke even. *Broke* being the operative word. Because our relationship, once solid, is now full of cracks.

Every tiny crack creates a new branch, multiplying, leaving fissures where we had both, at one time, found comfort.

And now, the weight of his disapproval bears down on me, eliminating the need for words. I've never needed to hear the words. There is no master list of the rules. No "sit down and let's talk" moments. It all goes unspoken. Communicated with looks. Through overheard conversations in which my parents cast judgment on others. Folklore about other Arab girls who brought shame to their families. Or about the kids around us growing up "lacking religion or morals." The words never need to be spoken directly to us. We all know. Daughters know. First-generation daughters especially know. Born with a foot in both worlds, we toe a line that is at once invisible and delicate.

"Can I come in?" Georgie asks from behind my bedroom door. I check my phone. It's still morning. And Saturday.

"Yeah," I mumble, sitting up in bed. She opens the door and light from the hallway assaults my tired, crusty eyes. "Could you close that?" I say, shielding my face with my hand.

She huffs out a laugh and shuts the door before sitting on my bed. "God I miss having the freedom to sleep in."

"What're you doing here?" I ask, my voice still hoarse from sleep.

"Nice to see you too," she says with a grin. "I want to take you shopping. New York City on Monday! You must be pissing yourself with excitement!"

"Where's Paulie?" I ask, deflecting. I've been afraid to show how happy I am to be going to New York. It feels like anytime I let myself get excited about anything or anyone, it gets taken away.

"With Zach."

"She's lucky *her* dad isn't a raging lunatic," I say, bringing my knees closer to my chest.

Georgie offers me a small smile, the kind that tells me she knows exactly how I'm feeling and what I'm thinking. She squeezes herself next to me like she used to before the pregnancy and Paulie and the wedding and moving out.

"Explain something to me," I say. "How could they let me date Theo and not John? Why was one okay but not the other? They didn't even give John a chance. And it's not like they really knew Theo. The *real* Theo. Because if they had, they wouldn't have let him near me."

Georgie laughs. "To them, Theo is safe."

"Theo wasn't safe," I say. "Not in the ways that are important to them. One of the reasons we broke up was because he wanted more, physically, than I could give him. But Mom and Dad seemed to think Theo wouldn't even have tried to kiss me until we were married."

She shakes her head like I'm some dense child. "They just chose to bury their heads in the sand. They knew that you and Theo did stuff. But they just didn't want to know, you know?"

"No?"

"Notice how they never gave you any lectures about him? Did they ever once warn you not to let him kiss you or touch you?"

"No. But I just assumed—"

"Right. You just assumed that they expected you wouldn't do anything. And they let themselves believe that Theo respected them too much to try anything. They wanted you guys together so badly that it almost didn't even matter. If the words aren't spoken, it never has to be true."

"I don't understand."

Georgie sighs and turns to me. "They want you to end up with Theo because they know what a future with him would look like. Visits every Sunday. A boatload of kids. You at home, taking care of things, and Theo at work, taking care of you. It's the life Mom and Dad have."

"You don't think Mom and Dad want more from me? Why else would Dad be pushing me to take all these math classes?"

"Think of Theo as a cloud. Somewhere soft to land," Georgie says.

"Do you really think they knew Theo and I were physical?"

"I think they just didn't let their minds go there. Because it's easier that way. Denial is a small price to pay to keep you in the arms of someone they approve of. Someone who would ultimately keep you close to them."

"Huh."

"Lennon, you can't seriously be this surprised. They have a daughter who got pregnant at seventeen. They were trying to control your love life while they still saw you as malleable."

What if Georgie's right? What if my father truly believes he's some kind of mastermind? A puppet master who brought me and Theo together. And the only thing that stood in the way of my father getting exactly what he wanted was, and still is, John Brody.

"I think I get it," I say, nodding.

"You could do worse than Theo Petropolis." She cocks a grin and I glare at her. "He's smart, and our parents love him. Easy on the eyes, too. But," she says, forcing eye contact with me, "none of that matters if you don't love him. Because you can't force love. It's either there or it isn't."

"Is it there for you and Zach?"

Before I can take back my intrusive question, she offers me a strained smile that answers it more than words ever could.

"Paulie is worth it all," she says. "But I want more for you. Everyone does. We all really love you. Everyone who knows you loves you." She takes my hand in hers and squeezes it. I swallow, squeezing her hand back. "You have this quality about you."

"My autism?" I snort.

"No." She shakes her head. "It's this sort of magical, ethereal *it* factor. This aura that draws people in. They give you their wild intensity, their truest, most honest selves, because they know you'll accept them. But it's a lot of pressure on you. Everyone wanting or needing you to be something."

"Why?"

She shrugs. "I guess it's a different reason for each person."

"What's your reason?" I ask.

"Remember that night we were in the backyard, and you made me stare up at the moon with you?"

I nod.

"My whole life was falling apart, and you had no idea, and yet you knew exactly what I needed. Your heart and intelligence are mixed with an old soul. You love very deeply and make everyone around you feel like they're the most important person in your life. And once someone gets a taste of that, they can't bear to let it slip away. So we all hold on tight to you, sometimes draining your beautiful energy, and it's not fair."

“Careful,” I say, swallowing down the tightness in my throat. “I may actually start believing in myself.”

Georgie smiles. “You know you’re special. You’ve always known it. Now get your special ass up so we can buy you some cute outfits for NYC!”

☾

The next day, Andie comes over to help me pack, though it’s more like watching me pack for New York. I leave tomorrow morning. We’ll be there for five days, and we’re allowed only one piece of luggage, and it has to be small. So much for that shopping spree Georgie made me go on yesterday. She did convince me to buy a two-piece for the first time, though, in case the hotel has a pool. I buried that in the bottom of the bag. Inside a pair of socks.

In a moment of weakness, I asked Mrs. Morales last week who won the scholarship seat, hopeful that maybe my words on the Ferris wheel had inspired John to apply. But it wasn’t him.

Andie’s lying on my bed, telling me a story about how she and Reid hung out with Eddie yesterday. She tried to convince Eddie to get the band back together so she could live out her dream and be a lead singer. But Eddie told her those days are over, and it’s all because of me.

“He had the audacity to blame the band’s breakup on you. Can you believe it?”

“It’s kind of true, though, isn’t it?” I ask, stuffing T-shirts into my duffle bag.

“No, Lennon. It’s not true,” she says, sitting up. “They can’t blame their issues on you. Besides, they sucked anyway.”

“They were okay,” I say. “From the little I heard.”

"Eddie says Theo isn't over you."

"Really?" I huff out a laugh. "I think he's had three girlfriends since we broke up."

"Exactly. It's so obvious he's trying hard to pretend he's over it. Hey." A devilish smile curves her mouth. "Did you ever see it?"

"Andie!"

"Please, I am dying to know. It's huge, right? He gives off BDE," she says before bursting into laughter.

"You're going to hell," I say, laughing with her.

She holds her hands out, parallel and slowly pulls them apart. "Tell me when to stop."

"Stop!" I say, throwing a pillow at her.

Andie looks down at her hands and frowns. "Really?"

She laughs hysterically as I pinch her sides. Sliding my bag away, I sit next to her on my bed.

"I was really attracted to him, and we did everything but . . . you know. The thing is, I always felt bad after."

"Like sore?"

"No." I push her, and she laughs again. "Like guilty. Like I did something wrong. But not just after, sometimes even during. I couldn't let myself enjoy being with him."

Andie's face scrunches up. "That sounds more like your own personal hang-up."

"Right, and I'd agree, but the thing is, I didn't ever feel that way with John."

Andie nods. "It's probably because you love John."

"But Theo loved me, so it's not like I felt used or anything."

"I think," Andie says, smiling back at me, "the way you feel about John is the way Theo feels about you."

"Maybe."

"So . . . you didn't happen to save any of those racy pics he sent, did you?"

We laugh so hard my bag falls off the bed. There's a certain freedom in being able to talk to Andie about Theo. But there's this other part of me that thinks it's something I should keep private. I just don't like the idea of people seeing me that way. Not that I viewed Andie any differently when she told me about her first time. It was with Reid a few months ago. She said once they had sex, he became a lot more attached to her, but it didn't really change her feelings for him.

"I wish you were coming to New York," I say with a pout.

"Me too. Alas, I'm not an artist. Just a wannabe singer."

"Aren't we all?"

"Any cute guys going?" she asks as I get up to finish packing.

"Cute? Yes. Straight and cute? Not sure."

"Well," she says, lifting one butt cheek off my bed and digging into her pocket, "just in case . . . here." She holds out her hand. I squint to get a better look at the shiny foil packet laced in between her fingers. A condom.

"Andie. Put that away," I say, my eyes shifting to the closed bedroom door.

"Okay." She sits up and sticks her hand deep into my bag. "There. I put it away."

I glance at the door again and lean down, whispering, "I'm not going to have sex with some random guy from our school in New York."

"Why not? It's New York City. If I could lose my virginity in New York City, I would."

“Even if it would be an incredible story,” I say, not wanting to admit it is something I may have daydreamed about, “I can’t do that with someone I barely know.” I sigh, flopping down on my bed. “I should have had sex with Theo and gotten it over with.”

“It’s not too late.” She winks and positions her hands apart while mouthing “This big?” We break into laughter again, and for the first time in months, the air surrounding me is light. I’m on the verge of something huge. Monumental. I can feel it in my bones.

Chapter Thirty

JUNE 9

I am moments away from boarding the bus, and my parents are clinging to me as if this is the last time we'll ever see each other. So many lectures and reminders to call. To text with Georgie because she'll relay all messages and pictures to my parents (that's comforting). Mom keeps asking if I have everything I need, as if I won't be able to purchase any forgotten toiletries in New York City. Then there's Dad reminding me to keep my eyes and ears open. Insisting I don't wear my headphones while I'm walking around, and "For God's sake, listen to the teachers and stay close to them."

The bus doors open and Mrs. Morales and Mr. Chang, the Art department head, step outside the bus.

Finally.

"You have everything?" Mom asks again, her hands wrapped around my arms, grasping me in these final moments before I'm free. Free from their constant supervision, but never quite free of their voices in my head. No. They succeeded at acquiring a permanent spot there.

"Yes. And I'll text Georgie and call you once a day, even though it will be long-distance."

Dad waves off the extra charges to my phone bill. My life sometimes feels like a conflict of privilege. An abundance of riches on one end—custom-built home, a debit card that gets refilled weekly to pay for school lunches and anything else I might want to treat myself to, expensive family vacations—paired with a life of microaggressions, unconscious biases, and claustrophobic limitations on who I am and who I want to be on the other.

I hug my parents once more before giving Mr. Chang my bag to load in the undercarriage. My backpack, which I'm allowed to bring on the bus, is filled with necessities like chargers and snacks, my passport, cash, credit card, a notebook, and, of course, books.

Once inside, I pick a seat in the middle of the bus. That's always been my preference. The back is too noisy and tends to be reserved for a certain kind of student. One of those unspoken rules. The front is too close to the teachers. Plus, I often catch myself watching the road closely when the windshield is in plain sight. Anxiety. Another thing I've inherited from my father. As well as being a very real side effect of autism.

As the bus fills, I glance out the window to find my parents still hanging around, even though everyone else's parents have left. I wave at them through the slightly tinted window, urging them with my eyes to leave.

The bus engine finally turns, and I watch as my dad takes my mother's hand in his, guiding her to the parking lot. I wanted this so badly, but watching them walk away kind of makes my chest tighten.

I'm sure I'll get over it.

I pull out my earbuds and place my backpack on the empty seat to my left. Maybe it's rude but there's no one on this trip I care enough about to spend over ten hours sitting next to. There's a buzz on the bus already. People filming videos and taking pictures. I message Andie that I really wish she were coming. There's something so incredibly depressing when you're reminded, once again, how few friends you have.

The driver, a native New Yorker, closes the door, and I sink into my seat, shutting my eyes. The bus is finally in motion, but for only a few seconds before it makes a sudden stop. I remove one earbud and crank my head slightly to see what's going on, holding my breath. I wouldn't put it past either of my parents to come racing to the bus, declaring they've changed their minds.

The door opens and I overhear Mrs. Morales say, "I'm so glad you decided to come."

I sit up and my lips part as I lock eyes with John at the front of the bus. Swear to god, I don't think I've ever experienced this many feelings at once. Relief. Excitement. Anticipation. Happiness. Instinctively, I remove my backpack and nod to my seat as he walks down the aisle.

"Hey."

"Hey," I say as he slides into the space next to me.

"Do you mind?"

"Yes. I mean, no. I mean . . . I want you to sit here."

"Good." He grins, placing his backpack between his legs. "I want to sit here too."

I force myself to restrain my smile, offering him just a small one instead, as I also jam my backpack between my legs.

"I signed up for the scholarship," he says, reading my mind. "I didn't get it, at first, but then the person who did had to opt out because of a family emergency or something, so it defaulted to me."

"Wow."

"Yeah," he says, running his hands through his hair. It's grown out, and I ache at the thought of running my own fingers through it. "It was all last minute. Otherwise, I would have warned you."

"No." I shake my head. "It was a nice surprise."

"Yeah?" he asks, a smile tugging at his lips.

"Yeah."

We're both jolted back slightly as the driver turns out of our school parking lot. I take out my other earbud, put it into its case, and stuff that into the pocket of the seat in front of me.

"You can listen to your music. I don't mind."

"I will," I say, choosing my words and actions carefully. We haven't spoken in almost half a year. For all I know he could have completely moved on. Perhaps with someone else. *I really hope not.* "How have you been?" It's a wildly generic question for someone I've shared some of my most intimate moments and thoughts with, but when time stretches two people apart, you need to start somewhere safe. Somewhere broad.

He nods slowly, his eyes to the floor. It's as if he's really thinking about what he wants his response to be.

"I have to tell you something," he says, shifting slightly, his arm bumping mine. He leaves it pressed against my bare skin. He is warmth personified. And he smells like the late-afternoon air of Halloween—sweet and crisp. I've tried so hard to push him and the idea of us out of my mind, but in this moment, I can't for the life of me remember why I ever needed to. Not when being around him fills in all the cracks left behind by others.

"What is it?" I ask, staring deep into his eyes. I can't help but let the smile escape my lips.

John pulls back slightly, studying my face. "I didn't want to bring up—" He stops to clear his throat before leaning in. "We have a long drive ahead of us, and maybe it would be easier if we ignored the elephant on the bus, but I don't want to do that."

"Okay." I nod, my eyes glued to his.

"It's been really hard not talking to you. And I guess . . ." He stalls again, releasing a breath. "A lot has happened, and in a way, the break was good for me. It gave me time to figure out things that I really needed to figure out. Even though I saw glimpses of you at school, I missed you. I had to stop myself so many times from coming up to you at your locker or sending you a text."

"I missed you too."

There's a lot more I wish I could say to him, but that's about as honest as I can let myself be in this moment. Because while the space might have been healthy, even productive, it didn't change things. It doesn't change who my dad is. What he expects. It won't erase the false first impression my father has of John. So maybe we leave it at that. For now. He missed me. I missed him. And now we're on a bus together for the next ten hours.

"It's kind of funny," I say. "We met on a bus, and here we are again, on a bus."

His lips offer a soft, genuine smile. "I'm always infringing on your personal space, aren't I?"

"Maybe that first time. But not today. I'm really happy you're here," I admit.

He looks down, then back up at me, smiling. "So am I."

It would be so easy to slip into old patterns and take his hand in mine, but I fight the urge. Just because he's happy to be here with me doesn't mean he wants to try again.

John nods to my earbud case. "What were you listening to? Or are you not going to tell me, like when we first met?"

"I never did tell you what song it was, did I?" I ask, grinning.

"No. In fact, you said, and I quote, that you don't share secrets with people who cut in line."

"Cut any lines lately?"

"Nope." He smiles. "I earned my spot here today."

I open my music app, searching for the song from that first bus ride together, and pass my phone to him. There's something so intimate about giving someone else access to your phone. A palm-sized device that is basically your brain, downloaded.

"'Keep On Loving You,'" he reads. "REO Speedwagon?"

I shrug. "It's a classic. It's catchy, too. Probably why I absent-mindedly started singing out loud."

"So you admit it, then?" he says, his mouth pulling up into a cute smirk.

"I admit nothing."

"And what books did you bring?" he asks, as he passes my phone back to me. Our fingertips find each other like magnets, but only for a second. My mind flashes back to that New Year's Eve party at Theo's. Me and John on Theo's bed. John's fingers exploring parts of me no one else ever had. An electrical current pulses through me and I beg my heart to regulate itself.

"I thought you'd never ask." I reach into my bag to pull out the four books I carefully curated to join me on this trip. He immediately picks up the last one.

"*The Sun Also Rises*," he reads. "Ernest Hemingway. Fancy."

"Actually, not at all. It's super accessible. And it's one of my favorites."

"Why?" he asks.

"Read it and find out for yourself."

"Okay," he says, glancing at what's written on the back cover. "I will."

I select my book, a young adult romance, and we lean into our seats, reading, bumping elbows, sharing snacks and earbuds for most of the ride. There's so much I want to say to him but there's no rush. For the first time ever, I don't feel like there's a ticking clock hanging over our heads. We have five whole days and an entire city to explore.

A fresh start. A new beginning.

I can't wait.

Chapter Thirty-one

For so long, New York City was a daydream. This very real place I'd created my own version of in my mind, made up entirely of images and videos I'd seen online or on TV and in movies, or read about in books. Sometimes it felt so close, so real, that I could almost taste and smell it. I worried that maybe I'd built it up in my head to be better than it was. And in some ways, I had. It's crowded here. And loud. The city streets are littered with trash and cigarette butts. People don't smile as much as they do back home. And everyone is always in a rush.

When we pulled up to the hotel, I had a moment of underwhelm. This city I'd been dreaming about for half my life, a city I planned to spend my college years in, was, for lack of a better word, squishy.

But something funny happened when I stepped off the bus and breathed in the gasoline-scented air: I came alive. A switch turned on, lighting me up from within. It didn't mean I stopped noticing the less-picturesque parts of the city, the parts the movies and books leave out. Instead, it left me with a new appreciation for a place that demands you must work harder to see the beauty that lies within.

And I had a feeling that I'd get there. Give or take five days.

We arrived late afternoon, and we were told to meet in the lobby of the hotel at six to explore the city on foot and find somewhere to eat. Before we got off the bus, Mrs. Morales reminded us that the boys' rooms would be on one side of the hall, the girls' on the other, and that she and Mr. Chang would be taking turns staking out the hallway at night. A very binary way of thinking, but it's not surprising.

I'm sharing a room with two seniors who are best friends. I try to fight off multiple pangs of jealousy watching them unpack and exchange inside jokes. They're nice enough, Claire and Maya, but I don't expect to be welcomed into their relationship. And I don't blame them. Andie and I would be the exact same. Not that we'd purposely ignore the sad third girl in our room. We just probably wouldn't even notice her.

One benefit is that I get my own bed.

As Claire and Maya take turns freshening up in the bathroom, I text Andie.

Me: Guess what?

Andie: You're in NEW YORK!

Me: Well, yeah but also JOHN BRODY IS HERE!!!!

Andie: NO DUCKING WAY

Me: YES DUCKING WAY

Andie: !!!

Me: My thoughts exactly!!!

Andie: Have you spoken yet?

Me: We sat next to each other on the bus. Ten glorious hours of just being with him. I'm so screwed. How am I supposed to get over him when he's here?

Andie: I say you spend the next few days trying to figure out how to get UNDER him 😉 And give me ALL. THE. DETAILS.

Me: I will. I promise. Not that I'm confirming anything will happen.

Andie: LENNON YOU ARE IN NEW YORK CITY WITH JOHN THE LOVE OF YOUR LIFE DO YOU KNOW HOW AMAZING THAT IS? IT'S GIVING 90s ROMCOM!

Me: I don't want to get my hopes too high.

Andie: Please do! You deserve it!

Me: I'll keep an open mind.

Andie: IM SO EXCITED FOR YOU!

Me: ME TOO!!!!

"Lennon?"

I look up from my phone to see Claire standing at the foot of my bed.

"Yeah?"

"The bathroom's free if you want to use it. We're going to head down now," she says. Maya is already by the door, her hand on the lever. "You have a key card, right?"

I glance to the nightstand. "Yep. Right here," I say, picking it up.

"Okay. See you in a few."

As Maya and Claire leave the room, I take in a deep breath. I'm here. In New York City. And John's here too. I grab a pillow to cover my face and bury an excited squeal!

☾

That first night, John sidled up next to me and stayed there as we all walked along the streets of Manhattan, searching for somewhere to eat. He asked if I minded him hanging around, and I could tell that even though he was trying to pass it off as a joke, he wanted to make it clear that it was up to me.

I considered his question carefully. John's going to graduate in a few weeks. This could be the last time we'd have to spend together, uninterrupted. So I told him that I wanted him there. I can't think of a better way to spend my first time exploring New York City than with someone who, regardless of what happens, will always be important to me.

Lying in my hotel bed that night, I text back and forth with John. The space between us is closing, and it's happening much more easily and much faster than I ever could have imagined. A lot can happen in five months. A lot of things can change. People change. Feelings can definitely change. Possibly fade away.

I'm falling again. And I think he might be too.

The room is still dark when I wake up. Claire and Maya are fast asleep. I blink my eyes open before reaching for my phone: *5:00 a.m.*

And there's a message from John, time-stamped only a few minutes ago.

John: You awake?

I sit up, trying to wipe the sleep from my eyes before typing.

Me: Yeah. Just now. What's up?

John: I'm too revved up to sleep any longer. Want to check out the hotel pool? It opens at 5:30.

Me: What about Morales and Chang?

John: We'll be back in our rooms before they even wake up. Our bus isn't coming until 9:30.

I stare up at the ceiling, mulling over John's invitation. I did bring a bathing suit.

And even if we do get caught, which isn't likely this early in the day, no one has technically told us we can't use the pool in the morning.

Me: I'll meet you by the elevators in fifteen.

John: Sweet.

I stumble around the dark hotel room, searching through my bag for my two-piece. I pull it out of the sock I stuffed it into. Using my phone as a flashlight, I tiptoe into the bathroom.

After a morning pee, face wash, and toothbrushing, I change into the raspberry-colored bathing suit. Studying my reflection in the mirror, I run my hands over my bare stomach. This is too much, and yet not enough. I wrap a towel around my body and go back to the room, searching the bag for my one-piece. Back in the bathroom I change into it. This feels more like me. I throw my hair into a high pony and slap on some face cream, hoping it will de-puff my sleep-deprived face.

I put my T-shirt back on, along with the sweatpants I slept in and grab my things before slipping out of the room, undetected.

John's already at the elevators when I arrive. Messy, tousled hair. Wrinkled white T-shirt. Teal swimming trunks. And not one pillow crease on his perfect face.

"Morning," he says, his voice a little scratchy. "How did you sleep?" He presses the elevator button.

"Okay. Sort of. I had kind of a hard time settling."

"Same." He nods. "I really needed this trip, though."

The doors open and he gestures for me to go in first. He presses the top button and smiles sweetly. "Rooftop pool."

"Nice."

Our ride up is silent, but comfortable. I follow John out of the elevator and down the narrow hallway toward the heavy doors that exit onto the roof. There's a sign that reads "NO LIFEGUARD ON DUTY. USE AT OWN RISK." I stall.

"What's wrong?" he asks, looking back at me.

"If something bad happens, we could get into a lot of trouble," I say. "Or get our teachers in trouble."

"We'll be careful," he says, in a calm, reassuring voice. "I'm a strong swimmer. So are you."

"But accidents happen all the time. People slip and fall and bang their heads on the concrete. Or what if we're looking out over the view and the railing collapses and we fall forty stories to our death?"

"Lennon, if you don't want to do this, we can go back to our rooms. I just thought it would be a fun bucket list item. Watching the sun rise over Manhattan from a rooftop pool. I mean, when are we ever going to have a chance to do this again?"

His jaw clenches as he waits for my response. I run through all the possibilities in my mind. John's lips curl into a smile, and the possibilities shift from scary what-ifs to exciting what-ifs.

"Okay," I say. "You're right."

He grins as we walk through the doors, together. He wastes no time pulling off his T-shirt and jumping in. I pick up his shirt and towel and place them on a lounger. When he surfaces, the pink and orange light of dawn bounces off his glistening, wet shoulders. He's golden. John swims to where I'm standing, his arms bent over the coping. "The water feels amazing."

I slip off my slides and remove my clothes before tossing everything on the lounger next to John's. I carefully step into the pool, taking in the view.

John swims up to me and holds out his hand. As soon as we make contact, goosebumps surface. I try to swallow back the nerves bubbling over. Before I can come up with something smart to say, he pulls me into the pool with him, wrapping his arms around my body.

Just like that. Two puzzle pieces clicking into place.

Without overthinking it, I hold him close to me, pressing my chest against his.

"Good morning," he says again, smiling down at me.

"Morning," I reply, my heart thumping in my ears. "You know . . ." I pause to swallow as his gaze lingers. "Greetings like 'good morning' and 'good night' don't come naturally to me. I know people say it, just to say it. To be polite, or whatever. But I only like to say it if I mean it."

John's eyes twinkle as he sucks in his cheeks. "Did you mean it?"

I bite on my lip and nod. "Yeah."

He closes his eyes, his chest rising ever so slightly. When his eyes flick open, there's a longing that is both intoxicating and familiar. "I really want to kiss you," he says, in a low, raspy voice.

"I really want you to kiss me."

John presses his lips to mine, our bodies completely entangled. Hands moving freely, mouths mashed together, hearts pounding. We melt into one another, pulling apart only to look up at the brightening sky. My breath literally taken away.

John kisses my neck before placing gentle kisses on my shoulder. The kind of kisses that make me grateful I'm floating in a pool, knowing the weight of his love would have me falling to my knees.

"This feels like a dream," I say.

He shakes his head. "This is better than any dream. This is real. You. Me. New York City. No parents. No timelines. Just us." He slides a piece of hair away from my face, kissing my cheeks, then nose, then lips again.

"What do they say? Right person, wrong time?"

"Do you believe that?" he asks. Drops of water rest on his broad shoulders, making his lightly freckled skin shimmer. My legs remain wrapped around him as we drift into the deep end of the empty pool.

"Timing. Opportunities. Chance. I don't know. I think that, for whatever reason, obstacles have been placed in front of us, and it's up to you and me to decide if we're worth fighting for."

He stares at me with deep intensity. "I've never thought you weren't worth fighting for, Lennon."

"Then why did you pull away? Why do you *keep* pulling away?"

John releases me with the question and I move to the pool ladder, looping my arm through the handrail.

He treads water across from me, his arms moving in large, slow strokes. A small ripple of waves travels from where he is to me. "My dad relapsed after Christmas. I didn't want to tell you because I didn't want to burden you with my shit. And I was embarrassed."

"Embarrassed?"

"I felt like such an idiot for believing he had changed for good after rehab. I thought once he returned to work, I could focus on my own stuff. But then he relapsed and refused to go to rehab or AA meetings or even meet with his sponsor. I knew it meant things would get way worse before they'd get better, *if* they'd get better. I walked away from you, from us, because I had to. Not because I wanted to, and not because of anything you did."

John swims to the shallow end and I follow.

"You could have told me," I say, wrapping my arms around myself. "I would have been there for you."

"I know you would have," he says, moving closer. "But it wouldn't have been fair to either of us. To start something up again with all this heaviness." He looks to the sky then back at me. "I have a hard time asking for help. Probably because I see my father constantly needing it and I don't want to burden people the way he's . . ."

He trails off and looks down.

I lower my eyes to meet his. "It's okay to be angry at your father."

"But it's a disease. You wouldn't be angry at someone for having cancer."

"It's not selfish to want more for yourself," I say. "To hope for things to change."

"Not selfish. Stupid, maybe. Hope hurts."

"No." I shake my head. "You can't lose hope. Without it there's nothing left. I almost lost hope for us, and then I saw you walk onto the bus."

"You did look pretty happy to see me," he says with a beaming smile.

John moves in close. He holds my face, the tips of his fingers threaded in my hair.

"I was a mess the entire time you were with Theo," he says, lowering his hands. "The worst part was the fear I had that you'd eventually see for yourself what everyone else saw. That you and Theo make sense. More than you and I ever could."

"You can't make sense with someone you don't love," I say, keeping my eyes on his.

"He loved you."

"But I didn't love him back. I've only ever loved one person," I say, fully pressing myself to him. "I knew I loved you after our first kiss. Almost two years ago. Probably even before that."

John's eyes search mine. "I love you," he says, just above a whisper. I hold my breath, focused on the water drops that have collected in the small dips of his collarbones. "I've always loved you. I've never stopped loving you, and I will never stop loving you."

We kiss again, slowly. Gently. Savoring one another as daylight takes over the sky. Beneath the sun's bright rays, we can't hide how we feel for each other, and I don't want to. We've spent too much time in the shadows, pushing away the potential of us. Everything we were and everything we could have been.

But no more could-haves. No more should-haves. I don't want to live my life that way anymore.

We fall into the water, bodies still intertwined, and I close my eyes, basking in this moment.

This one perfect moment.

Chapter Thirty-two

JUNE 10

We spend the day exploring New York City, following the teachers' perfectly planned itinerary to a tee.

"We'll arrive at the Met in about twenty minutes," the bus driver says, his thick New York accent punchy and raw. "Fucking traffic."

Mrs. Morales clears her throat disapprovingly.

"What's been your favorite part of the day?" I ask John, shifting to face him in my seat.

His mouth tilts up and his eyes shine. "I think you know."

I grin. "Okay, not including this morning."

John's smile, our eyes, the way our bodies move in sync—it all shouts in a whisper that we're keeping a secret. He presses a finger to my lips and exaggerates a shushing sound. I grab his finger, twisting it, and he tickles my side with his other hand. I squeal, and both John and I cover my mouth with our hands before breaking into a laugh.

Maya and Claire raise their brows then whisper to one another. Good. Let them. I want everyone to know John and I are . . . ?

"Question," I say, leaning in slightly. "Are we . . . you know . . . together?"

John takes my hand, interlacing his fingers with mine. "Do you want to be?"

I shrug slightly, a bit taken aback by his indecisive answer. "I kind of feel like we are. At least in the sense that I don't want to be with anyone else."

He smiles sweetly.

"But . . ." I begin.

"But . . ." he repeats, waiting for me to continue.

"It wouldn't be easy." I don't have to go on. He knows what I mean.

"But it would be worth it," he says, squeezing my hand. "If that's what you want. And hey," he says, tipping his head to mine, "we don't need to decide anything right now. We've got four days left. Let's leave all that back home and enjoy this time while we can."

I nod before leaning my head on his shoulder. *While we can.* My eyes squeeze shut, and I take in a deep breath, exhaling slowly. No matter how hard I try to be in the moment, my mind betrays me by taking me places I don't want to go.

I want to be carefree. I want to explore the world and John and myself. But every time I let go of the girl I think I'm supposed to be, the girl my parents expect me to be, in search of the girl I really am, I hear my dad's voice.

I feel his presence.

I see his eyes.

And dread fills my beating heart, pumping out shame, guilt, and years of rage.

At the Metropolitan Museum of Art, we're on a guided tour given by a woman named Elizabeth, who has white hair and kind, blue eyes.

We follow Elizabeth through the museum, listening as she tells us about the different wings and the current exhibitions. She shares, in passing, that the Met houses five thousand years' worth of art.

Five *thousand* years of history.

Five thousand years of people using art to express themselves, their cultures, the times they lived in, through painting, sculptures, drawings, photographs, carvings.

Visiting the Met is like being able to travel through time, but only as a visitor on a quickly expiring visa and with limited sensory details. We can look, but we can't touch.

As much as I'm enjoying being here with John, learning the history behind certain pieces and the vastness and impressiveness of the collections, part of me thinks about what it would be like to explore it alone. I picture myself two years from now, riding the subway to the Met on a rainy Sunday with my headphones on and a stomach full of New York City bagels and coffee. I'd walk through every room, slowly, taking my time, examining the pieces that speak to me and skipping the ones that don't.

I've overheard a few conversations from my peers who say New York is overrated and they can't wait to get back home to their spacious bedrooms. They miss being able to hop in a car and the quiet of our suburban streets. But I disagree. I love it here, and I've barely scraped the surface of everything this city has to offer. I could probably live here for a decade and say the same thing.

I want to study in New York City more than I think I want anything else in life.

I don't only want it, I need it.

"Everything okay?" John whispers.

I nod, my eyes on Elizabeth. She's telling us now about how

the Modern and Contemporary Art collection has become a lot more diverse since 2012, including art from all over the world. I think about how art has probably always been ahead of the times, but it's really something we can see only with the benefit of hindsight.

"It's interesting, isn't it?" I ask.

"What's that?" John responds.

Elizabeth tells us we have fifteen minutes to explore before moving on to the next exhibit.

"How every piece in this wing is so vastly different from every other. Like, when we were viewing the Medieval collection, or the Greek and Roman art, it was all pretty much cohesive. But here," I say, as I start to walk toward a wall of paintings, each one distinctive, "it's like they don't belong. It's kind of like the drawer where you put all your mismatched socks."

John sidles up next to me. "Maybe that's it, though. The pieces are so unique, they actually make sense. You couldn't put this," he points to the vibrant painting in front of us, "in the Egyptian section. But next to this," he says, pointing to a more minimalist piece, "it works. Kind of like—"

"New York City."

He smiles, but it's a little strained, as if I've given him the wrong answer.

I face him, feeling my emotions bubble over in excitement. "It's the most cliché thing to say, but I love New York! Being here makes me want to be creative. To make something timeless."

"You do have a certain glow here that I haven't seen before."

I study John's face and how it falls slowly at my excitement. "You don't like it here?"

He swallows, looking around us before responding. "I love it. I do. I just might not love it as much as you do."

"You can't see yourself living here?" I ask, but it comes out more like a statement.

"Not really, no. Which is fine because I'd never be able to afford this city." His eyes fall to the ground and a familiar wall forms between us. Me on one side, with riches in abundance but no freedom; John on the other, with all the freedom but no riches.

"Maybe I'm a little jealous."

"Of what?" I ask, my chest tight.

"The way you light up when you talk about a future here."

"Lucky for you my father will never let me come here for school anyway."

"I hope you don't let that stop you," John says, his voice low. "If you want to live in New York City, or study here, or whatever it is you want, you shouldn't let him stop you. You shouldn't let anyone stop you. It's your life, Lennon."

A familiar line. One that's easy for people to say. They like to remind me that it's my life. *My one life*. But it's just not that simple.

"Right, but he controls my life. All parts of it. I don't have a penny to my name. I need my parents' financial support. If it weren't for the way I grew up, I probably would never even let myself think about studying in another country. In one of the most expensive cities." I bite down on my lip, in shame. "I never realized what a spoiled princess I sound like sometimes."

"No." John shakes his head, his tone stern but loving. "You're not. You're someone who has big dreams. But if we're being honest, sometimes I'm not sure how I fit into your life and the big dreams you have for it."

I release a long breath and walk toward another wall. John follows. We study the colorful piece in front of us for a few minutes.

"Doesn't it seem like, in the past, everyone belonged in the same book, maybe different chapters, but the same book?" I say. "Now it's like every person is their own country. Their own era. We live in such a progressive time, and we're learning to celebrate our differences, and because of that, things move at a faster pace than they did before. It's ever-changing. What we've been conditioned in the past to believe about love, it's been challenged. Everything is a spectrum of faith and sex and identity, the way our brains work. But then, at the root of it all, we're the same. It's kind of like . . ."

"Art." I turn at his response and find him smiling.

"It makes me feel so small." I twist my foot into the floor, staring down at my phone, waiting for a reply from my mom. Her midday check in. "All these people, out in the world doing great, amazing, important things. And I'm just me."

"You are amazing and important, but I also think you're scared, and sometimes you use your parents' restrictions as an excuse not to push yourself outside your comfort zone."

His sharp words hit a nerve, deep inside. Because they're true. I'm nothing more than a spoiled, Canadian-born girl whining about my diasporic identity and parents who have seen and done more in their lives than I ever will.

And that's exactly what my parents want. They want to keep me safe because they've seen how the world can really be. They've experienced enough to believe that what I have should satisfy me. Maybe it is satisfying for some people. But not me. I see maroon, burgundy, cherry, rose, ruby, and scarlet. They only see red. They see blood. They smell fear.

I don't say much else as we make our way quickly through the rest of the wings.

It's late now, almost five. We're all hungry and cranky and tired as Elizabeth leads us to the Egyptian wing. She says a scene from *When Harry Met Sally . . .* was filmed here, and my ears perk up. I look across the room to find John standing in front of the huge windows. Elizabeth nods to him and says that's exactly where the scene in question took place.

My heart thumps out of my chest as my gaze meets his. He doesn't smile. He barely even flinches as our eyes remain locked on each other. Multiple sunrays surround him like he's the centerpiece, the focal point, the priceless piece of art.

I want a big life.

I want an intense love.

I want to make my parents happy.

I want to make a difference in this world and leave my mark.

I want it all.

But even I'm not pie in the sky, lost in the stars, naive enough to believe it will ever happen. Not all at once anyway.

With change comes discomfort. Upsetting the status quo. Disappointment. Making others disappointed in you. But on the path to love, success, serenity, one must walk on shards of broken glass. That is, if they're willing to.

I walk to John, my determined feet stepping on the shiny museum floor tiles and my insides both twist and burn with the speed of light. I know what I want. Now I just need to figure out how to get it.

Chapter Thirty-three

Our bus returns us to the hotel after a long, fun day—minus the traffic. Thankfully, tonight we'll be traveling on foot to the Empire State Building. Mr. Chang spent most of the ride back from the museum preparing us for how cold and windy it will be at the top.

I flop down on my bed while Claire and Maya visit their friends next door. They invited me to join them, but I have to call my parents and fill them in on the day's activities.

Almost as soon as I end the call, my phone buzzes with a text.

John: Do you have any snacks?

Me: I've got pretzels and chocolate almonds.

John: Mind sharing?

Me: You have the pretzels. Chocolate is mine.

John: be right there

John shows up at my door less than two minutes later. I open it and pass him the half-eaten bag of pretzels.

He doesn't take it. Instead, he looks past my shoulder.

"Where are your roomies?" he asks.

"Next door."

A grin paints his adorable face.

"What?"

"No teachers in the hall," he says.

"So?"

He slips inside the room. "Just for a few minutes."

Before I can stop him, he closes the door behind us and he's cupping my face, his soft lips on top of mine. I drop the bag of pretzels and wrap my arms around him, allowing my body to fall into his as we kiss.

We pull apart, my heart racing. John's fingers in my hair. My hands grabbing fistfuls of his shirt.

"Do you know how hard it is to spend the entire day together and not be able to kiss you?" he says.

Before I can reply, or kiss him again, a slight beeping alerts us to the door. Claire and Maya walk in, stopping at the bag of pretzels on the floor.

Claire picks it up and her eyes land on John and me, our backs up against the wall. She straightens and passes the bag back to me. "I assume these are yours?"

"Yeah," I manage to squeak out as I take it. "John was hungry."

Maya smirks. "Was he, now?"

Claire glares at me. "We're not supposed to have boys in our room, Lennon."

"I know. I was just giving him pretzels."

"Is there a problem in here?" Mrs. Morales asks from the other side of the half-open door. My eyes widen to Claire's, begging her telepathically not to say anything.

She squints at me, then John. Her eyes move to the gap in the door. "No, Mrs. Morales. Maya and I were just coming back from Phoebe and Hazel's room."

"You know, I don't love room hopping. It's harder to keep track of everyone that way."

"I understand," Claire says. "It's just Lennon had a headache, so we thought we'd leave her alone to rest."

"Is she okay?" Mrs. Morales asks, her voice becoming clearer. Closer.

Claire grips the door handle as John and I exchange fleeting, nervous glances. "She's fine. Just lying in bed."

"Okay. We're leaving in twenty minutes. Remember to dress warmly. And if Lennon needs an Advil, tell her to stop by my room."

"Got it," Claire says. She nods and smiles as she closes the door. Then her smile thins into a sharp line as her gaze finds mine.

She shakes her head. "Lennon, do you know that I'm up for valedictorian?"

"No."

"Well I am, and I'm not about to lose that position because I covered for some eleventh-grader who can't control her hormones."

John steps up to Claire. "Don't talk to her like that."

Claire rolls her eyes at John before focusing back on me. "The two of you? Weird."

"Weren't you with Theo Petropolis?" Maya asks from the foot of her bed.

My body stiffens at the mention of Theo's name.

"If it happens again, I'm not covering for you," Claire warns.

I can tell John wants to say something to defend me, so I grab his wrist tightly. He exhales and we both nod, silently agreeing to let it go. Claire steps out of the way and I open the door to check if the hall is clear. When it is, I give John the okay and he slips out.

I close the door and turn around to find both Claire and Maya looking at me.

"What?" I ask.

"Nothing." Maya shrugs. "Just surprised you can repeatedly land such hot guys."

"Thanks," I say dryly, walking over to my duffle bag by the window.

"John Brody is the kind of guy you mess around with, but Theo is the kind of guy you marry," Maya goes on. I'm not exactly sure who she's saying this to, so I ignore her. "Who's the better lay?"

"Maya." Claire steps in. "Enough."

I grab my outfit for tonight and walk past them both on my way to the bathroom. I don't know why, but I spend the entirety of my five-minute shower crying. I need to do better. I need to be better. I can't let myself lose control. I can't let myself get sloppy. *Smarten up.*

It's our last day in New York City, and I feel as though I'm carrying a bag of heavy emotions: euphoria, dread, anticipation, anxiety, liberation . . . each feeling a juxtaposition of the last.

Yesterday was spent at the Museum of the Moving Image, Radio City Music Hall, and Rockefeller Center, where we had a guided and mostly restricted tour of the TV studios.

This morning, we visited the 9/11 Memorial & Museum, and then we took a ferry to the Statue of Liberty. It rained the entire time.

We're all looking a little worse for wear after an activity-packed few days.

I woke up at five again this morning, thoughts racing through my mind. Mostly contemplating one last rooftop swim watching the sunrise with John. Time is running out. But after Claire's reaction to finding John in our room, I figured we'd be wise to play it safe. Trying to recreate a perfect moment is asking for disappointment anyway.

The good news is we have the entire afternoon free. The only rule is that we travel with a partner or group. And I know exactly what I want to do.

"A picnic in Central Park," I say to John on our ferry ride back from the Statue of Liberty. "And," I say, making sure I have his full attention as I get the words out, "a visit to Strawberry Fields."

"I love it," he replies. "But I was thinking maybe you'd want to visit Columbia? Just to see it in person."

"I thought about that, but there isn't enough time to do both. And I really want to go to Central Park. Besides, Columbia is probably just a bunch of buildings we wouldn't be allowed in anyway."

John looks up at the gray-blue sky. "And what do we do if it rains again?"

I hold out my arms. "This is New York. We could visit bookstores. Pretend we're rich and walk up and down Fifth Avenue. Eat a decadent lunch, or better yet, find a dive or a deli to eat at. Maybe take in a matinee of some Broadway show. Anything. That's the beauty of being here. There are more options than there is time."

John holds back a laugh. "Breathe, Lennon. You're young. You have lots of time."

Mr. Chang and Mrs. Morales repeat their instructions to us once we get off the ferry. Gathered by the pier, they remind us that we are to meet in the hotel lobby at 5:00 p.m. The plan is for one last dinner together before we depart tomorrow morning.

"So there's just one problem," John says to me as the group begins to thin out. "Strawberry Fields is at 72nd Street and we're, well, we haven't even hit the numbered streets. I'm thinking if we want to be able to have a picnic without rushing, we'll have to take the subway."

"Do you know *how* to take the subway?" I ask.

"No. But we'll figure it out. Together." He clasps my hand tightly and we begin to walk. The gray clouds are drifting away, and I wish my doubts could disappear with them.

☾

We make it to the subway station at Wall Street and John asks the employee in the booth for directions. We pay our fare and walk through the turnstile to wait for the subway to arrive. My parents would have a heart attack if they knew I was taking the subway here—and with John, of all people. I haven't texted since this morning, and if they try to reach me while we're underground they might not get through.

"Hey," John says, tilting his head to mine. "Where are you?"

"Just thinking about my parents."

"Don't." He smiles. "You'll see them tomorrow. Try to stay in the moment. You're the one who wants to live here one day. This could be part of your daily commute."

A soft laugh escapes me. "Who am I kidding? My parents are never going to let me come here. And if by some miracle they actually did, how would I figure everything out? I won't have you or anyone else to depend on."

He lowers his gaze to meet mine. "When you want something badly enough, you make it happen."

The lights of the subway glow in our direction, along with a warm gust of wind. When the train arrives and we squeeze inside, we find two empty seats. John wraps his arm around me and I lean into him, closing my eyes and resting my head on his shoulder. I wish I had as much faith in myself as he seems to have in me.

This day, which started out with so much hope, excitement, and anticipation, has taken a somber turn, and I'm not sure why.

"That's the building," I say, stopping dead in my tracks on the sidewalk. A few others have stopped to look too. "The Dakota."

Realization dawns on John's face and we stand quietly, observing the sandstone building in front of us where John Lennon was shot. A doorman eyes us warily, and John offers him a polite smile while mouthing "We should go" to me.

As we cross the street toward Central Park, a familiar song reaches us. We exchange looks and smile. The sun has come out now, and we enter the park to find tourists standing around the Imagine mosaic, taking turns posing for photos. A busker, who must be in his sixties, sits on a bench with his guitar, music stand, and instrument case open to collect donations.

We walk past the crowd toward the park.

"Here?" John asks. He's chosen a grassy area surrounded by trees, with a view of skyscrapers.

"Perfect."

I press my hand on the grass to make sure it's dry before we sit. We take out the snacks we bought from the bodega we found after getting off the subway. I pass John a bottle of pop, then I take a chicken sandwich from its plastic container and offer him half. He opens the bag of popcorn and props it between us.

"This is the quietest New York has been since we got here," he says.

"It's nice. Kind of like we found our own private island within an island."

He smiles, his eyes flitting up and around. "So? Is it everything you imagined?"

"And more."

His gaze shifts down to his sandwich, but he doesn't take a bite.

"What's wrong?"

"We're so different," he says, shaking his head. "In all these big, fundamental ways. But I still can't help wanting to be part of your world." He picks at his sandwich now, his mouth turned down in a frown. "Seeing you here, how you've come alive in this city, makes me think that maybe the differences between us are just too big."

"Too big to what?" I ask, afraid to hear his answer.

"I got into Shay College," he says instead of answering my question. "The carpentry program. I've accepted."

I sit up straighter and smile. "That's amazing. Congratulations."

"Thanks. It's three years, mostly apprenticeships, but I'm excited about it. I didn't realize how much I wanted it until I got my acceptance letter."

"I'm excited for you. I hope it's everything you want."

"Not everything." He clears his throat. "It feels so small compared to your dreams. I'm not saying this for sympathy or because I feel bad about myself, it's just, as much as I've loved being here with you in New York, I can't help but wonder if I'm enough for you."

I put my food down and move closer to John. "You are. You're more than enough."

"In this moment, maybe. But what about once we get home? In a few months I'll be in college. And next year you're going to be here, meeting amazing people and doing incredible things, and I'll just be some guy you knew in high school."

I shake my head at his words. "No. I've met amazing people and, to be honest, they're more amazing to themselves than they are to me. You have captivated me since the moment we met. We're not the same people we were three years ago. I've changed and so have you. But one thing hasn't. The way I feel about you."

He looks up at me, his eyes glossy. I don't think he believes me. But how could he not?

"You have such a romanticized view of life," he says, dipping his chin. "I wish I could see the world the way you do."

Suddenly inspired by an idea, I grab my bag, searching through it, almost desperate, and finally pull out my journal. I nod to myself before passing it to John, who hesitates a beat before accepting it.

"It's where I write all my thoughts. Song lyrics. Bad poetry. Short stories. You're the first person I've ever let *touch* this journal." I pause and take a breath. "Take a look," I say, as his eyes meet mine. "You might notice that a lot of what I've written over the last almost three years has been about you. You are the boy in the pages of my story."

John delicately thumbs the pages, his eyes tracing the words slowly. Reading. Sometimes stopping to look up at me and shake his head before he reads more. I watch as his Adam's apple moves around a swallow. His brown hair falls in front of his face as he turns the pages. I bite on my lip in an attempt to steady my racing heart as I hang on to every single movement he makes, trying to dissect the meaning.

When he comes to the last entry, his eyes lift off the journal to meet mine again. His lips are parted slightly as he studies me.

"It's too much."

"He won't get it."

"You can't trust your heart with him."

"You wrote these words . . . you wrote them about me?" he asks, his voice low but clear.

I nod and then force down my own swallow. "A lot of them."

"All this time, you've always known how you've felt. You've never wavered." He shakes his head again, fingers gripping my journal, now closed. "I don't deserve this."

"That's not true," I say, inching closer. "You've had a lot to deal with. You *have* a lot to deal with. And I'm a person who sits with my feelings. So much that it becomes too much, and I need an outlet for them. That's why I write."

"Thank you for sharing this with me." He stares at the journal as if he's just received the best present on Christmas morning. "You're a beautiful writer. And so talented. Honestly, I'm impressed and honored," he says as a blush turns his cheeks pink. He passes it back to me and releases a deep breath. "Can I share something with you?"

"Always," I respond.

John offers me a small smile before taking a sip of his drink. He wipes his mouth with the back of his hand as he straightens. "I think about my future a lot, especially when things are hard with my dad. It helps me, I think, picturing it. I see myself living in a house bigger than mine, but smaller than yours. And inside, all the trim work, anything to do with wood, will be because of me and my hands. I picture a workshop behind the house where I work on my clients' projects. Music is playing on overhead speakers, and the sun is shining through the windows when the person I love walks in on a Saturday, bringing me lunch because, if she doesn't, I'll forget to eat."

He has the sweetest look in his eyes as he tells me about this dream he has for himself. As I listen to him describe this random future Saturday and this nameless person, a pit grows in my stomach at the possibility of another girl in my place. Building a life with the boy I love. *The boy I loved first*, I want to scream.

"She puts the sandwich down on a dusty table full of wood shavings, teasing me about the mess, and I pull her to me for a dance."

John leans in, his eyes locked on mine.

"It's you I picture in this fantasy," he says, his face so close to mine I don't know if it's his breath making my hair move in front of my face or the warm breeze blowing between us. "The thing is," he begins, as he pulls away slightly, "we're back home. We're not in New York. We're not living in a fancy city condo. We have a house with a yard and maybe even a pool." He lets out a soft laugh as our fingers twine. "But I know that this is my dream, and it doesn't have to be yours."

I squeeze his hand. "It's a nice dream," I say, because it is. But I get it. I get why he has doubts, why he's afraid. "I know you have this idea of who I am and who I'm meant to be," I tell him, "but the truth is, whenever it's just the two of us, I never need anything more."

He lifts his head slightly, his eyes searching mine, as if he wants to believe me but can't fully trust himself, me, the universe. If only I could read his mind to find the exact right words to show how much I love him.

"We have this moment," I tell him. "It's ours. And the future. That will also be ours. The in-between . . . we'll figure that out."

John sits up straighter. "I don't want you to settle."

"Believe me," I say, burying a strained laugh, "choosing you would be the opposite of settling." It would be an earthquake.

John reaches out and weaves his fingers through my hair, pulling me toward him.

We kiss, and everything that's been weighing me down, and all the things yet to come, slip away. Because this feeling, right now . . . no one can take that away from us.

John stands. "There's something I want to do before we head back."

I get to my feet, and together we gather up and toss our trash. We follow the path back to Strawberry Fields, where there are only a few people now, hanging around the Imagine mosaic.

The busker is still there, playing the Beatles' greatest hits. We listen as he wraps up "Hey Jude"—one of Dad's favorites. John walks to the man and whispers something to him. He pulls out a ten-dollar bill and places it inside his guitar case. The man nods as John leads me to the mosaic. My heart expands as I hear the first few notes of "And I Love Her."

"Dance?" John asks, his expression so earnest, so sincere.

We dance across the black-and-white memorial, swaying slowly as the busker sings behind us.

John's breath tickles my neck as strands of his hair fall onto my cheek. I can feel his heart pounding against my chest, begging my own to beat in sync with his.

I wrap my arms around his neck, setting my cheek on his shoulder. He holds me close, and we barely move, still in this moment. Tears prick at my eyes. All the what-ifs race through my mind. How could I turn this away? This feeling. For what? To appease a father who will never be satisfied no matter how many times I try to win his approval?

If I choose John, my number one concern is *What will Dad do?* Will he disown me? I'm their second chance to get things right. But making things right for them only chips away at me and the person I'm meant to be. One day I might be someone they can parade around proudly, but I'll just be an empty shell. Being here with John in New York has built me back up, piece by piece, to the version of myself I want to be.

A version I'm not sure my parents will accept. Or love.

Chapter Thirty-four

JUNE 12

After leaving Central Park, John and I take the subway back to Midtown.

"Looks like rain again. Want to hang out in a bookstore?" he asks, his fingers locked with mine as we walk.

"My feet really hurt," I say with a pout.

"We could grab some ice cream and chill. There's that place next to our hotel."

I nod. "That sounds good."

"You're going to need some pretty serious footwear if you move here. I don't think I've ever walked this much in my life."

"Right? I'm not sure I'm built for this after all," I say with a laugh.

We walk for a bit, the warmth of the sun disappearing behind dark clouds. A drop of rain falls on the tip of my nose. Then another. And before John and I can even process what's happening, it's pouring down with the force of a million drumbeats while pedestrians dart in every direction around us.

"I think the hotel is around the corner," I say.

"Run?"

"Run," I echo.

Still holding hands, John and I maneuver around all the angry, wet New Yorkers seeking refuge from the monsoon-like rain pounding down on us. The hotel is less than a block away, but by the time we walk through the lobby doors we're soaked from head to toe.

The doorman eyes both of us and the small puddle our drenched clothes are leaving on the shiny floor of the lobby.

"We're staying here," I say to the doorman. "With our school."

"Then I'd advise you return to your rooms and change out of your wet clothing."

I fight an eyeroll, turning to John.

"You'd think this was a Five Seasons." John laughs.

"Four Seasons," I say, correcting him with a smile.

"Right."

I pull my phone from my back pocket. "It's three-thirty. Another hour and a half before we're supposed to meet up with everyone."

John lifts his shoulders. "It will give us a chance to shower and rest our feet."

"In separate quarters," I say, raising my eyebrows at him.

"Of course," he replies, his tone playful.

We walk toward the elevator bank and wait, my heart hammering in my chest, and we're silent for most of the ride up to the tenth floor.

"We really smell," I say.

"We really do."

The doors open and we head down the hall toward my room. We stall in front of my door, the change of scene making the silence feel more intense.

"Today was perfect," I say, swallowing down butterflies.

"It was more than perfect." John weaves his hand through my hair, and his thumb strokes the skin behind my ear. He tips his head down and kisses me softly. When we pull apart, John nods repeatedly. "Do you have, um . . . ?" He stalls, his eyes moving around the empty hallway. "Shampoo? I'm out, and the hotel for some reason never restocks it."

"Sure. Wait here," I say as I use my key card at the door.

Once inside our room, I place my backpack on the floor. The beds haven't been made. Claire will probably complain, but then again, she complains about everything. I grab the free hotel shampoo that none of us have used, catching my reflection in the bathroom mirror. I look like a wet dog. But a happy wet dog.

"Here," I say, opening the door and passing him the shampoo. "Only the good stuff for you," I tease.

"Thanks. I guess I'll see you in a bit."

I nod and smile. He nods and smiles back. I love him so much.

I close the door and lean my back against it, trying to regulate my heart. But it's not just my heart. My entire body is tingling. I bring my hand to my chest and close my eyes, picturing me and John dancing together in Central Park. Sitting in the sun, talking. Holding hands while walking, ignoring everyone around us.

Today was a fairy tale.

A knock at the door disrupts my reverie. I peek through the peephole to see John. I don't think he's moved a muscle. I bring my hand to the door lever and pause. My gut is screaming at me to open it. My head is telling me not to.

I push down on the lever, pulling the door open a crack.

"Can I come in?" he asks, his voice tinged with raw vulnerability. There are still drops of rain on his face and his hair is soaked.

He wants me to tell him yes. I want to tell him yes. But we both know if he steps inside this room, the few remaining barriers we have left in our relationship will be gone.

I can't get the words out so instead I just step back, opening the door wider. He bites down on his lip, fighting a smile. I know him well enough now to know what it means when his jaw clenches. When his eyes turn into little slits from laughter. When the rosy glow of his cheeks flushes all the way to the tips of his ears.

He closes the door behind him gently as I walk backward, farther into the room. The outline of his chest through his wet T-shirt makes my pulse quicken.

"I haven't had a chance to change yet," I manage to say as he stands by the door. There's about six feet between us. The final barrier.

"I can help," he says. It's a mix of flirtatious and sweet.

"I'm nervous."

"So am I."

"John Brody doesn't get nervous."

"Only around you." He takes a step closer, and the heavy rain hitting the window mimics my racing heart. "I know I'm not always the best with words. When I'm with you, I can't always get what's in here," he points to his head, "out the way I feel it."

All John ever has to do is look at me a certain way to show me how he feels. Meanwhile, I've filled an entire journal trying to make sense of my feelings for him. But right here, right now, I'm falling, and he's falling, and this time, we'll finally land in the same place.

"Can I come closer?" he asks.

"Yes." I swallow and stand still at the foot of the bed, waiting for him to make the longest trek ever from the door to me.

We're standing face-to-face now. The smell of New York City rain lingers, and suddenly it's the most beautiful scent that's ever tickled my nose. John brings a hand to my face and moves a wet strand of hair away.

"Confession," he says, tilting his head down to mine. "I sat next to you on the bus that day because I thought you were cute."

"You were using me to get away from Avery," I reply, dryly.

"If I was just looking to get away from her, I would have taken an empty seat near the front." He smiles. And my own cheeks ache, I'm grinning so hard at the memory. My entire life changed in an instant. When I opened my eyes and saw his blue eyes staring back at me, that was it. I was a goner.

It still takes my breath away.

He leans in to kiss me, and I pull back slightly. "John," I say, looking for a way out. Not because I want one, but because I'm testing myself to see if this is something all of me wants or just my body.

"Yeah?" he says, his head slightly cocked to the side.

"You've done this before. Does it . . ." I look down and clear my throat. "Does it change things?"

He laughs a bit nervously. "It didn't change things very much for me and Avery, but we were never in love."

"Has there been anyone else?" I ask, not sure if I want to know the answer.

He nods. "Do you want to know?"

"No." I shake my head. "Well, just one thing. Did you ever love any of them?"

"You're the only girl I've ever loved." His answer is so simple. Almost a little too simple.

Sex isn't simple. Not the way I've been brought up to see it, anyway. It's supposed to complicate things. It's meant to make things more serious. It's something you do because it's expected of you, not just because you want to do it. But only at the right time. Then again, who's to say when the right time is? According to my parents, the right time is when there's a marriage certificate.

"Are you afraid it will change things?" he asks.

I blow the air out of my mouth, then nod. "Yeah. But I also feel extremely ready."

John takes another step, and I swallow again. This is it. And it's with John Brody, someone I love so much it's bordering on obsession. He's not some random guy. This is not an impulsive decision. It's the way it should be. The way I want it to be.

I lift my eyes to find him staring back at me. How did I get so lucky?

John places a hand on my lower back, pulling me in. We kiss, and it's perfect. Like our first kiss. It's also our last kiss before . . .

We continue to kiss, standing at the foot of the bed. I think he's waiting for me to take the lead. He wants to be sure I'm ready. I am. It's always been him I wanted to share this with. I reach for the hem of his wet T-shirt and move it up. We pull apart long enough for him to get the shirt up over his head and toss it to the floor. I run a hand over his bare chest, my fingers trembling over his damp skin and firm body.

I pull off my own wet shirt. And then we kiss again, awkwardly kicking our shoes off while our mouths stay pressed together. The warmth of his skin against mine ignites every single pulse point in my body. I've fantasized about this a lot. The setting changes every time. The circumstances of how we end up alone also changes. But this isn't a fantasy. I can't orchestrate perfect moments in real life, but it turns out this is better than any made-up scenario my brain could have come up with.

His hands move to my waist, his fingers tiptoeing carefully to the button of my jeans, and soon they're unbuttoned and he's sliding them off. He's in shorts with a drawstring, so his come off with ease. Everything is always so much easier for guys.

Down to just our underwear, John's eyes shift to the bed. I sit on the edge and slide myself toward the pillow. He crawls on top of me, carefully. His body descends on mine and our kisses grow in intensity. All of him is pressed against all of me, and I can no longer fight the deep yearning. He's kissing my shoulders, his wet hair tickling my arm. John moves the straps of my bra down and I arch my back so he can reach behind and unclasp it. Our bodies crush into one another. He thrusts himself against me, and I rock with him in response as we kiss, slow and deep.

"I'm ready," I say, almost breathless as his mouth grazes mine.

"Are you sure?" he asks. I nod, probably a little too enthusiastically. "Shit." He pulls himself up slightly. "I don't have anything. Devon might. I can check our room."

"There's one in my bag," I say, pointing to my duffle by the window. "Don't ask," I add with a shaky laugh. "But it's in there, if you search for it."

He grins widely as he gets up and rummages through my things. His eyebrows rise ever so slightly once he's found it. He returns to where he was moments earlier, his nearly naked body on top of my nearly naked body. We kiss again, and then he pulls away to open the condom. This is all so real. I stare up at the water-stained ceiling and wait until my view of the ceiling is replaced with John's face. Those freckles. His blue eyes. The curve of his lips.

I slide off my underwear, and it feels like the most natural thing and, also, an out-of-body experience. John swallows as he takes in the sight of me.

"You're so perfect."

We kiss and I wrap my arms tightly around him. He moves his mouth off mine, meeting my eyes. "This might hurt a bit," he warns.

"I know."

"I'll go slow."

"Okay."

"We don't have to do this if you don't want to."

"I want to," I say, staring right back at him. "I've never been more sure of anything in my life."

"I love you," he says, melting away my remaining nerves.

"I love you back."

And then he's there, pressing against me. He keeps checking to make sure I'm okay every time he pushes a little harder, and I am. It hurts. And it's not that comfortable. But Andie warned me the first few times are like that.

"Can you just not move for a second?" I ask, trying to catch my breath. My muscles have tensed, and I know it's going to hurt more if I don't relax. He sweeps hair off my forehead before placing a kiss on my temple. I exhale. "Okay," I say, giving him permission to keep going.

He nods and I close my eyes. I pay attention to his breathing, like it's a song I can't seem to get enough of. It grows faster and I know enough to know that means he's close. I don't think I am, but it doesn't matter, because it's still perfect.

Eventually, John's tense shoulders relax as he lowers his weight onto me. I want to tell him to pull out because it hurts, but also, I don't want this moment to end. Because that's all it is at the end of the day. A moment. And it's already over.

My eyes sting and I try hard to fight back the tears, but they pool out of me.

John moves off me slowly. "Hey. You okay?"

"Yeah, just emotions. Good emotions," I assure him.

John brings the blanket to cover me, wiping my tears away. He kisses me sweetly before shaking his head, lying next to me.

"I can't believe we did that," he says taking my hand in his.

"Yeah. It's pretty wild."

We laugh, awkwardly, both of us staring at the ceiling.

"I should go shower," he says, like he doesn't want to leave me but knows he has to.

"Okay."

He rises and scrambles to pick up his wet clothes, throwing them over his body. I sit, hiking the blanket to cover myself.

Once John is dressed, he seats himself next to me, bringing my hand to his mouth and pressing a kiss against it. "I don't want to let go," he says.

I feel a blush creep up my cheeks and smile. "It's just for a little while."

"I'm so in love with you," he says, voice low, almost shaky. It's not the first time he's told me he loves me, but for some reason, this time his words steal my breath. John stands, looking down at me so sweetly. "I'll meet you in the lobby with everyone else."

"Okay," I repeat. I can fill a journal with all the ways I love this boy, but when he's in front of me, every single one of my senses battles for first place and the words never come out right. Sometimes they don't come out at all.

I wait for the door to click shut before getting up. I need a shower, but I also need to write about this before I forget any of the details. This is something I'm going to look back on, and I want to remember every single second of it. After the fastest shower of my life, I grab my notebook and sit at the hotel desk, my wet, tangled hair soaking my clean T-shirt. Pen in hand, I write all about our day. The park. The dance. Our first time. Every last detail. Reliving it sends tingles throughout my entire body.

I lean back and read over my entry, adding one last thought.

> *I feel like the luckiest girl in the world. Not everyone gets to find that person. The one who sets their heart on fire. Most people settle for something quieter, something that makes sense. We convince ourselves the fire will go out eventually, and instead we focus on how many ways the flames will hurt.*

Chapter Thirty-five

JUNE 13

"Is it just me or are people watching us?" I ask John on the bus ride home. We're not even doing anything obvious in terms of PDA. He's reading his book. I'm listening to music.

He puts his book down and sticks his head out into the aisle. "They are most definitely watching us."

Maybe we weren't so good at hiding our feelings over dinner last night. John was worse than me. In fact, he was downright giddy, and his face stayed flushed the whole night. And maybe we texted back and forth until 2:00 a.m., but it's not as if any of them would know that. When people's noses aren't stuck in a phone, they're too busy worrying about themselves and how others perceive them to realize I even exist.

Except, I seem to exist a lot more whenever John's around.

A shadow looms over our seats. I pause my music again, removing an earbud. Claire stands in the aisle, peering down at us, a shiny foil package flickering between her fingers. It's like that time Dad and I got into a car accident. A split second before impact we saw the car approaching ours but there was nothing we could do except brace for impact.

“You left this in the room. Thought you might want it back as a keepsake.” Her laugh echoes, silencing all other sounds around me, as the condom wrapper falls onto John’s lap.

I stand, pushing past John, and step into the aisle, causing Claire to trip backward in surprise.

“You are such a bitch!” The words fly out of my mouth before I can stop them.

“Chill the fuck down,” Claire says, the smile gone from her face.

“This is what you wanted, isn’t it? For me to react. Why else would you hold onto that and wait until this moment, in front of everyone, to slut-shame me?”

“It was a joke,” she says, all levity gone from her voice.

“I’m not stupid. I heard all the things you whispered to Maya when you thought I wasn’t paying attention. You’ve been judging me this entire trip.”

“You’re paranoid,” she retorts.

John is behind me, whispering something in my ear, but I’m too riled up to hear him. His arms wrap around my body, anchoring me in place, an attempt at defusing an already detonated bomb.

“I hate you.” The words spew out of my mouth as my fists engage.

When it looks like Claire is about to say something back, John steps in front of me, shaking his head at her. There’s a look in his eyes I’ve never seen before, and it’s a more powerful weapon than any of the words I could come up with. It manages to silence her.

She slinks back to her seat, and my focus shifts to the whispers and stares. I bury my face in John’s shoulder but I can still feel all eyes on us. I squeeze mine shut, trying, hoping, imagining myself somewhere else. Anywhere but here. It’s only a matter of time now.

Before I hear her say my name. Before another outside force takes John away from me again.

I fall into my seat, making myself as small as possible. John turns to me, his body acting like a shield. Soon, another body hovers. The heat of her breath wedges its way into the spot between my face and John's body.

"Lennon, you need to come with me."

I shake my head. *No!* I want to scream. *No, I will not go with you!*

"I'll come too," John says.

"We'll deal with you later, Mr. Brody. Right now, I need to speak to Lennon alone," Mrs. Morales says.

I shake my head again.

"It's okay." John's voice is gentle, soothing. "I'll be right here." His lips graze my ear as he whispers, "You didn't do anything wrong. We didn't do anything wrong."

I peel myself off John and follow Mrs. Morales to the front of the bus. She asks the students in the row behind hers to sit somewhere else. As if there's anywhere on this bus we could have a private moment.

"Lennon, do you want to tell me what happened?" she begins.

I'm seated next to the window, looking out. Cars passing. Greenery a blur. I flick my eyes up to catch the driver's in the mirror, and he quickly returns his gaze to the road.

Mrs. Morales holds out her open palm, the condom wrapper glistening in it. "Does this belong to you?"

When I don't answer again, she breathes out a heavy sigh. "We trusted you kids to spend an afternoon exploring the city. Not each other." She says those last words through gritted teeth, with a hiss. "Do you know that I had a conversation with your father on the phone? That he called a few days before we left to make sure that you were in good hands? I promised him you would be."

I stare down at my knees, where a small hole in my sweatpants exposes my pale skin. My head shakes but words don't come. They're all twisted in my stomach. The guilt, the shame, multiplying.

"Please don't tell them," I say in a meek voice, eyes still on the loose thread of my pants.

"I'm sorry, that's not possible. You put me and Mr. Chang in a very precarious position."

"Please. You don't understand. My dad will lose it."

"You should have thought about that before you and John . . ." She pauses and releases another labored breath. "I thought you were a good kid. I thought I could trust you."

I slump in my seat as Mr. Chang comes to the front of the bus with the rest of my things.

I turn away from Mrs. Morales to read the message from John on my phone.

John: I'll work on Morales. I'll explain to her that it's all a misunderstanding. I'll get her to promise she won't tell your parents. I don't care what it takes. I'll stay after school every day. I'll wash graffiti off the bathroom stalls. I'll do anything. I'm so sorry.

Me: it's not your fault.

Me: and it's too late. She knows the truth. She's going to tell them.

John: We have five hours left
of the ride. I can convince her.

Me: Don't. I deserve whatever's
coming to me.

I close the message with John, find my earbuds, stick them in, and hit play until I can almost imagine myself somewhere else. Anywhere else.

My life, what I knew of it, that girl, she's gone.

She may as well be dead.

Part IV

TWELFTH GRADE

Once upon a time lived a girl with a heart so big
and dreams so vast she needed to create
a different world for them to exist in.
But he wouldn't let her go.
Somewhere, in this alternate universe,
a boy waited for the girl.
Sending messages through the sky.
"He won't release me," she cried to the moon.
It didn't seem fair, the boy thought.
She created this world. She worked so hard for it.
Why did she have to sacrifice her happy ending
to give him peace?
If only the boy had a key.
But it was her world.
And only she could turn the lock.

Chapter Thirty-six

OCTOBER 10

Senior year. Time moves quickly and also stands still. I went from the greatest high of my life to living through my worst nightmare. Every morning, I wake up and want to scream when I remember I'm still living through this. This pain. This grief. Sometimes I wish I could feel less, and on my worst days I wish I could just make it all stop.

From having almost everything I wanted to losing it all. In an instant.

Like every morning since that day in June, I force myself out of bed because I don't have another choice. I wipe the sleep from my eyes and walk slowly to the bathroom to wash away the crusted-on tears that have become like a new layer of skin I grow every night and shed with the sunrise. I shower, return to my room to get dressed in whatever is clean or comfortable, preferably the latter, throw my too-long hair into a ponytail, and make my way down the steps.

I find comfort in the routine, in forcing myself to go through the motions, because every second I do is a second that I'm not being yelled at. Or being reminded of how ashamed they are, with just a look. Letting me know that my worth has been lost. How I'm lost.

My feet come to an abrupt stop a few steps from reaching the main floor. Dad is at the front door, key and wallet in hand. We don't typically come face-to-face in the mornings. He's usually gone before I come down.

Mom steps out of the kitchen to find the two of us, still, frozen. "Lennon, why are you just standing there? Yalla. You need to catch the bus."

I don't reply. Just shake my head and make my way down the final few steps, forced to pass my father on my way to the garage, where my shoes are.

"Do you need lunch money?" he asks, his voice even.

I stop and force out a silent breath. His question surprises me. Not because he hasn't been paying for my lunches for the last three-plus years, but because he's speaking to me at all.

"No, thank you," I reply. "I still have money on my card."

"How about breakfast?" Mom pipes in. "To go. I made those oat bars you love so much."

"I'm not hungry," I reply, and as it turns out, that was exactly the wrong thing to say to my father this morning.

He mumbles to himself, a familiar string of curse words in Arabic about how I'm being silly and milking the situation. How it's been long enough and that I'm only starving myself to punish them. "Eat something, damn it," he says in English. "You're killing yourself. It's not enough what you did, now you have to make your mother worry, watching you shrink away?"

"I'll get something at school," I lie.

"You can't keep doing this," Mom cuts in, standing in front of me and blocking access to the garage door.

"I'm not doing anything. I'm not," I say, eyes downcast. "I just want to go to school."

"Fine. Go to school. Starve to death," Dad says, walking out the front door and slamming it behind him.

The silence following his exit steals all the air from the room.

"Do you want me to drive you?" Mom asks, her frown deepening.

"No, thanks. Picking me up after school every day is more than enough," I say dryly, reaching for the doorknob.

My dad is still sitting in his car, idling in the driveway, when I step out of the garage. His eyes lock on mine, and I shake away the intensity of his stare before making my way toward the bus stop.

When the bus arrives a few minutes later, I watch out the window as my dad finally pulls out of the driveway.

He still doesn't trust me. I doubt he ever will again.

"Hey, baby girl," Andie says, her warm, comforting smile greeting me when I get off the bus. She does this every day. I think she's afraid of what I might do to myself if I don't have constant supervision. All I want is to be left alone, but Andie remains by my side—as much as someone who doesn't live with you can. She's the only one I listen to. The only one who reminds me on an almost daily basis that I didn't do anything wrong. The only one who keeps me from sinking further into depression.

"Hey," I say, swallowing down the searing lump in my throat.

She holds my hand as we walk into the building. The benefit of "the event" happening at the end of last school year means most of the people who were involved are gone now. Word got around, of course, as it does. High school is a silo.

Dad made it "easier" on me by forcing me to finish out the end of the school year at home. The only reason they let me return this year is because John's in college now.

"Why's it so dead around here?" I ask, gripping the strap of my backpack with my free hand.

"They're giving seniors the morning off to work on college applications if we chose not to attend the alumni presentations," Andie reminds me, as if there aren't signs everywhere, as well as an internal email that circulated to all of us every day this week.

I simply nod. Words strain to come out. After months of shouting and crying, fighting and arguing, I have nothing left.

I check my phone out of habit, and I guess because I keep hoping to see a message from John. But I was forced to block his number months ago, as well as disable my old email account. My eyes squeeze shut, and just like every day since June, uninvited thoughts play out in front of me, like a movie I can't turn off. I don't want to be here. I never want to be here but today, more than ever, it's like I *can't* be here.

"You ready?" Andie asks.

"For what?"

"The first session," she replies. Andie has been so patient and kind. But sometimes I just want to be alone. It's easier to suffer when you're alone. "Remember signing up for them together?"

"Vaguely. Don't we have to go to homeroom for attendance first?"

"Attendance is optional today. Come on, the first session starts after morning bell."

I allow her to lead me through the atrium and past the gym hall. We arrive in front of a classroom. The bell rings but no one else is here.

"Are you sure we're in the right place?"

Andie doesn't answer. Instead, she walks past me to the doors that lead outside and pushes one open. A moment later John walks through, nodding a thanks at Andie. I begin to back away, but then his eyes find mine and I stop. Everything stops. My racing heart serves as the only proof that this isn't just a fever dream.

Andie goes to open the classroom door and turns back to us. "It's empty. If you need anything, I'll be right outside," she says, looking at me.

"Lennon?" After months of not hearing his voice, John saying my name awakens something I've been failing to silence.

Without responding to either of them, I enter the classroom. John follows, and I watch as Andie closes the door behind us.

"I've been trying to get a hold of you," he says, cutting into the quiet.

"My parents made me block your number. They monitor everything I do."

"I came to school in September. Waited for you at your bus on the days I ended class early," John confesses.

"I know. Andie told me. My mom picks me up."

Eventually I had to ask Andie to block John's number because he kept trying to reach me through her and it was just too hard. Too tempting.

"I came to your house. I came every day for a week after we got back. I only stopped coming because my sister told me I was making things worse for you. That, and your dad threatened me with legal action if I didn't stay away." His words come out through a pained laugh.

"I know," I say again, because it's all I can manage to say.

"I just wanted to be able to fix it."

I shake my head, the tears threatening to spring loose. "You can't, though. The second Mrs. Morales told him what happened, we were done. We had to be."

"But you didn't do anything wrong," he says, taking a cautious step toward me.

I take one back.

He's always watching. He always knows.

"It was crazy of your dad to pull you out of school last year."

"He was trying to protect me," I say, studying the hole on the linoleum counter.

"From what?"

"You. And all the people who were talking about me and you and what happened."

"I would have defended you."

"I know," I choke out. "But you and I both know that guys don't bear the brunt of the carnage in these situations. No one saw you as a slut who let a boy into her hotel room. No one would look at you the way they looked at me."

"Fuck," he says, raking his fingers through his hair. "Was it bad?"

I swallow, then nod. Nothing will ever hurt the way it did when my father looked me in the eyes as Mrs. Morales told him about what she'd found. She made it all sound so seedy. So intentional. But it wasn't like that.

"My parents didn't speak to me for two days. And then, the bomb went off. All I could do was sit there and take it."

I had become my worst fear—a disappointment.

I fought back at first, trying to explain how none of it was planned, but there was no way out of the situation.

So I stopped.

They didn't care that I loved John.

They didn't think I was capable of knowing what love is.

I wanted to shout that I hated them.

I wanted to scream that I felt like a prisoner.

I wanted to blame them for forcing me to become this person even I didn't recognize.

I hated lying.

I hated sneaking around.

But I had no other choice. They'd left me no other choice.

"I know you don't understand, and I don't think you ever really will. It's like, you spend so many years doing what you're supposed to do," I say, forcing myself to look at John. "Focused on the goal. Their goals. You hit milestones. Applause. You reach achievements that separate you from the pack. More applause. Coupled with pride. It becomes this high, this goal of nirvana that you yearn to reach again and again. But it gets harder to find new ways to make your parents happy. Then one day you start to want different things. Things that set your soul on fire, but it's not in line with the vision they have for you. So you hide that part of yourself and you go on trying to find ways to make them proud. But in the end, you lose you."

"You don't have to hide who you are, Lennon. There are people who love the real you."

"But why does it have to be that way? Why does it have to be this push and pull of who I want to be versus who they want me to be? There's no way to win. You pick one, you lose the other. Either way, you lose."

"Or," John says, "you break the chain, and you set yourself free."

"What if I don't want to be set free? At least not completely."

He shakes his head. "I don't know if you can have both."

"I can't," I say.

"So that's it, then?" John asks, his even-keeled tone almost jarring. "You're just going to give up on us?"

"You think I'm giving up?" My throat is raw, like I've just swallowed a handful of razors, each word a sharp edge. "I went to hell and back for you. I fought a war where I lost not only you, but my dad's respect. I fought hard. The fact that I'm still here, still standing, I'm still . . ." My voice cracks. "I'm *still* fighting."

John studies me now like he sees me for what I really am: a soaked-through piece of paper, one miscalculated touch and another corner will tear off.

"I'm so tired," I say, looking right at him. "But I fought. Nothing I could ever say or do would be able to fix the damage I inflicted. I broke his trust. He has every right to be disappointed in me."

"You're not the only one who loses in this scenario, Lennon. I've spent the last four months trying to find ways to get to you, to get through to you. But I can't do it anymore. My family needs me. I can't let myself fall further behind in school."

"So you came here today to let me know you're moving on."

"That's not fair." John lets out a breath, his face softening. "I could spend the rest of my life fighting for you, but it won't change the truth: you will choose your parents' happiness over your own every time."

I throw an arm up in the air, my calm exterior slipping away. "What do you want me to do?"

"It's not about me telling you what it is I want. It's not even about us. This is about you. You need to choose yourself. If you don't, nothing will ever change."

He watches me, his expression still. He's stalling. He doesn't want to tell me what he's about to tell me. It doesn't matter how much distance or time is put between us, I know this boy in front of me. Maybe better than he knows himself. And he is mustering up whatever strength he has left to tell me something he thinks I need to hear. But it's only going to break both of us.

His jaw clenches as he takes a step closer. "I can't just stare at my bedroom ceiling every night thinking about you. It's not healthy."

I want to yell back, *Why not*? Because *I* do. I come home from school and I go to my room and lie in bed and just stare at the nothingness that surrounds me. But I guess John doesn't feel it necessary to punish himself. He just gets to continue existing.

"I wanted it to be you, Lennon." My eyes widen at his words. My name on his lips. His gaze on me. A spark of hope lights up the dark, narrow cavity of my heart. "I wanted it to be you, more than I've ever wanted anything. But I think it's time we both admit to ourselves that this thing between us isn't working."

The light goes out.

The thought of putting more distance between me and John both steals my breath and paralyzes me. It's like sticking my heart in a cage and throwing away the key. I want to scream. I want to grab his shirt in my fists and tell him he's got it wrong. He's so wrong. I want to explain. I want him to understand. I want to do all these things.

But there's no point telling him he's wrong. It won't change anything. It won't reverse the damage.

He's afraid. Of hurting me. Of hurting himself. Of getting stuck in this back-and-forth where we lose a piece of ourselves every time we break apart.

Fear makes us behave in ways we never would have thought possible. I've seen the result of what fear can do. How, if you allow it to, it can destroy you from the inside out before attacking the people in your life.

I am the result of my father's fear.

He created this.

It took a baby for Georgie to put an end to her cycle of fear.

I don't know what it will take for me, but I'm not quite ready to throw it all away. There's still some fight left, and I am not going to let fear steal my hopes, my dreams, or my life.

Chapter Thirty-seven

DECEMBER 8

"Get out of bed. We're going out."

I jolt up from the sudden disturbance. My eyes strain to adjust to the light, and I can just make out Georgie's silhouette in my bedroom doorway.

"What're you doing here?" I ask. It's six-thirty at night. On the rare occasion Georgie does visit from the city, she's always gone before rush hour. "Where's Paulie?"

"Mom and Dad are watching her. I'm staying the night, and you and I are going to celebrate your birthday."

December eighth. My seventeenth birthday.

"I don't want to go out," I say.

"Too bad. Andie's on her way. We're taking you for fajitas and virgin margaritas."

"Please," I say, trying to sink back into bed. "I just want to stay here."

"Tough shit. I'll be waiting in my room."

My room, she says. Like it still belongs to her. And it probably would have if she hadn't gotten pregnant. And maybe if she hadn't, I wouldn't have allowed myself to get so lost with John. I let myself believe in the love story—that John was my meant-to-be—but maybe he was just a distraction from everything happening at home. Or maybe I'd still be with Theo. He'd be taking me out for a fancy birthday celebration. And then he'd probably want to do it after. There's no escaping sex. Unless I stay here. In my room. Where it's safe.

"Let's go!" Georgie says, before slamming my door shut.

I sit up and run my hands over my face. My parents wished me a happy birthday over breakfast this morning, and I was pretty sure that would be the extent of the celebrations. Just another day. I forced down Mom's breakfast before going to school, to be nice, and I promised myself that I'd work on more college applications when I got home. But I couldn't bring myself to do it.

There's only one school I can see myself going to: Columbia. I even took the SATs back in October. Being locked up in my room for months left me with a lot of free time to take online courses and practice tests. One day I told Mom I needed a drive to a college fair at the community center, but instead I spent the afternoon writing the test. When my results were emailed two weeks later, I had no one but myself to celebrate my score of 1420 with. I did better than I expected. Way better. It was the first time it felt like maybe Columbia was more than just a pipe dream.

"How's it going in there?" Georgie calls.

Clearly, she isn't going to let this idea of hers go, so I pull myself out of bed, put on a pair of jeans and a forest green sweater to hide my shrunken frame, and throw my scraggly hair up in a messy bun. When I open my bedroom door, Georgie is there, waiting.

"Oh, good," she says, sizing me up. "Andie's already outside."

"What about Mom and Dad?" I ask, flicking off my lights and grabbing my things.

"I told them I was taking you out for your birthday with Andie."

"Did they give you the third degree?"

"No. I think they're just happy to see you leaving the house."

"Ha," I say. "Nothing ever makes them happy."

"Save it for dinner. Come on," Georgie says, taking my hand and leading me down the stairs.

"Are you going to finish that?" Andie asks, jutting her chin to my half-eaten cheese quesadilla.

I push it toward her. "I'm full."

"Half a quesadilla is filling?" Georgie asks as she takes a sip of her non-virgin margarita. She's twenty. Legal drinking age. Married. A mom. Yet somehow, I've reverted to that unsure, insecure, closed-off version of myself I was before my diagnosis.

"This is progress," Andie says. "Lennon barely eats these days."

"Mom was telling me." Georgie stares at me, her face almost ashen. "She says you've been starving yourself to punish them. Is that true?"

A puff of laughter escapes as my fingers coil tightly around my glass. "It's been almost six months. Where have you been?"

"What do you mean, where have I been? I've been taking care of a toddler and supporting Zach while he goes to university and works part-time. I'm sorry, but I have a life too."

"You canceled on me three times. You promised you'd help with my college essay."

"I know." Georgie nods as Andie's eyes move between us across the table. "I'm sorry about that, too. Things have been not that great on my end either. Zach and I went through a rough patch, but we're working through it."

"What happened?" I ask.

"Did he cheat?" Andie leans in, eyes wide.

"No." Georgie shakes her head. "He wouldn't. And nothing 'happened.' It's just hard. But this isn't about me. I should have been there for you."

I lift my shoulders before sinking deeper into my seat. "Wouldn't have made a difference."

"Give them time," Georgie says. "They can't stay angry forever. So, tell me, what did you decide to write your essay about? What school even asks for an essay?"

"About a time a worldview of mine was challenged," I respond as I rip a brand-new paper napkin to shreds.

The table is quiet until the three of us break into a careful kind of laughter.

"And it was only one school that required an essay," I say, kind of quietly.

"How about you, Andie? Did you apply to any out-of-province schools?" Georgie asks.

"I'm staying local. I figure why move to some small Canadian town when Toronto is at my fingertips?"

"You and Lennon should dorm together, downtown. Then the three of us could see each other more," Georgie says, like she's playing Barbies and creating idealized made-up scenarios.

"I didn't apply to any local schools," I say before taking a sip of water.

A beat of silence falls over the table as Georgie and Andie exchange looks. "Do Mom and Dad know that?"

"They asked if I applied to schools. I said I did. That was the extent of it. Dad probably thinks Mom paid my application fees, and vice versa."

"So what schools did you apply to?" Georgie shifts in her seat. I try to meet Andie's eyes but she's looking away. She already knows the answer to this question.

"Just Columbia. No other schools."

"Columbia University? The one in New York City? Lennon," Georgie says, lowering her gaze to me. "You're serious, aren't you?"

"It's the only school I want to go to."

"You knew about this?" Georgie asks Andie, and it comes out sounding accusatory.

"I tried to convince her to apply to some backup schools, but she refused."

Georgie places her hand on my arm, her grip tightening. "Is this about John?"

"It's about me," I say.

"They're never going to let you go," my sister says, her eyebrows forming a peak.

"If I spend my whole life only doing things that I have Mom and Dad's blessing to do, is that really a life worth living? You're always telling me to do what makes me happy," I point out, almost bitterly.

The waiter comes to settle the bill, and I excuse myself to the restroom. When I return, Andie and Georgie have their coats on, ready to go. I know they're both worried about me. Even I'm a little worried about me. But it's either go after what I want or spend the rest of my days holed up in my room. I've shown my parents that I'm capable of the latter, but the thing is, they don't know that all that time I was up there, I was plotting and planning, preparing myself for Act II.

Chapter Thirty-eight

DECEMBER 31

"Lennon?" Dad's voice calls from downstairs.

I rise from my desk chair where I've been writing all day and open my bedroom door. "Yes?"

He's standing at the bottom of the stairs, holding a bag of take-out. "I picked up Greek food for dinner. Hungry?"

My instinct is to say no. Food is one of the only weapons I have right now. But instead, I tell him I'll be right down, because if I want my life to move forward the way I need it to, then I must let go of some of this spite. It's not like holding on to it has gotten me anywhere.

I come down the stairs and follow him into the kitchen as he brings the food to the island, searching for scissors to cut the knot off the plastic bag. I open the drawer and pull out a pair for him.

"Where's Mom?" I ask.

"At Petra's house," he replies as he cuts the bag open.

"You're not going to spend New Year's Eve with your wife?"

Dad removes the takeout containers from the bag, and I grab us two plates from the cupboard.

"Here or the table?" I ask.

"Here's fine." He removes the lids to reveal chicken souvlaki, yellow rice, roasted potatoes, and vegetables. "I didn't want to leave you home alone tonight," he adds.

I choke down the knot in my throat as our eyes briefly meet.

"What are your plans for the evening?" he asks as he pulls out a stool. I pass him a knife and fork. "Grab a spoon for the tzatziki."

"Probably just going to read," I say, handing him the spoon before pulling out the stool next to him.

"No one is keeping you a prisoner here but yourself," he says, scooping rice onto his plate.

"Then why did you stay home tonight?" I stab a potato with my fork and pick up a skewer of chicken. He doesn't respond. "Is it because you're worried I'll invite him over?"

"I don't want to talk about him," Dad says, taking a bite of his chicken.

"I know you don't trust me." At those words, he puts his utensils down and turns to look at me. "And I understand why. I broke your trust. But there's a lot you don't know because you've been too angry to listen. To hear my side. And now that so much time has passed, it doesn't even seem worth it anymore."

I clench my jaw and breathe out through my nose. My heart is drumming in my ears. Trying to have this conversation with Dad brings me back to all those fights we got into after New York. The trauma comes right back, making it clear I haven't yet healed. But how could I have?

"It's over with John," I tell him.

He turns back to his plate and shovels a spoonful of rice into his mouth. I take a few bites of food, but it's a struggle to get it down.

There's been a constant tightness in my chest ever since June, and right now, it feels like there's a vise around my esophagus.

"I swear on my life and the life of Paulie that I didn't know he would be on that trip. And I know you would have preferred it if I'd ignored him, or maybe if I'd called to let you know, because lying by omission is still lying. I know you and Mom have strong feelings about . . ." I pause, unsure what word to use here, so I just let my sentence fade away. "But what's done is done. And I don't plan on doing that with anyone else."

Dad continues to eat as I speak, which I take as a good sign. He could have yelled. He could have walked away. But he's still here. Still eating. Still, hopefully, listening.

"I know that in order to rebuild your trust I need to be honest with you. This next thing I want to say isn't easy, because you won't be happy about it, and I'm really tired of being responsible for that constant frown on your face, but the thing is . . ." My voice starts to crack as tears prick at my eyes. *Push through. You're almost there.* "I have two goals right now. One, for you and Mom to forgive me. And two, to study Creative Writing at Columbia University. In New York City."

Dad puts his fork down slowly and grabs a napkin to wipe his mouth. I look down at the food on my plate, my heart thumping.

"Forget about it."

"Your forgiveness or Columbia?" Something fierce pulses inside me, forcing me to steady myself. For the first time in months, I feel alive. Awake.

"You're not moving to New York City for four years. You were there one week and look what happened. In four years, you'd be unrecognizable."

"Is that what you're so afraid of? That I'd change so much you wouldn't be able to recognize me?"

He lifts his gaze to meet mine. "What you did in New York was shameful."

"I don't understand. Georgie got pregnant and you managed to move on."

"Georgie isn't you," he spits out. "We expected more from you. We thought we'd raised you well enough not to allow some boy to take away your purity in a dirty hotel room."

"You make it sound so terrible."

"You broke our hearts," he says, his fist hitting the marble counter, "and our trust, and you made us doubt everything."

"You don't think I know that? I know that. And I'm sorry. I'm sorry. But I loved John. As much as it pains you to hear this, I loved him with all my heart. And it wasn't a decision made in haste. It was made from love."

Dad pushes out his stool, rises, and storms to the fridge. He pulls out a beer, twists off the cap, and tosses it with excessive force into the sink.

He points at me, his finger hanging in the air while his other hand wraps the neck of his beer bottle tightly. "This is not something you do until you're married."

"Says who? You? The Bible? Where exactly is this coming from?"

"Our beliefs."

"Come on, Dad. Do you really think anyone my age cares about those old-school beliefs?"

"I care," he says, pressing a finger to his chest. "I care. You're *my* daughter, and I care about the decisions you make."

"With *my* body," I remind him. "These are decisions I made with my own body."

He drinks a long gulp and then slams his beer down on the counter in front of me. I swivel my stool around and get up so I'm standing in front of him now.

"It's done, okay?" I say. "It's over. It only happened once. He's out of my life. I'm trying to rebuild. I'm trying to find out who I am outside of boys and love. I want to be a writer. And I want to study in New York. I can't do these things without your help, your support, your faith in me. Despite what you may think, I am a good person. I deserve happiness. I deserve your love and respect. I'm your daughter. I'm allowed to make mistakes. I'm allowed to make decisions you don't approve of. I'm sorry I hurt you. I can understand why you're so upset. But making me feel like a terrible human being every time we're in the same room together doesn't help anything or anyone. I miss you." My voice catches but I press on. "I miss being your friend. Your daughter. I miss listening to Beatles records together. Barbecuing in the winter. Going for long drives to expensive grocery stores to buy fancy cheese." The tears have sprung loose, and I allow them to fall. "I'm a good person, Dad. I am. I made a mistake, in your eyes, and I'm sorry I upset you. But I am a good person, and I'm tired of feeling like I don't deserve to even live anymore."

My father's gaze drops to the ground as he lets out a deep breath.

"Don't you think I've paid enough? It's been six months. Look at me, Baba. I'm skin and bones. I can't eat. I either sleep too much or not at all. I have one friend left in this world. Georgie is busy with her own family. The only boy I ever loved is moving on without me. And I'm always alone in my room, reliving the moment I lost my father's respect. It wasn't only *your* heart that broke that day."

I have no clue if I'm getting through to him at all but the fact that he's still here tells me that this is my best chance to be heard, so I just keep talking.

"The only thing that's kept me going and kept me hopeful, that's kept me alive, is my writing. I'm punished for wanting things almost everyone on this earth wants. But it's wrong when I want it. When I want love, when I express my dreams, they're silly. They're insignificant. Face it, you're disappointed in me not only because of what I did in New York, but because I'm not your perfect daughter who will fulfill your life's ambitions. And now you don't know what to do with me. I'm tarnished. Not worthy. You act like I murdered someone. I never chose to fall in love. My heart made that decision. But my head decided to do what I did that day, and I refuse to feel any more shame over it. I will not apologize for my actions anymore."

"Are you done?" Dad asks, stoic, still.

My heart plummets to my stomach. All those words are just making an emotional graveyard at his feet, sinking into the ground, failing to penetrate that thick, stubborn head of his. I shrug slightly in response because I don't know what else to do. I'm all out of words.

"You're my daughter and I will love you no matter what. It's very upsetting to hear how much you've been struggling. But I don't know what you want me to say, because I've been struggling too. I had one job as a father, and I failed. Twice."

"No." I shake my head. "You're wrong. You didn't fail me because of the choices I made for myself. You failed because of how you treated me after I made those choices. I love you, Baba, and I respect you. But I'm going to mess up and do things you don't approve of. It's what makes me human. It's what makes me an individual."

I sit back and stare at the food, my stomach churning at the sight of it. I get up and bring some plastic wrap so I can put it in the fridge for later, but we both know I won't eat the food.

Just as I'm about to leave the kitchen, I turn to my father, who is still standing, unmoored.

"I will continue to work toward these goals. I want to study at Columbia. And if I don't have your financial support or your blessing, then I'm still going to pursue this dream, and I'll do whatever it takes to make it happen. I wasn't put here on earth to live my life for someone else. None of us were."

Our eyes briefly meet, and maybe it's wishful thinking, but I can almost see a slight nod from my father.

"I hope we can both resolve to put aside our differences and enter the next year as father and daughter. You know where to find me," I say, before heading back to my room, the adrenaline of the conversation keeping me upright.

When the clock strikes midnight, I usher in the new year alone in bed.

No message from John.

No apology from my father.

But that's okay, because fear is not going to win this time.

Chapter Thirty-nine

MAY 9

I take the train into the city to visit with Georgie and Paulie.

When Georgie invited me to her condo, I simply came downstairs with my bag packed and announced that I was going to her home for the weekend. I didn't wait for their response. Or their permission. I didn't even say goodbye. I just left.

The problem with sticking it to my parents this way is that I derive no satisfaction from being so miserable. I just want to be able to move on. But neither of us will ever forget the way we made each other feel. You can't glue together a glass vase that has shattered into a million tiny pieces and not expect there to be gaps left behind.

Georgie and Paulie are waiting for me when I step outside Union Station. It's an unseasonably warm day for May, with a gentle breeze. I bend down to Paulie's stroller to kiss her cheek. Georgie tells me I can stick my bag in the undercarriage. When I'm done, I playfully nudge my sister aside so that I can push the stroller.

I breathe in the city air. It may not be as clean as the air in my home, but I take it in more easily.

"Are you okay to do the aquarium before we eat?" She stops herself just then and takes in the full sight of me. "For fuck's sake, Lennon. You've completely withered away."

My grip tightens around the foam handle of the stroller. We're stopped on the corner, waiting for the light to change. "Things suck at home."

I spent most of the winter hibernating in my room, writing, and sometimes hanging out with Andie. I haven't attended any of the senior year functions or events. But in my own way I've been doing the work, building something that's just for me.

Georgie pauses, her eyes welling up, shaking her head. "This is my fault. I should have helped more."

"It's not. You have your own life. And winter makes things harder, especially with a kid."

"I can do better. I *will* do better," she says as we cross the street. "It's been almost a year since New York. Are they still making you feel guilty?"

"We don't really talk. I tried to with Dad over New Year's. I told him about Columbia. Said I applied. I think I just made things worse."

"And Mom?"

"I don't know how to approach Mom," I say as pedestrians speedily weave around us. "I expected Dad to act like this, but Mom never once stuck up for me. Never attempted to hear me out or come speak to me alone. She just 'stood by her man.' So grossly stereotypical, it makes me sick."

"Yeah. Mom was a giant disappointment to me, too, when I got pregnant. I think she's afraid that he'll turn on her. Or maybe she just feels sorry for Dad because he has no one else."

"Probably both," I say.

"Say what you will about Mom and Dad, and there's a lot we can both say about them," she laughs, "but they really do love each other. And I don't know if it's fair of us to expect that they would ever choose a side if it meant going against one another."

"Is that how it is with you and Zach?" I ask. "Why you've chosen to spend more time with him and Paulie and less with us?"

"It wasn't about choosing," Georgie says. "Life just happens. It gets busy, and priorities shift. Not that I'm saying you're not a priority, but Paulie is so dependent on me. And so is Zach, in a different way. It's funny. I went from my life being mine to now being the most important person to two other people who need me in ways that can sometimes feel suffocating. But other times? I love my life. It's confusing, I know," she says with a laugh.

I get why Georgie married Zach, even though I never believed she truly loved him. She needed to leave that house. It was for her survival. I see that now. Because Columbia is my version of survival.

"So Columbia. Have you thought this through?" Georgie asks as we arrive at the aquarium.

"What's to think through? It's my dream. I applied. Now I wait."

"And if you get in? There's no way they're going to let you go, and we're too well off to get any financial aid," Georgie reminds me.

I push the stroller up the ramp to the entrance, not responding to my sister's concerns. Concerns I have tried to block out of my mind for months. Delusional? Maybe a little. Probably another survival tactic.

"Have Mom and Dad found out yet that you didn't apply anywhere else? Are you prepared to brave the shitstorm again?" she asks as we walk through the front doors.

"Applying to other schools would have created a safety net," I say. "And if there was a safety net, they'd make me use it."

Georgie exhales a heavy breath. "Your stubbornness is going to ruin you, you know that, right?"

Or save me, I think, but don't dare say out loud. Because then maybe Georgie will think I'm just as crazy as my parents think I am. And I never once said to her that having a baby would ruin her life, even though I thought it—and much worse. Why does it feel as if no one is ever on my side? Maybe I am delusional. Maybe I'm the problem.

I pull back the stroller canopy so that Paulie can take in the full view of the colorful lobby. Crouching next to my niece, I point to the aquatic mobiles and giant fish tanks. Georgie goes to the counter to buy our tickets, and I take in another deep breath. When she returns and passes me my entry ticket, pity is etched across her features.

We don't talk about anything having to do with me, Dad, or college the whole time we're there. We focus our attention on Paulie and all the sea creatures. Taking pictures by the jellyfish, pointing up at the sharks as they swim above us, reading about the old sea turtles. We make a pit stop at the gift shop before leaving, where I buy Paulie a pink jellyfish stuffie.

Once we're back outside, Georgie stops to take a call and I walk around with Paulie, showing her the CN Tower. "Look up, up, up!" I tell her. Her big, brown eyes go wide. As my gaze falls again I freeze. *John?* I stand up straighter, arching my neck, my eyes fixed on the person standing just a few feet away. He smiles when he catches me staring. I don't reciprocate. It's not him.

Georgie catches up with us and bends down to kiss Paulie. "Dinner?" she asks as she straightens.

"Sure."

Paulie grows increasingly cranky over dinner, so we eat quickly and walk back to Georgie's condo.

"Where's Zach?" I ask as we step inside her home. Georgie unbuckles the stroller straps for Paulie, who immediately runs to her play area. I follow my sister to the kitchen, where she prepares Paulie's nighttime bottle. A surge of nostalgia courses through me. I miss those early days when Georgie and Paulie were still living with us and I got to be there every night to help give Paulie her bedtime bath and, if I was lucky, her bottle.

"No bath tonight?" I ask.

"She doesn't get one every night anymore."

I swivel the stool I'm seated on at the kitchen counter to watch Paulie play.

"Zach's spending the weekend with his parents at their cottage," she finally answers. "They're opening it up for the summer."

When the bottle's ready we head to the family room. I sit on the couch, and she passes me the bottle, smiling. I smile back and hold it out to Paulie, who runs clumsily to me, a telltale sign that she's exhausted. I cradle my newly three-year-old niece, breathing in her baby scent, which is slowly fading, as she drinks her bottle.

"I know she's too old for a bottle," Georgie admits as she sits on the coffee table. "But she still loves it. Fuck the rules."

"Fuck the rules," I echo, stroking my niece's slightly sweaty hair as she drinks her warm milk.

"I'm worried about you," my sister says, watching me with her daughter on the couch. "I just feel like maybe you're not being realistic."

"It'll all work out," I say gently, my eyes filling up as I study my niece's soft features. If Paulie has taught me anything it's to trust the process.

"You didn't do anything wrong, Lennon. If you hadn't got caught, you'd still be their perfect daughter."

"But I did get caught. And so did you," I say, running a finger along Paulie's rosy cheeks. "And I think, in a way, it was necessary. Because it broke the good girl facade, you know?" My eyes meet Georgie's.

"But you *are* good. So am I. It's not our fault that our parents' values are twisted up in some weird purity culture that they use religion to justify. It's not about religion. It's not even about our culture. It's about controlling us."

"I see that now," I say, nodding. "And that's why I'm doing what I'm doing."

"Except you're hurting yourself in the process. Don't deny yourself a postsecondary education just to make a point. Don't take your anger at our parents out on your body. You have to take better care of yourself and plan for your future in a way that is . . . more viable. I love Paulie. I love being a mom. But I regret not being able to go to university."

"You can go once Paulie's in school."

She offers me a sad smile. "Maybe."

"Mama, I'm tired," Paulie says once her bottle is finished.

Georgie rises from the coffee table and picks up Paulie, but not before I sneak in a goodnight hug and kiss. They disappear into Paulie's room, and I sink into the couch, reaching for my phone. There are a few messages from Andie. She's at another party without me. She sends me a couple of pictures of her and her newest boyfriend, Thom with an *h*. As I click on her images, my heart stalls. I bring my fingers to the screen to expand the photo, zooming in on the people in the background. Theo and John. It's like seeing a ghost. Two of them.

Me: John and Theo are there.

Andie: Yeah, how did you know?

Me: They're in the background of your photo, genius.

Andie: Ah fuck me. Sorry, babe.

Me: How are they?

Andie: Good I think. They appear to be friends again. I only spoke to them briefly. Theo asked about you. He's home for the summer from UBC.

Me: How did John seem?

Andie: Sullen. As usual.
You should text him.

Me: Andie! That's like telling an alcoholic to enjoy a beer with dinner. I can't.

Andie: lol, I don't know why you two are being so stubborn. He's your person. Everyone knows it so why fight it?

Me: Because I'm focusing on myself this year.

Andie: That's bullshit. You don't do anything for yourself. You don't even come out. That's just a lie you've been telling yourself. You need to snap out of it. Life is passing you by. TEXT JOHN.

Me: Only you could speak to me that way and get away with it.

Andie: I know. And you can call me a bitch and I'll still loe you.

Andie: Love*

Andie: TEXT HIM. It won't hurt to talk to him.

Andie: Also, I hate how hot Theo is. He makes Thom look like a skinny British boy-bander.

Me: lol. Theo is annoyingly hot.

Me: FYI I am out of my house. I'm visiting Georgie and Paulie. And we spent the day in the city.

Andie: Good! Get used to going out because whether you like it or not you're coming to prom with me!

Me: I'll think about.

Andie: luver you

Me: luver you too

Andie: TEXT HIM!

Georgie returns from Paulie's room with the baby monitor. The condo is so small I'm surprised she feels the need for one. She picks up the empty bottle and I help tidy up the play area. We snack on popcorn and watch an old movie together before Georgie turns in for the night. She's given me sheets and a blanket for the couch, preemptively apologizing for the sunlight I'll be waking up to thanks to her floor-to-ceiling windows. Amazing views. Not the most practical for sleeping late.

Nuzzled into the couch, I flick off the TV and stare up at the ceiling. Andie's words echo in my head. *TEXT HIM!*

If only she knew how many times a day I almost do.

The other thing I haven't been able to bring myself to do is sign in to the Columbia admissions portal to check if I've been accepted. I know the answer lies within a few clicks but the longer I don't know the answer, the longer I can keep the dream alive. Instead, I study the photo Andie sent with John in the background. My heart cracks seeing his unsmiling face. Those lips that once belonged to me, if only for a moment. I close my eyes, remembering the two of us on the cool Central Park grass, the sun beaming down on us.

The one butterfly I have left, the one who hasn't let my depression push it away, flutters in my stomach, its wings sending a wave of bravery to rush through me. I choose to seize this moment—one I know will be fleeting—and sign in to the portal.

Congratulations . . .

Chapter Forty

MAY 16

I've been sitting on my good news for a week, trying to process what it all means. It could mean everything changing (for better or for worse). It's been nice having this little secret to myself for the past seven days. A reason to hope again. To dream. To get excited.

I wait until I know it's just me and Dad at home. Mom's brunching with Petra. She does this every Sunday when the weather is nice.

Dad's sitting on the front porch, cup of coffee in hand. I sit next to him on the swing chair. We don't talk, just sit side by side as birds chirp, taking turns at the feeder. The occasional car drives by, and clouds slowly move through the sky, easing the force of the sun.

"I got into Columbia," I finally say. "I wasn't sure if I would. Their acceptance rate is pretty low, but my SAT scores were good. I have you to thank for my above-average math results. If you hadn't forced me into taking advanced courses the last few years, I would have bombed for sure."

Dad nods, the corners of his lips turning up ever so slightly. "I'm glad to know I didn't completely ruin your life."

“Is that sarcasm?” I ask, because I’m honestly not sure.

He lets out a long breath. “I haven’t been a very good father to you this last year. Somewhere along the way, I forgot how to be the man you needed me to be.”

He’s right, and part of me wants to tell him he is, but the creases on his forehead and the frown lines around his mouth remind me that he’s just a flawed human, one with a bit more life experience than me. Our eyes meet for a moment before his flit away. His grip on his coffee cup tightens so much that the tips of his fingers turn white.

“I got wrapped up in my anger, my disappointment, like it was a disease I couldn’t see outside of,” he continues. “Why was it my default to make my daughter suffer? What is so broken inside me that I would choose to behave this way to my own flesh and blood?” His voice cracks, and I watch his Adam’s apple move down his throat, slowly, like it’s caught on something.

“When my older brother passed away . . .” He pauses before clearing his throat. “I was very young, but not so young that I didn’t remember what it was like to have him around. The aftermath of his loss was so profound, so devastating, that things were never the same. We were completely broken. That’s when my parents turned to religion. And so did I.”

My father runs a hand up and down his thigh, and I sit still, silently taking in every word like it’s catnip. I didn’t realize how much I missed hearing him speak to me like I was his best friend.

“Religion saved us,” he says. “We not only built a new, or maybe I should say different relationship with Christ, but we found community. It was the community that helped patch us back together and ultimately led to me meeting your mother. Most of the other children of immigrants at that time were trying to assimilate into Canadian culture, but once I found religion and community I embraced it fully. It felt safe, you know?" He looks at me, almost searching for approval, or maybe understanding. "Within our tight-knit group, I knew I'd be surrounded by people who not only had the same beliefs I did but who also got me. It gave me this feeling of control. And when I lost my parents, I clung even tighter to religion. The fear inside me kept growing. I was so worried about who or what I'd lose next."

I'm almost certain that if I were to ask my dad he'd admit that everything—his anxiety, his past trauma, all of it—became heightened when Georgie announced she was pregnant. Learning about me and John must have been his tipping point. I'm not saying what he did or how he treated me was right, but sometimes I can almost see why he reacted the way he did. The question is, how do we move through all the pain and hurt?

"I saw myself in you the first time I held you in my arms," he tells me. "We were both the second-born and youngest in our families, and even though a parent should probably never admit this, I felt closer to you when you were only a few seconds old than I'd felt to Georgie in all her three years. The first child, you don't know what you're doing. You just want to keep them alive and hope you don't screw them up too much. But when you were born, I was a more relaxed parent, in some ways." He laughs. "And I guess I saw you as this fresh canvas. My little buddy. Maybe I wanted you to fill the gap my brother had left behind. My brother was the big Beatles fan. He's the one who introduced me to them. It's why you got the cool name," he says proudly, elbowing my side slightly.

"I didn't know that." I wring my hands, taking in his words. They're heavy but they're honest.

"If my brother liked something, then I liked it ten times more." A faint smile leaves his lips. "Mom and Georgie had their own special bond, and you and I had ours. That's why, when Georgie was pregnant with Paulie, I was upset, obviously, but I didn't feel as betrayed as I did when I found out about you and . . ." He stalls, as though saying his name is painful. As if even admitting he exists is too much for him. "You and John."

"I wasn't trying to betray you."

He nods. "I understand that. Now. But it took me a while to get here. I don't know if my way of thinking can ever change when it comes to this subject. I don't believe you should be doing that with anyone before marriage. Perhaps I am a little judgmental, considering some of the things I participated in growing up."

We both let out a small laugh.

"You're allowed to have your own belief system," I say, because it's true. If he wants to believe the sky is yellow, it's not for me to tell him he's wrong. What's wrong is him telling me that he sees a yellow sky and therefore so should I.

"If I could have gone on being the perfect daughter, I would have, but that girl doesn't exist. If I'd tried to force it, I would only have ended up resenting you." I turn slightly toward him, still struggling to meet his eyes, so I look just over his shoulder, focusing on our neighbor's mulberry tree instead. "This last year has been really hard on me. I've lived with this constant pit in my stomach reminding me that I had disappointed you. But also because my rock, the person I always turned to when life got hard, the person I ran to with my good news first, was no longer there for me."

A meaningful silence settles after I speak, the birds filling in the quiet between us. I try to find a way to say the next thing without upsetting him.

"We can't go back. We just . . . can't. All we can do is move forward."

"And you want to move forward by going to school in New York?"

I nod. "For the first time in months, I'm excited about my future. I'm hopeful. I know what you want for me is different from what I want for myself. But I can't be forced to be someone I'm not." I finally brave eye contact, and I'm surprised to see how much his face has softened since the start of our conversation. "If I stay here, it may buy us a few more years together as father and daughter, but it would all be a facade, one that would eventually shatter into a million unfixable pieces. I've also come to learn over this last year that I still need you. I still need a father. I need your guidance, faith, and support to help me become the person I've always dreamed of becoming. Someone who, I hope, will make you proud one day."

My eyes burn, and while I'm able to control my quivering lips, tears roll down my face. The words I've said, I didn't realize how true they were until this very moment. Sitting here next to my father, I can't help but grieve the time we've spent apart.

In a move that takes me by surprise, Dad places his hand on top of mine.

"I'm sorry." He says it so simply, but those two words are powerful. He doesn't say them often or easily. "You're right. I held you to a higher standard than Georgie. An impossible one. I want you to be happy, and I want to be part of your life. Lennon," he says, turning slightly in his seat to face me, "I believe in you. I've always believed in you, and I think that's part of why I held on so tight. I know you are capable of big things. But doing big things means you'll be taken away from me."

"And now?" I ask, hope sparking in my chest. "Do I have your blessing to chase after my dreams? To study in New York? Because," I say, our eyes locked, "the truth is, you hold all the power here. I can't go without your help."

He nods slowly, swallowing again, his hand still on top of mine. "If you love someone, you need to set them free. And if they come back to you . . ." He looks down, his eyes red-rimmed. "If they come back to you, if you come back to us . . ." He sniffles, trying to fight back the tears.

"Does that mean I can accept this offer?" I ask, my breath hitched.

"Congratulations, habibti. You're going to New York."

I collapse into tears, and my father wraps his arms around me as I feel a deep, guttural cry released from within. I did it. He's given me his blessing. I'm going to Columbia University.

Sitting up slightly and wiping away my tears, I manage to say, "Thank you."

"Thank you for forgiving me," Dad says. "You'll visit, right?" he asks, his voice raw with emotion. I realize now I never confirmed if I'd come back, and yet he still gave me his blessing.

"All the time," I promise.

We sit, with my dad's arm around my shoulders, me resting my head on his.

After a few minutes pass, he clears his throat. "Did you love him?" he asks quietly.

"Yes. I do love him. And he loved me enough to set me free. Just like you."

"Do you think one day you might go back to him?"

I stare ahead at a robin pecking through our garden in search of a worm. "I don't know," I say, letting out a heavy breath. "We don't talk anymore. For all I know he's in a serious relationship with someone else."

"What is meant for you will come to you," Dad says simply.

I really want to believe he's right.

For me, it's worth giving my parents another chance. I'm not as religious as them and I don't have the strong ties to my culture that they do. Not yet, anyway. It's something I might cultivate over time. With experience. Not because someone told me I should. But I do believe in the strength of family. Maybe that's the part of our religion and culture that has rubbed off on me. Maybe all of this was growing pains. Maybe we'll get past it. Maybe we won't.

I'm choosing to forgive my parents. I don't expect to forget. I'm not sure we can ever forget the things that alter our brain chemistries. I've tried.

So far it hasn't worked when it comes to John. I've attempted to shift my thinking into learning how to live a full life without him. He's not blood. He's not family. He's not even a friend.

But he just may be the other half of the moon.

Chapter Forty-one

SEPTEMBER 7

Sometimes we get so focused on our end goal that we forget to think about what might happen if we get there. Watching as a dream you've worked toward for years comes to fruition and realizing it won't just be this idea in your head anymore is something you can never fully prepare for. Finally, you get to step inside the story and live within its pages. The pages you designed. The pages you drew up. The life you always wanted, right there, within your grasp.

And it's terrifying.

What if it's not everything I imagined it to be?

What if New York isn't what I so desperately *need* it to be?

What if I realize three weeks in that I hate it? That I want to go home? That I want to live a comfortable life with my family studying something that I know will lead to a stable, well-paying career?

What was I thinking? Creative writing? What am I going to do with an arts degree? How could I ask my father to spend all this money, his hard-earned money, just so I can write made-up stories?

And for who? Who is going to read these stories?

I'm scared.

I'm petrified.

And I'm so goddamn excited I can barely breathe.

"Lennon, you ready?" Mom stands in the open doorway of my bedroom.

"I think so," I say. I'm looking at half my life packed into open suitcases, while the rest of my things will sit untouched and wait safely for my return, when I visit. The meaningful juxtaposition is not lost on me.

Mom comes in and stops when she steps on clothes that didn't quite make it into my suitcase. She bends down to pick them up and, seemingly without thinking, clutches them and brings them to her face to inhale their scent.

"Sorry. I'll make sure to tidy up before I leave," I say, assessing the current tornado status of my room.

Mom simply smiles as she places the extra clothes on my bed. "Daddy and I built this home for the four of us, and soon it will just be two."

"I'll be back," I say, not really sure if I'm talking about visits or moving home after I graduate. I've learned not to overpromise on things I can't predict. A lot can happen in four years.

She nods. "It won't be the same as it was, though."

"But maybe that's a good thing," I say. The subtext of my words weighs heavy in the space between us. It's easier to forgive someone when you know exactly what you're forgiving them for. With Mom, she wasn't the one who dealt my punishments. She wasn't the one who inflicted the most damage to my heart. But she was the one who stood by the person who did, and because of that, I've struggled with how to let her back into my life.

"I was around your age when I moved to Canada," she says. "Leaving home is a very big moment in a young person's life. It's like drawing a line between who you used to be and who you're becoming. It's a lot scarier when you're a parent watching your child leave the home you built for them, though."

"You and Dad believed that giving us freedom would mean losing us. But that's not how it works. You're not going to lose us in exchange for giving me and Georgie autonomy. You'll lose us if you *don't* give us that freedom. Even if sometimes our choices lead to mistakes or decisions you don't approve of."

"I know it doesn't look like I stood by you last year, but when you weren't looking, I was working on him. Maybe it would have meant more if I'd done that in front of you."

"Dad isn't the easiest person to stand up to. But if anyone can do it, you can," I say with a small smile. The room settles into silence as Mom and I seem to search for our next words. "Do you think you can help me with this mess tomorrow morning? I'm struggling to decide what to bring and what to leave behind."

"Yes. We'll figure it out together," she says, eyes glistening.

I drop the clothes in my hands and reach my arms out to hug my mother. She wraps hers around me, her soft body like being encircled by the warmth of the hot sun on a cool day.

"I promise to make you proud," I say, my words muffled against her neck.

"You already have."

"Yalla," Dad calls from the front door. "Everyone is waiting for us."

Mom and I pry ourselves away from one another, wiping our tears. I search for my phone and check the time.

We've been invited to Theo's for a barbecue/going-away party. This is my last night at home before we fly to New York tomorrow.

Both Mom and Dad are coming to help me get settled in. I'm trying not to think about the part where I walk them out of my dorm and kiss them goodbye. My throat burns every time the thought crosses my mind. I keep swatting it away, but there's no denying that it's going to happen. Because it has to happen.

On the drive to Theo's, I sit in the back seat with the window open, breathing in the late-summer air. Tomorrow at this time I'll be in New York setting up my new life, Book Two in the series. Maybe Three? I think at this point John deserves his own stand-alone.

It's been almost a year since we saw or spoke to one another, and yet he still exists in my everyday. I'll be fine, going through the motions, working toward my goals and dreams, rightfully proving to everyone, including myself, that I don't need him. And then I'll think about something he said, or a moment we shared, and it takes my breath away, reminding me of the cavity that still exists in my heart.

Dad turns onto Theo's street, and I spot Georgie's car parked at the curb. I get out, closing the door behind me while taking in the sight of the Petropolis home. So many pivotal moments have happened in and around this house. It seems fit for me, in an ironic kind of way, to have a goodbye party here before leaving this part of my life behind.

Music blasts from Theo's backyard. I spot him by the barbecue, a beautiful girl with dark skin by his side. Our eyes lock, and he smiles so broadly that I can't help but smile back. We meet halfway, embracing in the kind of hug reserved for people who hold a special place in your heart.

"Hadid," he says, and my heart warms.

"Petropolis," I say, nodding to the girl who is now at his side as we pull apart.

I called Theo after my dad and I resolved things. Just to let him know that I wasn't holding on to any resentment from our relationship. Said I wanted to be friends again, if he was okay with letting bygones be. We talked for a while, and it was nice. Making room for people who are important to you feels good. Relationships will always mean a little bit of extra effort on my end, but when someone's worth it, you do the work.

Theo drapes an arm around the girl next to him, pulling her in, and she blushes hard. "This is Raychelle."

"Hi," I say, forcing myself to make eye contact. Meeting people is still a challenge. "When Theo told me he had a serious girlfriend, I almost didn't believe him."

Theo's face is completely flushed as he glances between us.

Raychelle grins. "I'm taking all the credit for Theo getting over you."

"Ray," Theo says, glaring at her like an embarrassed toddler.

"Oh, be for real, Theo. Everyone knows you were hung up."

"Swear to god, my next girlfriend is going to be a meek person who worships the ground I walk on."

"You'd be so bored," I say, burying a laugh.

"Right?" Raychelle smirks.

"So, you go to school together?" I ask.

"Yeah. I'm from Vancouver Island. I've been here for a couple of weeks to visit and wrangle him back to B.C. with me."

"I did the long-distance thing for almost three months," he says with a pout.

"Poor you," I reply, rolling my eyes.

"Can you blame me for having a hard time being away from this beauty?"

There's something so sincere about the way he speaks about Raychelle that it makes me genuinely happy to see he's found his match. Still, I can't help but think about how that could have been me under Theo's arm, family and friends surrounding us. It wouldn't have stopped us from going our separate ways tomorrow, though. Maybe in another universe we would have stayed together, but that would have meant both of us giving up our dream schools and our dreams.

My dad waves Theo over, leaving me and Raychelle alone to talk.

"Are you also getting a Business degree?" I ask.

She huffs out a laugh. "Hell no. Business is dry as fuck. I'm studying Philosophy and Greek Mythology."

"Oh god, Theo must tease you nonstop. My thoughts and prayers are with you."

She places a warm hand on my arm and squeezes it. "I appreciate that."

We both laugh, but then her face grows serious.

"Theo said you had a tough year. He feels bad about not being there for you, but given your past together and how hard it was for him to move on, he wasn't sure *how* to be there for you."

"I wouldn't have let him in anyway," I say, lifting my eyes to hers. "I needed time to process things on my own."

"That's completely valid. And the great thing about Theo is that once you're in his life, that's it. You're in. So maybe don't hesitate to reach out?"

"I will. Besides, it'll be fun ganging up on him over the holidays and teasing him about our useless degrees."

"If he wants to make all the money to support my creative endeavors, I'm down." Raychelle looks over my shoulder and smiles.

"Looks like Theo could use my help with the barbecue. Talk to you later."

As Raychelle walks away, my body jolts suddenly backward. Andie's arms are wrapped around my waist, hugging me from behind. I grasp her arms and sway back and forth, taking in the force of her embrace.

"I can't believe you're leaving me, you bitch," she says playfully.

We release one another and our eyes meet. Our lips have matching pouts as our foreheads touch. "I *am* a selfish B. I'm sorry."

"Don't be sorry. You're doing what I've wanted you to do since the moment we met. You're putting yourself first."

I pull Andie to me and we hug. She really is the best friend I could ever have asked for. In the four years we've been friends, she's never pushed for me to meet her at her level. She's always met me where I was. She knew I had my own path to follow and, often, pave. Her love and companionship have always been unconditional. Friends like her come along once in a lifetime, and for that reason I will hold on tight to what we have and make sure it withstands the four years I'll be in New York.

Ever since I told Andie about Columbia she's been glued to my side, soaking in every moment before I leave. She's staying local, going to school part-time to test the waters. Part of her wants to be an entrepreneur, but the other part doesn't want to have to work as hard as her parents have.

We went to prom together, danced to all our favorite songs, and skipped the after-parties. Instead, we had an old-school slumber party at my place. The last three months of healing have been exactly that: healing.

Except there's one area of my heart and mind that remains in a perpetual state of grief. Maybe, eventually, hopefully, I'll be able to look back on my time with John and remember only the parts that made me happy.

We spend the afternoon at Theo's eating hamburgers and hot-dogs, swimming, and reminiscing about old times. My parents take off around seven, and Georgie, Zach, and Paulie leave shortly after. They're spending the night at our home so that they can take us to the airport tomorrow and see me off properly.

There's a heaviness in the air as the sun begins to set. No one wants to say goodbye, but we know we have to. I hate goodbyes. But, as they say, every goodbye leads to a new beginning.

Andie keeps looking at me as if I've broken her heart, and we wipe one another's tears as Theo and Raychelle go inside to help Petra clean up.

"It's been a good run," Andie says. "I've never put up with anyone else for this long. Probably never will." She pulls me in tighter, squeezing me. "You're never getting rid of me."

"Same." I pull back slightly to wipe a tear away. I try to smile, but my lips are quivering too much.

"I know I've said it before, but it bears repeating." Andie takes my face in her hands, her eyes laser-focused on mine. "I am so, so proud of you. You have this fire inside of you, Lennon. I have one too. It's why I latched onto you all those years ago." She grins. "And I know you are going to do amazing things. Mark my words: you're going to change the world. I can just feel it."

"Any fire I have inside me has only grown since meeting you. You are my favorite person, Andie Smith-Johansson. The most beautiful girl I've ever known, inside and out."

Andie begins to sob, which triggers another flood of tears from me as we embrace again.

"We'll text. And FaceTime. And you bet your ass I'm visiting you in New York every chance I get."

"I know people say that all the time, but let's mean it, okay?"

"Okay," she says, nodding, eyes glistening. "I love you."

I nod back, tears falling. "I love you more."

We stand and hug for what feels like forever, but when it ends, all I want to do is hug her again.

She squeezes my hand and kisses me on the cheek before releasing her grip and walking out of Theo's yard. Standing alone, I rub the spot on my hand that Andie was holding only moments ago.

Theo comes out a few minutes later, a sympathetic smile on his face.

"Did Andie leave?" he asks.

"Yeah. I guess I should head home then."

"Yeah." He nods, seeming to fight back a grin. "But as it turns out, I can't drive you."

"Oh." I shake my head. "That's fine. I'll call Andie and ask her to circle back."

"You won't need to do that," a deep voice says from behind me.

I turn to find John standing by the backyard gate. My heart stutters to a stop as our eyes lock.

Theo lifts his chin to John before leaning in and whispering, "Think of it as a going-away present from me."

I smile back at Theo, leaving a quick kiss on his cheek. "Thank you," I mouth before making my way to John.

Chapter Forty-two

"Hi," I say, my eyes lifting to meet John's. His eyes shine, despite the darkness of the night sky.

"Hey." His smile is so wide that little crinkles form around his eyes, making him look slightly older.

I want to ask him so many questions. I want him to wrap his arms around me. I want to walk out of Theo's yard with John and go somewhere only we know.

"Are you here to take me home?" I ask.

John nods as he brings a hand to my face, stroking my jawline with his thumb. My knees buckle at his touch, both foreign and familiar. "If you'd like."

"I would love that."

For the millionth time tonight, my eyes burn. Luckily I don't need to worry about mascara running down my cheeks, since I've spent most of the day in the pool. It's only now that it occurs to me how rough I must look, as I run a hand through my frizzy hair. But you wouldn't know it from the way John is gazing at me.

His smile is small and bittersweet now. My heart aches as I watch it fade.

"Can we make one stop first?" he asks.

I only nod, because my throat is tight. We both know we're going to have to say our goodbyes soon. It feels like all we ever do is say goodbye.

As we walk to his car, there's a part of me that is tempted to navigate the hard conversation we need to have by bulldozing over it with small talk—"How was your summer?" "Your family?" "What did you do last year?"—but we both deserve more than that. We deserve closure.

At his car, we stand in silence for a moment. Space and time between us. He opens the door, and I get inside. His eyes latch onto mine. My heart races, trying to think of everything I want to say to him, but there's not enough time. There's never enough time.

He gets in and turns the ignition. An old, familiar song plays in the background as he shifts his car into drive. I look back at Theo's home one last time before facing forward.

"I'm leaving tomorrow," I say. The air between us is so thick my words struggle to cut through.

"I know," he says, then he clears his throat. "I'm happy for you. And I'm so proud. I'm not sure how you convinced your parents to let you go," he says with a small laugh. He comes to a red light and turns to look at me. "You know, despite all the differences your father and I have, we both share a deep love for you. And I think," he glances at the street before turning his gaze back to me, "part of me felt comforted in the fact that, because of how protective he is, you would never be too far from me. His little bird." John shakes his head. The light turns green, and he continues to drive. "I hate the fact that part of me wanted to keep you caged up so I would always know where to find you."

"It took me a long time to realize that when we said goodbye last October it really was goodbye. I'd gotten so used to all our back-and-forth that I almost expected you to come back for me. But then you didn't," I say, around a tight swallow.

He doesn't respond, just keeps driving. Every now and then the streetlights we pass briefly spotlight his face, like he's a still image in one of those old black-and-white silent films. He turns the car into a subdivision, driving past cookie-cutter homes and fire hydrants painted like little people. My heart clenches at the simplicity, a view that will be foreign to me for the next four years.

You really never know what you have until it's gone. Or until it's taken away from you. The finality of losing something or someone never hits until it's too late. You always believe there will be at least one more time. A moment when you'll be able to say everything you want to say perfectly. So you hold back. And then, just like that, you've reached the end and there are no words left to be said. No moments left to be had. Only memories. Along with would-haves and should-haves. Regrets, they slice sharper than a knife.

John pulls into a small parking lot and turns off the engine. He rests his arm on the center console and it bumps mine. I breathe in the feel of his warm skin pressed against my arm.

"Want to go for a walk?" he asks.

I remain still, afraid to blink for fear he'll be gone again. "Yeah."

We get out of the car and he takes my hand as we walk along a gravel path. "I kept my distance in part because it was practically impossible to reach you," he says, finally responding to my words from earlier. "But also because I needed time to figure things out for myself."

"And did you?"

"You want the truth?" John asks.

We've come to a footbridge, and we stop halfway across. He drops my hand before leaning his elbows on the railing. It's hard to see past our own noses in the dark, but every so often the glow of the moon lights up his face, and I fall in love with him all over again.

"Yes. The truth," I say, matching his pose.

"Okay," he says, blowing air out of his mouth and nodding. "The truth is, I was completely lost after what happened between us in New York. I felt terrible, like I'd messed up your life and taken something important away from you. I didn't feel worthy. And that's always been *my* issue, it wasn't fair to make it yours. I hated that I couldn't protect you from what happened. Even worse that I had something to do with it." He pauses, shaking his head. "A silver condom wrapper broke us apart."

I clasp my hands, looking down at the water below us. "You've never given yourself enough credit for what an amazing person you really are. You made it through high school while your home life was falling apart. You were the glue that kept your family together. You're the one who got your father the help he needed, time and time again. You raised your little brother when you needed someone to raise you. And you," I touch his face and turn it to mine, "you made me feel like I was the most important person in your universe. You saw me in a way no one ever has before, or since. You have this ability—you've *had* this ability, since day one—to peel back all my layers to get to the real me. You have been my safe place, and I have zero regrets about letting you into my life." I straighten and take John's hands so that he's facing me. "Being with you in New York was a fairy tale. I would never take back that moment. It was perfect. You were perfect. *We* were perfect."

John releases my hands and pulls me into a hug. My cheek presses against his chest as his lips meet my forehead.

"I hated saying goodbye to you in that empty classroom last year, but I know it's what we both needed," he says, the warmth of his breath passing over me.

I pull away slightly, keeping my gaze firmly planted on his face. "What do you mean?"

He swallows and looks down at me. "If you and I had tried again, it would have only caused more friction with your father, and we'd have continued to be in the same, constant, heartbreaking loop. Something had to change. Despite every fiber of my body yelling at me to ask you to try again, I walked away. And clearly it was the right decision, because look at you now." He smiles so broadly that his scar disappears. "Columbia. New York City. You're about to live out your dream."

I shake my head, even though everything he's saying is true. "I prayed every night for you to come back to me. You were supposed to come back to me."

"I did, Lennon. I'm here now."

"Now," I say, with a bitter laugh. "Hours before I leave."

John brings both hands to my arms and grips them. He lowers his head to mine again. "The path may not have been ideal, but you're about to get everything you want."

"Not everything," I say, meeting his gaze. I get lost in his blue eyes. The little frown in his forehead. The shaggy brown hair. The face I see every time I close my eyes. "Do you have everything you want?" I ask.

"Mostly." He exhales another sharp breath. "Tomorrow, I start year two of the carpentry program. This year will be mostly apprenticeships. I love it, Lennon. I've found my calling. When I'm in the workshop with music on, I'm in the zone. I lose track of time. And that's what I want—not to be watching a clock. God," he says, raking a hand through his hair, "the number of times I wanted to call you and tell you about how much I was enjoying the program, how it felt like you were part of the reason I was doing what I loved."

"I'm happy for you. And your family?" I ask. It's the kind of question no one wants to ask, but the kind of question that must be asked in order to move forward.

John places a hand on the back of his neck and sighs. "Dad relapsed. Again. This time it was really bad." His eyes shut tight. "He hit rock bottom last September. Alcohol poisoning."

"Oh my god. Is he okay now?"

"The doctor in the emergency room said if he didn't stop drinking, immediately, the damage to his liver would . . . he was close to death. Like he was at the top of a waterfall, and if he took one more drink, he'd tip over and there'd be no going back. He stopped drinking that night."

"I'm so sorry," I say softly, wishing I could take away all his pain.

"We didn't tell my sister or Mikey at first. We sprang into action to get him clean. Got him back into rehab after they detoxed him. It felt like we were all in survival mode. He's working the program now. We can't be sure what the future holds. His body sure as hell can't take much more, but like they say in AA, one day at a time."

"And there's me wallowing in self-pity, and I had no idea you were going through all of that."

"No one did. When someone in your family is sick, it becomes your whole life. Between my dad, my family, and school, I had nothing left to give. It's why I was able to walk away from you last fall. But as we slowly crawled our way back to the surface, I started to think about you and me again. Then Theo told me that you were going to Columbia, and all I knew was that I had to come and say goodbye before you left."

"So where does that leave us?" I ask, the words escaping my lips.

"You're about to go on a big adventure. You're finally choosing yourself. Beautiful bird, you need to fly." He takes my hand and holds onto it so tightly it almost hurts.

"The caged bird only flies away if it wants to," I say, my voice quiet.

"Do you want to?" he asks, tipping his head down to meet my eyes.

"Yeah." I nod and then follow that with a deep exhale. "Yes. I want to. But I also want you."

He runs his fingers through my tousled hair and smiles.

"I have this dream," he says, his voice soft, hopeful. "In it, I walk up to your door and instead of knocking I let myself in. Your father greets me with a handshake. You come down the stairs and our eyes meet. We smile because you're where you want to be and I'm where I want to be. No what-ifs. No secrets. No regrets. Just the future ahead of us. Our future."

"Sounds nice," I say with a small smile. "But putting more distance between us won't make things easy. And what if I don't end up coming back home after graduating? What if one of us gets hurt or . . . even worse? A lot can happen in four years."

"We're connected," he says, around a smile. His smile, I know all too well, is just for me. "We always will be. No matter what."

"No matter what," I echo.

"On the last page of *The Sun Also Rises*, Lady Brett Ashley says to Jake, 'We could have had such a damned good time together.' And Jake responds, 'Yes . . . Isn't it pretty to think so?' I don't want that ending for us, Lennon. I don't want any what-ifs to haunt us. I don't want that to be our last page. Or this. I love you."

"I love you too," I say, looking up at him. I press my lips against his, my fingers digging into his back. My body falls into him, my knees unable to support the intensity of his mouth on mine again. We pull away for a second, and wisps of my long, dark hair cover my face. Our chests rise and fall as rain begins to pour down on us. John takes my hand and we run back to his car, the parking lot now deserted, the sky inky black.

He opens the door to the back seat and we tumble in. Rain pounds on the roof, streams down the windows, shielding us from the world outside. We very clumsily try to remove each other's clothing. I climb on top of him, and we move in sync, our bodies falling together like embers at the end of a long-burning fire.

I pull back slightly, studying the curves in his face, trying to remember every line. "The person I am with you might not be the best version of myself, but it's the most real. Mask off," I say.

His hands clasp me tighter, clinging to me, while the raindrops mimic the beating of our hearts as we come together as one.

Our eyes open and latch onto one another's. When we're together, minutes move faster than seconds, and when we're apart, every minute lasts a lifetime.

"We see the same colors. Colors other people don't see. We hear the same songs. Songs other people don't hear. Lennon." John places his hand on my face, and I can't help but lean into it. His voice is soft, his breath is warm, as he brings his lips to my ear. "It's always been you."

Nestling my head into his shoulder, we hold one another even tighter. I could say it back. Promise him the world and my heart. But I don't need to. And I don't think he needs me to, either.

For most of my life, everything I did, every move I made, came back to my dad. How would he feel? What would he think? Am I making him proud?

Then I met John, and for the last few years, everything has kept coming back to him. How could he and I make it work? Could I be happy if I chose him over everyone?

But it wasn't really about John, or me and John.

It wasn't even about my dad.

It's always been about me. I've been the common denominator. I just wasn't able to see it before, not when the hopes and dreams of others were pinned on me.

Love shouldn't come with conditions.

Love can't exist without acceptance.

Love starts from within.

My eyes meet John's again, as if his are my North Star. I'm not sure of many things, but I know when I look up to the night sky the moon will be there, whether I see her or not. Despite clouds or wind, rain or snow, she'll be up there, her beautiful incandescent light grounding me. And whether John and I are in the same room or a million miles away, our love will always be there. Always existing. Always beating. Always.

Always.

Always.

Isn't it pretty to think?

Acknowledgments

I wrote the first draft of this novel in three weeks, back in 2020. It was an adult romance at the time, with two POVs (Lennon's and John's) and two timelines (then and now). The characters, their words, their complex relationship poured out of me. A lot has changed since then, and a lot hasn't.

At its core, this is a coming-of-age story that explores love (self-love, romantic love, familial love, among other forms) and identity. It attempts to start a conversation that distinguishes the often-intertwined polarizing subjects of culture and religion, and how girls especially experience shame over feelings and desires that they have been taught to believe are "impure" and "bad."

It took me many years, many attempts at writing this novel, and raising daughters to articulate, or at least attempt to articulate, the effect on me of growing up in a world, community, and culture that paints a very black-and-white picture of what makes a girl "good." I struggled with feelings of being unworthy for a long time, and I don't want that for my daughters, or others. And if you experienced the same, or are experiencing the same thing now, I hope this story helps you.

I believe in my heart that there is an audience for this book, and it is my hope that it finds those readers. Hopefully you.

To Lynne Missen, thank you for believing in this idea when it was just a spark. You have never made me feel shame for wanting to tell stories the way I do (whether the main character is "boy crazy" or curious) and I appreciate you always being a safe place for me and my leading ladies.

To Evan Munday, thank you for your support through three books. It can be challenging trying to get mainstream media on board to talk about young adult books, especially from marginalized authors, and I appreciate all the work you do to get my book in front of the right people.

Thanks also to Katie Heeps for your thoughtful feedback on this novel, and for reading it so many times!

Extended thanks to Catherine Marjoribanks, Jennifer McClorey, Zeena Baybayan, Bharti Bedi and Tundra Books / Penguin Random House Canada.

Kim Myatt, you have created the most stunning portrait of Lennon. I am so in love with this cover. You masterfully matched the essence of Lennon and this story. Thank you so much.

I have been spoiled with the most gracious and beautiful blurbs from authors I deeply admire and am in awe of. Thank you to Alena Bruzas, Jesmeen Kaur Deo, CG Drews, Zoulfa Katouh and Racquel Marie. I am so grateful and proud to have your words and names on my book.

To Jim McCarthy, thank you for believing in me and taking me and my books on. From one anxious bundle to another, I feel so secure and at ease with you at the helm of my career.

Stacey Donaghy, you continue to take care of me and my first three book babies, and I am so grateful to you for that.

Maren Soderbeck, I don't know what I'd do without your presence and support. Every July 27, I'm grateful we found one another.

Julia Foster, I'm so happy I weaseled my way into your life. You push me to be better and do things I don't always want to that always make my stories stronger.

Teresa Moore, throughout every iteration of this novel you cheered me on, pushed me to keep going, and assured me that this was a story that needed to be told. Thank you for your steadfast belief in not only me but Lennon and John.

Extended thanks to those who read early versions of this novel: Elizabeth Kessick, Julia Foster, Anne Putnam, Maren Soderbeck, Heather Dixon, Crystal Hill, Lindsay Maple, Natalie Kikić, Bonnie Jo Pierson, Amanda Nelson, and Sky Regina.

To my SP writing group: what a fun-gi time we have together. Get it?

To Rob, Elsie, Emma, and Pearl, you are the grounding I need. You are my home.

To my family and friends who continue to stick by and support me, maybe skip this one.

To my readers, we are three books in now, with (knock on wood) more to come. I love doing this and I wouldn't be able to do it without your support. You probably don't realize when you message me or tag me in kind posts how much it makes my day. How it gives me the drive to push through all the challenges and disappointments. I appreciate you all so much.

Until we meet again . . .